PRAISE FOR *BIT FLIP*

"In *Bit Flip*, Trigg aims some wickedly smart satire at the dark, beating heart of Silicon Valley, and exposes a lot of moral gray areas along the way. This is the kind of book that'll make you very afraid—and very angry—about the win-at-all-costs ethos at the core of our self-righteous tech culture."

—**ROB HART**, author of *The Warehouse* and *The Paradox Hotel*

"In *Bit Flip*, Trigg shines a light on the often-toxic tech community and walks a fascinating tightrope, deftly mixing insider knowledge with an outlier's moral observations. Just as 1's switch to 0's and back again, Trigg's characters challenge us to examine the complicated, false binary between right and wrong."

—**ADAM NEMETT**, author of *We Can Save Us All*

"A searing exposé of one man's journey into the heart of Silicon Valley darkness. Trigg, with heart, levity, and deftness, portrays a culture driven by one seemingly innocent question: 'Why can't that happen to me?' A culture where there is no failure, there is only trying again, and again, until all the Kool-Aid is gone. One might think it preposterous if it wasn't frighteningly real. A slow burn that sneaks up and bowls you over in the end."

—**JACKIE TOWNSEND**, author of *Riding High in April*

"As much a compelling narrative as it is a critical analysis of contemporary capitalism, this story worries over the coming future, in which technology could take over much of what people used to do. This helps to make *Bit Flip* an engrossing novel that satirizes the pretensions of tech bros and billionaires."

—*FOREWORD REVIEWS*, 5 stars

". . . a worthwhile, humorous take on the moral infirmities of the tech industry."

—KIRKUS REVIEWS

"Mike Trigg's novel *Bit Flip* is exceptionally well-written, with a satisfying balance of action, intrigue, back story, characterization, and description. He weaves together several compelling story elements, some of them technical in nature, with ease and the manner in which he wraps up the narrative is both concise and provocative."

—INDIEREADER, 5-star review

BIT FLIP

A NOVEL

MIKE TRIGG

Published by SparkPress, a BookSparks imprint,
A division of SparkPoint Studio, LLC
Phoenix, Arizona, USA, 85007
www.gosparkpress.com

Published 2022
Printed in the United States of America
Print ISBN: 978-1-68463-177-3
E-ISBN: 978-1-68463-178-0
Library of Congress Control Number: 2022901445

Formatting by David Provolo

Author website: www.miketrigg.com
Facebook: fb.me/MikeTriggAuthor
Twitter: @mike_trigg
Instagram: @mike_trigg254

bit \ 'bit \ [binary digit]

noun

1. *computers:* a unit of computer information equivalent to the result of a choice between two alternatives (such as yes or no, on or off, 0 or 1).

bit flip \ 'bit, 'flip \

noun

1. *computers:* the act of switching a bit from 0 to 1 or 1 to 0. Also refers to the changing of one's mind 180 degrees.

CHAPTER 1:

GREENROOM

THE BUZZ OF THE AUDIENCE was audible even from the greenroom backstage in which Sam Hughes sat with the other panelists. All of them pretended to be preoccupied with their phones as they picked at pastries and fruit salad. Something that sounded important was announced over the loudspeaker from the main stage, but Sam couldn't make it out—like someone shouting underwater. The excitement in the speaker's voice was perceptible, but the actual words were indecipherable. The lost message—information he wondered if he needed before he went onstage—only intensified his anxiety, tightening the knot in his chest.

When he left the house that morning, Sam didn't know he would be speaking to an audience of over a thousand people. The day started typically enough, indistinguishable from thousands of others like it in the twenty-year journey he called his "career." He and his wife, Heather, orchestrated a tightly choreographed dance each morning, orbiting each other like planets, starting in the bathroom, culminating in the kitchen, striving to get their three children out the door in time for school, before she left for work and he embarked on his hour-long commute to San Francisco.

During his drive that morning, Sam reflected on the previous start-up companies he had worked for, each so promising at the outset but now blurred together in his memory—one year here, two years there, their sequence and significance only recalled accurately if he consulted his LinkedIn profile to jog his memory. Some were modest successes, but most ran out of money, or never shipped product, or never generated revenue, or all of the above. Sam had managed to jump from rung to rung, opportunistically grasping increasingly senior positions at the next company before the previous one fizzled out, lost in the detritus of venture-backed implosions. But his current company, Ainetu . . . *This one has potential*, Sam thought as he drummed his fingers against the steering wheel, trapped in the crippling helplessness of bumper-to-bumper traffic along the Embarcadero, inching toward his office in the SoMa district. An endless parade of bicycles, motorized skateboards, electric scooters, and other wheeled contraptions passed him on the sidewalk as he stood still, watching the traffic light again cycle to yellow, then red, with only a car or two making it through the intersection.

Sam was busy convincing himself this job, this commute, this *career* was all worth it when the unexpected phone call from Hannah Goodwin, the PR person at Ainetu, blared across his car speakers. Her call was initially a welcome distraction, but her urgent appeal was not.

"*Sam*! I'm so glad I caught you. Where are you?" she asked.

"Uh . . . right now I'm in gridlock on the Embarcadero."

"Oh, thank *God*! OK, you need to go straight to Moscone Center," she said. "You're speaking on a panel at SaaStr in twenty minutes."

"Wait, *what*?" Sam asked, but Hannah was already gone.

Now, here he was in the greenroom, dutifully awaiting his moment onstage to opine on a panel discussion about . . . *Wait, what was it about again?* He thumbed through the event guide and reread the buzzword-laden description but felt no more prepared. Looking up from the program, he regarded the twentysomething guy across from him, with his feet sprawled on the coffee table, wearing pink Chuck Taylor high-tops and a black T-shirt with all-caps white lettering that read, "I SAY WHAT EVERYONE ELSE IS THINKING."

Bet you wouldn't say what I'm thinking now, Sam thought.

This had to be Cory Campbell, who, according to the program and Sam's vague recollection, was the twenty-four-year-old founder of an AI analytics software start-up called Marvel.io that was supposedly competitive with Sam's company. Having just raised a huge round of venture capital, Marvel.io had timed their announcement perfectly to maximize buzz at the high-profile conference. The other panelist Sam had met before, Danny Liu—the founder of a smaller company in the space called Red Sparrow that was acquired by Prism Systems, the huge enterprise software conglomerate where Liu was now some midlevel VP of "AI Innovation." Apart from curt greetings, the three panelists hadn't exchanged any further words. The crowd laughed at something inaudible onstage as Cory took a selfie with his arm raised to full extension and his face in a sly, contorted pose.

Sam tried not to visibly roll his eyes. He didn't want to be there, but as chief operating officer, he didn't have a choice. His boss, the founder and CEO of Ainetu, Rohan Sharma, had originally agreed to speak on the panel but abruptly deemed it beneath him earlier that morning. As usual, Sam had to clean up the mess. Rohan's likeness peered up at Sam from the program, dozens of which were splayed across the table, soiled with coffee rings and croissant remnants. Sam had a million other things he needed to be doing, but placating his boss always seemed to trump everything else. He wasn't prepared for the event, but he knew the routine—he had done it more times than he cared to remember. The dog and pony show of humble brags and restrained amazement at your own company's incredible growth trajectory. Peacocking for the audience, the press, the analysts, and anyone else who gave a shit about your little corner of the vast tech landscape.

"OK, we're ready for you guys," an event planner in a headset and armed with an iPad announced through the greenroom door. Sam followed his fellow panelists past the production equipment, where a tech wired them up with lavalier microphones he clipped to their shirts, tucking the transmitters into their pant pockets.

Kyle Kawala, their gregarious moderator, intercepted the trio back-stage. "*So?* Are you guys *psyched*?" he asked, greeting Cory with a bro shake with his right hand accompanied by a back-thumping half hug with his left. An associate at one of the big investment banks, Kyle was a ubiquitous fixture on the conference circuit. His diminutive stature was simultaneously exacerbated by an impossibly skinny gray suit and elevated by a meticulously tousled mane of jet-black hair.

After greeting Danny with the same exuberant ritual, Kyle turned to Sam and asked, "So . . . *who* are you again?"

Hannah, who had somehow slipped backstage without anyone noticing, interjected before Sam could answer. "He's COO at Ainetu. Sam is the number two."

"So, Rohan couldn't make it?" Kyle asked, giving Sam a cursory inspection.

"Unfortunately, no—he had a . . ." Hannah started her practiced excuse.

"He's so full of shit," Kyle interrupted. "I don't know why I invite him to these things. So, he sent this guy?" Kyle asked rhetorically, as if Sam were an inanimate object at a flea market, worthy only of disdain.

"Sam's awesome. He's going to do great!" Hannah insisted. Then, turning to Sam, she said, "I'll be live tweeting the whole event. Thanks for filling in at the last minute. You'll do great!" She clenched Sam's arm in a manner that was unclear if the encouragement was meant for him or herself, then slipped back between the curtains toward the auditorium.

Kyle and Cory snickered in a quick sidebar conversation as the voice of God announced, "And now . . . please welcome to the stage our next panel, 'The Age of Knowing Everything,' moderated by Kyle Kawala of Bronson & Associates!"

Kyle strode onstage to the welling of applause and high-energy pop music. Spotlights captured each of the panelists as they took their desig-nated seats, crossing their legs and opening bottles of water as the walk-out music faded. Sam knew the room was big from attending the event in the past, but with the bright lights of the stage he could only make out the first row or two of people. It was an unsettling effect—like being in front of a one-way mirror knowing thousands of people were on the other side.

After effusive introductions of each of the panelists and all their accomplishments, along with an acknowledgement of Sam's substitute status, Kyle directed his first question at his party buddy, Cory. "So, Cory, let's start off with you. Where did you get the inspiration for Marvel.io?"

"That's a great question," Cory said with a coy smile and a sudden affect in his voice that was vaguely British. He sat sideways in his chair with one leg casually bobbing over the armrest. "I just looked at the landscape of tired legacy vendors and thought, '*We can do better.*'" The shot, presumably directed at the other panelists, seemed off base to Sam, given Ainetu had been founded only seven years ago. Of course, Cory was in high school seven years ago, so maybe Ainetu did deserve to be lumped in with the dinosaurs.

"Congratulations on your recent big series A financing. What was it? Twenty?"

"Yeah, twenty million on a hundred million pre," Cory replied.

"Nice, *mate*!" Kyle smiled conspiratorially, extending a quick fist bump. "Great valuation. You can do some damage with that!" A ripple of envious laughter coursed through the audience.

"Yeah, we're making incredible progress," Cory said. "We've developed the world's first unsupervised deep-learning algorithm on over a thousand individual behavioral attributes. We know what you're going to buy, say, or do before *you* do."

"So, what do you plan to do with all that fresh gunpowder?" Kyle asked.

"Go after the big boys," Cory said with a nod down the dais, landing another jab at his fellow panelists. "It just shows, if you build something truly innovative and disruptive, good things happen."

"We love you, *Cory*!" a young woman's voice shouted from the back of the auditorium. Cory pointed into the darkness in recognition of his admirer.

"I'm sorry," Danny, the VP from Prism, interjected, eager to defend his entrepreneurial street cred. "I'm not sure you can call yourselves disruptive when you barely have a product or any customers." The remark didn't land as intended. Too snarky, coming from a conscripted foot soldier of the old guard, lobbed into an audience partial to the perpetual march of innovation and disruption.

"OK . . . I *like* it!" Kyle encouraged. "Mixing things up! This isn't just going to be some boring, put-you-to-sleep, get-me-another-cup-of-coffee panel," he said, turning to the audience to incite a reaction. "So, tell us . . . why did you sell little Red Sparrow to a behemoth like Prism?"

Danny sat upright in his chair, cleared his throat, and paused to heighten the drama of his response. "I'll tell you, Kyle . . . it was . . . bar none . . . one of the toughest decisions of my life. No doubt. I tell you. We had so much momentum. We were growing *so fast*! But I just felt we could do so much more with the resources of a big company behind us. It just made *sense* for us, you know?"

"OK, fair enough," Kyle acknowledged, sensing the murmur in the audience as begrudging approval. "It's nothing to be ashamed of. You guys had a nice exit. What was the price again?"

"Ha! Nice try, Kyle. You know the terms weren't disclosed," Danny said, shuffling in his chair. "I'll tell you, though, if there's one bit of advice I'd share with all those budding entrepreneurs out there, it's that companies don't get *sold*, they get *bought*. I mean . . . if you're building something of *value*, then eventually someone's going to want that value, *you know*?" Danny said, cupping his hands to the word *value* as if carrying something precious. "As soon as you start *selling*, you're trying to convince people to do something they don't want to do. You seem *desperate*. Buyers want confidence. They want swagger. If there's no FOMO, you're not going to get the deal you want. Simple as that."

"That's a great point," Kyle said. "So, how are you going to keep that swagger now that you're part of such a big organization? How are you going to remain disruptive now that *you* are the incumbent?"

"Disruption can come from anywhere," Danny said. "One of the reasons I did the deal is we've been given a lot of autonomy within Prism. We have the nimbleness of a start-up but the resources of a global organization."

Sam had tried to retain the appearance of being involved in the conversation that had thus far transpired without him. His head politely turned from left to right like a spectator at a tennis match to follow the self-congratulatory volleys. Under the harsh spotlights, he felt beads of sweat precipitating in his armpits, threatening to roll down his rib cage and dampen his shirt. Then he caught a glimpse of his face, delayed by a barely perceptible millisecond on the giant projection screen hovering in the corner of his eye. Realizing he looked disinterested, he contorted his face into a forced expression of engagement, as if profound points were being made.

"What about you, Sam?" Kyle said, snapping Sam to attention with the abrupt redirect. "What's your perspective on all *this?*"

"My perspective on what?" Sam asked, thinking he had been adequately following along but now realizing he was distracted. He saw a look of concern flash across Hannah's face in the front row. Her thumbs suspended over her phone in a temporary halt of her live tweeting.

"Well, you're kinda caught in the middle—both figuratively and literally," Kyle said, gesturing to Sam's position between the two other panelists. "Ainetu's not a start-up anymore, but you're not a big company either. You're like a tween."

The audience laughed.

"Oh . . . ," Sam said, his tone changing, slightly perturbed at the joke. "I didn't know what you meant by 'this.' Maybe you meant this panel, or this room, or this whole event—or maybe even this area or this industry. There's lots of interpretations of '*this*,' Kyle."

"Interesting," Kyle said, taking a beat, measuring how to react as a ripple of discomfort reverberated through the audience. "Well, let's pull that thread. Which 'this' would you like to talk about?"

Sam looked out toward the crowd, silhouetted by the glare of the spotlights. About half were absorbed in their phones or laptops, their faces illuminated in miniature spotlights of their own. The other half that was actually paying attention looked at him expectantly. He knew what he was supposed to tell them. He was supposed to say how great Ainetu was doing. Boast about their latest round of funding at a sky-high valuation. Commend his tireless, bright, hardworking team for all the momentum they had generated. Marvel at their visionary founder (who, sadly, was too focused on building the world's next billion-dollar business to join them this particular day) for his extraordinary prescience. Conjure their envy by alluding to how big their exit was going to be. Declare without a hint of irony or misgivings how Ainetu was disrupting the status quo, shifting the paradigm, *changing the world*. But he couldn't do it.

"Sam?" Kyle prodded.

Sam began tentatively. "I don't know . . . I know what you *want* me to say—what the SaaStr audience wants to hear. You want me to pound my chest in that distinctly faux-modest Silicon Valley way, about how we're *crushing* it. How we're going to be the next to join the Unicorn Club. But some days it seems like the only thing we're 'crushing' is ourselves. Grinding away at the elusive, life-changing exit that, for most of us, never comes."

"Oh, c'mon, Sam—you just told me backstage that Ainetu is doing amazing. Don't be so modest," Kyle said, attempting to stem the buzz-killing monologue by referencing a conversation that never happened. Sam could hear shuffling in the audience, see heads leaning together to whisper snide remarks. Some started livestreaming the stage with their phones.

Sam conceded a melancholy smile toward Kyle. His thoughts suddenly flashed back to his first glimpse of the San Francisco Bay, framed by the glow of the setting sun, as he descended from the Altamont Pass in his U-Haul from college. Breaking away from his Midwestern familial obligations to pursue a career in Silicon Valley. It was his Eden—a land where brilliant young entrepreneurs conjured transformative products, disrupted every facet of the global economy, and generated overnight fortunes as a well-deserved reward. He had been so idealistic. So genuine in his belief that the dawn of the internet was a once-in-a-lifetime opportunity. That he was part of something bigger, part of something that was making the world a better place.

That sentiment seemed so distant and gullible to him now. It had been a long time since he had sincerely felt that way. So long that he barely remembered what it even felt like anymore. That idealism, that hope, that purpose had all dissipated long ago. All that remained in its place was his bruised ego after two decades of forgettable start-ups. The financial and professional windfall he assumed awaited him, that seemed so easily attainable, never materialized. Exacting a psychological toll along with the bleak financial reality of bounced payroll checks, mediocre healthcare, and onerous mortgage payments—barely getting by, even as a dual-income couple. Did he really think Ainetu would be any different? Sam clasped his hands, cleared his throat, and leaned forward in his chair.

"Maybe I've just been here too long and gotten a little cynical. But we're all fed this narrative about success when we come to Silicon Valley. I remember sitting out there in the audience and watching people like us talk. We use the language of humility and virtue and modesty, but, really, we're all just bragging. We remember how envious we felt about those lucky ones who raised big rounds or had successful exits. So now we want you to feel that same envy, that jealousy. To hold us in high esteem for our amazing accomplishments. That's the fuel that keeps the Valley going. Greed and envy and pride and all the other deadly sins are the core flywheel of who we are. We may sugarcoat it in rhetoric about making the world a better place. But, for the most part, that's *bullshit*. We're motivated by fame and fortune, just like everyone else. *More* so than everyone else. Without your naive optimism, your willingness to take the riskiest, one-in-a-million bets, Silicon Valley doesn't exist—the machine stalls. The story you're told by entitled entrepreneurs, and your friends at other companies, and investors, and the tech press, is just that . . . a *story*. Ostensibly to inspire you, but, in reality, it entraps you. Destines you to expend your energy and creativity for the enrichment of investors. Measures you only by the size of your exits. Values you only by the esteem of others. Don't let yourself be a victim of that one narrative."

Sam unscrewed the cap of his water bottle and took a long sip. He wasn't sure himself if he was trying to regain his composure or letting the room stew in the juices of his diatribe. Maybe both. The dais was silent. The other panelists exchanged furtive glances. Kyle's expression indicated he wished he hadn't baited Sam down a conversation-killing rathole. Hannah pressed her hand into her forehead.

Finally, Sam stood and said, "And that's all I have to say about 'this,' Kyle." He unclipped his lavalier, walked off the stage, and returned to the greenroom.

CHAPTER 2:

FIRE ALARM

SAM HAD NEVER NOTICED the fire alarm before. He had been in that conference room a thousand times, maybe more. But he had never noticed the transparent piece of plastic, jutting an inch or two from the wall, emblazoned with a single word in vertical red lettering down the side, *FIRE*. He vaguely recalled a false alarm one day, a year or two ago maybe. The pitch and wail of the alarm was intolerable. Employees plugged fingers in their ears as seizure-inducing strobe lights illuminated the floor. No doubt the flashing lights emanated from mechanisms like the one Sam now regarded, but he hadn't noticed them at the time. Like psychedelic disco balls, hiding in plain sight, just waiting for the moment to activate.

"Do you know what I mean?" Sam's boss, Rohan, asked, facing Sam but avoiding eye contact. The question sounded rhetorical, so Sam didn't feel immediately compelled to reply. Biding his time to engage in the conversation that really did seem to be unfolding, Sam again gazed around the glass-walled conference room. He noted their director of HR, Jessie Hernandez, lingering awkwardly outside the conference room door. Any ambiguities about the point of this conversation were eradicated by her presence. Sam noted more mundane details around the room—the pen trough below the whiteboard filled with multicolored dust from the erasable markers; the stained, orphaned conference room chair that didn't match the others; the little plastic plug in the tabletop to conceal wires running to the electrical outlets below. Details he had been too busy to notice before, now seen, likely, for the last time.

"No, I'm not sure I do know what you mean," Sam finally replied. "It just doesn't seem like a big deal to me."

Rohan let out an exasperated sigh. "You may not think so, but it reflects poorly on Ainetu, on *me*, to have you storming out of one of the premier tech conferences. We're trying hard to portray a certain image as a business, and losing your shit onstage is inconsistent with that image."

"I just wasn't in the mood to partake in all the bullshit," Sam said. "I didn't say anything negative about Ainetu, or *you*. I was just speaking my mind. Besides, if it was such a big event, why did you bail at the last minute? The only reason I was there was 'cause you couldn't be bothered."

"Well, the message it sent to me is that your head isn't in the game. That you're not committed. That Ainetu isn't your number one priority," Rohan said, still without making eye contact. For all his bravado and rhetorical bullying in groups, Rohan could become awkwardly conflict-averse in interpersonal conversations. "See, sometimes companies outgrow their executives, and a change becomes necessary . . . to do what's best for the company."

Sam felt his face flush with anger. His outburst at the event was a mistake, but it was also an outlier. Outwardly, his default role had always been that of the dutiful lieutenant—implementing orders, rectifying problems, achieving objectives. Ensuring the company was positioned for success, often in spite of the founder's arbitrary edicts. Rohan had been dropping knives at him for months, and Sam had caught every single one.

"Are you *really* firing me over this?" Sam asked. "After everything I've done to make this company successful—to make *you* successful. After cleaning up the mess and getting the company back on track, you're *firing* me? For what? Telling the truth?"

"I just can't trust you anymore."

The reality, Sam knew, was that Rohan had never trusted him. Maybe he was right not to. A founder always looks over his shoulder at a second-in-command, particularly one placed there by an interventionist board. Though Sam had ruminated about assuming control someday, now wasn't the time to break the facade of his loyalty.

"That's ridiculous! You've trusted me with every aspect of running this business for over two years. This is a complete overreaction—totally unexpected," Sam said, staring incredulously, trying to remain calm. "Why are you doing this?"

"Jessie can go over all the details with you," Rohan replied, twirling a pen in his hand. "It's probably best to talk with her."

"Talk with *Jessie*? I'm not asking how to enroll in COBRA," Sam said sarcastically. "I'm asking you why you're really letting me go. There's no justification for it."

"It's already done," Rohan said with a wave of his hand. "I'm interviewing your replacement in ten minutes." Sam immediately deflated with the realization that this wasn't the usual impulsive Rohan decision, but a premeditated plan. "How do you think we should position this?" Rohan asked after a prolonged pause.

Sam was dumbstruck, still absorbing what was transpiring. Was Rohan *really* asking him how to position his own firing to the rest of the company without even giving him the courtesy of a rational explanation as to why this was happening?

"What do you mean?" Sam asked.

"Well . . . I was thinking, if you want to tell people you decided to quit, I'd be fine with that," Rohan said.

Sam realized then that Rohan actually understood just how tenuous his control of the company was. That if he told the employees he fired Sam, he could have a mutiny on his hands. Hence the offer, under the veil of letting Sam save face, to position his murder as a suicide.

"No, I think we should tell people the truth. That this was *your* decision," Sam said. "That you decided the 'best thing for the company' is to let me go."

Rohan remained silent, looking down again at his spinning pen just as it slipped from his grasp and clattered across the table. Then, stealing a glance at Sam, he said, "OK, Jessie is ready to talk to you now."

■ ■ ■

Jessica Hernandez perfectly fit the prototypical HR person—eager to please, but incredibly risk averse and uncomfortable with conflict. Sam had had the unfortunate responsibility of letting other employees go at Ainetu. Rohan was never willing to do the dirty work himself. To mitigate the risk of an employee lawsuit, Jessie was always involved in those firings, delivering the news in a sterile but nervous monotone.

Sam exited the conference room to the awaiting Jessie without exchanging further words with Rohan. Other employees who had noticed the discussion through the glass walls of the conference room and the unusual formal presence of Jessie holding a manila folder started whispering to each other and gravitating toward the conference room— trying to discern what was going down.

"I'm sure Rohan told you that today will be your last day at Ainetu," Jessie began once they sat down in the adjacent conference room, as if reading from a script.

Sam's thoughts raced. *Am I truly powerless to stop this? Has Rohan cleared this decision with the board? They hired me to keep Rohan in check. Surely they will have my back, right?*

Jessie's face flushed under the thick base of foundation and rouge that spackled over her pockmarked complexion. Her perfume was over-powering in the small room. She continued, "We appreciate your service to the company, but I will need to collect your key card and employee ID today. Here is a copy of your termination letter and final paycheck," she said, sliding the envelope across the table. "I have put a box near your desk so you can collect your belongings and turn in your laptop. You will be eligible for continued healthcare benefits under COBRA. There is information on how to enroll in this packet."

Sam interrupted the monologue. "Jessie, I know the routine. I've been through it a dozen times on the other side. I helped you write those damn talking points," he said disarmingly, finally getting Jessie to let down her guard.

With an exasperated exhale and tears welling in her eyes, Jessie broke out of character. "Look, Sam. I just . . . I just can't believe this is happening. I told Rohan this was a terrible idea."

"Yes, you're right. It's a terrible idea," said Sam, discharging some of his still-churning anger in her direction. Every emotion was compelling him to go apeshit—wipe everything off his desk, declare at the top of his lungs that they were all fucked, and stomp out of the building in a blaze of glory. But he had to keep his composure. As unjust as he felt this dismissal was, he wanted to handle it as he had handled every other irrational impulse from their mercurial founder, with dignity and grace.

It's nothing personal. You're just not who we need at this stage. We've decided to go in a different direction. Every line, every lame rationalization, all of which he'd delivered himself to other unwitting victims he had axed, echoed through the disoriented chambers of his mind. He recognized them now for what they were: insincere platitudes, conjured to assuage the awkwardness, to provide air cover for at-will employment, to mitigate the legal risk. Sam took the termination packet and stood up as Jessie wiped tears from the corners of her eyes. "It's just not fair," she muttered, subduing a sob.

"No, it's not. But I guess that's the role of the COO—to be the fall guy. Nice working with you, Jessie. Keep in touch."

As he returned to his desk, Sam was conscious that the entire office was only pretending to work at this point. Rohan was still in the conference room, now on his phone in agitated conversation. Jessie remained in the other conference room blowing her nose into a Kleenex. Both were awkwardly visible through the glass walls as Sam picked up the moving box Jessie had not-so-discreetly left near his desk and commenced filling it with his personal items. As he did, a palpable buzz circulated through the cubicles as speculation was now in full force. Instinctively, Sam checked his email only to discover his account had already been shut down. *Two years of building trust at this company, and I'm shut out of the network in two minutes.*

Amanda Augustine, their head of sales, was the first to approach him. "Sam, what the *fuck* is going on?" she asked, the urgency in her voice implying her disbelief at what she suspected. He paused and gave her a look that said it all, before putting a framed picture of his family into the box. "Are you *kidding* me?"

With Rohan and Jessie still occupying the only two conference rooms, Sam nodded Amanda toward the copier room to speak with her privately. Everyone called it the copier room, even though making photocopies was not something anyone ever did in it. Instead, it now housed their lonely printer, office supplies, miscellaneous remnants of past employee birthday parties—and, most importantly, it served as their informal third conference room.

"Rohan fired me," Sam said.

"I literally don't understand the words coming out of your mouth right now," Amanda stammered. "*Why?* Because of the SaaStr thing?"

"Apparently."

"Sam, you're *running* the goddamned company. He can't do this. The place is going to fall apart!"

"He *can* do it, and it's *not* going to fall apart. Because you're still going to be here to keep it on the rails." Amanda was Sam's first hire when he joined Ainetu. They had worked together at a previous company where she was a regional sales manager with obvious potential. It was a big promotion to lead Ainetu's sales organization, but her impact was immediate—building the sales team, winning several key accounts, and repeatedly beating their quarterly revenue target.

"People are going to lose their shit," Amanda said. "What are you going to tell them?"

"I'm just going to tell them the truth—that it's been a great run, but the best thing for the company is for me to move on." Sam shrugged. Amanda, for one of the first times Sam had ever seen, was speechless, staring at him in disbelief as the reality of what was happening further set in. "You'll do great. And if you ever need a sounding board or just want to vent, I'm always just a phone call away."

"Thank you," Amanda said, suddenly wrapping Sam in a tight hug. "Thank you for believing in me and giving me this opportunity. I've learned so much from you." Then, as she pulled away with a wistful smile, dabbing the corner of her eye with her finger, she said, "And I'll definitely be calling you. You're not getting rid of me that easily!"

A couple sales reps cautiously peeked into the copier room. "Hey, guys—what's going on?" one of them asked. With Rohan still sequestered away in the conference room, Sam stepped out of the copier room to discover dozens of expectant faces forming an impromptu company meeting. Unsure what to say, he defaulted to his instinct to disarm the situation. "Look, it's going to be fine," Sam reassured everyone. "Today will be my last day at Ainetu. We've decided to go in a different direction. But you all will be fine. Just stay focused, keep executing, and this company will be a huge success."

Suddenly, Rohan, upon realizing the crowd that had assembled, abruptly dropped his phone and burst out of the conference room. "What the hell are you still doing here?" Rohan shouted at Sam. "Jessie, I thought I told you to retrieve Sam's laptop and escort him out of the building. What are you all looking at? Get back to work."

Sam swallowed, the humiliation swelling like regurgitation in his throat. He recognized in that instant all the times he had placated Rohan. Buffered his insufferable rants from the rest of the company. Rohan was a genius, no doubt, but he was toxic. Why was he enabling him? He was tired of being the dutiful lieutenant—the ever-loyal company man. Perhaps Sam was helpless to change this decision, but the company was going to die with Rohan at the helm. Sam couldn't let that be his epitaph at Ainetu.

"Rohan's right," Sam began, turning back toward the assembled employees. "Get back to work. That's what you're all here for. To work your *asses* off—24-7, 365. You're here to get rich, *right?* You've got your stock options. We feed you. We hop you up with Red Bulls and kombuchas and free Philz coffees. Whatever it takes to keep you awake and at your desks. So get back to them!" Sam threw a backhanded wave toward their cubicles, then continued, "Oh . . . here's a little fun fact, though. Those stock options you have are most likely *worthless.* Scenario one, which happens to nine out of ten venture-backed start-ups, is Ainetu goes belly-up, and you all lose your jobs. Scenario two is that we muddle along and manage to break even, which means the investors get their money back and you're lucky to still be gainfully employed. Scenario three is the one-in-a-million moon shot. Maybe that's us! But even if Ainetu is a huge success and is acquired or goes public for some massive, eye-popping valuation, most of you will barely make enough— after dilution, and preferences, and carve-outs, and lockups, and all the other bullshit that peels away what was already such a miniscule percentage of the company that you need a calculator to keep track of that many zeroes—to pay the fucking alternative minimum tax on your hypothetical windfall! So good luck! Godspeed! And, if you're smart, get out while you can."

The room was silent. The rant was out of character, but it was his second in two days. Sam couldn't believe what he'd just said, let alone that Rohan had permitted him to complete his monologue without interruption. Maybe Sam's words rang true even for him. Sam threw a stapler into his box, which no doubt belonged to the company, but there was nothing else on the desk left to pack. He handed his laptop to Jessie. Then, with every employee staring at him, he picked up the box in one hand and slung his empty laptop bag over his shoulder.

Rohan watched contemptuously, then returned to the conference room as employees shuffled back to their desks. Approaching the lobby, Sam saw their receptionist handing a chilled bottle of water to a sharply dressed middle-aged man. She led him toward the conference room as Sam passed, carrying his box of office supplies. Standing alone in the lobby, Sam waited for what seemed like an eternity for the elevator.

Then, there it was again—another previously unnoticed fire alarm.

He intently pondered the red lever with its thin glass bar.

He glanced over his shoulder, still alone—momentarily marveling at how instantaneously he had become a pariah. No one willing to associate with him. He wanted the world to stop. He wanted to undo what had just happened. He wanted to wipe Rohan's smug expression off his face, to scuttle his replacement's interview, to cast everyone scurrying down the stairwells with alarms blaring. Impulsively, he reached his hand to the alarm and yanked it downward. If he'd had his faculties, he would have anticipated what happened next. In addition to the shrill screech and flashing lights, dozens of sprinkler heads simultaneously unleashed a torrent of water.

Sam was too stunned to move.

He heard people shrieking through the din of the alarm and cascades of water. His hair, clothes, and box were all immediately saturated, as if he had plunged into the deep end of a pool. Which, in a way, was exactly what he had done. The sound of employees running toward him finally broke him from his motionless state. With his dripping box still in his hands, he turned his hip to burst through the emergency exit into the descending stairwell.

CHAPTER 3:

VALLEY POOR

Three Months Earlier

"DID YOU TALK TO ANDY ABOUT THE lack of progress?" Sam's wife, Heather, asked, glancing at him in the mirror as she applied mascara.

The remodel had seemed like a good idea at the outset, but it was rapidly becoming a pile of debt with no end in sight. Their house at 806 Richardson Court was barely big enough for their three kids when they purchased it for over $3 million a few years earlier. But the three-bedroom, 1,800-square-foot layout was starting to feel tight. The boys were too old to still share a room.

They contemplated a move. Sam set up push notifications on one of the real estate apps, which dutifully let him know each time a new house was listed that they couldn't afford. Maybe they could find something opportunistically—like an unincorporated parcel or a foreclosure, if they were lucky. But spec builders were scooping up properties as soon as they listed with all-cash offers and no contingencies. Many were teardowns. Even as a dual-income couple, a move just wasn't financially feasible. So they took out a home equity loan, demolished the walls, and embarked on the remodel.

"Yeah, he said seven or eight weeks tops," Sam said, hesitantly repeating the promise of Andy, their contractor, that he doubted himself.

"Seven or eight *weeks*? I'm going to go crazy if we don't have a working kitchen and bathroom for that long."

"I know, I know. Me too," Sam said. "I had to wipe my ass with a dry baby wipe last night. I couldn't find any toilet paper."

"How did you find a baby wipe? That thing must be five years old," she said, her softened tone acknowledging his attempt at comedic relief.

"I know! It felt five years old. I'm not sure I'm going to be able to sit down today. Anyway, I stressed with Andy that we need to bring in that time frame. So keep your fingers crossed."

"OK. Well, there's not much we can do at this point," she said with the resignation of a homeowner who knows the options are few. "But stay on him, will you?"

"Yes, of course. I'll stay on him. Like facial hair on a hipster," Sam said with a half-hearted chuckle at his own joke.

"I don't know what that means," she replied flatly.

"You know . . . how every hipster has facial hair?" Nothing. "It's just a metaphor. Or maybe an idiom."

"Is it?"

"Yeah, like 'white on rice,' you know?" He paused again for acknowledgement. "Whatever. Point is I'm on it."

"Thanks," she said, pecking him on the cheek. "I've got to get to work."

Sam walked down the hall to their gutted kitchen. A tap on his wrist from his digital watch reminded him it had been twelve days since his last workout. His two sons were eating cereal from Styrofoam bowls with plastic spoons, both engrossed in their devices. Connor, the oldest, was sitting at a folding table finishing homework on his laptop. Mason was pulling a carton of orange juice from the refrigerator while watching a sitcom with wireless headphones.

"Good morning, guys. How'd you sleep?" Sam asked.

"Fine," said Connor, briefly glancing up from his keyboard. No response from Mason. Sam waved a hand in front of Mason's face to get his attention.

"Can you pause that for a second? I asked if you had a good night's sleep."

Mason pulled down his headphones with a slight huff. "Fine."

"OK, OK . . . no need to get into an argument. Where's your sister?" Sam asked as he noticed her burrowed into a nest of pillows in the corner of the couch watching a cartoon on her iPad while feeding Cheerios to their dog.

"Riley, sweetie, don't feed too many of those to Baxter. It's not good for him," Sam said. "I have a breakfast meeting, guys, so I need to drop you off at school a little early."

"OK," said Mason. "Where are you going?"

"The Four Seasons. I'm looking forward to a hot meal for a change," Sam said.

They went outside and got into his Audi. He was a little self-conscious about driving a car nicer than anything his dad ever owned, but the ubiquity of Audis in the Bay Area made it seem less fancy—a Honda in Silicon Valley. As they pulled up to the school in a queue of Teslas, Jaguars, and BMW SUVs, any bashfulness about the car quickly dissipated. Inching their way to the appointed drop-off spot, Sam could see in the rearview mirror that Riley had a question on her mind.

"Dad," Riley started with curious innocence. "Are we poor?"

Sam was taken aback. "That's a stupid question," Mason admonished his sister.

"No, we're not poor, sweetie," said Sam, chafing at the notion that a girl being chauffeured to school in a $50,000 car would think she was poor but trying to retain a calm demeanor. *Teaching moment.* "Why would you think that?"

"Haley Whitaker said because they have two stories and we only have one that we must be poor," said Riley matter-of-factly. The Whitakers, their next-door neighbors, had purchased the two-story McMansion that loomed over the Hughes's fence. Sam could practically hear those words coming out of the mouth of Haley, their pretentious only child.

"Oh, OK . . ." Sam considered his next words for a moment. "Don't worry about what Haley says," Sam said in a measured tone. "She's just trying to put you down to feel better about herself."

"Courtney thinks we're poor too," Riley said bluntly.

Well, you can tell Courtney to go fuck herself. "OK, well, I'm sorry they were giving you a hard time, but don't worry about it. We're not poor."

The car finally came to a halt at the designated drop-off spot, and the kids popped out with their backpacks and lunch boxes. "Bye! Love you guys!"

"Love you too, Dad," they said in chorus before shutting the doors. Sam lingered a moment and watched them merge into the river of children toward the school, wondering in his mind if his kids' sense of reality was permanently distorted from life in the Bay Area. How do you explain that not having a gate code and full-time house staff makes you *normal*, not poor?

Sam realized Riley was just picking up on his own anxieties in the perceptive way children sometimes can. The house purchase and remodel had strained them financially. Although he and Heather were both well-paid, an "exit" seemed increasingly necessary to stay financially afloat in the Bay Area. Sam tried calming his nerves about their growing debt load with the recognition that their financial situation could change in a heartbeat. As a senior executive at Ainetu, his stock options could be worth millions if the company was acquired or went public. Such an event would not only solve their current financial pinch but enable them to live what amounted to a normal middle-class life in the Bay Area. Though he was cautiously optimistic about the company's prospects, he had to be patient. The stock options today were illiquid. A lottery ticket, worth nothing until it hits.

■ ■ ■

Sam exited Highway 101 at University Avenue in Palo Alto, an area formerly known as Whiskey Gulch. The now-gone two-block stretch of road had been the only portion of Palo Alto's sister city, East Palo Alto, that was on the *west* side of 101 when Sam first moved to Silicon Valley twenty years earlier. Whiskey Gulch was the closest thing "EPA" residents had to a downtown, populated with liquor stores, Laundromats, and check-cashing stands bunkered behind bulletproof glass. In its place today was his destination, the Four Seasons hotel.

To anyone who lived in Palo Alto prior to 2005, the very phrase "Four Seasons East Palo Alto" sounded like the punch line of a joke—as incongruous as the Four Seasons Compton or the Ritz-Carlton Harlem. In the 1980s and '90s, East Palo Alto had been one of the most violent neighborhoods in the country. The freeway that cut the two communities in half separated two worlds—palm tree–lined driveways on one side, drive-by shootings on the other. As the first dot-com frenzy escalated in the '90s, something about East Palo Alto seemed like it couldn't last. Sure enough, in 2004 the dam broke. Developers acquired the entire neighborhood and the bulldozers followed. Gone were the storefronts selling lottery cards and bail bonds and in came a massive ten-story office complex housing several of the top venture capital and law firms in the country—all anchored by the Four Seasons, which Sam approached, navigating through Ferraris and McLarens to the valet.

His breakfast meeting was with Kamal Jha, their most recent investor and board member at Ainetu. It was a relatively routine affair. Polite handshakes followed by innocuous banter and a $100 breakfast. Spotting each other with a nod across the large dining area, Sam was led by the maître d' to the table. Kamal's nearly empty coffee cup suggested he had been there a while, even though Sam was ten minutes early.

"Great to see you, Sam," Kamal exclaimed, somewhat overenthusiastically.

"Great to see you too," said Sam, gesturing toward the nearly empty cup. "Looks like you got here early."

"You know how it is. Holding court," Kamal said in a deliberately self-deprecating tone.

They sat as Kamal summoned the waiter. "We're ready to order." Then, turning to Sam, "Go ahead, Sam."

Feeling rushed, Sam quickly scanned the menu, "Oh, I guess I'll just have some scrambled eggs with wheat toast, please. And a coffee."

The waiter diligently scribbled down Sam's order, then turned with some trepidation to Kamal. "And for you, sir?"

"Yes," Kamal said, glancing over his glasses to ensure he had the waiter's full attention. "I'll have half an avocado, sliced. With fresh ground pepper, no salt. I can't have salt. No toast."

"Would you like an English muffin instead?" asked the waiter.

"No—no carbs. I can't have *carbs*, Miguel," he said, glancing at the waiter's name tag. "Just the avocado. And I've been waiting for my coffee to be refilled for ten minutes now."

"Yes, sir. Right away. Anything else, sir?"

"Yes. I need a spoon. This table wasn't set properly," Kamal said, his hand extending over the table to indicate the presence of a fork and knife, but no spoon. "There's no spoon."

"Yes, sir. Right away, sir," the waiter said as he hurried off.

Kamal rolled his eyes, then returned his gaze to Sam as a smile returned to his expression. "So, Sam . . . Rohan tells me you guys are *crushing* it!"

"Oh, yeah," Sam said, modestly looking down to reposition his napkin. "It's going really well." His mind scrolled through what new information Rohan might have shared with Kamal since their board meeting only three weeks earlier.

"I'd say! I'm getting calls from my guys at Goldman and Morgan. They're itching to kick off a process," Kamal said, referring to the process of shopping a company for potential sale. "Or, if the public markets stay strong, maybe even file for an IPO."

"Well, I want to see how Q1 goes first. It won't be a layup," Sam said, trying to temper expectations. The quarter had been one of their toughest, and they still needed to close several big deals to hit their revenue target.

The waiter discreetly placed a spoon next to Kamal, who picked it up without looking at the waiter or the spoon. He then peeled the top off what appeared to be a plastic pudding cup that he had pulled from his briefcase. Sam couldn't immediately discern if it was part of a diet or maybe some sort of prescription or maybe just a pudding fetish. Kamal set the foil top on the table and ate a spoonful. Sam tried to ignore the ritual, as if grown adults eating pudding cups at the Four Seasons was commonplace.

"I'm on a strict diet," Kamal said, noticing Sam's apparent curiosity out of the corner of his eye as he lifted another spoonful to his mouth, his words muffled by the pudding. "Rohan tells me Q1 is in the bag. I've already connected him with a bunch of bankers."

"Oh . . . OK." Sam was mildly irritated Rohan was already talking to bankers. As the number-two executive at Ainetu, Sam expected to at least be consulted about such a major decision. Further, *What the hell was Rohan telling the bankers?* Sam wasn't at all confident that Rohan wasn't getting carried away with the attention, exaggerating the company's metrics in an attempt to impress would-be suitors and accelerate the process.

"Don't be so conservative, Sam," Kamal said with a smirk, as if he was calculating his firm's IRR. "With the momentum you guys have, Rohan will nail this."

Rohan had founded Ainetu in 2014 with his friend, Sasha Kuznetsov, from Stanford's computer science program. As one of the first machine learning data-modeling systems, they rode a wave of investor enthusiasm around leveraging artificial intelligence to predict security threats. They quickly raised a $2 million seed round, followed shortly thereafter by an $8 million series A, both led by Preston Lawrence at Ellipsis Ventures, based on promising customer traction. Within a year, Preston convinced Ben Bentley at Wellington Ventures, whom he had coinvested with on another deal, to lead a $20 million series B round. Flush with capital, Rohan spent heavily in pursuit of growth, but after their early success, the company started to move sideways. His constantly changing manic impulses had overextended the business. Each "pivot" deepened the sense internally that they lacked a strategy.

Unfortunately, Rohan's supercilious personality was making a bad situation worse. Reacting to the setbacks like a petulant child, he would go on condescending tirades with his senior management team. The friction led to executive departures—first Rohan's cofounder, Sasha, who had been almost solely responsible for coding the initial version of their platform but could no longer tolerate being blamed for all the product's deficiencies; then the head of sales, Brian, after refusing to sign up for an aggressive sales target he knew they would miss. Rohan seized on the departures to blame his lieutenants for the company's struggles—throwing them under the proverbial bus both with the board and at the company all-hands meetings.

Ainetu was running low on cash and struggling to raise their next round with shaky metrics and questions about Rohan. A solution finally came in the form of Kamal's firm, OakGrove Capital. Rohan had gotten them interested in investing, but privately Kamal expressed trepidation about the CEO situation. To secure the investment, Ben proposed bringing in a "seasoned number two" to help Rohan regain his footing and return the company to a growth trajectory. He called Sam, whom he knew from a previous company, and persuaded him to join Ainetu as COO. With a new leadership team, OakGrove led a $30 million series C round.

The waiter returned to the table with a vibrant green avocado perfectly fanned out on a large white plate and a pepper grinder under his arm. Sam's eggs were nowhere to be seen. "Please let me know how much fresh ground pepper you would like, sir."

Kamal watched each twist of the pepper grinder intently, then raised his hand in a prompt vertical motion to indicate a sufficient amount of pepper had been applied. "What varietal of avocado is this, *Miguel*?" Kamal asked.

"Sir?"

"Yes. Do you know what a 'varietal' is?" he asked, pausing not long enough for Miguel, whose family had probably picked avocados for a living and knew every varietal grown in the state, to respond to the rhetorical question. "Is it a Hass or a Fuerte or perhaps a Pinkerton?"

"I believe it is a Hass avocado, sir. But I can confirm with the chef."

"No. No, it looks too long for a Hass," Kamal said assertively, examining the fruit. "Maybe a Reed or a Gwen."

Jesus Christ, thought Sam. *Are we really going to sit here and listen to him pontificate on avocados?* Ostentatious displays of knowledge on obscure topics was a common VC behavior trait. Over the years, he'd heard similar blustering on every possible area of expertise, from Italian bicycle parts to Cambodian green teas. All Sam could think when he heard such monologues was, *How do you possibly have time to obtain such depth of irrelevant information?* while outwardly feigning interest in whatever asinine fact was being recited. *Oh, you're right! You really can tell that this tea is only picked by Buddhist monks on the third Tuesday after the full moon.* It was all peacocking to establish social status. My dick is bigger than yours because I can name forty varieties of avocado.

"I will check with the chef, sir," the waiter said, deflecting the confrontation by turning to Sam. "Your breakfast will be up in just a moment, sir." The two of them exchanged a brief glance to acknowledge their respective need to genuflect to the avocado king.

Kamal began cutting his avocado with an inverted fork in his left hand and a steak knife in his right.

"Please, go ahead and eat before it . . ." *Before it what? Turns more room temperature?* "Oxidizes." Sam chuckled at his poor attempt at humor, but Kamal simply stared at Sam and chewed without a reaction, his mind apparently going in a different direction.

"You've made a big impact at Ainetu, Sam," Kamal said with an impaled piece of avocado in midair. "It was Rohan's vision that I invested in, but you've brought a much-needed discipline around execution. You deserve every bit of the financial reward ahead of you."

"Thanks, I appreciate that." *This is my chance*, Sam thought. "I just hope we can keep it on the rails until then."

"What do you mean?" Kamal asked.

"Rohan's . . . *management style* is causing a lot of tension. You know we already lost Sasha and Brian, but I'm afraid practically everyone on the executive team is a flight risk."

"Two eggs scrambled with wheat toast, sir," said Miguel as he placed an immaculately presented plate of food in front of Sam. One that cost thirty dollars for about fifty cents' worth of ingredients.

"Thank you," said Sam, noticing that Kamal, who was already finished with his avocado and his pudding cup, was providing his undivided attention. "I just don't want a bad situation to get worse. Regardless of what Rohan has told you, this quarter is going to come down to the wire. If we start down the path with bankers and immediately miss our number or have a bunch of executive departures, we may not get a second chance for a while."

Kamal contemplated Sam's comments with his legs crossed and his coffee cup perched on his arched knee. "I'm not worried," he finally said. "I have every confidence you will get it done. You always do."

CHAPTER 4:

UNICORN DREAMS

FOG COMPLETELY SHROUDED the Golden Gate Bridge, obscuring any sign of land as Sam approached his destination like a pilot descending toward a runway through a bank of clouds. With the end of the quarter looming and a board meeting two weeks away, Rohan had insisted on an executive team off-site that week at Cavallo Point, a former military officers' compound just underneath the Marin side of the bridge that had been converted into a luxury resort.

With his breakfast with Kamal a few days earlier still on his mind, Sam knew the timing couldn't be worse. He and Amanda, their head of sales, were frantically trying to close deals before the end of the week to meet their lofty quarterly revenue target. Rohan was never very mindful of such things. Expensive off-sites were one of his favorite activities. If he wasn't under such pressure to hit the number, Sam would have valued the chance to talk strategy with the team. But there rarely seemed to be time to do that. Most of the agenda was filled with routine departmental updates and team-building exercises. At the last off-site, Rohan had hired a professional facilitator, at a cost of $10,000, so he was unburdened from the task of even preparing an agenda.

Sam had to admit that Rohan's swagger hadn't been entirely detrimental. In the right setting, like an analyst briefing or investor pitch, Rohan could exude a combination of self-confidence and prescient vision that VCs found captivating—enabling Ainetu to raise capital well ahead of what was rational based on their fundamentals. That same projection of assurance along with carefully nurtured media connections enabled Rohan to play an outsize role in the tech blogs, which amplified his eccentric personality and professional accolades, portraying him as a mystical entrepreneurial savant. That brash public persona Rohan worked so hard to portray could fade in social settings, revealing a fragile psychological core riddled with insecurities and doubt.

Pulling into the valet at the resort, Sam arrived just in time to get another cup of coffee before taking his seat around the horseshoe-shaped conference table. Rohan was late, in spite of his email laden with capital letters and exclamation points the night before insisting that everyone be on time. They killed time checking email and filling plates with breakfast pastries. Sam and Amanda discussed the latest on a big pending deal with Green Gate Technologies they were still hoping might close before the end of the quarter. GGT had been Amanda's white whale for a while. As a developer of custom software for banks, they were a prime candidate for Ainetu's AI-based security analytics, but Sam was skeptical. They had visited Chicago twice to meet with Carl Downey, the head of IT and lead decision maker at GGT. He talked a big game with Amanda about a multimillion-dollar purchase, but Sam couldn't help but think that Carl was just relishing the attention of an attractive woman. Watching Amanda laugh at every lame joke Carl uttered was like watching the prom queen flirt with the pocket-protector nerd to get a ride home in his car.

Bill Johnson, Ainetu's CFO, was urgently working on his laptop, barely acknowledging the rest of the team. He was first on the agenda and seemed stressed as he looked at his screen with a furrowed brow. Bill was well organized, detail-oriented, and diligent, as you'd expect of a CPA. He was also a constant worrier, pessimistic in his outlook, and passive-aggressive in his interpersonal interactions, as you might also expect. In temperament, he was ill-suited to the ups and downs of a start-up.

He had almost certainly been the first person in the room that morning, dressed in one of his endless repertoire of nondescript blue Brooks Brothers button-downs. Bill was one of only two members of the executive team who reported directly to Rohan rather than Sam, the other being their chief technology officer, Zhang Wei. This made Bill a bit of a thorn in Sam's side, particularly around the end of the quarter when Bill would grow agitated if the bookings didn't precisely meet the forecast in his spreadsheet. His consternation was higher than usual his morning.

Rohan finally burst through the double doors of the conference room, finishing a phone call on his Bluetooth headset. "Uh-huh," he said to whomever he was speaking. "Totally!" Another pause as he filled a cup with hot water from the buffet. "*Dude*, you're so right!" All other conversations in the room stopped as Rohan continued with the call that would no doubt be the stated reason for his tardiness. "OK, I gotta run to this off-site thing. I'll call you about it tomorrow."

Rohan hung up the call, removed the sunglasses he was still wearing, and sat at the front of the room dipping a tea bag into his mug. "Hey, guys. I had to take that call," he said. The rest of the team shuffled to their seats around the table, sipping coffee and opening laptops. "Bill, get us started," Rohan said, offering no further preamble about the agenda or goals of the off-site.

"Before Bill gets started, if I could just take a second," Sam said. "First, welcome, everyone. Thank you for making time for this important off-site, particularly during the end-of-quarter crunch. We have a lot to cover today. You all have a copy of the agenda. Bill is going to start off with the numbers. I think we all know that this last quarter was tougher sledding than we've had in the past. So the goal of today's meeting is to get a better sense of where we can improve going forward to get the business firing on all cylinders again. Anyone have questions before we kick off?"

The group glanced around the room at each other. Nobody seemed to have any questions; they nodded in agreement. Rohan was already typing on his phone. Looking up peevishly, he said, "OK, no questions. As I said, Bill, get us started."

Bill plugged his laptop into the projector, and a spreadsheet in an incredibly small font came up on the screen. "As you can see, the financials aren't where we want them to be for Q1," Bill said. He then quickly ran through various numbers, toggling between worksheets. With a dizzying array of columns and rows on the screen, it was doubtful anyone in the room, save Sam, who'd had the benefit of reviewing the spreadsheet earlier, could follow along.

"So new bookings for the quarter should come in at about 80 percent of the financial plan," Bill said. "Unless there's a miracle with GGT closing this week, I can't see us closing that gap. There just aren't any other big-enough deals. Any new news, Amanda?"

"No, unfortunately," Amanda said, shaking her head. "They're talking about only doing a pilot, but Sam and I are still working on them."

"So there you go on the bookings side," said Bill, returning to the spreadsheet. "We still have a shot at making our revenue target since the revenue recognition from these deals is a little complicated, but if we keep missing our bookings, it will really screw up our financial forecasts for next year."

"You guys need to get this fixed," Rohan said, gesturing his phone toward Amanda and Sam but not looking up from his screen.

"Unfortunately, we also have a problem on the expense side," Bill continued, toggling to a different spreadsheet. "We were way over budget in Q1 by over 30 percent, mostly due to unplanned new hires in the engineering org and the offshore professional services team in Hyderabad. Our sales head count was also above plan, and we ran up pretty hefty legal fees related to the patent lawsuit." A patent troll had come after Ainetu, asserting the company had violated some decade-old patent they had acquired from a defunct company. After initially fighting the frivolous suit to the tune of $400,000 in legal fees, they changed tactics and settled with the plaintiff for $500,000. Nearly a million dollars flushed down the drain.

"For you non-finance types, less revenue and more expense is not what you want," Bill quipped while remaining expressionless. "Given the lackluster results this quarter, I reran our cash-out analysis, and we have less runway than we planned at the start of the year. At our current course and speed, we're out of cash in seven months."

"That's not true, Bill," Rohan said dismissively, finally looking up from his phone to make the remark. "We have a $10 million line of credit from Silicon Valley Bank. We can just draw that down if we need to."

"It's not quite as simple as that," Bill responded. "As I have explained before, that line of credit has a number of covenants. The first of which is that we need to hit our bookings plan, which we will not do this quarter. The second, and more important, is that we have a cash balance of over ten million, which we did not as of the end of Q1. Plus, we've already got five million in convertible debt. So that line of credit is effectively unavailable to us."

"Then why do we even have it?" Amanda asked. "What use is a loan if you have to have more money than the amount of the loan?"

"Good question," chimed in Anton Larsson, their Swedish-born head of marketing, as others nodded in agreement.

"It's not really meant for operating expenses," Bill explained. "It's for stuff like purchasing equipment."

"What equipment?" asked Zhang Wei, their CTO. "We run on AWS. Besides laptops, we don't buy equipment."

Bill didn't react to the remark except to stare at Zhang for a moment. Rohan seemed to have lost interest again in the conversation, returning his thumbs to his phone. Bill looked at Rohan for several seconds, trying patiently to regain his attention.

Sam felt compelled to get the meeting back on track. "Look, Bill is right," he said, standing to walk to the screen. "This is our head count expense line. We're about ten engineers ahead of plan, which equates to about $3 million of additional burn annually. And the Hyderabad team is costing us another million per year that wasn't in the plan."

"We need those engineers and the offshore team to hit our new feature deadlines," Zhang said in his thick Mandarin accent. "We have less staff than we need for the current product roadmap."

"I know, I know, Zhang," Sam reassured him. "I get it. We have an ambitious product vision, and we all agreed that hiring more engineers and ramping up the Hyderabad team were the right things to do. But we also didn't expect the patent lawsuit, and . . . other expenses." Sam looked around the room at their surroundings, indicating to all, except Rohan, who was still immersed in his device, what he meant. "We also had several large customers cancel this quarter, which hurts us on revenue recognition."

"Yes," Bill said. "I didn't mention that, but, as you all know, three of our big accounts canceled, so we have a revenue gap to close from that."

"Why did they cancel, Sam?" Rohan dropped back into the conversation, again not looking up from his screen, as if the question were rhetorical.

"Well," Sam said, "for Cantilever Gaming, we couldn't integrate to their back end."

"Which is why we need the professional services team in Hyderabad," Rohan interrupted.

Sam continued. "Tetra Bank said we didn't have the security certifications they need for their EU division, as we discussed."

Rohan dropped his phone on the table in exasperation. "That's not true, Sam! Their CIO told me your customer support team was the worst he ever worked with!"

The customer support team was a favorite scapegoat for Rohan. He fancied himself the product visionary, but he lacked the organizational discipline to execute on any coherent plan. Constantly shifting priorities, he would insist engineers pull all-nighters on pet new features no customers seemed to want. If a deal was lost or a customer canceled, it was never the product's fault—blamed instead on the customer team's inability to explain the latest failure to deliver promised features. The pressure had already caused their top two customer support managers to quit. As the gap had widened between the external perception of Ainetu and the internal reality, Rohan's agitation and unpredictability intensified. He had always been impetuous, but the tirades had become more frequent and less cogent.

"Look, we don't need to relitigate what caused these accounts to cancel," Sam said, trying to disarm the confrontation, which was really just a proxy war over where to lay blame for their recent struggles: the product team or the customer team. "The fact is, they did. And I think all Bill and I are saying in this meeting is that we need to adjust the financial plan accordingly."

"Exactly," Bill said. "If we even want to think about filing an S-1 to go public in the foreseeable future, we need to deliver consistent growth. But realistically, I don't see us being ready for that. We need to be thinking about raising another venture round, and soon."

"We're only doing a round if we can get a billion-dollar valuation," Rohan proclaimed. "Otherwise, it's too much dilution."

Ah, the magic number: one billion dollars. Price of entry to join the "Unicorn Club." This term was originally coined to characterize the rarity of a private company with a valuation of more than $1 billion. Now there were over five hundred Unicorn companies. Entrepreneurs saw the Unicorn Club as affirmation that their company was elite, even if the stock wasn't liquid just yet. Venture investors pointed to Unicorns as proof that deal values were too high, yet they themselves were the very force perpetuating the phenomenon—bidding up valuations and pushing founders to overcapitalize due to the VCs' need to fully allocate their huge funds by writing bigger checks.

Sam again tried to avoid escalation. "We're fortunate to have great investors. They're not going to let us run out of cash. They will do a bridge round if we can't get the valuation we want. All that matters is getting back to our operating plan in Q2. If we do that, we'll be fine."

"Well then, you and Amanda better start delivering, because the board meeting next week is going to be ugly," Rohan said, looking directly at Sam. *Start delivering?* Sam had delivered eight straight quarters of beating the plan, but now wasn't the time or place to push back. He knew continuing with Rohan as CEO was untenable. Sam had already put the gears in motion to usurp him. Now he just needed to be patient.

"We will," Sam said. "We will."

CHAPTER 5:

FREE FALL

Present Day

SAM BURST OUT of the emergency exit into an alley. Disoriented, he couldn't believe what had happened. Thoughts flooded his mind. *What is Rohan thinking? What is Heather going to say? Did I really just pull a fucking fire alarm?* He walked briskly down the alley, looking back at the doorway from which he knew his former colleagues would soon emerge. Once around the corner, he pulled out his phone and texted his wife, "*I just got fired.*"

Sam watched the gray bubbles, awaiting her response. "*WHAT!?!?*" Before he could read to the last punctuation mark, his phone rang with Heather's caller ID.

"What *happened?*" she asked as soon as he picked up, with a blend of agitation, sympathy, and disbelief.

"Rohan fired me," Sam said, choking slightly on the sentence. "He just told me."

"What do you mean he fired you? *Why?*"

"I don't know. I guess I sorta lost my shit at a conference yesterday."

"You mean the SaaStr thing?" she asked after a moment of silence.

"Did I tell you about that?"

"No. I saw it on Facebook. Someone posted a video from the conference and tagged you," she said. "I was so embarrassed."

44

"Embarrassed? Why?" Sam asked, looking around the corner at the much bigger embarrassment he had just created—the alley starting to fill with drenched Ainetu employees, sirens of fire engines growing in the distance.

"Meet me at the Starbucks on Market," was all she said in reply, and she hung up.

■ ■ ■

"Holy shit!" Heather said when she first saw Sam, sitting alone on the patio with his cardboard box, cradling a venti latte. "Why are you soaking wet?"

Sam leaned forward and pulled his damp button-down shirt away from his chest, where it had adhered to his skin. He was suddenly self-conscious about the box, realizing it immediately broadcast the story of his recent termination, and that the only item of sentimental value it contained, a framed photo of their family, was ruined. He set the box on the ground and slid it under his feet, as if it held all his worldly possessions.

"Well, you know . . . that's a reasonable question," Sam said, realizing that in his haste to meet her and tell her about the incident he had neglected to come up with a plausible story to explain his soggy state. "The sprinkler system malfunctioned in our office. Just as I was leaving. With my box."

Heather stared at him as if he were deranged. "Are you feeling OK?" she finally asked.

Sam sat upright and tried to straighten his thinning hair. He was coming down from the manic euphoria that had propelled him out of the Ainetu office in a blaze of glory. Disheveled and humiliated, he was now grappling with the wreckage. He looked down at the detritus in his box—random business cards, an Ainetu-branded mug, the stapler. Hard copies of strategic plans and board presentations he had invested countless hours preparing were now irrelevant garbage—bloated and heavy from the water they had absorbed.

"I'm feeling fine," he said, still looking down at the box. "I just don't think I can do this anymore."

"Do *what* anymore? What are you talking about?"

"*This,*" he said, as if the explanation were obvious, gesturing at the bustling tech workers passing on the sidewalk, faces buried in their phones. "I just don't think I can do another start-up. I've been bucked from the horse too many times. Something happened to me on that stage. It was like an out-of-body experience. The futility of this thing I've been chasing for twenty years was suddenly obvious. The realization that, even if I win, somebody else gets the prize."

Heather's look of dubious concern had remained unchanged. Breaking her frozen expression with a sigh of exasperation, she asked, "So what are you saying? What are you planning to do?"

"I don't know," Sam said, looking her in the eye for the first time since their encounter. "Maybe we should sell the house. Move back to Ohio."

"I'm not from Ohio," she bluntly reminded him.

"True, but we could afford an insanely huge house there."

"What would we *do?*" she asked skeptically.

"We'd reboot our lives. I'd take over the family business. That's what my dad always expected me to do. You wouldn't have to work. The kids could ride their bikes to school. We could grow our own vegetables, raise chickens, sell the eggs at a local farmers market . . . or something."

"Sounds miserable," she said. "Sam, you're romanticizing a life you couldn't wait to get away from. Our lives are here. We can't just uproot the kids. I'm not quitting my job to pursue some . . . some *Rockwellian* fantasy!"

Sam leaned back in his chair. "I just don't know if I can get back on the horse."

"Well, you're gonna *have* to! We can't make it on one income. We're in the midst of a remodel we can't afford. We have medical bills for Riley.

We have three kids to put through college," she said, counting off each financial strain on her fingers.

"What am I supposed to do?" he asked.

"Get another job! Or fight to get your job back. But don't just feel sorry for yourself."

"Thanks for being so understanding."

Heather stood with a hurt expression, slid her chair under the table. "I need to get back to work."

■ ■ ■

Sam trudged the several blocks back to his parking garage, his shoes still squishing with each step. He threw the box into his trunk and slumped into the front seat as he pulled up Ben Bentley's contact information. As the lead investor in Ainetu's series B financing round, Ben had first introduced Sam to the company. If anyone would have his back, Ben would. He clicked "Call" and listened to the ring coming across the car's speakers.

"Hey, Sam!" Ben said with rehearsed enthusiasm. "Good to hear from you. What's up?"

"I was hoping *you* could tell *me* that."

"I take it you talked to Rohan?" Ben asked.

"Uh . . . yeah. He just gave me the news this morning. It was completely out of the blue. There was nothing to suggest this was coming."

Ben was silent for a moment. "Well, not quite *nothing*. There was the SaaStr thing."

"Why is everyone making such a big deal out of that?" Sam asked. "Sorry for piercing the veil and telling the truth for a change."

"Look, this all went down really suddenly," Ben said. "I was actually on vacation in Saint Barts when I got the email from Rohan about this."

"So, did he give a *real* reason why he wanted me out of the company?" Sam asked.

"He just said he didn't think your head was in the game after your little outburst."

"Why? Because I didn't sufficiently genuflect at the altar of greed?" Sam asked. "I got this company back on track, and now I'm getting swapped out like a dead spark plug."

"Look, Sam—you know I think you're a rock star. The whole board does. We're all *huge* Sam Hughes fans."

"So why didn't you have my back? Why didn't you stop him?" Sam asked. "Wasn't getting a number two *your* idea? Wasn't that how you convinced Kamal to invest?"

"I guess we just felt that if we told Rohan no on this, that it was a vote of no confidence in him as CEO."

"Do you *have* confidence in him as CEO? Do you really think he's doing a good job running the company?"

"C'mon, Sam—you know how unpleasant it is trying to remove a founder," Ben said. "He could make a scene. He could steal employees. He could bad-mouth us with other founders. Hell, he could sue us. It's just too delicate right now."

"Did the other board members support this move?" Sam asked, acknowledging in his tone this fight was one he couldn't win.

"It's not like we took a vote on it, but we all agreed it was either you or him."

Sam just couldn't comprehend how this had reached the point of irreconcilable differences—why the first step wasn't a discussion among adults about how to work together more effectively, rather than hastily jumping to termination. There really wasn't much more for Sam to say.

"Don't worry about it. Let's grab coffee next week after all this has blown over," Ben suggested cheerily. "I'd love to find a role for you at one of our other portfolio companies."

CHAPTER 6:

PRINCESS BIRTHDAY

SAM SIPPED HIS IPA to the din of an industrial-strength blower. A crew of five tattooed men tended to the straps and anchor points of the three-story inflatable play structure—complete with pink turrets, a princess-themed jumpy room, and a fifty-foot "magic carpet" slide. He watched the pack of shrieking fourth graders as they bludgeoned each other with foam swords and hurled themselves against the various castle-inspired obstacles.

This . . . *thing* could barely be called a jumpy "house." More like a jumpy mansion. A jumpy chateau. "Available for birthdays, bar/bat mitzvahs, and quinceañeras," Sam noted the promotion on the side of the thirty-foot delivery truck, wondering how many families could actually fit this structure in their yard. Despite its impressive stature, the jumpy chateau only occupied a small corner of the palatial backyard of this Atherton estate. In addition to the pool and tennis court, other accoutrements included a full-size soccer goal, a giant stone firepit with Adirondack chairs for twenty, and a two-story jungle gym replica of the Eiffel Tower.

It had been three weeks since Sam's flameout from Ainetu. He felt like a poster child of the "Five Stages of Grieving." The first day or two was Denial. *Did that really just happen? Surely this is a mistake.* But after he thought about it more, he quickly transitioned to Anger. *That weaselly motherfucker! I'm gonna burn the place down!* The Bargaining stage soon followed, as Sam tried to negotiate a better exit package. *Three months of severance is the least you can do. Can I have a year to exercise my options?*

Lately, Sam felt the onset of the fourth stage: Depression. He tried to distract himself—to enjoy his "time off." He'd played golf for the first time in over a year, nearly hurling his 7 iron into a ravine in frustration. He rekindled his love of basketball by joining an over-thirty pickup league, then spent the next three days icing his partially torn hamstring. He felt rudderless. Like he didn't belong. Like what he'd spent his whole life pursuing wasn't important to him anymore. *Maybe I'm just not good enough. Maybe I deserved to be fired. Maybe the company is better off without me.* The voices of doubt grew louder with each passing day. It didn't help his mood to be at a ten-year-old's birthday party only a week ahead of his own forty-fifth birthday.

"How's it going, Sam?" interrupted the recognizable voice of Reid Costa, the host of this extravagant affair. As he turned mid-sip, Sam wasn't prepared to witness Reid in his full regalia, consisting of a black low-cut tank top and matching black yoga pants. Sam nearly spit out his beer at the sight. "Can you believe how fast our little monsters are growing up?" Reid asked, gesturing to the multistory inflatable structure. Sam could only nod his head in agreement as he tried to process the banana hammock Reid was sporting. *Who wears that to a ten-year-old's birthday party? Did he just return from a Bikram yoga class? Is he a registered sex offender?* Sam tried not to look down.

"This is quite a . . . spread," Sam finally mustered. *Spread? Really? You couldn't think of another word to use?* "It's impressive . . . I mean, it's huge!" *You've got to stop talking now.* Sam pointed his beer at the jumpy chateau to clarify he wasn't referring to Reid's spandexed crotch.

"Yeah, you know, anything for my little princess!" said Reid as they both watched a group of girls in one of the turrets typing on their phones, isolated from each other. "She only turns ten once!" he said of his daughter, Isabella, who stuck out in Sam's memory for having once slid Mason a tightly folded note in class that read, "You suck and EVERYONE hates you!"

Sam nodded in agreement, as if turning your backyard into a medieval carnival was the least a father could do. Reid and his wife, Stella, had made their money by acquiring a failing biotech company called Covansys with Stella's father's fortune. The company had a patent on an oral pill that claimed to be an alternative to Botox. They reformulated the drug, and, despite lackluster clinical trials, including pronounced increases in diarrhea, depression, and melanoma, sold the company for nearly $500 million. Reid and Stella owned 80 percent of it.

"You guys are staying for the concert, right?" Reid asked enthusiastically. Sam noticed for the first time a stage and dance floor set up on the far end of the lawn.

"Oh, yeah . . . I'm sure we are," said Sam, trying to calculate the amount of money Reid must have dropped on this party. Just in time to up-level his calculation, a white-clad server presented them with a tray of hors d'oeuvres.

"Gentlemen, would you care for an ahi tuna tartare on fried taro root?"

"Sounds delicious!" Reid said, grabbing one.

"Thanks," Sam said as he popped the perfectly prepared morsel into his mouth. "Wow, that's delicious." He nodded to both the server and Reid simultaneously. "Pretty fancy food for a bunch of fourth graders. We usually just serve them pizza at our birthday parties."

"Oh, that's the best part," Reid said with evident delight. "We're serving pizza too, only from our own wood-burning brick oven." Reid pointed across the vast gardens to a large brick structure being attended to by a cluster of caterers. "This oven was built by my great-grandfather on my nonna's farm in Montepulciano. Just like her, we moved it here, brick by brick. It cost me a fortune, but we precisely reassembled it."

"Oh . . . wow." Sam struggled for the appropriate reaction, torn between the sentimental gesture of preserving a family heirloom and the ostentatious display of wealth it required to transport it halfway around the world.

"Yeah, I finally got that thing fired up just in time for her ninety-fifth birthday," Reid said. "She couldn't chew it, but she got a slice of pie just like back in the old country." Reid lovingly contemplated the brick oven from across the lawn. "Unfortunately, she died the next year, but I know it meant a lot to her. We tossed her ashes right in there!"

"Wow," Sam said, joining Reid's stare at the oven. "She must have been . . . very proud."

"Yeah . . ." Reid trailed off. "So! Heather tells me you're in between jobs," Reid said, shifting topics. Heather seemed to have an increasing tendency to share Sam's situation with an expanding circle of acquaintances. Perhaps she was networking. Perhaps she thought Sam wasn't networking on his own. Regardless, Sam chafed at the topic.

"Yeah, things didn't quite work out at Ainetu. So I'm looking for my next gig," Sam said, tilting his head self-consciously.

"Come meet some of the other dads. They're all tech guys like you."

"Oh . . . OK." Sam begrudgingly followed Reid and his tightly swaddled ass across the patio to a cluster of dads tossing bocce balls. His favorite activity—getting career advice from a bunch of pretentious nozzles.

"Guys, this is Sam Hughes. Mason's dad." Reid introduced Sam to everyone, though to no one in particular. Sam shook hands with the dads, certain not to remember any of their names.

"So, what do you do?" was the first question asked by the last dad Sam shook hands with before everyone else returned to the bocce game.

"Oh, actually, I'm in between jobs," Sam said, taking a deliberate sip of his beer and letting the awkward silence just hang for a second.

"I see," the dad said, trailing off with an expression intended as empathy but that felt more like pity. "What were you doing most recently?"

"I was COO at Ainetu," Sam replied.

The dad's ears perked up. "Oh, yeah—Ainetu. I've heard of them. AI analytics, right?"

"Yes, that's right."

"That's a pretty hot company. Why did you leave?" The dreaded question. The professional equivalent of, *Did you* mean *to get pregnant*?

"I just didn't see eye to eye with the founder, I guess." Sam shrugged. "He's also a bit of a dick, honestly." The two shared a conspiratorial laugh for a second, reflecting on all the collective dicks the two of them had likely worked for over their careers. "What do you do?"

"I'm at Google," the dad replied without elaborating.

"I think I've heard of it," Sam said sarcastically. "What do you do for them?"

"It's a new skunkworks project. Super exciting, but can't really talk about it, you know." Sam relented with a nod as the dad turned to toss his bocce.

Another dad stepped away from the game and turned to Sam. "So, it was Sam, right?"

"Yes, and your name again?"

"Brian. Brian Erlebacher, but you can call me the Bach," the dad replied with a broad smile and firm handshake. "I feel like I know you. Have we met before?"

"Mmmm . . ." Sam feigned jogging his memory since the fellow dad didn't look familiar at all to him. "I don't think so."

"No, I know you from somewhere," the Bach said, squinting at Sam as if trying to place him. "Are you a video blogger or something?"

"Um, no," Sam said, growing uncomfortable with the scrutiny.

"I know! You're that guy who lost his shit at the SaaStr conference!" the Bach declared emphatically, slapping Sam on the shoulder. "That was fucking hysterical! We watched that like five times in my office."

"Oh, yeah . . . guilty as charged," Sam said, mustering a meager smile at his internet fame.

"I'm going to grab another beer. Do you want one?"

"No thanks, I'm good," Sam replied despite his now-empty bottle. The Bach strode toward the bar, laughing at his encounter with social media celebrity.

With no one else to talk to, Sam pretended to be interested in the kids on the jumpy chateau again, noticing the birthday girl, Isabella, in a halter top and miniskirt posing with two friends for a selfie in one of the turrets, then hurriedly posting it to Instagram. In that act, Sam saw a microcosm of what he increasingly found intolerable about Silicon Valley—it didn't matter what you thought about yourself; it only mattered what *other* people thought of you. The esteem of others was the real currency of Silicon Valley. He was no different—posting content crafted by his PR firm on his personal LinkedIn account, ostensibly to show how great Ainetu was doing but really just trying to impress his colleagues.

A third dad approached. Despite his well-intentioned expression, Sam braced himself for another dead-end conversation when his current unemployed state was inevitably revealed. Maybe he could really weave a yarn this time—assert he was an artisan cannabis curator, or a third-generation shoemaker from Austria. "What do you do, Sam?"

"Hey, it was Gabriel, right?" The dad gave a curt nod, as if he was accustomed to being recognized. "I was most recently COO at Ainetu," Sam replied, trying to bolster his street cred.

"Hmm," Gabriel said, pursuing his lips. "Never heard of it. Are you guys a start-up?"

"Well, not really a *start-up* anymore, I guess. We're a series C company, so pretty established now," Sam said, trying not to sound too defensive.

"So, what does the Aneti do?"

"It's actually *Ainetu*. We're an AI analytics platform."

"Oh, so B2B?"

"Yeah, we sell to companies looking to detect security threats using deep-learning analysis of big data," Sam said, instinctively wanting to brag about their success but stymied by the fact he was no longer at the company.

"Cool . . ." Gabriel nodded, clearly uninterested in learning more. Sam contemplated the logical next question in the conversation: *What do you do?* Before he could ask, the answer was volunteered. "I lead the VR team at Facebook. Virtual reality is really the next frontier in social. We're changing the way the world communicates," Gabriel said.

Sam, who could barely stand scrolling through his news feed of self-aggrandizing humble brags in its 2D format, winced at the idea of consuming it strapped into ridiculous virtual reality goggles. *Great, now I can see my neighbor's cats in 3D.* "Sounds exciting," he said instead.

Evidently dissatisfied with Sam's failure to demonstrate the proper amount of awe, Gabriel took a sip of his Moscow mule in its obligatory copper cup and peered at Sam. "Connect with me on Facebook, and I'll send you a headset and access to our beta release so you can check it out," he finally said—intoning, *I'll make a believer out of you, pagan.*

"That would be great. I'd love to check it out," Sam replied, shaking Gabriel's hand while thinking, *I don't want your fucking goggles, or your beta, or your patronizing attitude.* With a faint grin, Gabriel returned to the bocce game. Sam checked his watch to estimate how much longer they'd need to stay at the party. When he was gainfully employed, Sam hadn't fully appreciated how these social get-togethers were really just games of one-upmanship, scored by the relative importance and wealth-creation potential of their respective careers. Without a job to talk about, there was . . . *nothing* to talk about.

He wondered if Heather was faring any better. He could see her on the patio led by their hostess, Stella, with a cluster of other moms. Stella's attire offered a stark juxtaposition from her husband's athleisure look, sporting a silver sequined top, sleeveless but with a high collar, and a long fuchsia pleated muslin skirt. Sam was unsure if it was high fashion or an attempt at princess attire befitting her daughter's party theme. The ladies had just concluded a tour of the estate, including the full-size home theater, wine cellar in a proper cave, and personal yoga studio. *Maybe that explains Reid's yoga pants.* Stella pretended to tend to the expansive buffet, which, in reality, had already been meticulously prepared by the numerous catering waitstaff.

It struck Sam as odd. Here in the "liberal" Bay Area, everyone gave lip service to progressive values. But the day-to-day facts on the ground were more traditional gender roles. The men were the breadwinners—held in higher regard by their peers the more bread they won. The women were the homemakers—doting over their kids and their houses, even if their staff of nannies, tutors, and housekeepers did all the work. Sam caught Heather's attention from afar and exchanged a subtle eye roll. Both of them felt like fish out of water here, but they had to stay a little longer. Plus, there was a full bar. Sam split from the bocce crew to refresh his beer when he finally spotted a friendly face—his college buddy, Justin Placer.

"Paging Doctor Hughes!" Justin jested in a mock PA voice and his usual gregarious tone as he joined Sam at the bar and ordered himself a drink. Like Sam, Justin had caught the start-up bug when the two of them were at Illinois together. Sam had ventured to the Bay Area first, but Justin moved out a year later and they shared a bachelor pad in the city. Justin was married with two kids now himself, so they saw each other less often but immediately clicked back into a joking repartee when they did. Justin was one of those people who seemed to know everyone. As a result, he was incredibly well-connected even though his own career as a midlevel sales manager had been lackluster. Sam had confided in Justin about the whole Ainetu fiasco during a school band concert the previous week. "So, how's the job search goin', buddy?"

"Christ, Justin, lower your voice," Sam whispered in mock horror as they shook hands. "You might as well be asking, 'How's the syphilis?' in this crowd." The two shared a laugh and toasted beverages, then turned to survey their surroundings.

"This place is ridiculous," Justin said, gesturing at the sprawling grounds.

"Yeah, no kidding." Sam nodded toward the jumpy chateau. "I think that thing has more square footage than my actual house."

"So, seriously, how is the job search going?" Justin asked with sincerity. "I'm sure you'll find something awesome soon."

"Oh, you know . . . There are a ton of companies out there, but it's hard to find the role you want at a company that isn't hyping complete bullshit."

Justin gestured to the group of dads still playing bocce. "This is a great place to network. The dads here are like the Silicon Valley elite. I can make some intros for you."

"Thanks, but I'm not in the mood to network for my next job at a ten-year-old's birthday party," Sam said, recalling his awkward conversations at the bocce court.

Suddenly, Stella appeared with a tray of brownies cut into small squares. "Gentlemen, can I interest you in an *adult* brownie," she asked with a wink, suggesting they were actually edibles.

"Absolutely!" Justin smiled, selecting his square and eagerly popping it in his mouth.

"I'm good for now." Sam graciously waved his hand, feeling the scene was already trippy enough without cannabis enhancement. Stella just as quickly vanished, offering up her treats to other guests. "Hope the kids don't tuck into that batch," Sam said, snickering at the thought of a party full of stoned fourth graders.

Then, Sam froze as he saw Anton Vogel from Pantheon Ventures approach the bar. *Oh, shit!* He tried to turn, but it was too late to avoid the encounter. Anton had been a particularly abrasive investor and board member at Arbor.io, an ill-fated subscription-payments platform that Sam had served a short-lived stint at before determining the depth of the technology was almost as shallow as the commitment of their venture backers. Anton was fit and slender for a man in his late fifties, well-manicured with precisely styled gray hair and meticulous attire. He was evidently just as contentious in his personal relationships as his professional ones, now on his third, and much younger, wife, Katya, whose child, Roman, from her first marriage was in the same class as Mason.

Justin, who, of course, somehow knew Anton as well, eagerly reintroduced them. "Anton and Katya—great to see you both! Have you met Sam Hughes?"

"Yes, we are already acquainted," Anton said as he shook Sam's hand.

"Oh, right, what was the company again? Arbor-dot-I-O or something?" Justin asked.

"Arbor-*ee-ooh*," Sam corrected. "Like the rice."

"Right! Like the *rice*," Justin said. "An ancient symbol of wealth for a payments company. Very clever! Well, I'll let the two of you catch up. Sam, let's grab a drink soon." Justin headed toward a group of parents with cannabis-inflected laughs near the firepit.

"Good to see you, Anton," Sam said, embarking on what, with Anton, always seemed to be a strained conversation. "How have you been?"

"Outstanding. So, I heard you're out of Ainetu."

How the hell does he know that? "I guess word gets around fast. Things just weren't clicking with Rohan."

"That's unfortunate," Anton said as he indicated a drink order to the bartender. "So, what are you going to do next?"

"Well, you know, looking for a C-level role at a B2B start-up, something in the series B to C stage with momentum," Sam said in the nonplussed tone of a successful Silicon Valley tech executive who could afford to take his own sweet time to find the perfect next job.

"Hmmm . . . ," Anton said pensively, peering over the rim of his perfectly prepared gin and tonic. "You don't think you've aged out? Still have another start-up in you?"

With the remark, Anton effortlessly cut to the insecure core of Sam's career anxieties. He *wasn't* sure he had another one in him. Filled with folkloric stories of college dropouts creating multibillion-dollar businesses, Silicon Valley start-ups didn't feature a lot of fortysomething entrepreneurs. The path for "seasoned" executives Sam's age seemed to be either a career in venture capital for the successful ones or getting put out to pasture as a midlevel manager at a tech dinosaur for the less successful ones. The idea of getting back on the merry-go-round for yet another ride at yet another venture-backed start-up did seem increasingly exhausting to Sam, but he put on a good face. "Yeah, definitely. It's what I love doing."

"Well, in that case, I may have something for you," Anton said, taking another sip of his drink. "We invested in a company called Sentient Systems recently. The founder, Stu, is a genius, but he needs some adult supervision. We're trying to get a strong COO in there to help him out. I'll have the recruiter connect with you to set something up."

Sam smiled graciously, not quite able to respond verbally yet. He felt like a pawn in a rich man's game. An interchangeable part plugged in to prop up a founder who was in over his head. To help justify their investment by turning a check written to a socially awkward wunderkind into a real business. "Sure, sounds great," Sam finally said.

They shook hands, and Sam watched Anton turn with Katya still in tow and descend the steps to the manicured lawn. He never knew a children's birthday party could be so emasculating.

"*Can we go now?*" he texted Heather.

CHAPTER 7:

DOOMSDAY LUXURY

"ARE YOU GOING TO GET UP?" Heather asked as Sam tapped the snooze button on his phone for the third time. She had already returned from an early morning spin class and fixed the kids' breakfast.

"Eventually," Sam murmured with his face buried halfway in his pillow.

"Don't you have that meeting with Peter Green today?" she asked.

"Mmm . . . yeah," Sam said unenthusiastically.

Peter Green was the founder and CEO of FusionCommerce, where Sam had worked earlier in his career. When the company was acquired for over $4 billion in the dot-com boom, it made Peter a billionaire. Unlike Sam, Peter had the foresight to sell much of his windfall before the crash. But his good luck didn't stop there. Through the early 2000s, he made multiple investments, including one in a little company called Google that probably doubled his net worth. Then in 2007, Peter bet big against the housing bubble by shorting mortgage-backed securities, earning him another massive payday when the market crashed. Peter's latest Midas-esque investment was a huge position in a cryptocurrency that increased more than ten times in two years. On paper, Sam estimated Peter was worth more than $20 billion—enough to make him one of the top fifty wealthiest people in the world. As his wealth grew, however, Peter had become increasingly reclusive. He was an entrepreneur and investor of fabled status within Silicon Valley circles, but he never appeared on the annual *Forbes* list of billionaires. He preferred to operate in the shadows.

As a newly hired product manager, Sam was a relatively junior employee at FusionCommerce, but he had the opportunity to work closely with Peter as the company prepared to go public in late 1999. This experience gave Sam a front-row seat to how Peter's mind worked—incredibly visionary and, at the same time, able and willing to exaggerate reality to the hairy edge of outright fraud. Sam found himself continually rephrasing Peter's rhetoric in the business section of their S-1 to accommodate their lawyers' discomfort with untruths. Peter usually won these debates with the attorneys, pushing the envelope. But he grew an appreciation for Sam, who had a way of threading the needle with his phrasing—capturing the inspirational vision in just such a way that assuaged the legal concerns.

Sam had occasionally reconnected with Peter in the nearly twenty years since their FusionCommerce days. Peter's myriad investments and connections represented countless opportunities to become part of his ecosystem. So Sam had reached out as part of his networking efforts to find a new job. After three unacknowledged emails, a curt response came finally from Peter's assistant that simply said, "Tuesday, 9:00 a.m. at Valhalla."

Sam made his way through the rural tree-lined streets and palatial estates of Woodside for his meeting with Peter at Valhalla, which he discovered after receiving the meeting invite was the name Peter had given his sprawling compound. Pulling up to the gate, Sam clicked the buzzer as security cameras loomed over his vehicle. "How can I help you?" a man's voice asked bluntly over the intercom.

"Sam Hughes for Peter Green." After a prolonged pause, he added, "He's expecting me."

"ID, please," the voice said.

"I'm sorry?"

"Your ID. Please hold it up in front of the camera."

"Oh . . . uh . . . OK." Sam fumbled for his wallet and finally produced his driver's license and held it in front of the camera on the intercom.

Without further courtesies, the gate opened, revealing a long arching driveway through a grove of mature oak trees. As Sam approached the house, he noticed two security guards with earpieces on the lawn. The mansion was palatial, with a roundabout that led to a five-car garage, a canopied entryway, and a cobblestone road that wrapped around underneath the main house and appeared to be some sort of service entrance for staff. Sam was unsure where to park, so he pulled to the side of the driveway about thirty feet from the main entrance. He took a deep breath and walked up to the door as the security guards exchanged commentary over their radios.

Dogs began barking after Sam pressed the doorbell, and a middle-aged woman in a fitted gray skirt suit with dark hair pulled back in a bun answered the door, which towered nearly twenty feet above them. "Welcome to Valhalla, Mr. Hughes," she said expressionlessly as Sam entered. "Please remove your shoes."

"Excuse me?"

"Your shoes," she said, pointing to his feet. "You can leave them under this settee," she said, gesturing to an upholstered seating area with cubbies underneath, designed specifically for this purpose, located in the grand entryway that led to a spiral staircase to the second floor.

"Oh . . . of course." Sam crouched to remove his shoes. *The guy owns a $50 million home he names after the Nordic gods' hall of heaven with a staff of twenty and he makes me take off my fucking shoes?* Sam tucked his shoes under the bench.

"Right this way," the woman said, guiding Sam through an ornate living room that looked like Versailles. Giant tapestries and gilded mirrors adorned the walls. Sam tried to look dignified but felt like a child ice-skating in his socks on the cool marble floor. They stepped down a few stairs at the end of the living room, passing an expansive dining room with seating for twenty on one side and a bar area on the other, with full-length sliding doors that opened to an outdoor loggia that itself led down more steps to a sprawling swimming pool with fountains. Across the pristine lawn was a separate huge pool house that appeared large enough to accommodate a family of twelve. Beyond that was a greenhouse, in which Sam could see a man in chef's whites harvesting herbs, and what appeared to be a full-size exercise studio.

Finally, they walked down a hall, passing an intimate office ordained with Persian rugs and a cozy fireplace, and entered a library with thousands of books accessible by sliding ladders along the walls. "Please, have a seat," the woman instructed, gesturing to a burgundy leather sofa upholstered with brass nailheads. "Mr. Green will be with you in just a moment. Would you like anything to drink?"

"No thanks," Sam replied, taking in the room that felt as if it could have been transported straight from Oxford, with mahogany tables under green reading lamps, a wraparound balcony halfway up the two-story interior, and ornate windows of interlocking clover shapes overlooking the sprawling lawn and oak trees outside. By the time he turned, she was already gone. Sam sat and began flipping through a copy of *National Geographic* that was arranged neatly among the large-format Taschen books on the coffee table in front of him.

Several minutes passed. Sam's mind wandered as he contemplated the room. *Are all these books real?* There were thousands. *How many of these has he actually read?* At Sam's pace of about four books per year, his lifetime library of read work would barely fill a bookshelf. Not wanting to leave the couch, he squinted to discern some titles from the pristine volumes adorning the walls. *What kind of stuff is he into?* His curiosity stoked, he was just about to walk to one of the shelves when a voice startled him from behind.

"Hello, Sam," Peter greeted him. *Where the hell did he come from?* Sam had not turned his back from the entrance, so Peter was either already in the room when Sam came in or had entered through some secret passage, as there appeared to be no other discernible doorways.

"Oh, geez. You startled me," Sam said.

"It's good to see you. Thanks for stopping by."

"Thanks for inviting me over," Sam said. Then, unsure what one says to a multibillionaire about his ostentatious house, he added, "Your place is incredible."

"Please, sit," Peter said, again indicating the couch from which Sam had instinctively stood up at the discovery of Peter. Without breaking eye contact, Peter sat in a huge tan leather chair with a high back and a matching ottoman onto which he placed his socked feet. "Hopefully you didn't have a hard time getting in."

"Yeah, that's quite a security detail," Sam said.

"I know. I hate it, but I'm afraid it's necessary. Ever since those Occupy Wall Street motherfuckers burned an effigy outside Strom Thornton's house down the block, I've buttoned things up around here." Strom Thornton was the CEO of a bank that had settled charges of predatory lending practices, and then, afterward, he exited the company with a $100 million golden parachute. "I'm worth 100X what that guy is. It's only a matter of time before they come after me with pitchforks." Sam imagined the Occupy protesters with homemade signs getting mowed down by automatic weapons' fire from Peter's security detail. "I had to get an armored Escalade and two matching decoy vehicles just so I can go anywhere," he said with a sigh, exasperated at the inconvenience of it all.

Despite working with him at FusionCommerce for almost three years, Sam didn't know much about Peter's personal life. Nobody did, really. He had read in one of the tech gossip blogs that Peter was again divorced, and he recalled from a passing comment years ago that Peter was estranged from his three children—two with the first wife and one with the second. Sam knew this fact from Peter's request to his assistant at FusionCommerce to buy the kids some Christmas presents. When she asked what they might like, Peter replied brusquely, "How the fuck would I know? I haven't spoken to them in years!"

"So . . . ," Peter asked with a shrug of his eyebrows, cutting to the chase, "what did you want to discuss?"

"Oh, well . . ." Sam paused, realizing he wasn't even sure himself what his big ask was. "I left Ainetu recently, so I guess I'm looking for my next gig."

"Good," Peter said. "That company was a piece of shit."

Sam politely objected, "Well, we actually were doing pretty well. We were even hoping to go public in the next year or two."

"That's never going to happen with that shit-stick founder," Peter said dismissively. "Anyway, the market isn't big enough. It was never going to be a ten-figure valuation. You dodged a bullet by getting out of there while you could."

With his signature crass tone and impulsive decision-making style, Peter had an uncanny knack for success—always in the right place at the right time. His decisions were never forged by extensive analysis or thoughtful strategy, but by instinct. He could incisively zero in on exactly why a company or a person or a market or an investment opportunity was fantastic or destined for failure. It was black or white for him—there was no persuasion or second-guessing or rationalization. He would just instantly form a gut instinct and go all in behind it with complete faith in himself. And why not? Whether they were instincts, biases, or prejudices, it was a philosophy that had served him well.

Even though he hadn't spoken to Peter in years, Sam decided to be forthright in the circumstances of his departure from Ainetu. What did he have to lose? Besides, if he wanted Peter's help, it didn't make sense for the situation to seem self-inflicted. "Yeah, although it wasn't exactly my choice," Sam said. "Rohan fired me."

"Really?" Peter asked. "That seems like an interesting decision on his part. Weren't you basically running the company?"

"I was technically the number two—the COO. But, yes, it did feel that way sometimes."

"That's the reason," Peter said. "He was threatened by you. Shortsighted on his part—a smart entrepreneur needs all the help he can get. I remember when I was running Fusion, I would have done *anything* to make that company successful."

Sam recalled the reality distortion field he'd entered with Peter during their preparations to go public, and later to get the company sold. Within six months of the FusionCommerce acquisition, Peter was gone and the rest of the employees were left holding the bag—trying to justify to their new overlords the multibillion-dollar price tag built on Peter's exaggerations. As Peter cashed out, Sam and other employees realized what a tiny fraction of the company they owned. Although Sam's shares had a high initial value on paper, it was hard to capture that monetary value. Between his exercise price, lockouts, vesting, and taxes, his actual realizable profit was much smaller. These were all high-class problems—until the dot-com crash. Sam watched the value of his paper portfolio diminish to practically nothing within a year—like grains of sand slipping through his fingers.

"So, what are you going to do next?" asked Peter.

"I'm not totally sure yet," Sam conceded. "I'm reconnecting with colleagues like you to learn about new opportunities that may be on your radar. I've looked at a few things—mostly C-level roles at venture-funded start-ups. Nothing very interesting so far."

"It's amazing how many crappy companies get funded," Peter interjected.

"Yeah, and then the ones that show any momentum quickly get over-capitalized raising crazy-huge rounds," Sam said. "It can become really difficult to live up to the expectations inherent in those huge valuations."

Peter nodded. "That's why I'm not doing a lot of venture stuff at the moment. I'm into other asset classes. The cryptocurrency space is exploding, so that's been an incredible place to apply capital," Peter said, as if he were just putting money into a 401(k) plan. Sam contemplated that, given the volatility of the various cryptocurrencies, Peter had to be seeing daily fluctuations of his net worth in tens of millions of dollars. "I can hook you up with some companies in that space," Peter offered.

"Yeah, honestly, the whole Bitcoin thing is a mystery to me. I'd be useless!" Sam said self-deprecatingly. "Actually, this whole situation has prompted me to reassess where I'm going with my career. I'm even thinking of pursuing something outside of technology."

Peter regarded Sam for a moment with a slightly quizzical squint in his eye, then asked, "What do you mean?"

"Just that I'm looking at a lot of technology companies and not feeling the same passion and excitement that I used to feel. So I'm wondering out loud if there's another industry that I might find more interesting."

Peter again paused, as if he was contemplating how to deliver bad news. "But, Sam . . . there *is* no other industry."

"Oh, I know—so many of the job opportunities here in the Bay Area are in tech," Sam acknowledged.

"No, that's not what I mean," Peter interrupted. "I mean, technology *is* the economy. There are no other industries. I don't even really know what you're talking about. Nothing else matters. Technology is gobbling it all up." It was Sam's turn to look confused. Seeing Sam wasn't tracking, Peter continued, "Everything has become digital. And all things digital are governed by technology. Therefore, all things are technology. The microprocessor, the personal computer, the mouse, the modem, the internet, the search engine, the social network—all these things and many more were invented right here. Modern life as we know it wouldn't *exist* without Silicon Valley. Technology isn't just a sector or an industry, it is the *entire economy*. Sure, people may think they work in financial services or healthcare or manufacturing or retail, but tech is absorbing all those legacy industries. The financial services industry doesn't matter anymore. No one trades stocks in pits on Wall Street—it's all done algorithmically on computers in nanoseconds. The retail industry doesn't matter anymore. Physical big-box stores are closing because we buy everything now on apps and e-commerce sites. The entertainment industry doesn't matter anymore. No one shoots movies or records albums in studios—it's all done on laptops. The hospitality industry doesn't matter anymore—it's being replaced with Airbnb. And on down the line. There is no industry that hasn't been completely obsoleted by technology. We're in the third phase of the technology revolution. The first was transformation—making legacy industries more efficient at delivering the same goods and services.

The second was disruption—where legacy industries were forced to revisit their fundamental business models in light of new technologies. Now we're in the final phase: *replacement*. At the end of the day, it's hard to cannibalize yourself. The legacy incumbents just cannot change fast enough to accommodate these technological sea changes, and they're being driven out of business by digital-native companies that are replacing them."

Peter grinned conspiratorially, as if he were letting Sam in on a secret world-domination plan of the global elites. "Even warfare is online now," Peter continued. "And I don't just mean that every plane, tank, and missile is wholly dependent on technology to function, which they are. I mean the actual battleground is digital. Those legacy physical assets are being rendered irrelevant. The new warfare is hacking communications networks, dismantling electrical grids, exploiting and extorting world leaders, spreading disinformation—control of these technical levers means controlling the world."

Sam felt himself recoiling slightly from Peter's increasingly diabolical peroration. Of course, he'd heard all this self-important rhetoric before, about how Silicon Valley was "eating the world." But Peter spoke with a conviction that Sam found unsettling—as if delivering a treatise or prophecy. Sam wasn't sure how to respond, so he didn't say anything.

"And you know who is going to take control of those levers?" Peter asked rhetorically. "It's going to be the Chinese, or the Russians, or the Indians. Those countries were the ones who forced their youth to study math and write code. Unlike previous generations, American kids didn't answer the call. They were too busy playing Xbox and drinking Red Bulls and getting strung out on pain meds. Now all these other countries are kicking our ass. We've lost our abilities, and it's only a matter of time before we lose our independence as a result. And the worst part about it? *We're enabling it!* By importing workers from all these countries with H-1Bs and training them on the best tech, and then they return to their home countries and enact propaganda and aggression toward our way of life." Peter let his words hang in the air a moment. "So that's why I got this," he added with palpable self-satisfaction. Peter pushed in Sam's direction a glossy folder with a picture of wide-open foothills on the cover that had been sitting on the coffee table.

Sam apprehensively opened the folder and regarded what appeared to be information about a luxury condominium, but peculiarly adorned with American flags in the corners and a picture of a man straddling an ATV in combat fatigues while holding an automatic weapon. Sam glanced up from the brochure with a confused look.

"It's a private bunker in South Dakota," Peter explained. "Ten thousand square feet in a former nuclear missile silo. It's fully furnished to my specifications and completely off the grid—entirely solar powered. It has a two-year supply of food and water, and there isn't another human being for two hundred miles in any direction." As Sam struggled to process Peter's doomsday preparations, he returned his attention to the other leaflets in the packet. One had a diagram of the expansive floor plan, another showed photos of a happy family sharing stories in front of a simulated fireplace, another explained how the microparticle ventilation system and LED-simulated sunlight would "replicate a gorgeous summer day from two hundred feet underground."

Sam fumbled for words. "Why do you . . . *need* this?"

"Don't be naive, Sam," Peter said. "Shit could get real in an instant. It wouldn't take much—an earthquake, a wildfire, a pandemic. It could tip at a moment's notice. Once civilization starts to crack up, who do you think the crazies are going to come for first? *Me*," he said, pointing emphatically at his chest. "My stuff, my house, my money. I need to be prepared for that scenario. It's why I have a bug-out bag packed in every room," he said, kicking what appeared to be a backpack under the ottoman he'd been resting his feet on. "It has three days of food and water, a multi-tool, flashlight, first-aid kit, radio, sleeping bag, and, of course, a pistol. All ready to go at the drop of a hat. And if I can't take the Escalade caravan—because there could be gridlock traffic, of course, or mobs of people—I have a fleet of motorcycles ready for me and my security detail. It's five minutes to the airport, where the Gulfstream is always fueled and waiting, and two hours from there to the private airstrip in South Dakota."

"What if the pilot can't make it to the airport?" Sam asked.

"I have a bug-out bag and motorcycle for him too, and his family," Peter replied, having clearly thought through his doomsday scenario to the most intricate detail. "The compound has accommodations for my pilot, my security team, and all their families. We could stay there pretty much indefinitely."

Holy mother of God. The envy Sam had felt at Peter's wealth, power, and privilege was suddenly overcome with a feeling of pity. Here was this man who had achieved what Sam considered the ultimate professional success, but what had it led to? Multiple failed marriages, estrangement from his kids, and now, quite literally, confinement in the trappings of his own wealth—relegated to live out his days cloistered in his mansion or burrowed into a missile silo in the Black Hills.

"Sounds like you've got it all planned out," Sam said.

"If there's one thing I've learned through all my success, it's to be prepared. You need to stay one step ahead of everyone else."

Sam nodded and stood somewhat abruptly to take his leave, before the entire compound went into lockdown and he was trapped there permanently. "Well, I don't want to take up any more of your time," Sam said, conscious of the loaded firearm underneath the ottoman.

Peter stood as well and shook hands as an idea flashed across his face. "You know, Sam. There's a knowledge management start-up we're investors in, maybe through my family office. I don't know much about it, but I think they're looking for someone with your profile. I'll connect you with the recruiter."

"Oh, OK—that would be great," Sam said as the woman who had led Sam to the library suddenly reappeared at the door without being summoned.

Peter turned as if she had been standing there the entire time and asked, "What's that knowledge management company we're investors in again?"

"Aegis Knowledge," she said.

"That's right. Introduce Sam here to their recruiter." She acknowledged the request with a curt nod, though Peter wasn't looking at her. "Oh, and Sam," Peter added as they approached the threshold, "find out the *real* reason you were fired."

CHAPTER 8:

INTERVIEW DAY

SAM AWOKE ON THE FAMILY ROOM COUCH. He sat, momentarily disoriented, then remembered the argument the night before that landed him there. Another discussion with Heather—about the cost overruns on their remodel, unpaid healthcare bills, the dwindling balance in their bank account—had escalated into an argument about his lack of employment. Her position wasn't unreasonable. They needed the second income. But Sam couldn't overcome his ambivalence. His speech on the dais at SaaStr had broken something inside him. Or perhaps revealed it. *It's hard to motivate to find a new job when you don't know what you want to do.*

Earlier in his career, recruiters flocked to him with job opportunities—hungry for up-and-coming executive talent with the pedigree of a company with a huge exit like FusionCommerce. This time around, the headhunter calls weren't coming. Maybe it was the videos of his onstage meltdown. Maybe it was the taint of his ouster from Ainetu. Maybe he was just over the hill. Aged out of an industry biased toward the unbridled enthusiasm of youth. In spite of his passivity, Sam had lined up several promising interviews in the city that day. He figured if he was going to make the one-hour trek, he might as well make a day of it. So he mustered the enthusiasm to shower and put his best foot forward.

The first interview was at Sentient Systems, a company that did some sort of natural language processing (NLP) for speech recognition.

Anton Vogel, the VC who intercepted him at the birthday party, had followed up, gushing about how the company was "blowing up" with a "disruptive" technology for speech recognition and "absolutely *crushing* it." Anton made the introduction to the founder and CEO, Stuart Prichard, so Sam could join this "rocket ship."

Standing outside what he thought was the address, Sam saw no sign for Sentient Systems, or anything that looked like an office on this decidedly sketchy block of the Tenderloin district. A cluster of homeless people in tents lingered down the block to his left, and a strung-out woman was slumped on the pavement in front of a dispensary to his right, repeatedly flicking an empty lighter in a futile attempt to ignite a bowl. Sam checked his phone again to make sure he had the correct address. He studied the blank stretch of wall where he expected the entrance to be, looking for any indication he was in the right place. In the next doorway down, he noticed a discarded pair of pantyhose and what appeared to be human feces. Under his feet crunched the tempered glass pebbles of shattered car windows along the curb near where he'd parked.

Wondering if his Audi would be converted to a heroin den by the time he returned, Sam reflected on this notoriously rough neighborhood. No place else in the city brought to focus the story of extremes that San Francisco had become. Tech-company wealth had already gentrified low-income neighborhoods from the Mission and SoMa to Dogpatch and Potrero Hill. Where the worlds still collided, like in the Tenderloin, the juxtaposition was disorienting—needle exchanges next to artisan coffee houses, dingy hotels that charged by the hour across from sparkling new condominiums, passed-out bodies at bus stops where tech intelligentsia waited to be whisked away to their offices in sleek, tinted-glass coaches. Marginalized residents tried to fight back, organizing human chains around tech company buses, wiping dog shit on electric scooters parked outside coworking offices, picketing new housing developments that tore down rent-controlled apartments. None of it slowed the inexorable tide of gentrification.

A homeless man with a golf-ball-size protrusion oozing from his eye, clad in multiple winter coats but no pants or shoes, was staggering across the street—shouting incoherent expletives to no one in particular. Sam inconspicuously shuffled down the block and regarded a solid steel utility door he had initially overlooked. On closer inspection, he noticed a small electric doorbell with just the number "28" written on it—the address he was looking for. *This can't be right.* But he pressed the button.

A chipper young woman answered, "Welcome to Sentient Systems, how can I help you?"

Sam leaned toward the device, which appeared to also have a camera. "Sam Hughes here to meet Stuart Prichard."

"OK, *awesome*! Come on in!" The door buzzed, allowing Sam into what felt like another world from the street outside. Skylights brightened an internal courtyard with living plant walls and a fountain, complete with a koi pond. Cement pavers led entrants across the pond to the front desk, made from an entire cross section of a giant tree trunk framed in rolled steel.

The woman who greeted him on the intercom emerged from behind a fern wall with an iPad in her hands. "Welcome to Sentient Systems," she said as she handed Sam the tablet. "This is our guest registration and nondisclosure agreement. Just review and sign it with your finger. Can I get you a green tea or a nitro brew or something?"

"No thanks, I'm good," said Sam, fumbling with the iPad to achieve something that vaguely resembled his signature.

Retrieving the device, she enthusiastically instructed Sam to follow her.

Beyond the reception area, the office expanded into a large industrial-chic warehouse space with high ceilings and whitewashed brick walls. Employees were scattered across all manner of ergonomically designed office furniture, from mesh chairs to standing-height desks. Several engineers in shorts and flip-flops were congregated along a bar preparing drip coffees, while others lounged in upholstered pods mounted against the walls or talked on video conferences from clear soundproof booths illuminated by multicolored LED lights.

The receptionist led Sam across the bustling open-concept space and deposited him in a clear-walled conference room. "Stu will be with you in just a moment," she said. Sam watched two employees playing shuffleboard while another flirtatiously took aim at the departing receptionist with a Nerf gun as she squealed and ran back to her desk.

"Hi, Sam," said a slender man cloaked in a Sentient-branded hoodie like a disgruntled teenager, somehow startling Sam upon his entrance even though the door was transparent.

"Hi, you must be Stuart." Sam stood to shake hands.

"Call me Stu. Only my mom calls me Stuart," he said, taking Sam's hand in a limp, damp half shake. Stu slumped into a chair and leaned back. His dark hair was matted on one side as if he'd just rolled out of bed, with tufts of a splotchy beard on his pockmarked chin. "So, tell me about yourself. Where did you go to school?"

A bit of an odd question to start. Nobody had asked Sam where he'd gone to school in years. *Who cares? Want to know my GPA too?* Besides, it was right there on his resume and LinkedIn profile if the guy had bothered to read it. "CS degree from University of Illinois," Sam replied.

"What's the most important thing you learned in your last job?" Stu immediately shifted gears without any further exploration of the education question.

"Probably the importance of establishing product-market fit," Sam said, trying to make eye contact with Stu, whose glance nervously darted around the room.

Before even quite finishing his reply, the next monotone question came: "How would you grow this to a hundred-million-dollar business?"

"Before I answer that, it would be great to get a better understanding of your business," Sam said. "For starters, what's your revenue model?"

"We're freemium," Stu abruptly replied, picking up a dry-erase marker from the table and fiddling with the cap. "With an API."

"OK . . . so how long do you allow people to use the product for free?"

"As long as they want. We don't believe in time-based trials," Stu dogmatically replied.

"I see. So do you have feature upgrades or paywalls of some sort?" Sam asked, trying not to sound overly pedantic. "What catalyzes users to pay for your product?"

"The product is *killer*," Stu said, picking up a second pen and conjoining it with the first. "Nobody else is doing what we're doing with NLP. Not even close. We can pick up millions of semantic attributes and align them with sentiment analysis, topic detection, automated diagnostics, and more—all without any training data."

"Yeah, I've heard the tech is amazing," Sam said. "That's what sparked my interest. I'm just curious what your business model is. How you price it, who sells it—that sort of stuff."

"That's what *you're* supposed to figure out," Stu said, staring several feet to the right of Sam's head, compelling Sam to briefly steal a glance over his shoulder to make sure an employee wasn't pressing their open mouth against the glass wall behind him.

"Fair enough," Sam smiled, trying to disarm the perceived threat while bolstering his credentials. "Fortunately, I've done a lot of that type of work in my career. Having rock-solid tech that customers love is always the foundation," he said, stroking the founder's fragile ego. "If you have that, there are a lot of different business models that could work."

"Let me show you," Stu said, suddenly leaning forward and sending the double-length marker rolling across the table. He pulled forward a wireless keyboard, igniting the large flat-screen on the wall beside them. More comfortable with a keyboard than a conversation, Stu eagerly jumped into a live demo showing Sam how easy it was to modify "just a few lines of code" to embed Sentient's product into "any application." He then directed Sam to "say anything" into a microphone mounted on a pencil-thin stand on the table.

Sam thought back to Ms. Krantz, his sixth-grade typing teacher, and her go-to phrase using every letter of the alphabet: "The quick brown fox jumps over the lazy dog."

Stu furrowed his brow in annoyance as if Sam had just uttered a sentence in Swahili. "No, this is simulating a customer support center. You have to say something that makes sense—like your iPhone just broke or something."

How many people calling into a customer support line say something that makes sense? "Uh, OK." Sam thought for a second, then got into character. "Hi, yeah, so my iPhone, like, won't turn on. It's just, like, *not* working. At all. And, like, I totally charged it and everything, but the screen is just, like, black."

Sam paused to see if his performance as the ignorant caller was up to Stu's standards. Stu just maintained an unwavering stare at the monitor, interrupted finally by a female computer-generated voice. "I'm sorry. I didn't understand you. Could you repeat the question?"

"You were talking too fast," Stu quickly rationalized. "Say it again. But don't say 'like' so much."

My kids can't get out four consecutive words without interjecting "like." "OK, so do I have to say it the same way?"

"No, just say it the way a normal person would."

Sam thought he just *had* said it the way a normal person would, but he cleared his throat and leaned into the microphone again. "Hi, my iPhone won't turn on. It's not working. I charged it, but the screen won't turn on. Can you help me?"

Sam watched the screen and Stu expectantly, waiting for a response from either. Then the subservient voice asked, "I think you're calling about a cracked screen. Is that right?"

Mmmm . . . not exactly. Stu, undeterred and anxious to gloss over the obviously underwhelming demo, pointed to the screen. "And see here, we give every caller a sentiment score across multiple emotional dimensions, like anger, happiness, frustration, and more."

See if you can tell my sentiment now, thought Sam.

The interview didn't last much longer. Stu was obviously uninterested in bringing on a COO to bother him with low-brow questions like how to make money, and Sam was equally uninterested in daily jousts along the Asperger's spectrum. "Let's keep in touch," Sam said as he navigated his way back across the koi pond. *Thanks for nothing, Anton.*

■ ■ ■

Sam's second meeting of the day was at Aegis Knowledge. Peter Green's assistant had promptly made an introduction to the company's founder, Brandon Watts. Sam wasn't entirely sure what they did from reading their website—some sort of enterprise knowledge management, but the site was so chock-full of buzzwords it was hard to decipher. The company was early stage, having just raised a seed round, albeit a substantial one at $5 million. They had been incubated by Poseidon Ventures, where Peter was a limited partner, and now resided in a shared workspace near the San Francisco Giants' ballpark.

Brandon got his business degree at Harvard before joining the esteemed management consulting firm Bain, where he became one of the youngest to be named partner. Through a family connection, he then relocated from New York to San Francisco to join Poseidon Ventures as an "EIR," or "entrepreneur in residence"—a fancy acronym that basically just meant hanging out at the VC offices looking at deals until you decide on some company to join or found, in exchange for the firm having first dibs on investment. So Poseidon's substantial seed financing was a bit of a foregone conclusion, even though Brandon lacked any actual hands-on start-up experience.

Sam's introduction was to Sally Moreno, the in-house executive recruiter at Poseidon. She was a little vague about the exact role—something between a COO, a CFO, and a CRO (or chief revenue officer). C-level titles at this stage of a company were all a little inflated and self-important anyway, given the entire company was probably fewer than a dozen people. But Poseidon had some impressive companies in their portfolio. If they incubated Aegis, they must have seen something compelling about it. So he agreed to take the meeting and learn more.

Sam exited the elevator on the fifteenth floor of a gleaming new office building and entered the hip coworking space with floor-to-ceiling windows overlooking the baseball diamond. Millennials with wireless Beats headphones lounged on an array of modern furniture. A frantic game of ping-pong occupied one corner of the spacious lobby adjacent to a bar featuring citrus-infused water and draft beer on tap. Sam took a stool by the bar and soaked in the panoramic views of the bay to the calming beat of chill house music.

"You must be Sam Hughes," Brandon said, gripping Sam with a firm handshake.

"Hi, Brandon. Nice to meet you."

"Call me 'B.' Did you get some of the grapefruit-mint water? It's delicious." Sam held up his compostable plastic cup of the ice-cold beverage. "Great—let's find a conference room."

For the next few minutes, the two men tried to find an available room, but every one of the glass-walled cells was occupied by people working on their laptops, or on a video conference, or showing slides on the flat-screen monitors. Finally, they gave up and resigned themselves to a table and two stools in the large open space near the reception area.

"So, it was my fourth year at Bain when I had the idea for Aegis." Brandon, a.k.a. B, started into the backstory with no particular prompting. "I was on a project at one of the big energy companies, and our team was interviewing a bunch of their execs, as well as scientists, field technicians, guys working the pipelines with soot all over their faces and hard hats on." He gestured to his head as if putting on a hard hat. "Anyone we could talk to about the business. It was so amazing how much knowledge all these people had, but just about their little part of the overall puzzle. And then it hit me: What if you could capture all this knowledge and make it immediately accessible to everyone?" Brandon paused dramatically to let the gestalt of the concept seep in.

"Oh, yeah—that would be amazing," Sam said, feeling obliged to concur but not sure yet exactly what it was they were talking about.

"I know, *right*?" Brandon's eyes bulged out like he had struck gold that was right under everybody's noses. "So I got hooked up with the Poseidon guys, and their minds were completely blown, and they said, 'Come out to California and show us you can build this thing and we'll fund it.' So I was like, who's the smartest guy I know? And that's when it hit me," he said with the requisite smack of his open palm on his forehead. "*Sergey*! This crazy Ukrainian dude had been coding circles around everyone else on a bunch of different projects at Bain. So I got him on board, and we rounded up a dream team of developers—I'm talkin' Stanford, Carnegie Mellon, MIT, all the best CS schools—and started building this thing!"

Sam still wasn't sure what "this thing" was, so he probed on that topic. "Do you have a working version of the product yet?"

"Oh, no—this thing is crazy complicated. We're still at the prototype stage."

Sam nodded. It wasn't unusual for a seed-stage company to still be pre-product. "So what's your mechanism for the knowledge capture?" Sam asked.

"That's the best part," Brandon said, leaning in with a conspiratorial smirk. "We capture it *passively*."

"What do you mean?"

"We capture it passively," Brandon repeated himself. "You know—from phone calls, emails, conversations around the office."

Sam squinted his eyes slightly, trying to make sure he comprehended what Brandon was proposing. "So how are those phone calls and emails and conversations actually collected?"

"Well, we just install a little snippet of code on the employees' laptops and cell phones, and some microphones and webcams around the office, and we aggregate everything we collect, discern the underlying meaning, and then translate it all into one enterprise knowledge base. We can tell you everything about everyone—from who is working on a formula for a new fuel additive to who has the best Fourth of July pie recipe!" Brandon declared with victory.

So, basically, you're spying on all your employees, Sam thought while outwardly nodding in forced agreement at the eminent brilliance of the idea. "So . . . would you get employees to consent to having their communications monitored?" Sam asked.

"Technically, yes—we'd bury it in their employment agreement. Nobody ever reads those things. And, if they do, then *find another job*!" Brandon joked darkly. "And there are all sorts of other applications—you can understand which employees are the greatest flight risk, or which might have marital strife or a substance abuse problem that is impacting their work, or which managers really have the best ideas so you can promote them more quickly. Once you get the infrastructure in place, the possibilities are limitless! With this unique data set, we can use AI to mine it for any number of insights that we can monetize."

This entire idea could only be the brainchild of a man who had lived in a world of management consulting and business school case studies. The impracticality and unethical nature of surveilling employees in order to get them to unwittingly contribute to a company-wide knowledge base, even if ostensibly for a legitimate purpose, was troubling. The fact that Poseidon Ventures had enabled it with their $5 million investment was terrifying.

"So where are you at with the development process?" Sam asked, curious how close to reality this abomination to civil liberties was.

"We're just testing a prototype now, but I expect we'll be ready for our first customer deployments by the end of next month," Brandon said—optimistically, Sam thought. A product this complex would likely take years to be ready for customer usage and years more to overcome its legal liabilities. Sam found Brandon's overconfidence immediately off-putting. The conversation continued like this for nearly an hour, with Brandon unilaterally proclaiming how "disruptive" their product was, without actually having a product; how "massive the TAM" was, without defining what the market even was; how "transformational" it would be to companies, without having any customers. The whole diatribe was so lacking in substance and specificity that Sam couldn't fathom why Poseidon had invested. Then it hit him why he was there.

"So, I'm looking for a solid number two," Brandon finally stated with only a few minutes left in their interview. "Tell me about yourself."

Sam sat upright on his stool and summoned the energy to describe his twenty-year career in their remaining two minutes, knowing that there was zero chance he was going to take this job, whatever the job was.

■ ■ ■

Sam hoped his final meeting of the day would be more promising. FrontRange and the company's charismatic twenty-eight-year-old female founder, Haley Kentworth, had received disproportionate buzz in the tech blogosphere. As with Sentient and Aegis, it was a little unclear exactly what FrontRange *did*—he'd heard it described in press articles variously and ambiguously as "next-generation sales enablement" and "analytically driven sales process optimization" and "sales pipeline acceleration through AI." So . . . something about sales.

The introduction had come through Portia Lambert-Jones, the über Silicon Valley recruiter and grand dame of the executive search firm Lambert Shaw & Associates. Portia had placed CEOs at some of the hottest tech companies. "Marc" (Benioff, CEO of Salesforce.com) and "Larry" (both Ellison, CEO of Oracle, and Page, CEO of Google) were on a first-name basis. So, when Portia called, Sam answered. "This company FrontRange is absolutely on fire," Portia effused. "They just did a $20 million round and were oversubscribed with every VC in town. I'm sure you've read about Haley in *TechCrunch* and *Wired*—she's been everywhere. She's just absolutely brilliant."

"Yeah, they've got a ton of buzz," Sam agreed. "What's the role?"

"CEO, darling—you'd be perfect for it!"

"So . . . what's happening to Haley?" Sam asked. "Does she know there's a search going for her replacement?"

"Oh, she's totally fine with it. She really wants to be more the public face of the company, not get mired down in the day-to-day."

"I see," said Sam. "So what will her role be?"

"She'll stay on as chairman or president or something. Some role that gives her the title so she can do what she does best: generate buzz and raise money. Just maybe when you meet with her, don't mention the CEO role specifically," Portia said. "Tell her you'd be an advisor or something. This is just a first meeting to see if you two are a good culture fit."

So, in other words, the board was pushing Haley aside. Whether she knew it or not, the gears of her ouster were in motion. Sam realized Portia would never work directly for a twenty-eight-year-old female founder, particularly one who was in the prime of her beauty and reminded Portia of her younger days, before plastic surgery and early morning boot camps. The board, probably Paul Fleming from GrayWillow Ventures, had hired Portia directly, perhaps even going behind Haley's back. Sam cringed at the thought of himself as the old white guy, hired by a bunch of other old white guys, to push one of the few female founders out of her own high-profile company. But CEO roles at hot start-ups were hard to come by, so Sam agreed to the meeting.

The FrontRange offices were tucked into one of the many alleyways in SoMa, next to a Michelin-starred restaurant that previously was an auto repair shop. A young Asian woman with long eyelashes accented with swipes of glittering purple eyeshadow that extended to her temples greeted Sam when he entered. Summoned by the sound of a visitor, an enormous shaggy-haired dog emerged, immediately burying his muzzle deep into Sam's crotch. As he tried to fend off the canine molestation with his left hand, he clumsily attempted to sign in with his right. The receptionist did nothing to discourage the 150-pound personal-space invader, now slobbering on Sam's extended hand.

"Haley's expecting you," she said, and she led Sam up an open staircase to a balcony area overlooking employees sitting at reclaimed-wood desks. His new best friend bounded up the stairs as well, following Sam into what felt like a kids' loft but appeared to be Haley's office, with a bead curtain entrance, Persian throw rugs, and a large sofa accented with bright-colored silk pillows. "She'll be right with you," the receptionist said.

Sam glanced at the artifacts in the space. A wall of framed photos of Haley at various exotic destinations—in hiking shorts and a bikini top at a tropical waterfall, in a Jeep on safari with a possible ex-boyfriend, at the top of what appeared to be Mount Everest. The room was adorned in an eclectic array of decorative accoutrements—various ornate tapestries, the lingering smell of incense, a small shrine of bulbous waxy candles guarded by a miniature bronze Ganesh, the plump Indian god with the elephant head. To Sam's dismay, the dog jumped up onto the couch next to him and commenced licking his hand as a poor man's alternative to his crotch, which Sam defended vigorously.

"Sam Hughes—it's so great to finally meet you!" Haley said as she bounded through the bead door. "I've heard *so* much about you!"

"All good stuff, I hope!" Sam said, trying to wipe the dog slobber off his hand before shaking hers. "Sorry, I got the full puppy welcome."

"Oh, I'm *so* sorry! Buster, get down!" She waved the dog off the couch and he reluctantly complied. She was smartly dressed in a designer pantsuit with long chestnut hair. Removing her suit jacket, she tossed it on the back of her desk chair to reveal a billowing sleeveless silk blouse and toned bronze arms. Self-confident with deep hazel eyes, Haley commanded attention. She had the poise of a celebrity and the appearance of an heiress adorned with jewelry and high fashion. Sam wondered if her fundraising prowess had more to do with her stunning looks than her business plan. There weren't many female founders in the Valley. Sam had seen female founders with PhDs and impressive ideas pitch every

VC on Sand Hill Road without getting a nibble. But Haley, with her coquettish attractiveness, had done it effortlessly, despite nobody really understanding what the company did. "Thanks for coming in. I'm glad we're able to get some time," she said with a broad smile, crossing her legs gracefully like she was assuming a yoga pose.

"Of course! I'm excited to be here. I love your office," Sam said, gesturing toward the photo wall. "Looks like you've been to some amazing places."

"Oh, yeah. Those are some great memories." She smiled wistfully, looking at the wall. "Bali, the Great Wall, Machu Picchu, so many incredible places. Do you like to travel?" she asked with a suggestive lilt, as if they should leave together for someplace that afternoon.

"Definitely, but hard to find time for it with three kids," Sam replied with a shrug. At this point, Buster decided he'd been on the floor for the requisite amount of time and climbed back on the couch next to Sam. "What kind of dog is Buster?"

"He's an Irish wolfhound, and he's a *bad boy*." Haley mockingly scolded the gigantic beast. "I've had him since he was a puppy."

"Must have been a big puppy!" Sam joked as Buster sidled in closer to him.

"Do you like dogs?" Haley asked, like the response was an incisive judge of character.

"Yeah, we've got a little Labradoodle named Baxter," Sam said.

"*Awww* . . . sounds cute," Haley replied. "So, tell me about yourself."

Buster was starting to pant lightly as Sam replied, "Well, I've been in tech since the original internet boom." He realized Haley was around eight years old at the time. "Most recently, I was COO at Ainetu."

"*Great* company!" Haley interjected, hoisting her shoulders forward in a mini shiver to underscore how amazing she thought they were. "Tell Rohan I say hi. So, why did you leave?"

Always a tough question to answer when the reality was that he had been fired. *Do I clarify that I was let go, or do I let her continue with the assumption that the departure was voluntary? She knows Rohan, so she'll just ask him.* Sam decided to shoot straight. "Well, honestly, Rohan decided to go a different direction," Sam said with a barely perceptible grimace. "He and I didn't see eye to eye about our product-market fit, so we parted ways."

Haley took in the response, nodding slightly in apparent appreciation of his candor. "Sounds like a difficult situation," she said.

"Yeah, it was a little frustrating, but it's his prerogative, and it affords me an opportunity to find my next big adventure," Sam said. Buster's panting had intensified, and Sam stole a glance at the dog occupying two-thirds of the sofa.

"Well, Paul says you did an amazing job there," Haley encouraged him. Sam barely knew Paul, the GrayWillow partner, so the comment struck him as an indication that his introduction had come via Paul rather than Portia. "What are you looking to do next?"

"Well, I'm looking for something very similar to FrontRange. I'm less concerned with the role than I am with the opportunity," Sam said, treading lightly around the question of what capacity in which he might get involved with the company. "I want something that has real potential to disrupt a major market."

With that, Buster's heavy panting escalated to retching. "I totally agree," Haley said, not seeming to notice her dog's escalating convulsions. "If it's not a huge market, then what's the point?"

Sam glanced at Buster, who was now hunched on the couch. He tried to continue without being distracted. "So, tell me more about your solution at FrontRange."

Buster's heaving had become too much to ignore. "I'm sorry, is he bothering you?"

Yes, he's fucking bothering me! I'm trying to do an interview, and this freakishly large dog is about to barf! "Oh, no—he's fine," Sam said, wondering when Buster would finally consummate his retches with a proper vomit. Then it came, a full-fledged spewing all over Haley's ivory-colored couch. Sam felt a wave of nausea come over him as the smell hit his nostrils.

"Buster!" Haley scolded. "I'm *so* sorry; he's on a new medication that obviously isn't agreeing with him."

"No . . . no problem," Sam said, giving a wave of reassurance as he fought back the gag reflex. *Are we going to continue the interview amid this stench? Do we evacuate the room? What were we even talking about?* "So, tell me more about FrontRange," Sam finally mustered, his mouth filling with saliva.

"One second, I'll be right back," Haley said, exiting quickly through the bead door. *I think we're probably done here*, Sam thought as Buster started lapping at his own pool of vomit. Sam stood, contemplating the distance to the nearest bathroom. He parted the bead door and hastily descended the stairs back toward the reception area. Haley was returning with a roll of paper towels. "I hate to do this, but I need to take Buster to the vet. Can we reschedule this for another day?"

"Of course, no problem," Sam said, trying to demonstrate what a sympathetic "dog person" he was. She was clearly less concerned with him than she was with Buster.

"Great, thanks. I'll have my admin reach out to you to schedule another time," she said before bolting up the stairs to Buster.

CHAPTER 9:

THE ALIBI

SAM PEERED OUT THE AIRPLANE WINDOW at the patchwork of farm fields below him. They were starting to make their descent to the Columbus, Ohio, airport under cloudy skies. The bright green fields below were cobbled together in irregular shapes that just slightly deviated from a square grid, stretching to the horizon in all directions across the perfectly flat landscape. He thought he could pick out Lima, his hometown, to the north as they made their final approach, but it was hard to tell. Except for the Columbus skyline, it all looked the same from ten thousand feet.

Heather and the kids were not with him. She had work and the kids had school, and nobody wanted to take vacation days to be there. This trip was one he felt he needed to do alone anyway—to get out of Silicon Valley and regain some perspective. Increasingly disillusioned by his lack of job prospects and estranged from his family, Sam found himself compelled to return to his roots. He wasn't sure why. Part of it was the family business, even though Sam knew, rationally, it was a lost cause. The debt-laden equipment-rental company Sam's grandfather had started was struggling, all the more so since Sam's dad was forced to cut his hours after being diagnosed with coronary artery disease. Guilt was another driver. His mom's salary as a part-time Walmart cashier earning just above the state's minimum wage was their main source of income. With no nest egg, limited earning potential, declining health, and imminent retirement, they would require financial support. Sam was their only safety net, and he was slipping deeper into the red.

Bob, Sam's older brother by two years, had offered to pick him up at the airport. He lived in Dayton, where he worked as a pharmaceutical sales rep. He had married his high school sweetheart, but it didn't last. She and their two daughters lived in Columbus. Bob only saw them on weekends.

"How the hell are ya?" Bob greeted Sam, intercepting him at the security gate.

"Great to see you," Sam said, giving his brother a hug.

The two conversed about the weather and various Ohio sports teams as they walked to short-term parking. Climbing into Bob's gray Chevy Impala—a company car, he explained—they exited the garage in a light rainfall and embarked on the two-hour drive north.

"So, when was the last time you were home?" Bob asked with an inflection in his voice that Sam perceived as intending to provoke guilt.

"Gosh, it's probably been three years," Sam said, not taking the bait. "I came out with Heather and the kids for Aunt Mae's funeral."

"That's right," Bob noted. "But that was down in Wilmington. Did you even get back to Lima then?"

"I don't think so." Sam thought back further. "Damn. It was probably 2012 for my twentieth high school reunion."

"Go Spartans!" Bob extended a fist bump in honor of their alma mater, Lima High School.

"Christ, I'm old!" Sam said.

"Not as old as me!" Bob countered. "OK, that settles it. I'm taking you to the Alibi."

"Wow, throwing me right into the deep end!" Sam laughed. The Alibi Lounge was one of the seedier dive bars in Lima. Occupying a narrow strip of sidewalk between a sewing shop and an empty lot, the Alibi had a tall facade like an old-time saloon. The single-story interior was a fire marshal's worst nightmare—a tangled web of Christmas tree lights daisy-chained by the dozens into a single ungrounded outlet underneath the multitiered chockablock of high-proof alcohols. All tended by a barkeeper and clientele who had apparently missed the memo on Ohio's statewide ban on smoking indoors. It was a favorite haunt during their high school years in Lima, thanks to its seventy-five-cent highballs and willingness to serve anyone, regardless of ID.

Sam followed Bob up the cracked cement steps of the Alibi, past a Stroh's beer sign. The flood of memories hit him the moment they stepped inside. The place was frozen in time. From the vintage beer cans adorning the walls to the lacquered bar top to the pinball tables and dart boards in the back, it all was completely unchanged from Sam's memory. The kind of place that has a warm, comforting glow if you're a local but a cold, intimidating vibe if you're not. Sam wasn't sure which he was.

As they made their way toward two empty seats at the bar, Sam was practically tackled by a large man who had tipped toward him off a bar-stool between a cluster of friends. "*Hughesie*! How the hell are ya?"

Startled but feigning recognition, Sam engaged the man in a hearty handshake. "Hughesie" was a tip—they must have gone to high school together, since that was the last time anyone had called him by that nickname. "Hey!" Sam said, churning through his memory banks to no avail. The man was tall, probably six feet three but heavyset—pushing three hundred pounds. He had a leathered countenance under a dingy mesh trucker's cap, and his weight pulled down the skin below his eyes and jowls like a softening candle, making him more difficult to identify.

The man stood in a soiled Pearl Jam T-shirt, smelling of cigarettes, with a look of realization that Sam didn't know who he was. "It's Joe," the man said. "Joe Schneider."

"Holy shit! Of course, Joe Schneider!" Sam proclaimed, suddenly distinguishing a faint resemblance to his memory of the man. They had actually been friends in junior high but fell into different crowds by high school. Sam recalled that Joe had been a decent athlete. Tall and slim, he was the starting center on their freshman basketball team. By sophomore year, he was off the team—already drinking beer constantly and smoking two packs a day. Sam hadn't seen him since graduation. "How are you?"

"I'm doin' all right." Joe shrugged indifferently. "I've been down at the Ford plant since high school, but they cut our hours back. Everyone thinks they're gonna shut it down. Who knows?" he chortled with a smoker's rasp. "These are some of my buddies from the plant." Joe turned to introduce his friends. "This here's Rick and Jimmy, and of course you know Chuck from Lima High." Sam did not recognize Chuck either.

"You remember my older brother, Bob?" Sam asked.

"Of course, Bob Hughes—you were quite the stud athlete in high school," Joe remarked while Chuck nodded in agreement. "Where you at now?"

"Working for Pfizer down in Dayton," Bob replied.

"Cool . . . ," Joe said and took a sip of his beer. Then he turned to Sam and asked, "So how're things with you, Mr. Silicon Valley Hot Shot?"

How does he know I'm in Silicon Valley? Sam wondered. He hadn't thought of Joe once since junior high, but Joe apparently was aware of his whereabouts. *Fucking Facebook.* "Oh, things are going OK," Sam said. Then, realizing he had an opportunity to make his situation seem more relatable, he added, "Actually, I got laid off recently."

"No shit," Joe said with deliberate astonishment. "They movin' your job to Mexico too?" he jested, and the whole group cracked up.

Sam winced with a perfunctory smile at being the butt of the joke.

"Nah, he was just working for an asshole," Bob said, coming to his brother's defense.

"Anyway, Bob and I are going to catch up. But good seeing you, Joe," Sam said, shuffling down the bar to gain some distance.

Joe murmured something under his breath then returned his prodigious ass cheeks back to the stool that Sam presumed had hefted his bulk for more than one evening.

"They're just bitter 'cause you got outta this shithole," Bob reassured as he ordered them two draft beers.

"I didn't even fucking recognize the guy," Sam said, shaking his head. "I'm not trying to be an asshole. I guess I've just moved on with my life since high school."

"There aren't many guys from Lima working out in Silicon Valley," Bob said. "You're kind of a big deal."

"Fuck you," Sam said, countering the wisecrack and taking a deep gulp of his beer.

"I saw someone else you knew in high school the other day," Bob said, relishing his impending divulgence.

"Oh, yeah? Who's that?" Sam asked.

"Stacey Albright," Bob said, letting the name of Sam's high school girlfriend linger.

"Wow. That's a blast from the past. How did she look?"

"A little wear on the tires, but pretty damn hot still," Bob said.

"Yeah, I follow her on Instagram, but you can never tell if it's just filters or flattering angles or something."

"Nah, man—she's cute. Why did you guys break up anyway? You dated for, like, a year, right?"

"I don't know, Bob," Sam said, getting perturbed at the line of questioning. "I was seventeen. I was going to college. What are you saying— that I should have married my high school girlfriend like you did? How did *that* work out?"

Sam immediately regretted the unintended harshness of the comment. A pained expression flashed across Bob's face as he looked up at the TV. Their fraternal rivalry could flare up quickly, but their lives had been on separate tracks for so long that it was no longer a fair fight. When they were kids, Bob and Sam had conspired in their ambition to move to New York City or California when they graduated. Bob didn't cast his stone quite so far. He attended Wright State University, less than an hour from their home. But Sam stuck to his determination to attend college out of state. He was accepted at Carnegie Mellon, but they couldn't afford the tuition, so he instead enrolled at the University of Illinois. Sam was self-conscious about the divergent paths their lives had taken, but he was never apologetic. He had worked hard for what he had achieved. Rationally, Sam knew he couldn't harbor remorse for the decisions his brother or high school friends had made, but that was no reason to rub it in their faces.

"Sorry, that was out of bounds," Sam said. Then, wanting to change the subject, he asked, "So, how are Mom and Dad?"

"Oh, you know . . . getting by, I guess." Bob sighed. Sam's parents, Bob and Connie, had always arguably been an odd couple. They'd met in college at Ohio University and were married within a year of graduation. For their introvert dad, it was the only period of his life outside of Lima, to which he promptly returned to work at the equipment-rental business founded by Sam's grandfather. When Bob Junior was born, Hughes Rentals was doing well enough that the young couple was able to afford a down payment on a modest house. Sam arrived two years later. The brothers were close growing up, but their family life was strained. Their father was distant, always harboring a low-simmering resentment about being coerced into the family business.

Despite living only a few miles apart, they saw their paternal grandparents infrequently. Dinners at their house consisted of their grandfather sitting silently in his oversize lounge chair with a tumbler full of bourbon, while their grandmother, always wrapped in an apron, earnestly served old-fashioned dishes like calf livers and ambrosia salad that the boys could barely gag down. When their grandfather, the patriarch of Hughes Rentals, died prematurely, their father discovered substantial debts, mostly punitive loans from farm-equipment manufacturers, that had them on the brink of insolvency. Sam and his brother worked long hours without pay through high school to keep the business afloat.

As the older brother, Bob Junior was under greater pressure to continue the family business. He worked there a few years after college, managing their few remaining big accounts, but eventually had a falling out with their dad and quit. The two had barely been on speaking terms since. Over the years, their parents' situation had only grown worse. When the mortgage crisis hit, they were forced to sell their home, downsizing to a dilapidated house on a treeless street somewhere on the dreary grid of city blocks. Though Sam would be staying with his parents, it was an unfamiliar dwelling. Sam didn't even know how to get there. He would be sleeping in their second bedroom during his stay. Although it was technically home, it no longer felt like it to Sam.

"It's weird being back here," Sam admitted, looking around the bar at the setting that was at once familiar and foreign.

"Yeah, how so?"

"I don't know." Sam paused, choosing his words carefully. "It's different from how I remember. It just . . . doesn't really feel like home anymore."

"Oh, I see," Bob said, again looking away at the TV above the bar.

"What?"

"You think you're better than us." It was the tear-down comment—assertion, really—that Sam had heard a hundred times since he'd left Ohio. If not verbalized, the sentiment always seemed to swirl under the surface—in the inflection of questions, the pregnant pauses in conversations, the overt innuendos. The phrase was so revealing in its simplicity. An emotional grab bag of resentment, jealousy, hurt, envy, frustration, bitterness, and spite, intended at once to alienate its target while elevating the person who said it. It hurt all the more because Sam had always felt a lingering guilt about leaving Ohio. As if he had somehow betrayed his family and friends. Denied his roots. Contributed to the "brain drain" in the "flyover states" with their best and brightest leaving to pursue better opportunities. Though he was still a Midwesterner at heart, he was aware of how his tastes and style had changed. How his political views had been shaped. He found it harder and harder to relate to the opinions he'd hear each time he returned home—couldn't help but feel they were isolated, xenophobic, and uninformed, filled with more jealousy, prejudices, and outright spite than he remembered. Or maybe it was his perspective that had changed. Maybe he had become the "coastal elite" that they constantly railed against.

Sam stammered defensively. "That's not what I meant."

"But it's what you were thinking," Bob said, sipping his beer while still training his eyes on the TV.

"No, it wasn't," Sam insisted. Yet, there it was—part of him *did* feel he was better than them. Why was it that he had wanted to leave Lima so badly? Implicitly, it was to get away from . . . *this*. From *them*. To pursue bigger and better opportunities. By the time Sam graduated high school, the town just felt defeated and depressed. If you had any ambition, you got out of Lima. Success *meant* leaving—fleeing to Columbus, or Chicago, or the coasts. As Sam's determination increased to pursue a career in technology, he eschewed any financial obligation to his father and took out student loans. Four years later, he packed up a truck and moved west. Silicon Valley was full of transplants like him who felt they'd successfully escaped their hometowns, whether in Ohio or India. But when confronted by family and friends with their emotions of jealousy and envy, it felt hostile.

"OK, my bad," Bob said, again disarming a potential conflict. They were silent for a few minutes, both pretending to watch a baseball game.

Suddenly, Sam felt a pang in his gut at the realization of his own hypocrisy. The envy and jealousy he felt toward the Silicon Valley billionaires was no different than the envy and jealousy his friends and family from Lima felt toward him. From Sam's vantage point, the success of the billionaires was the result of good fortune. His why-can't-that-happen-to-me impulse would discount the skill, hard work, and sacrifice involved in their success, instead attributing it to luck, favors, or nepotism. But perhaps that was exactly the same rationalization that others went through about him—ignoring his effort, since that would require an acknowledgement of his achievements, and exaggerating his luck, since that was easier to unabashedly resent. The reality for Sam, and for the billionaires, was that his success was a combination of intermingled effort and luck—impossible to attribute which had contributed more to an end result. It was life. Wallowing in his envy of the Silicon Valley elite wasn't benefitting him any more than his hometown harboring petty resentments toward him.

"Well, we should probably get you *home*," Bob said, emphasizing the word as if their parents' home were any more familiar to him.

"Yup," Sam agreed, finishing off his beer and starting toward the door.

"See you later, Mark Zuckerberg," Joe said as they passed.

"Take it easy, Joe," Sam said with a nod.

CHAPTER 10:
HOMECOMING

HIS PARENTS WERE ALREADY ASLEEP by the time Sam came in through the unlocked back door. Avoiding an encounter with them undoubtedly had been part of Bob's calculus in stopping for a drink. It was only eleven, but they were creatures of habit and nine thirty was their typical bedtime. Sam tiptoed into the kitchen, feeling as if every move was disrupting the silence in this small, creaky house. On the counter was a plate of food wrapped in aluminum foil with a Post-it Note from his mom that read, "Welcome home, Sam!" He appreciated the gesture, but he wasn't hungry, and this unfamiliar house wasn't really his home anyway. He picked at the meal to make it appear at least half-eaten, then wheeled his suitcase to the spare bedroom on the first floor.

He awoke to the sound of brewing coffee and his mom's one-sided conversation emanating from the kitchen. "Well, there he is!" she announced as he entered the room, embracing him in a hug. Seated at the kitchen table, his dad briefly acknowledged Sam before returning to his newspaper. "So, your brother actually remembered to pick you up at the airport last night?" his mom asked, handing him a cup of coffee.

"Yup. We even stopped for a beer at the Alibi and caught up."

"You boys still go to that old place? There are so many nicer restaurants in town now."

"We were just grabbing a drink," Sam said. "Thanks for leaving some food out for me, by the way."

"Oh, I just figured you might want a little somethin' to tide you over after your long trip," she said.

Sam heard his phone pulse with the arrival of a text message, so he checked the display with one hand as he sipped his coffee in the other. He stiffened when he saw that it was from Carl Downey at Green Gate Technologies, the white whale customer they had been trying to close. He shuffled into the sparse living room to read the message: "*Hey, Sam—everything OK? I tried emailing you the contract but it bounced.*"

Emailing me the contract? Sam wondered if Carl had finally agreed to a deal at GGT, as it dawned on him that Carl must not know yet that he was no longer at Ainetu. He paused for a moment, curious to get the details of the deal but feeling guilty about misleading Carl. His curiosity got the better of him.

"*Hey, Carl—sorry, don't have access to my email right now. Can you text me the link to the contract?*" he replied.

"*Sure, one second,*" Carl responded. "*Here you go.*"

Sam clicked the DocuSign link to pull the agreement up on his phone, realizing as he opened it that he wasn't sure which outcome he was hoping for—the originally promised $1 million deal, which would yield a huge commission for Amanda, or some substantially smaller amount, which would screw over Rohan. He swiped down on his phone screen to scroll to the end of the contract where the dollar amount would be. And there it was: $200,000 total contract value. *What an asshat.* Carl had screwed them again—going from a promised deal of $1 million to a pilot of $50,000, and then only ultimately signing a deal for $200,000.

"*Have you sent this to Amanda yet?*" Sam texted.

"*Yes, I copied you both,*" Carl replied. "*Figured you needed to sign it.*"

"*Amanda can sign it,*" Sam typed. "*I'm sure she'll get to it today.*"

Sam set down his phone briefly and took a sip of his coffee, overhearing his mom speculate about what he was doing and that it "must have been important" as his dad grunted monosyllabic responses.

He then picked up the phone and shot off a text to Amanda: "*Carl just texted me about the GGT deal.*"

As always, Amanda was quick to reply. "*Oh, yeah? Did the troll tell you how much $?*" Then after a moment: "*$200K!!! I think I spent that much in airfare visiting that fat fuck! You were right about him.*"

"*Sorry,*" Sam replied with a frown emoji.

"*It wasn't enough that he screwed us last quarter. He had to come back and finish the job this quarter!*" Amanda continued her rant.

"*What did Rohan say?*" Sam asked.

"*He was surprisingly calm about it. I guess he has bigger fish to fry.*"

"*I guess so,*" Sam replied, then added, "*Let's grab a drink next week when I'm back. I'm curious how Rohan is going to spin this with the board.*"

"*Sounds good,*" she answered.

Sam set down his phone and returned to the kitchen. "Sorry about that. Just some work stuff," he offered in explanation for his absence.

"Work stuff?" Sam's dad asked with a humph, his first real words of the day. "Didn't they make it clear you don't work for them anymore?"

Sam smiled wryly as he wondered to himself how Rohan had handled this latest setback. No doubt, Sam was still being propped up as a scapegoat, even in absentia. Or maybe he was backing the bus over Amanda now, though he was surprised she hadn't heard that from Rohan. Maybe he would be able to find out more when they had that drink. He took a seat at the linoleum built-in table in the kitchen across from his dad, and his mom promptly placed a heaping plate of scrambled eggs, hash browns, bacon, and toast in front of him. "Just trying to tie up some loose ends," Sam said.

The two men ate in silence for a few minutes before his dad stood from the table and announced, "I gotta head down to the warehouse." Sam watched him gather his wallet and keys from the kitchen counter and step out the back door without elaborating further.

As the pickup truck backed out of the driveway, Sam remarked sarcastically to his mom, "Well . . . it was great catching up with Dad."

His mom sat at the seat across from him. "Now, Sam, you know how hard things have been on your father. The business is dying, and he barely has enough energy to work at all, let alone get things back on track. He needs help from you or your brother, but he's too proud to ask for it."

"That ship has sailed, Mom," Sam interjected with frustration. "Bob already tried that, but Dad made it clear he didn't want his help. And I live two thousand miles away."

"Yeah, but since you're not working now, maybe you could just do it for a little while. Stay at home here till things are going good again," she said with heartbreaking earnestness.

"Mom, it's not *going* to get good again."

"He needs to retire, but there's no one to take over the business. Maybe you could help him sell it?"

"There's nothing to sell. The only assets are the equipment and the warehouse. But the equipment was already outdated when I was in high school. Most of it would just be hauled off for scrap metal. And there are loans against the warehouse, so he'll be lucky if he breaks even on that. He's better off just riding out whatever cash flow is left."

She stared pensively out the window, as if contemplating how she would navigate this latest predicament. Sam liked to think he had some of his mom's remarkable resolve. Raised in Maysville, Kentucky—somewhere between Louisville and Cincinnati along the Ohio River—Connie was the oldest of five siblings and grew up working at her father's chicken hatchery. Although she had to fend for herself from an early age, she got good grades and managed to earn a scholarship to Ohio University, the first in her family to go to college, where she met Sam's father.

The financial stress of the business took a toll on their domestic life. But Sam's mom had a knack for finding a way to keep the family together—even if it meant calling the occasional time-out. When the boys were in junior high, their parents temporarily separated. She took them with her to Maysville that summer, where they helped their cousins at the hatchery—cleaning chicken shit from cages, scraping the trampled carcasses of runt chicks from the wire floors, and tossing any chicks that came out deformed into a white pail at the end of each row, where they would lie helplessly layered on top of each other until the end of the day when the bucket was filled with water. They returned to Lima in time for the start of the school year, and their parents reconciled with no further discussion.

But Connie's resourcefulness was no match for the downward trajectory of their hometown. The exodus had the feeling of inevitability to it—like a low tide retreating from an inlet. One by one, factories closed, farms foreclosed, and storefronts shuttered, never to be reoccupied. The Walmart Supercenter snuffed out what few shops were left in the downtown. The impact on Hughes Rentals was inevitable—with no construction, farming, or manufacturing, there was no one to lease their equipment. As the clients dwindled, the business languished. Unable to afford investments in new equipment, they took out bank loans to keep it afloat, falling deeper into debt.

"Can't you just go down to the warehouse and meet with him?" she said, looking pleadingly into Sam's eyes. "Get a sense of the place, that's all. He's running out of options."

"OK, sure," Sam relented, taking another sip of his coffee.

"Thank you, dear," she said, placing her hand on his shoulder. "So, how are Heather and the kids doing?"

"Uh . . . fine." Sam felt off guard at the sudden change of topic. "You know—work and school. Nothing much new."

"You got a good one with her. I hope you know that."

"Yup," Sam said, wondering if the same sixth sense that had kept her own marriage intact enabled his mom to sense he and Heather weren't on speaking terms at the moment.

"I don't know how she does it—raising three kids and a successful career on top of it. Y'know, women couldn't really work full-time out of the house in my generation."

"Well, we probably couldn't make it without two incomes in the Bay Area, so it's not really an option for one of us to stay at home," Sam said. "Which is why I need to get a job soon, or maybe we *will* move back here." Then, after a pause, he added sheepishly, "Speaking of jobs, Bob told me you're working nights as a cashier now. Are you doing OK? Y'know, financially?"

Her expression artificially brightened at the question. "We're doin' just fine," she said, attempting a reassuring smile. "We don't make much, but we don't *need* much. I get about thirty hours a week, so that helps. Plus, they have Uber in Dayton now. I started doing some drivin' with them, so if money's short at the end of the month, I can make ends meet that way."

Sam had a hard time picturing his mom, who could barely manage the complexities of her iPhone, navigating the streets of Dayton on behalf of Uber. "Well, if you ever need help, let me know. I won't tell Dad."

"What would help me is if you help your dad. Besides, I don't want you givin' us money when you're out of work yourself," she said. "By the way, you never told me why you left."

"It wasn't exactly voluntary," Sam said.

"*What?* You mean he *fired* you?" she asked. Sam shrugged his eyebrows and nodded. "Why on earth would he do that? I can't believe that horse's ass fired you without any reason at'all! He should be ashamed of himself!"

"It wasn't exactly *no* reason. Maybe I deserved it. But it's OK, Mom. I'll be fine," Sam said, trying to stem her instinctive escalation into hillbilly saltiness.

"It's *not* OK," she protested. "People like that are ruining this country."

"There are a lot of people ruining this country," Sam said, not wanting clarification of what "people like that" meant to her.

"Well, I never trusted that fella," she persisted. "Whatever his motives, he disrespected my baby," she said, putting a hand to Sam's cheek. "And you know what we do when someone disrespects a Hughes, don't ya?"

"Shame them on social media?" Sam cracked.

"Take a twelve-gauge and shoot his dick off," she said without missing a beat. Her unsmiling expression left Sam not entirely sure she was joking, triggering memories of her stories of long-lost uncles and half cousins settling scores with familial rivals back in Kentucky.

"Well, unfortunately, I don't own a twelve-gauge, and California isn't an open-carry state, so . . ." He paused for comedic effect. "Maybe I can tote yours back in a violin case or something."

"Don't be such a prick," she scolded. "I'm not sayin' you actually need to shoot the shithead—just fight back a little. There's a reason he did what he did, even if he won't fess up to you."

"I'll take it under advisement," Sam said.

"*Advisement?*" she echoed. "When did you get so fancy?"

"It's a fairly common word, Mom. I'm not trying to be fancy."

"You don't even talk like you're from here no more," she said ruefully. Her Appalachian accent always thickened when discussing matters of family pride.

"Why, 'cause I don't say 'warsh your dishes' and 'please?' when I didn't understand what you said?" Sam asked.

She gave him a melancholy gaze. "I just wish we could all be together as a family again. It's nice having you home." Sam looked at her a moment, seeing in her eyes an expression that took him back to his childhood. Reminding him how long it had been since he'd been back in Lima.

"It's nice to be here," he finally replied. *There's no place like home, but this isn't it anymore.*

CHAPTER 11:

DITCHES

THE SUN-BLEACHED YELLOW SIGN of Hughes Equipment Rentals hung slightly askance over the chain-link fence that encased the multifarious contraptions on the lot. Weeds pushed through the cracks in the pavement at the front of the establishment, like fingers dragging the whole property back to its rural past. Sam tried the door, but it was locked—in the middle of the afternoon on a Tuesday. He cupped his hand to the window to see if his dad or anyone else was inside. Seeing nothing except a dusty bell on the counter and a three-year-old calendar from an automotive-parts manufacturer, Sam walked around the side of the cinder block building to the service gate.

He saw his dad's pickup parked inside near the warehouse, so Sam pulled at the gate—also locked. He regarded the chain enclosure and padlock, thought for a moment of the hundreds of times he had opened that gate, and recalled the combination. Straining slightly to slide open the rusted enclosure, Sam entered the compound. He started to close the gate with the intent of locking it back up, but then stopped—*What's the point?* Sam glanced up and down the abandoned block, noting his mom's dusty Ford Taurus, which he had driven over, as the only sign of life. He probably wouldn't be there very long anyway.

Sam could hear the gas-powered engine of the pressure washer roaring in between blasts. The chore had always been a favorite of the brothers. They would roshambo for the privilege, with the winner knowing full well he could soak the loser, if not inflict bruises and cuts, with the industrial-strength nozzle the moment their dad looked away. Turning the corner, Sam found his dad wielding the rod, pointing at the jagged-toothed blade of a ditch digger. With a broad handlebar in back and oversize knobby tires, the contraption looked like a mutant Harley-Davidson whose front wheel had been replaced with a six-foot chainsaw. His dad hadn't heard Sam approach over the din of the pressure washer, each pulse of which sent chunks of dirt flying through the air. A river of mud wound through the other equipment toward the drain.

Sam shouted, "Dad!" but got no response. Not wanting to startle him, Sam tried to maneuver into his line of sight. He waved his arm to get his attention and shouted "Dad!" again. This time his dad instinctively swung toward him with the pressure washer cocked like a rifle.

"Jesus *Christ*, Sam! You scared the shit out of me!"

"Sorry."

"I told you guys when you were kids, you gotta be careful around here. I could about take your head off with this thing."

"That's why I was trying not to surprise you," Sam said, indicating his peripheral approach.

"Well, it didn't work. I about shit myself," Bob Senior said, returning his attention to the ditch digger, which he proceeded to blast several more times with the pressurized water.

"Someone digging a drainage trench or something?" Sam asked in an awkward attempt to make conversation.

"Grave."

"Oh . . . that makes sense, I guess."

"Why the hell are you here anyway?"

Sam thought for a moment. Since his mom's urging earlier that morning, he had reflected further on the business. Perhaps it wasn't the lost cause he had assumed. Maybe if they set up a commerce website and enabled clients to reserve equipment with a mobile app, they could resuscitate it. Sam even started speculating they could use this yet-to-be-built app to manage the inventory of other equipment-rental businesses, offering on-site delivery—like an Uber of equipment rental. As Sam was prone to do, he let his enthusiasm for his own idea grow quickly. Even if all he ended up doing was offering his dad financial advice, it was still worth it—fulfilling his mom's request and helping to assuage his guilt at not working a day at Hughes Rentals since his last summer of college.

"I figured since I'm here for a few days, maybe we could take a look at the books together," Sam said, his long pause giving the comment a twinge of insincerity.

Bob Senior regarded Sam for a moment through squinted eyes, as if he expected Sam to admit he was kidding. Determining it wasn't a joke, he dubiously asked, "Why would you want to look at the books?"

"I don't know—I guess just to see if there's some way I can help. You know, like with financial advice or something." Sam realized the remark sounded condescending, though that wasn't his intent.

"What do you even mean by *books* anyway?" Bob asked, blasting the pressure washer again. "We got a checkbook, but the last person to balance that was probably your mother. I have a stack of bills you can go through if you want."

"Sure," Sam said, trying to seize any opening to help out.

Bob dug into his pocket and fished out a set of keys that he tossed to Sam. "Top drawer in the office. Knock yourself out," he said, returning his attention to the ditch digger.

Sam walked back across the yard, cluttered with cement mixers, back haulers, and scaffolding, toward the office. He unlocked the back door and passed through a room filled with smaller equipment—power generators, leaf blowers, ice drills, shelves full of various handheld tools. The door to the office was ajar already, so Sam pushed it open and entered cautiously. Although he had spent countless hours in the warehouse, equipment yard, and storefront, he had only been in the office a handful of times. The cramped space was filled with filing cabinets and a large metal desk that looked as if it could survive a nuclear Armageddon.

Sunlight from a narrow ceiling-height window illuminated the dust floating in the air. Sam sat at the desk and opened an ancient laptop computer the thickness of a dictionary. The battery was long dead, and Sam couldn't find a power cord, so he closed it and instead opened the desk drawer to discover it jam-packed with unopened mail. He wrenched a handful of envelopes out of the drawer and set them on the desk.

His phone suddenly vibrated with an incoming text. It was from Amanda. "*I got my hands on something I think you'll find interesting.*"

"*Great—can you send it?*" he replied.

"*No. Only have hard copy. Meet me at 6PM Thurs at Sand Hill Court bar.*"

"*It's a date,*" Sam replied.

He placed his phone on the desk and rifled through the first stack of bills, sorting them into piles—bank statements, utility bills, past-due notices. He pulled out another stack, emptying the first drawer. Several envelopes were unpaid invoices sent by Hughes Equipment Rentals marked "Return to Sender," which he put into another pile. In the second drawer, Sam found a large spiral-bound ledger. He set it on the desk and opened it, revealing pages of the torn-off perforated edges of checks with handwritten entries. The last check written was dated almost a year earlier. He grabbed the most recent bank statement and wiggled it open with his finger. As Sam started deciphering the various accounts, his dad suddenly appeared in the threshold.

"Figured it out yet?" Bob Senior asked.

"Oh, *crap*!" Sam snapped his head up. "You scared the hell out of me!"

"Got you back, then," his dad said as he took a seat in a cracked vinyl chair in the corner.

"Dad, this is kind of a mess. It looks like you haven't paid any bills in over a year."

"We've paid a few, using our personal checking."

"You have to account for that," Sam said. "You can't just mix your bank accounts."

"You think I don't know that? It's just temporary—till we get paid on some of these open invoices," he said, indicating the "Return to Sender" stack that Sam suspected had a 0 percent chance of being paid. "I don't know why I let you come in here. It's not your problem."

"It sorta *is* my problem, Dad. You're going to get foreclosed if you don't deal with this stack of bills."

"We'll figure something out," Bob said with a dismissive wave of his hand.

"*How* are you going to figure something out? Mom said the medical expenses are getting out of control."

"Your mother worries too much. We've been keeping things going like this for a while now. Shiftin' money around to make it work. We're both getting Social Security checks now."

"She's driving for Uber, Dad! Besides, how much longer are you going to have the energy to work at all?"

"What? Cause of the CAD? That's nothin'—half the people I know have heart issues."

"Look, all I'm saying is you need a plan. You need to take care of yourself. And, someday, you're going to need to retire. Have you thought about selling the business?"

"There's nothing to sell, and no one who'd buy it."

"Mmmm," Sam said in agreement. "That's what I told Mom."

"Why are you and your mother talking about all this anyway?" Bob asked, his irritation mounting. "Like I said, it's not your problem."

"I'm just trying to help, Dad."

"Well, you're *not*. Sometimes I think you forget you're just two generations removed from having running water and an in-house toilet. A couple of unpaid bills are a high-class problem."

"Look, it may sound crazy, but I had an idea today for how you could get things back on track." Sam took a breath and continued. "We could build a website and mobile app. They're not very expensive to develop these days. I could do most of it myself. I'm not working anyway, so I could stay here a few weeks while we get everything done. Then, who knows—maybe we start managing the online presence for other equipment-rental businesses too."

Bob Senior was leaning back in his chair staring at Sam with his hands clasped on his arched stomach. "Have you lost your fucking mind?" he asked.

"Yeah, it might be ambitious to manage other companies' inventory," Sam admitted. "But there have to be other distressed equipmentrental businesses like ours who could benefit from an app. They just need to modernize their IT."

"I'm not talking about your app idea. I'm talking about you coming back to Lima and wading into this 'mess,' as you called it. Tech isn't the solution to everything. Even if it was, is this where you'd want to spend twelve hours a day?" Bob asked, gesturing around at the office. He leaned forward in his chair. "You listen to me. I worked my *ass* off to give you and your brother a shot at getting out of here. To do what I never got the chance to do."

"What are you talking about, Dad? You made us work here *all the time.* You told us that if we weren't taking over the family business, we could pay our own tuition. You made Bob come back again after college, and he still practically won't talk to you."

"I *never* wanted you boys to come back here! I didn't want you to feel trapped, the way I did my whole life. Bob Junior worked here because he couldn't find another job. This is a dying business in a dying town run by a dying man. You want to be drowning under this pile of bills? If you're dumb enough to come back here, I'll drown you myself!"

"So you're telling me that I've felt guilty my entire adult life for no reason?" Sam asked. "Why didn't you tell me this, like, twenty-five years ago?"

"There are plenty of things I never told you," he said, then suddenly chuckled at a recollection. "You remember that time I made you and Bob clean out the carcass of that pig that got run over by the combine?"

"*Remember?*" Sam asked. "It scarred me for life. Neither of us could stop vomiting hosing that thing down."

Bob let out a loud laugh. "That was just some spoiled pork shoulder and a bucket of pig blood I got from my buddy at the butcher shop."

"Holy shit—are you *kidding* me?" Sam asked, beginning to laugh incredulously himself.

"I figured if I made you guys do that, you'd never want to work here another day in your life. Mostly, I was right. I knew if I didn't push you out of it, you'd get sucked into it. Everyone wants a better life for their kids. For my dad, this business got him out of the fields. Gave him something to hand down to me. Even though I hated it, my life was better because of what he did. I got a lot of good years from this business. Made a living my whole life here. But I knew this wasn't the life you boys wanted, or deserved."

"I always thought you expected Bob or me to take it over. I felt like I let you and Mom down when I left," Sam said.

"The day you packed up that U-Haul and drove west was one of the proudest of my life. Sure, I was sorry to see you go, but I knew you were going to make it. You always had that determination you got from your mother. Especially when anyone told you that you couldn't do something."

Sam watched dust particles drift lazily in the lone beam of sunlight, refusing to meet his father's gaze in order to maintain his composure. "I don't know . . . I don't feel like much of a success right now," Sam said. "I just got fired from my job. I'm over the hill at forty-five. We're barely keeping it together financially. Heather isn't currently talking to me. And the kids think I'm a giant loser."

"Sounds familiar," Bob said, and they both laughed. Sam dabbed at his eyes, welling with tears. "Frankly, that's life. You play the hand you're dealt and fight through it the best you can. Feeling sorry for yourself isn't going to solve anything. You think I feel sorry for myself? There's always a way, Sam. You just need to find the path."

CHAPTER 12:
FEELING PHILANTHROPIC

SAM AND HEATHER EASED FORWARD behind a line of cars, waiting their turn for the valet at Fort Mason, the complex of renovated military buildings turned high-end venue on the San Francisco Bay waterfront. Out of each luxury automobile disembarked men in black tie and women in impeccable designer evening gowns. They watched the couples as they shuddered in the bracing ocean breeze, the daylight descending into evening.

"Dang, people are decked. Glad I can still fit my fat ass into my tux," Sam said with a self-deprecating glance.

"You look nice," she said.

"Not nearly as nice as you," he said, taking her hand. Heather looked spectacular in an elegant form-fitting evening dress in a slightly iridescent deep blue reminiscent of the darkening sky. "Men are mere accessories at an event like this."

The unexpected compliments were the culmination of a gradual rapprochement that began after Sam's return from Ohio the previous day. A lingering glance, an involuntary smile, and all the other micro-reconciliations of a long-married couple had eased the tension between them and reminded Sam why they had fallen in love in the first place. When he fastened her necklace, Heather elegantly suspending her hair with both hands, he couldn't resist kissing the back of her neck.

Their destination for the evening was the annual black-tie gala organized by Patrick Tierney, a tech billionaire turned philanthropist to a wide range of pet charities. Each year, Patrick would select a different newfound organization as the beneficiary of the annual campaign and embrace it with a zeal that rivaled a teenage girl's celebrity crush. This year's honoree was called Hemp, Not Heroin, an organization providing "transitional training" to farmers in Xalisco, Mexico, so they could grow hemp instead of poppies.

"So, how was Ohio?" Heather asked.

"It was good. I'm glad I went. I think I figured some things out."

"Oh?" she asked with an optimistic raise of her eyebrows.

"Yeah. I think I'm ready to get back on the horse." Sam smiled and squeezed her hand. The valet opened the car door and handed him a ticket.

Upon entering the venue, Sam and Heather were immediately met by servers—one with a silver tray filled with flutes of champagne, the other with a platter of "caviar blini tacos, in honor of Mexico," it was explained. Patrick was a huge benefactor who had donated millions and raised millions more, but the extravagant gala was as much a showcase for himself and those in his orbit who wished to be seen as this generation's Rockefellers. Sam hadn't attended the event for years, not willing to pay the $1,000-per-person admission. This year, however, they were attending as guests of Paul Fleming, the venture partner from GrayWillow Ventures who had introduced Sam to FrontRange and their wolfhound-loving founder. Since then, Paul had introduced Sam to two other opportunities in his portfolio, so when the invite came, they felt obliged to attend.

The format of the event was a silent auction, followed by a live auction, which Patrick emceed with a professional auctioneer calling out the bids. Sam and Heather perused the items for sale as they sipped their champagne and nibbled on passing trays of appetizers—stopping to contemplate various sports memorabilia, wine offerings, and vacation getaways but balking at the already-astronomical bids written on the sheets.

"So, what exactly do you mean by 'get back on the horse'?" Heather asked, glancing at him curiously above the rim of her flute.

"You know—like you said. Get back in the game. Find my next job. Speaking of . . . ," Sam said, trailing off as he made eye contact with Paul, who had invited them to join his table for the evening. The two shook hands vigorously while introducing each other to their respective spouses. "Thanks so much for inviting us," Sam said.

"Of course! We're so glad you could make it." Paul then turned conspiratorially to Heather and said, "I'm determined to get your husband into the GrayWillow ecosystem. He'd be a perfect fit at several of our portfolio companies. Come, let me introduce you to the rest of our table."

Paul led them across the ballroom, navigating through the twelve-person tabletops that cost upward of $20,000 apiece for the evening, and proceeded to introduce Sam and Heather to the other couples—the middle-aged white CEO of one of their portfolio companies and his young wife; Constance Jones, the buzz-cut matriarch of GrayWillow and her rather elderly husband who seemed borderline comatose; a junior partner at GrayWillow and his recently engaged fiancée; and a mixed-race lesbian couple of unclear connection. Sam and Heather took their seats, and moments later a chilled asparagus vichyssoise arrived, onto which servers shaved a gluttonous portion of black truffles—just as the ornately printed miniature menu at their place settings described. Looking across the table, Sam noticed the junior partner had scooped the truffles out of the soup and placed them on his side plate. "Not a fan of truffles?" Sam asked.

"Oh, no—I'm just trying to trigger ketosis," the associate replied.

"Sorry, what?" Sam thought maybe he had misheard him in the din.

"The truffles have too many carbs," the associate explained. "I'm on the keto diet. Strict no carbs. I've been on it a couple weeks and it's amazing what it's done for my metabolism. I'm really close to achieving full ketosis!" he said proudly.

"It means his body is burning fat for energy," Heather interjected, having overheard the conversation and observed Sam's obvious confusion.

"Yeah, I'm almost there," the associate said. "My breath stinks, my energy level is spiking, and I have insomnia every night. I'm trying to get to a ketone level between 3.0 and 8.0 millimoles per liter. I check my level every day using urine strips."

"I see, uh . . . congratulations," Sam said. Mercifully, an announcer interrupted over the loudspeaker. "One minute before the silent auction closes. One minute! Last chance to get in your final bids." Eager to pivot from his urine-strip conversation, Sam turned his attention to the other side of the table, where the CEO and his obsequious wife demonstrably hoped their $10,000 bid for a basketball autographed by all the members of the Golden State Warriors would prevail. Sam assured them that such an acquisition would be a lifetime memento and could only appreciate in value—besides, all the money went to charity.

As the next course was served, the lights dimmed, and the same voice announced the silent auction was officially closed. A member of the crowd whistled into the ensuing silence before raucous hip-hop music reverberated through the room. Spotlights in a rainbow of colors swept across the crowd as the music crescendoed and Patrick emerged from behind a curtain in a billow of smoke. Patrick could only be accurately described as obese. At a weight likely approaching four hundred pounds, he labored onto the stage as he waved enthusiastically to the crowd under his signature tangled tuft of red hair. Unapologetically and flamboyantly gay, Patrick was one of those men like Elton John or Liberace that Sam always wondered how other men could possibly find attractive. Pale white with ample jowls that cascaded into a torso that resembled a slumped beanbag, Patrick donned a gender-neutral combination of a fuchsia jacket with long tails and gold-fringed epaulets that looked as if it were stolen from the set of the *Sgt. Pepper's* movie over a muumuu in a bold lavender flower motif.

"Hello! Hello!" Patrick shouted, waving to the crowd. "I'm *soooo* glad you could be here on this very special night!" He waddled to the front of the stage like a walrus nudging its way to a food trough. "How many of you are here for the first time tonight?" he asked, his voice modulated by his laborious breathing. A handful of hands went up. "Well, you're in for a special evening. This is the twelfth-annual Patrick Tierney Charity Auction and Gala, and each year it gets better. So, who's ready to spend some mo-*nayyy?*"

Paul turned to the rest of the table and declared, "Classic Patrick!"

"I'm so proud of this year's charity, Hemp, Not Heroin! This organization just spoke to me. As many of you know, I fought my own dark battle to overcome the pernicious craving of opioid painkillers to help with my chronic back pain."

"I wonder why he has chronic back pain," Sam whispered to Heather, who giggled but nudged him to be quiet.

"Thank God I never succumbed to black tar heroin to subdue the demons of addiction, as so many Americans of lesser means have been forced to do," Patrick continued. "As the heroin epidemic gutted our heartland and took countless lives, I thought there should be a special place in hell reserved for those heroin growers. But then my eyes opened up. These people weren't criminals. They were *farmers*. They were growing the crop they'd always grown, not realizing just how addictive and destructive their crop was."

Patrick panned his gaze around the room dramatically as a picture of a Mexican farmer in a straw cowboy hat appeared on the screen, accompanied by Latin music in the overdramatic tone of a telenovela. "Now, finally, thanks to HNH, there's an alternative. Hemp is a true miracle crop—it's medicine, it's fabric, it's fuel. And it sure can take the edge off, am I *right*? This is Victor Jiménez, a farmer I met in Xalisco who has completely converted his family's five-acre poppy farm 100 percent to sustainable, organic *hemp*. Thanks to HNH, this dream is becoming a reality for dozens of farmers like Victor!"

"Such a *great* cause," the nameless CEO asserted as applause rippled through the crowd, ostensibly to his wife but loud enough to be audible to the whole table. Sam sipped his champagne and watched the CEO continue to kiss up to Paul, adding earnestly, "This organization is really transforming these communities."

"I'm going to let you finish your dinners before we start the live auction," Patrick continued. "Spoiler alert! The lobster thermidor is ah-MAAAY-zing! But before I do, I want to announce the winner of our most coveted silent auction listing: the all-expenses-paid luxury camp suite for Burning Man! This crew will pitch a tent that would make an Arabian prince jealous—a 2,000-square-foot main tent with private suites for twelve adults, complete catering, running water, electricity, and air-conditioning, plus private jet and limousine service to *the* bohemian arts and culture event on everyone's bucket list! Drum roll, please!" Patrick said as he opened an envelope with a game show host's flourish. "And the winners, with the top bid of $175,000, are Dave and Susie Parsons!" A portly couple in their late fifties stood from their table, hugged enthusiastically, and waved to the crowd. "Congratulations to you both! I claim one of those suites!" Patrick said, smiling mischievously. "Thank you to everyone who bid in our silent auction. If you didn't win, the main event is coming right up, so get those auction paddles ready! Refresh your drinks, enjoy your entrées, and I'll be back for the live auction!" Patrick exited to a soundtrack ripped from the Oscars as the din of conversation ensued.

"Wow," Sam mouthed silently to Heather, who laughed discreetly. She looked down coyly to hide her smile, pretending to adjust the napkin in her lap. "I'm going to go get us some drinks."

Sam wove his way through the tables toward the bar, beating a rush of people looking to refresh their drinks during the intermission. "That was quite a show," Sam heard a voice say over his shoulder. He turned to discover Quinn Randall, a reporter with *TechWrap*, the venerable technology blog.

"Hey, Quinn. Yeah, Patrick is the consummate showman," Sam said, immediately familiar with the reporter he'd briefed dozens of times in mostly unsuccessful attempts to get coverage in *TechWrap*. "Have you been to one of these before?" Sam asked, gesturing toward the gala.

"Oh, sure. Patrick always invites the press to his annual gala. If you don't get press, what's the point?" Quinn mused. "It's like the tree that falls in the forest—if there was no press coverage, did it really happen?"

"Well, I'll tell you what *did* really happen," Sam said. "Someone just dropped a hundred and seventy-five grand for VIP service at a festival espousing anti-consumerism."

"Yeah, good point." Quinn chuckled and ordered himself a drink. "I guess I'm so jaded I don't even notice the hypocrisy anymore."

"How long have you been in tech, Quinn?" Sam asked.

"Oh, shit . . . Too long to remember. Since '99, I guess."

Sam grinned and reached out his glass to toast. "Me too."

"A lot has changed since then," Quinn acknowledged. "It feels like, at some point, something flipped. We stopped being the good guys who were changing the world and turned into . . . something else."

"I've kinda been feeling the same way lately," Sam said.

"Oh, yeah, I saw your rant at the SaaStr event on Twitter. Is that why you left Ainetu?"

"Indirectly, I guess," Sam said, taking a sip of his drink.

"What's going on there? We're getting some interesting emails into the tip line," Quinn said, putting on his innocent reporter's demeanor.

"More than you want to know," Sam replied. Then, wanting to change the subject, he said, "By the way, congratulations on your exposé on Pathway Systems." Pathway was a hot tech company in the online-ad remarketing space that turned out essentially to be a multilevel marketing scam. Exposed initially through Quinn's investigative reporting, the company went from unicorn to bankrupt in the span of a month.

"Thanks," Quinn replied with earnest modesty. "I was really proud of that reporting. Those guys were breaking the law for years and nobody called them on it. There's no board oversight. The regulators are a joke—they're completely asleep on the job. It's up to the press. We're the last remaining check and balance on these guys. Unless there's public outcry, nobody calls them to account. But we're a dying breed. Most so-called journalism is just a constant stream of click-bait to drive page views, regurgitating press releases, or contorting our content into advertorials. Any *real* journalism, if it's even remotely negative about a company, gets immediate pushback and our editors usually buckle, slaves to our few remaining advertisers."

"The irony is that true journalism gets labeled 'fake news' by those exposed, while everything else is essentially propaganda for a company or some other special interest."

"It's a goddamn shame, and I'm not sure how much longer I can do it," Quinn admitted. "Maybe I'll do PR."

"Shit, and go to the *dark side*? Don't do it!" Sam implored demonstrably.

"Well, I guess I might have a few more big stories in me first," Quinn intimated with a conspiratorial look. "Look, if what we're hearing is true, there could be a similar situation going on at Ainetu. So, if you ever want to share what's *really* going on there, off the record, of course, I'd be all ears."

"I'll keep that in mind," Sam said with a noncommittal grin.

Quinn chuckled briefly, then said, "I know I've given you my card a hundred times, but just in case the mood strikes you." He tucked his business card into the breast pocket of Sam's tuxedo jacket. "Enjoy the gala."

"You've got to save me," Heather whispered through a faux smile when Sam returned to the table. "I'm getting a minute-by-minute ketone-level update from this guy."

Sam laughed. "Sorry that took so long," he said, handing her a chilled martini. "I was having an enlightening conversation with Quinn Randall from *TechWrap*."

"Oh, really?" she replied with interest. "What about?"

"He was fishing for dirt on Ainetu."

"*Is* there dirt on Ainetu?" she asked, balancing her cocktail as she brought it to her lips.

"Possibly," Sam said, peering at her. "I accidentally got some information when I was in Ohio. Some sales contracts that seem off. I'm meeting Amanda this week to learn more."

"That's interesting. Would you ever tell him anything off the record? A story like that could really change things."

"Not sure anything I'd say could truly be off the record," Sam said. "They'd immediately suspect it was me, but I'm not sure I care. If what I think is happening is really happening, then this would be the leverage I never had when I was there." Sam looked around at the room of tuxedo-clad socialites. "Anyway, it's a long shot and I should probably move on with my life. Maybe I could follow Patrick's lead and do charitable work."

"Right, because you're such a big philanthropist," Heather gently teased.

"Well, maybe it would help me be less envious of these billionaire douchebags if I was doing something for someone other than myself for a change."

"So basically you'd be doing philanthropy for completely selfish reasons. Why don't you start by bidding on something in the auction," she said as she slapped him playfully in the chest with the auction paddle.

"Are you kidding? We can't afford any of this stuff."

"At least your heart is in the right place," she said with a smile as they held each other's gaze momentarily.

Just then, the lights dimmed, the music swelled, and Patrick returned to the stage with his arms extended over his head. "Welcome back, ladies and gentlemen!" Patrick shouted. "Now for the main event of the evening—the live auction!"

As the buzz of anticipation reverberated through the crowd, Sam rested his right hand on Heather's knee, then slid it underneath her napkin to find a patch of her warm skin. His pulse quickened from the simple act of affection as the audience turned their attention to the auctioneer onstage. The activity in the room faded into the background as Sam concentrated on the sensation of their contact. Caressing her leg, Sam gradually moved from her knee to her thigh, sliding her dress up just slightly under the cover of the unfurled napkin. Heather reached down, taking his hand in hers to curtail his advance but giving him a flirtatious look as if to say, *Stop that.*

Bidding started on the first item, a two-night stay at a five-bedroom, 6,000-square-foot ski chalet in Aspen, at an opening bid of $25,000. As the auctioneer stirred the crowd into an anticipatory frenzy, bidders began raising their paddles—increasing their bids in $5,000 increments as he shouted out their numbers. Sam turned, pretending to get a better view of the stage, and moved his right hand to the back of Heather's chair, resting it nonchalantly on her exposed shoulder. With his left, he crept farther up the outside of her thigh, hiking her dress up slightly more until he was able to slip a finger underneath the string of her panties high on her hip.

Heather shifted in her chair and Sam thought their first intimate foray in months might be over. But instead, still facing the stage, she reached back and placed her hand on Sam's knee, then held the auction paddle over her lap, creating a blind. Sam leaned forward close to her neck, also facing the stage, trying to mimic the enthusiasm of everyone else at their table with his attention apparently trained on the escalating auction, already over $50,000. He followed the line of elastic from her hip forward and downward as she subtly parted her legs and rose to meet his touch. Finding her already wet with anticipation, Sam gently pulled her open with his fingers and slid one inside her. He was close enough to hear her gasp quietly at his entry.

Heather's fingernails clenched Sam's knee as the bidding continued— sixty thousand, sixty-five, seventy. "Do I hear $75,000?" the auctioneer bellowed as Sam quickened the pace and intensity of his circular motion. The crowd was transfixed with anticipation as a paddle rose to accept the latest offer. "Seventy-five thousand dollars to Bidder 235! An incredible weekend away in Aspen—and a bargain, I might add, at $75,000.

Anyone at eighty? No? Anyone? Going once at seventy-five! Going twice! *Sold*!" Heather allowed herself a soft moan as she climaxed, masked by the applause. She spun in her chair toward Sam, her face flushed from the thrill of their lust in plain sight. Leaning in, she whispered breathlessly in his ear, "Let's get out of here."

CHAPTER 13:

JEWELRY EXCHANGE

SAM WATCHED HIS TWO SONS shooting baskets at their outdoor hoop. From the living room window, he marveled at the fact that they both seemed to have grown perceptibly just in the week he was in Ohio. Sam was finding his conversations with the boys were less frequent and more strained as they became teenagers. Responses to his questions tended toward the monosyllabic—"OK," "Umm," and "Huh?" were common responses. Sam recalled playing at that hoop with them for hours when the boys were younger, but it had been a while—particularly as he grew increasingly busy with work. Inspired by his own recent father-son communication breakthrough, he laced up a pair of sneakers and ventured outside, trying to capture a bonding moment before the remaining window of childhood closed.

"Hey, guys," Sam said, interrupting their one-on-one game by grabbing a rebound.

"*Dad*, we're in the middle of a game!" Mason said. Connor rolled his eyes and held up his hands, beckoning to get the ball back.

"Riley's at a friend's house, so I thought we could hoop it up a bit," Sam said, clanking a shot off the iron.

"There aren't many games for three people," Mason said.

"Horse?" Connor suggested.

"Nah, c'mon—I want to get some exercise. Me versus you two," Sam said.

"Are you sure?" Connor asked.

"We'd kill you," Mason added.

"How about you two against me," Connor, their oldest, proposed instead.

"OK, bring it!" Sam said, grabbing the rebound and dribbling to the top of the key. "Check up."

Connor promptly stole the ball from Sam on the opening possession and swished an uncontested three-pointer. Sam then airballed a shot on the next possession. After which Connor effortlessly drove past him for an easy layup. Quickly, it was ten to zero and Sam was bent over with his hands on his knees, sweating profusely.

"Dad, can we just go back to our game?" Mason, his visibly frustrated teammate, asked.

"Sure," Sam said, panting for air. "When did you guys get so good?" The boys immediately resumed playing. "I need to take a shower anyway."

"Why, are you going somewhere?" Connor asked as he dribbled the ball between his legs, pondering his move. Sam saw in Mason the same younger brother's determination that he recognized in himself to match up to his taller, stronger, faster sibling.

"Yeah, I'm meeting Amanda from work for a drink. You guys can order a pizza for dinner." Connor and Mason stopped playing and gave a knowing look to each other. "What is it?" Sam asked.

"Oh, nothing," Connor said, resuming his dribble.

"I don't think Mom likes her," Mason confessed.

Connor quickly explained, "The day you got fired, she said something about Amanda fending for herself. Like she didn't want you working with her anymore."

"I see," Sam said, considering the remark. He had never thought of Heather as jealous.

"Why are you seeing her? Is she helping you get your job back?" Mason asked.

"No, it's just to catch up as friends."

The boys exchanged another look. Then Connor asked, "When are you going to get a new job? It's been, like, three months already."

"I'm working on it," Sam said. He returned to the house as they resumed their game.

■　■　■

The valet parking at the Sand Hill Court Hotel was already studded with Porsches and Lamborghinis around the circular drive when Sam pulled up. Following up on their text exchange in Ohio, Amanda had set the location with the tantalizing promise of "something big" she'd discovered at Ainetu. Handing his keys to the valet, Sam noticed a sputtering circa-2000 Honda Accord pull up behind him, out of which decamped nearly a half dozen middle-aged women in heavy makeup and short skirts. Central Valley cougars on the prowl for VC sugar daddies. A typical scene for Thursday night on Sand Hill Road—the equivalent of Wall Street for Silicon Valley venture capital firms.

He spotted Amanda on the terrace overlooking the sunset behind the redwood-crowned mountains to the west. The bar was packed, and she was fending off encroachers on the spare seat she'd saved for Sam, like a lioness fighting off a pack of hyenas. Relieved to see him, she eagerly waved at Sam, dashing the hopes of her would-be suitors.

"So good to see you!" she said as they hugged and pecked cheeks.

"Good to see you too," Sam replied. "Looks like you had to resort to hand-to-hand combat to save this seat."

"Just about! I should have known better than to suggest the Sand Hill Court on a Thursday night." She surveyed the room as she held the stem of her glass of chardonnay. "This place has gotten a little . . . slimy."

"Yeah, just don't let anyone give you a piece of jewelry," Sam advised.

"Why's that?"

"Because they'll expect something in return," he said.

"They always do!" Amanda laughed, pushing an errant lock of her auburn hair over her ear. "But what do you mean, exactly?"

"Rumor is the jewelry store here in the lobby is a front for prostitution," Sam explained. "A guy buys a fancy necklace, gives it as a 'gift' to his chosen lady of the night, and then she returns it to the store for cash—with the store taking their restocking fee, of course. Gives everyone plausible deniability."

"*Really?*" Amanda asked in astonishment.

"Well, not like I'm speaking from experience, but that's the scuttlebutt."

"Wow, I'm in the wrong profession," Amanda said. "I get fucked every day, but no one ever gives me a fancy necklace."

Sam was immediately reminded of Amanda's charm—a captivating combination of striking good looks wrapped in self-confidence and tomboyish brusqueness. She was simultaneously the untouchable super model and one of the guys. A study in contrasts—alluring and crass, beguiling and off-putting, gentrified and approachable. Their relationship always had remained strictly professional, but now that they no longer worked together, Sam suddenly realized that the specter of HR lawsuits was no longer an impediment. As these thoughts ran through his head, one of his neighbors recognized him from across the room. "Hey, Sam—how's it goin'?" Chris Parks, an investment banker, said as he eagerly closed in to shake hands.

"Hi, Chris," Sam said. "This is Amanda. We worked together at Ainetu."

"Pleasure to meet you," Chris said, delicately accepting Amanda's handshake as he stared suggestively into her eyes. Sam thought for a moment he might kiss the top of her hand.

"Nice to meet you too," she said, retracting from his grip.

"We're just catching up about work stuff," Sam somewhat awkwardly offered. Then, trying to cut the conversation short, he said, "Let's grab coffee next week."

"Christ, I thought he was going to kiss my fucking hand," she said, rolling her eyes.

"Yeah, I thought so too. The Sand Hill Court brings out the phero-mones. So, what's the big news?"

"Oh, right," she said, pulling up her purse from a hook under the bar and extracting a hardcover book. "Before I forget, will you give this back to Heather for me?" The reference to his wife curtailed any notion this could be the start of an extramarital affair.

Sam took the book and examined the dust jacket. "Sure, what is it?"

"It's just a novel she loaned me for our reading group." Amanda then removed a clasped stack of paper that she tossed on the bar top. "This is what I have for you. It fell off the back of a turnip truck."

Sam regarded the front page of what was now revealed to be a slide presentation with the title "Ainetu Q2 Board Meeting."

"Shit," Sam said. "How'd you get this? Were you in the board meeting?"

"No, are you *kidding*? Rohan has the board meetings locked down like Guantanamo. Nicole left the original in the copier and I snagged it." Nicole was their less-than-capable executive assistant who had been with Rohan since the beginning.

Sam picked up the document. "Have you read it yet?"

"Of course," Amanda said.

"Anything fishy?"

"Not that I saw." She shrugged. "You know I could lose my job if Rohan found out I'm talking to you, let alone giving you this presentation."

"I know. I appreciate you doing this." Sam looked around the bar for anyone else he knew, then cracked open the document and flipped through the pages, each footnoted with the Ainetu logo and the dis-claimer "Confidential—Internal Use Only." The first twenty or so pages were the usual board-presentation flotsam, which Sam skimmed over to reach the main event—the profit-and-loss statement for the current quarter. "So you guys beat your revenue target for Q2?" Sam asked.

"Yeah, barely," Amanda replied.

"I'm a little surprised, given GGT came in at only 20 percent of the forecasted deal size."

"Yeah, but we only recognized about a month of revenue from that deal in Q2," she said. "Where that hurt us was bookings, which was below target. And Rohan won't let me forget it."

Sam nodded in agreement. In software companies, "bookings" were the total contract value of a deal over a period of time, usually between one to three years, while "revenue" was the amount recognized in their financials for a given quarter as the subscription term progressed. He turned the page and found a list of Q2 deals. Scanning the list, he found GGT with the deal size of $200,000 next to it—the same number in the contract Carl had inadvertently sent him. "And all these deals are accurate?"

"Yup."

"Did you sign the paper on all these?" Sam asked, referring to the customer contracts.

"Most of them. All the big ones."

Sam puzzled over the numbers. *How could they be missing their bookings targets but still hitting their revenue?* Even with the lag in revenue recognition, that would catch up with them eventually. "Well, good for him, I guess," Sam said, referring to Rohan as he closed the slide deck. "Looks like he pulled a rabbit out of his hat. Bill must have been relieved," he said of their tightly wound CFO.

"Actually, not so much," Amanda corrected. "He was more stressed out than I've ever seen him before this board meeting. One of our sales guys told me he walked into the men's room and Bill was vomiting in one of the stalls."

"*Really?*"

"I know, *right*? I guess he's freaking out about the bookings miss. I don't know why that stresses *him* out so much. *I'm* the one who has to hit the fucking number." She laughed.

"Curse of the VP of sales," Sam said.

"I think I'm only safe for one more quarter," she said, the smile fading from her face. "We can't miss the bookings again in Q3. Rohan read me the riot act last quarter. If we miss again, he'll either fire me or I'll quit. I can't face that again," she said, unexpectedly placing her hand on Sam's knee.

"Sorry I can't be there to deflect some of the heat," Sam said, trying to remain nonchalant about the physical contact.

"It's not your fault," she dismissed, removing her hand. "I just may have to resort to begging to get deals. Or selling my body." She smiled with a sideways nod toward the jewelry store. "I practically had to sleep with Carl to get him to sign that deal. Not only did it take forever, but the conniving twat finagled me down to one hundred K," she said, shaking her head.

"Wait." Sam paused. "I thought that was a $200,000 deal."

"Well, yeah, but over two years. He wanted it for a hundred per year, and I told him the only way I'd go that low is if they signed a two-year deal," she said with sarcastic pride.

"That's *it*," Sam said. "That's what he's doing!" He ripped open the board presentation and hastily flipped to the slide on Q2 deals.

"That's what *who's* doing?" Amanda asked.

But Sam was too possessed to answer. Finding the list of deals, he asked, "Wave Logic was your biggest deal this quarter. Was that a one-year or two-year deal?"

"Two-year."

"What about Frontier Bank, Alta Home Mortgage, and Carlton Hotel Group?"

"All two-year deals," Amanda replied. "It's how we're trying to hold our ground on pricing. Rather than discounting further, we make them sign a two-year deal to get the annual price they want. We did a bunch of two-year and even three-year deals the last few quarters."

Sam put a hand to his forehead in revelation. "That's how Rohan is manipulating the revenue number," he exclaimed. "He knows he can't lie about the bookings number, or you'd find out since you sign all the contracts. These are all multiyear deals," he said, pointing to the list of customers. "But he's accounting for them as one-year deals so he can recognize all the revenue earlier."

Amanda's expression suggested the light bulb had gone off for her too. Pulling the page from Sam's hands, she scanned the list. "You're right. There are one-year, two-year, and even some three-year deals on this list, but they're all jumbled together as if they're single-year deals. The only thing we get compensated on in sales is the booking number, so we don't pay much attention to the revenue recognition."

"He's probably been doing this for a quarter or two. That's why the revenue number is still ahead of plan."

"Holy shit, Sam!" Amanda leaned back on her stool. "This is serious. This is like shareholder-lawsuit-type stuff."

"That's probably why Bill is barfing in the men's room," said Sam. "He must be in on it."

"What should we do?" Amanda asked.

"Right now, nothing. Look, you didn't manipulate any numbers, so you're not culpable," Sam said. "The board needs to hear about this, but if we're going to blow the whistle, we need proof. Can you pull all the customer contracts for Q1 and Q2 and send them to me from your personal email?"

"Sure. They're all on my laptop."

"Then we've got to get the revenue recognition spreadsheet from Bill. All that's in the board presentation is a summary of the total revenue. We need to see which deals comprise that revenue number, so we know if this is the smoking gun we think it is."

"How are you going to get that?" Amanda asked.

"I'll call him. Meet him for coffee. He owes me," he said. He picked up the board presentation. "Can I hold on to this?"

"Yeah, sure—just don't tell anyone where you got it, or my ass is toast."

"OK, I need to get home. Great seeing you," Sam said as they exchanged another peck on the cheek.

As Sam waited for his car at the valet, an obese, balding, pale-white man arrived in a convertible Bentley with two apparent prostitutes, one in the front seat and one in back. As the valets held open his door, the man posed with the two hookers for a selfie. Sam handed his claim ticket to another valet as the man stumbled out of the car, evidently inebriated and sweating profusely. Under each arm were large wet patches in his armpits and the two amply breasted women in tight-fit-ting miniskirts. He slurred something incoherent to the valet before staggering into the lobby of the hotel, passing the jewelry store on the way to his room.

■ ■ ■

Back at home, Sam's discovery had transformed into indignation as he ranted with Heather, who was propped up on their bed watching Netflix on her laptop with a glass of wine. "Can you fucking believe that?" Sam asked after relaying the alleged evidence of Rohan's fraudulent behavior. "Now I know what he's been up to. The guy's not only a weasel and an egomaniac; he's an outright criminal!"

Heather was unfazed. "I don't know." She shrugged, trying to return to her show. "Just seems like a bunch of numbers. Don't people do that all the time?"

"Do *what* all the time?" Sam asked. "Blatantly manipulate their rev-enue to make it look like they're beating their number when they really *aren't*? I didn't do that *all the time*. I hope none of the companies we own stock in are doing that *all the time*. What does that even *mean*?"

"Are you done?"

"I just think this is a big deal. I finally found the *real* reason I was fired. He knew once we missed Q1 that he was going to have to start cooking the books and that I wouldn't go along with it, so he had to find an excuse to push me out."

"*You* were trying to push *him* out! Be realistic, Sam—this isn't going to change anything. The board won't care. He'll lie and just say it was . . . a typo or something, and—"

"A *typo?*" Sam interrupted. "He *doubled* the revenue they recognized on dozens of deals. You'd have to have your head up your ass to believe that's due to a typo!"

"You're really starting to piss me off."

"I'm sorry. It's just . . . ," Sam sputtered, looking for the words. "It's just so fucking *unbelievable*. And yet, so *believable* at the same time. The guy is a slave to his own pride. Of course he's going to do whatever it takes to manipulate his way to a big exit," Sam said, gesturing his arms wildly. "I can't let him get away with this. I knew he was up to something but never knew what. I got so sick of being the number two—always covering for him. For two years I said the emperor has no clothes."

Heather's face took on a quizzical expression. "You mean you said the emperor *had* clothes when he really *didn't.*"

"No, I'm talking about that children's fable about the emperor who has no clothes."

"Right. But in your analogy aren't you the one saying the emperor *does* have clothes, not that he *doesn't?*"

"It's a metaphor, not an analogy, and I'm not a literary expert on Hans Christian *Fucking* Andersen. The point is—"

"Actually, it was Andersen who was speaking metaphorically about the emperor. You're just using a literary reference."

"Shit, Heather. You're killing me with the English lesson."

"All I'm trying to do is point out that you're barking up the wrong tree. You're chasing a red herring. Pick your metaphor."

"I think those are idioms," Sam said deadpan.

"And I think you're an *asshole*! If you'd let me finish my point, I don't know if what you found is the smoking gun you think it is, and it may be distracting you from what really matters. If you're going to go after Rohan, you better know what you're talking about because he outmaneuvered you before. So you need to have him dead to rights."

"You're right, I know," Sam agreed.

"You're also putting Amanda at risk. How is she doing anyway?"

"She's doing fine. She gave me some book to give to you," Sam said with no elaboration, his thoughts obviously still lingering on Ainetu. "I'll reach out to Bill and see what else I can find out."

Heather nodded pensively. "Just pull the thread a little more and get your facts straight, that's all I'm saying," she said. Then she closed her laptop, set it on the floor, and reached over to turn off their bedside light.

"Pull the thread," Sam repeated at a whisper in the darkness. "That's definitely a metaphor."

CHAPTER 14:

LEVERAGE

SAM COULD ENVISION THE SPREADSHEET in his mind. Bill would grill him about it every quarter to make sure their revenue was accurate based on the customer contracts. Without a copy of that now, Sam didn't really have proof of anything. Even if he did have proof, who would he report this alleged financial wrongdoing *to*? Was this technically even a crime, given that Ainetu was still a private company? He thought for a moment about the blank stares he would receive from the Palo Alto Police Department. Could they give less of a shit about some founder lying to his wealthy VC investors about their revenue? No, this was a job for the Feds. But which "Feds"? The SEC? The FTC? The FBI? Who the hell would even care about this enough to investigate it?

Sam realized his only leverage was to use this knowledge to compel the board to fire Rohan. But if he was going to go to the board, his case needed to be irrefutable. This thought process led Sam to one person: Bill Johnson, the Ainetu CFO. He was the only person Sam could think of who *must* be in on the scam but could conceivably flip. And if he was going to persuade Bill to flip, he needed to get him in person—and maybe apply a little pressure.

Sam pulled up Bill's contact information on his phone and sent him a text: *"Hey, Bill—it's Sam. Can you grab coffee this morning?"*

Sam watched his phone, hoping for a quick reply. He waited several minutes, then Bill responded, *"About what? I'm busy."*

Sam attached a photo of the list of deals from the Ainetu board presentation, then wrote: "*Meet me at Café Borrone in 30 mins.*"

■ ■ ■

Sam arrived at Café Borrone in Menlo Park and ordered a cappuccino. The café was bustling with a mix of Stanford students, professionals, and moms chatting over smoothies after their morning Pilates classes. Sam spotted Bill trying to be discreet in a corner table of the outdoor courtyard.

"Hi, Bill," Sam said as he approached.

"Hey," Bill said, glancing around furtively. "You could have picked a more low-key place to meet."

"I figured if we met by a dumpster in a parking garage, people would get suspicious," Sam joked, trying to lighten the mood. This had always been part of his repartee with Bill—gently teasing him about how uptight he was, but in a vaguely self-deprecating way that didn't make it seem malicious. Bill, for his part, never really partook in the banter.

"Where did you get that slide?" Bill asked in his usual matter-of-fact style.

"Geesh. No foreplay or anything?"

"Did Amanda give that to you?"

"It doesn't matter how I got it," Sam said. "What matters is what it says."

"What do you want, Sam?"

"Fine. I'll cut to the chase. I was surprised to hear you guys hit your Q2 revenue number. Particularly since the GGT deal was only for one hundred K."

"The GGT deal was for two hundred K," Bill said.

"Sure, but over two years. It's one hundred K *per year*. I saw the contract. Carl sent it to me by mistake. Pretty big gap from the $1 million per year we forecasted from that deal, don't you think?" Sam let the question hang for a moment. "And that's not the only deal that came in below forecast. Yet, somehow, you guys still managed to hit the quarterly revenue goal. I just can't for the *life* of me figure out how that could have happened. Can you?"

After a long pause, Bill said, "Revenue recognition is complicated, Sam. There are a lot of accounting rules we need to factor in."

"Wouldn't accounting rules cause revenue recognition to be *delayed* rather than *accelerated*?"

"Well, yes, but . . . the deals you're talking about all just closed this quarter, so their impact on revenue is minimal. How do you know what our Q2 financials were anyway?"

"I don't. I just heard through the grapevine that you made the revenue number."

"That's confidential information," Bill said. "You don't have the right to any of that information anymore. Particularly since you signed a confidentiality agreement. Whatever you've seen or heard is proprietary company information. You aren't entitled to anything. No financials. No board presentations. *Nothing*."

"Look, Bill," Sam said with a change in his tone. "I know what's going on. You know better than this. You're one of the good guys."

Bill sat silently and looked around the café. "I don't know what you're talking about."

"You're falsifying revenue by recognizing multiyear deals in a single year," Sam said, unambiguously leveling the accusation. "If this comes out, you don't think Rohan will have you take the fall for this? You'll never work in the Valley again. Or worse."

"It's not going to come out," Bill said.

"You can't cover for him, Bill. I know—I did that for too long, and look what it got me."

"No, no, no," Bill repeated, seemingly to himself.

"Are you willing to get sued? To go to *prison*? This isn't just about losing your career; it's about losing your savings and your freedom."

"This wasn't my idea," Bill said with a quiver of desperation in his voice.

"I know it wasn't. And I know this is hard, but you need to help me prove what's happening and blow the whistle on this."

"Blow the whistle to *whom*?" Bill said, his resolve deteriorating. He'd obviously had the same realization as Sam—that nobody was really in charge of investigating relatively minor alleged securities fraud at privately held companies whose sole shareholders were wealthy VCs and a handful of overpaid employees.

"Look, at least protect yourself. Gather all the proof you can that you were coerced. That way you'll be prepared to make the case if you have to. And, if it ever blows up, which it very well could, you'll have the evidence."

"I already did that," Bill said, demonstrating the preparedness of a meticulous CFO. He reached into his briefcase, pulled out a USB drive, and set it on the table in front of Sam.

Sam looked at the thumb drive for a moment before picking it up. "What's on here?"

"Everything," Bill said, pressing his fingertips into his temples. "The customer contracts as they were signed, showing the amount and term of each deal. Along with our full quarterly financials and the spreadsheets we used to calculate our revenue recognition, on a deal-by-deal basis."

"And?" Sam asked.

"The numbers don't foot. It's exactly what you suspected. We've been taking all the revenue from multiyear deals this year. It's had the effect of inflating our current fiscal year's revenue by over 20 percent. And that's just the start of it. There's more, *much* more."

Sam tapped the drive on the table. "Who else knows about this?"

"Besides me and Rohan? Really nobody. Amanda is suspicious, of course. She knows the deal terms, but she doesn't have access to the rev-rec spreadsheets. It's the opposite for the folks on the finance team. They know our financial statements, but they don't have access to the sales contracts."

"What about the board members? Do they know?" Sam asked.

"I think they're in 'don't ask, don't tell' mode," Bill said. "Obviously, they've seen our bookings numbers come in on the low side for a few quarters now, but revenue continues to beat our targets. No doubt they're wondering how that's possible, but none of them seem to want to really ask that question."

Reflecting on his conversations with each of their board members, Kamal, Ben, and Preston, Sam understood Bill's insinuation that they were perhaps slow-walking their fiduciary responsibilities. Sam looked up at Bill, who was cradling his coffee in two hands as if to hide his face. He shot sideways glances around the courtyard, clearly unnerved by the admission he had guarded so privately for months.

"You're doing the right thing, Bill," Sam reassured him.

"What are you talking about? I'm not going public with that," Bill said, indicating with his eyes the USB drive.

"What do you mean? Why did you give it to me then?"

"I didn't *give* it to you. I was *showing* it to you," Bill said, reaching out his hand to retrieve the device.

"Bill, I can't prove anything unless I see what's on this drive," Sam said. "Let me hold on to this, just for a day or two. I'll keep it 100 percent confidential. I promise. In the meantime, you really need to think about coming forward with this to the board, or you could be implicated."

"I don't have any choice," Bill insisted. The color had drained from his face.

"You *do* have a choice. You can't let yourself be a victim in all this. You don't even need to necessarily expose it. You could just leave the company. Find another job. I'll help you."

"You haven't found a job for yourself yet. How are you going to help me?" Bill remarked, revealing a hint of levity.

"I'm going to find a job, and it's going to be *great*. The best job you've ever heard of," Sam sarcastically overpromised, trying to further lighten the mood. He paused, momentarily distracted by the buzz of his phone indicating an inbound text message. He glanced at the screen and froze. It was from Rohan.

"*What the fuck do you think you're doing?*" was all it said.

Sam's heart skipped a beat. He instinctively looked around the café to see if they had been discovered. "*Shit,*" he muttered.

"What? What is it?" Bill tentatively asked.

"You didn't tell Rohan we were meeting today, did you?"

"Are you kidding? No way. He's been more paranoid than ever. Why, is that him?"

Sam didn't respond as he typed into his phone, "*Hey, Rohan. What are you talking about?*"

Sam watched the bubbles, awaiting Rohan's reply. "*I know you're meeting with Bill.*"

Sam looked around the café again, suddenly aligning with Bill's opinion that he shouldn't have picked such a public venue. Who could say what surveillance Rohan was doing? At the very least, he probably had installed employee-monitoring software on everyone's computers—tracking email and text messages, capturing keystrokes, analyzing network traffic. But Sam suspected Rohan's paranoia might have inspired him to do much more—bug phone lines, track geo-location, hire private investigators. "Well, he knows we're meeting," Sam said.

"Uh-oh . . . ," Bill said.

"Yeah, uh-oh—we've got to tell him we were meeting about something benign. Tell him Heather's expecting another baby."

"Aren't you guys too old to have a baby?" Bill asked.

"Bill, you're fucking older than me!"

"I wasn't taking a crack at your age. I was just trying to make sure the excuse was plausible."

"Yeah, you're right—that doesn't make any sense," Sam admitted. "I know!"

Sam texted, *"Just trying to decide whether to exercise my remaining options :)."* *Did I really just send a smiley face emoticon?* Sam thought, scolding himself over his possible tell.

"Reminder: You signed an NDA and nondisparagement agreement. So . . . ;)."

Did he really just reply to my smiley emoticon with a winky emoticon? *"Is that like 'wink-wink' I'm cooking the books?"* Sam typed, but then thought better of it and deleted the message. Then he simply replied, *"Of course."* Sam set down the phone.

"What did you tell him?" Bill asked.

"Just that I had a question about exercising stock options," Sam said.

Bill's face tightened. "Seriously, though—what are you going to do with that?" he asked again, looking apprehensively at the USB drive.

"I'm not going to do anything before letting you know. I'll keep everything confidential. The board can figure this all out themselves if they're properly motivated, so I don't need to give them a thing. But knowing I have proof, I can push them harder now to do the right thing."

"I just don't know if any of those guys will do the right thing," Bill said, visibly anxious.

"Well, then maybe we need to go to plan B," Sam said with a shrug.

Bill wiped his hands across his face in a pained expression. "That's what I'm worried about."

"Bill, I won't share this with anyone," Sam reassured. "I promise."

CHAPTER 15:

WINE COUNTRY

"JUST PROMISE ME YOU'LL BE NICE," Heather said to Sam as she checked her makeup in the vanity mirror before closing the visor. Gravel crunched under the wheels of their car, sending billows of dust across the vineyard.

"I'll do my best," Sam said, pulling their car under the shade of an oak tree.

It had been Heather's idea to arrange a day of wine tasting in Sonoma with her college friend, Jennifer Stoltz, and her husband, Todd. Normally, Sam would have enjoyed a day sipping wine under sunny skies, but the purpose of this occasion was to celebrate a big promotion for Todd, who had just made senior partner at Goodman & Wilson, one of the top venture law firms. Tall and athletic, Todd displayed the preppy demeanor of his Ivy League education and had cleared enough money over his tenure at the firm to afford a palatial home in Marin County. Jen, as everyone called her, didn't work and spent most of her time doting over their two daughters. Petite and brunette, she had the fit, bronzed figure consistent with her Southern California upbringing, sustained by her time on the tennis court and in the yoga studio at their club.

Their arrival announced by a text message from Heather, Todd and Jen walked down the steps from the tasting room, glasses of wine already in hand, to greet them in the parking lot. "Oh my God! How *are* you guys?" Jen squealed, giving them both big hugs while balancing her rosé and bending back the rim of her fashionable straw sun hat.

"I'm so psyched to see you guys! This is going to be so much fun!" Heather said, exchanging hugs and a peck on the cheek from Todd. "And congratulations, Todd!"

"Oh, thanks," Todd said modestly. "It's so nice of you to organize this little celebration. Let's get you guys some wine," he added, leading them back up the stairs to a beautiful sun-drenched patio with cushioned outdoor seating under a vine-draped trellis, expansive umbrellas, and dappled sunlight. Todd poured two glasses of rosé from a bottle in an ice bucket, taking the opportunity to top up his and Jen's glasses as well.

"To a great day of wine tasting with great friends," Heather said, raising her glass.

"*Cheers*," they said in unison.

"That's delicious," Heather said after a sip of the perfectly chilled rosé.

Sam and Todd noticed a group of millennials that had just arrived in a black limousine loudly roll up to the patio as if they were arriving at a night club in Las Vegas. The girls, decked in oversize sunglasses, short skirts, and high heels, immediately struck poses in front of the vineyard view, taking selfies. Meanwhile, the guys, one in a fedora hat with rolled-up sleeves revealing ornate arm tattoos, got the attention of the hostess to seat them at their reserved table on the terrace.

Todd nodded toward the crew and said, "That's Kurt Lowe, the founder of DoorBuzz. You know—that alcohol-delivery app. They're one of my clients, so I should go say hi. Excuse me one second."

They all watched Todd stand and walk toward the group, gregariously greeting Kurt and his posse with bro hugs and high fives.

"He's always bumping into clients wherever we go," Jen explained. "He did all the acquisition docs for DoorBuzz, so those guys love him. He's built up such an amazing practice."

"That's so great," Heather said. "He totally deserved to make senior partner." Sam silently watched their boisterous conversation from a distance and took a sip of his wine.

Returning to their corner of the patio, Todd asked Sam, "So, how's work going?" Heather shot Sam a glance, revealing she hadn't shared the news of his termination.

"Actually, I left a couple months ago," Sam said.

"You *did*?" Jen exclaimed.

"That's big news," Todd said. "What happened? I heard Ainetu was a hot company, maybe even an acquisition target."

"Well, it wasn't entirely my decision," Sam said. The admission hung in the air for a moment like a cancer diagnosis.

"Sorry to hear that," Todd said, breaking the silence. "You know, one of my clients is looking for a chief operating officer—BloomStamp. They're killing it as a demand aggregator in the pay-per-click performance marketing space. You'd be perfect for it."

"Yeah, I know about those guys from Paul Fleming. They're a Gray Willow portfolio company," Sam said of their benefactor for the charity auction. "He's been trying to persuade me to interview for that job for weeks."

"You didn't tell me that," Heather said.

"There was no need, because there's a 0 percent chance I'm doing it," Sam said.

"Honey," Heather paused. "I thought the whole point of attending that charity gala was to get a job at a GrayWillow portfolio company."

"Well, things have changed," Sam said.

Jen shot Heather a knowing glance at Sam's perfunctory remark. Steering away from the evidently sensitive subject, Todd pulled the dripping bottle out of the ice bucket. "Well, you'll find something soon, I'm sure. Let's have some more wine. You know what they say?" Todd asked rhetorically as he poured the last of their second bottle. "Rosé all day!"

The hostess returned on cue to retrieve the empty bottle. "I see you liked the rosé," she said with a wink. "Well, you're definitely going to like what's next. You're in for a real treat—our estate pinot noir flight paired with appetizers prepared by our in-house executive chef."

"*What* did you do?" Jen asked Heather gleefully.

"Oh, just a little something to celebrate Todd's big promotion," Heather said.

"You shouldn't have," Todd insisted as other servers arranged stemware in front of them.

The hostess began pouring. "I'm going to start you off with a very special wine, the 2016 Carneros Reserve. This is 100 percent estate-grown pinot noir. As I'm sure you know, the 2016 vintage was an unusually challenging growing season with a warm spring and very little rain. But the result was incredibly intense fruit, small and super-concentrated with complex flavors that yielded this incredible wine. Today, the chef is pairing this wine with a sage-marinated spring lamb chop with feta and a mint-walnut pistou. Enjoy!"

"This is amazing, Heather," Todd said, toasting her with his glass.

"Of course! You deserve it," Heather replied, returning the gesture.

Sam surveyed the spread as Todd eagerly bit into his lamb chop.

"So, what are you going to do next?" Jen asked Sam, picking up the conversation as if she had tapped in for Heather.

Sam gave her a circumspect look for a moment. "Well, I've done a bunch of interviews, but every company is run by some conceited dick who thinks he knows everything. I'm too old to be a babysitter to a bunch of kids. I'm not doing the whole 'parental supervision' thing again."

"C'mon, Sam," Jen pressed. "Don't be so sour. There are so many great companies out there."

"Like *DoorBuzz*?" Sam said. "Yeah, that's just what the world needed—another booze-delivery app."

"Sam, you're being rude," Heather said. "Jen's just trying to be supportive."

"I moved to Silicon Valley because I believed in a bigger purpose. I wanted to make the world a better place. How is booze delivery making the world a better place?"

"Fewer drunk drivers," Jen said. Sam scoffed.

"They're creating jobs," Todd said.

"Sure," Sam said. "Delivery jobs that don't pay a living wage, with no overtime or vacation or benefits. How are you supposed to live on that in San Francisco?"

Jen shrugged. "No one's forcing them to be a delivery person."

Sam shook his head. "Where did our Silicon Valley idealism go? We no longer talk about how we're going to change the world, except in trite, self-serving mission statements. The rhetoric I hear is more like how we're going to *dominate* the world. People call us 'Big Tech' now, like Big Oil or Big Pharma. They hate us. But like gas-guzzling SUVs or pain meds, there's nothing they can do about it. They're *addicted*. So instead of innovating, we're giving the world booze on demand. Anything to keep them fat, dumb, and lazy."

"You can dismiss DoorBuzz all you want, but they're laughing all the way to the bank," Todd said.

"That's *exactly* the point," Sam said. "Making money is the only goal that matters anymore. Each generation of entrepreneurs who has flocked here from all corners of the world has become more and more divorced from the original mission. All they care about is making money."

"So, are you saying I should only take clients with a higher mission?" Todd asked.

"Not at all. *I've* lost that original mission myself. I see these douchebags who think they're such big swingin' dicks." Sam nodded toward the DoorBuzz crew farther down the patio. "I may roll my eyes, but I'm chasing the same thing. I'm part of the problem. *I'm* just as much of a douchebag! I drive a nice car, I wear fleece vests, I even drink fucking kombucha, for *Christ's sake*! Every day, I further perpetuate the cliché that I can't stand. If I'm going to play the part, then I might as well embrace my inner asshole."

The hostess arrived with another bottle of wine as servers again descended on their table. "Up next is our Russian River Valley estate pinot. We only produce two hundred cases of this wine, so we limit purchases to two bottles at $120 per bottle," she explained. "We're pairing this with a Wagyu beef carpaccio with fingerling potato crisps, daikon radish, and truffle aioli."

"So that's your goal? To be an asshole?" Heather asked Sam after the hostess left.

"I just feel like everything I've told myself for the last twenty years has been a lie. I pretend to have this higher purpose, but really what motivates me is envy of other people who have more success, more esteem, more money. I worked so hard to make it here. I sacrificed so much for this dream of coming to Silicon Valley and changing the world and making millions while doing it. Yet here I am with nothing to show for it. I'm like a gerbil on a wheel, just running my ass off but never getting anywhere."

"Don't be ridiculous," Todd objected. "You've had a great career. Maybe you didn't have that grand-slam windfall, but—"

"*All that matters* is the grand-slam windfall!" Sam interrupted. "Easy for you to say after you just got promoted for the DoorBuzz acquisition. Nobody gives a shit about the guy who's had a '*great career.*' Success means liquidity events. Otherwise, you're just another nice guy. I've been too naive—spent my whole career trying to do the right thing, being the dutiful executive, kissing up to customers and investors and board members. I'm sick of it. I want to be in charge for a change. I want to be the one making all the money while everyone else fights for table scraps."

As their banter grew in intensity and the pours of wine got bigger, an older couple at an adjacent table got up and moved to another corner of the patio.

"OK, but you still haven't said what you're going to do next," Jen said. "You can't just bitch about the world and feel sorry for yourself."

"Oh, I know what I'm going to do," said Sam. "I have some loose ends to tie up at Ainetu."

"Loose ends?" Jen asked.

"Sam has some conspiracy theories," Heather explained.

"They're not *theories*," Sam objected. "What's going on there is called *fraud*. They're deliberately misstating their financials. That's why I lost my job."

"Oooh. Now you're getting into my area," Todd said, smiling and rubbing his hands together after a bite of carpaccio. "Can you prove it? Maybe you could file a wrongful-termination suit."

"I don't want to go the legal route," Sam dismissed. "That will put a taint on the company. You know how it goes with start-ups—either you're a rocket ship or you're swirling in the dead pool. There's no in-between. Once there's any hint of scandal, it's just a matter of time before it's a punch line in a joke. You know, 'You don't want to pull an Ainetu!'"

"Good point. So what's your strategy then? You're not employed there anymore. What are you going to do? Sneak back in at night and *correct* the financial statements?" Todd joked.

"No, I'm going to use it to get Rohan fired," Sam said matter-of-factly. Heather shifted her attention toward the vineyard, sensing the onset of a tirade she had already endured several times.

"*Why?*" Jen asked. "Just for revenge?"

"I'm still a shareholder," Sam said. "I want my stock to be worth something someday. And Ainetu is my best shot at an exit. So I'm going to play some hardball."

"I don't know, Sam . . . ," Todd said skeptically. "The board is pretty unlikely to fire a founder they've put that much money behind. I don't really see what you stand to gain. Let them fix whatever is going on internally. Move on with your life."

"Sam's having a hard time moving on," Heather said, returning to the conversation. "He's been ranting about conspiracies like Alex Jones."

"Yeah, you sound a little paranoid," Jen concurred.

"I need this," Sam said. "I can't be associated with another flameout. This company might be my last best chance at success."

"Sure, but, Sam, you have to do it responsibly," Todd said. "Remember the Google mission statement: 'Don't be evil.'"

"*Don't be evil?*" Sam echoed incredulously. "That's such *bullshit*. Do you really think that's the credo of Big Tech anymore? As an industry, we've just kept moving the goalposts of what constitutes 'evil.' Developers obsess about how to make their apps more addictive to users. Websites force visitors to sign up for newsletters then spam them incessantly. Online services make it practically impossible for people to cancel their subscriptions. Advertisers siphon personal data and compromise our privacy. Data aggregators scrape personal data about us from social media websites. And hackers exploit this entire treasure trove of information to perpetrate fraud, from identity theft to fake news. I think most people would call that stuff evil, but as an industry we present them as 'best practices.' We just keep weaving a more and more elaborate lie. Pretending we're not facilitators . . . *enablers* to forces that are corrupting our society. And, meanwhile, those are the companies that are having multibillion-dollar IPOs. Every day, there's just more and more proof: you need to be evil to win. And I'm tired of losing!"

"You're starting to scare me," Heather said.

"I'm starting to scare myself!" Sam said with a sardonic smile.

With Sam's tirade still reverberating, the hostess approached their table and uncomfortably asked, "I'm sorry, but would you mind speaking a little more quietly? Your conversation is disturbing other guests."

Todd apologized and assured the hostess they would lower their voices, but Jen reacted coarsely. "Who the hell are they to tell us to shut up?"

"Let's get the fuck out of here," Sam said as he tipped back the remainder of his wine.

"I agree," Jen said as she stood with her wine glass still in hand. "I want to go someplace where people aren't so uptight."

"We still need to pay the bill," Todd explained, trying to summon the hostess as Heather let out an exasperated sigh.

"Well, I'll meet you by the car," Jen said, turning toward the staircase to the parking lot with her wine glass at her lips.

"I'm sorry, ma'am, but you can't bring your wine with you," the hostess said, catching up to Jen near the stairs.

Jen spun around and glared at the hostess as if she'd just told her she had saggy tits. "This is wine country, bitch, I'm taking this to go!" Jen shouted.

"I'm sorry. You can't take alcohol in an open container out of the winery," the waitress explained sheepishly. "It's the law."

"You listen to me," Jen snarled. "We just spent a shit ton of money here, so I'll take my goddamn wine wherever I goddamn want!" At this point, the manager of the tasting room had arrived to try to defuse the situation.

"Hi, folks, what seems to be the matter?" he asked, innocently walking into the buzz saw of Jen's fury.

"I'll tell you what's the matter." Jen glared at him while stabbing her index finger at the hostess. "This bitch won't let me take my wine with me, which I would add cost one hundred twenty fucking dollars!"

"Yeah, I'm sorry—that's not our rule," the manager explained. "That's county law. I can pour it back into the bottle for you and cork it up."

Jen glared at him, then glared at the hostess, then gulped down the remainder of her wine in a swift chug. "Are you happy now?" she asked as she thrust the empty glass into the manager's hand.

"C'mon, let's go," Heather said, seizing the opportunity to usher her drunk friend to the car. Sam was already down in the parking lot fumbling with his keys.

Seeing the bill placed in front of Todd—the only one of them still seated—Jen staggered back to the table and insisted, "Do *not* give that bitch a tip!"

"I'm sorry," Todd said to the hostess as he scribbled his signature and stood to take his leave. "We've all had a little too much."

CHAPTER 16:

WHISTLE BLOW

PASSING ROLLING HILLS dotted with oak trees, Sam came upon the Old West–style facade of the Pioneer Inn, welcoming him to the upscale rural community of Woodside. The two-block stretch of historic buildings and wooden sidewalks culminated in the one-stoplight intersection between Woodside Road and Cañada Road—the heart of the modest downtown for one of the wealthiest suburbs in the country. Sam had arranged to have coffee with one of the Ainetu board members, Preston Lawrence from Ellipsis Ventures. They were meeting at Buck's, a kitschy restaurant that was a favorite of both fleece-clad VCs and aged horse-ranch owners.

As the first investor in Ainetu, Preston was a critical board member. Sam had always found him to be an entitled prick, exploiting his father's massive media conglomerate, Paragon Enterprises, to create his own fortune. His new-media offshoot, BroFest, was notorious for its misogynistic exploits and editorial content. The sale of the company to one of his father's friends was as much a bailout as a strategic acquisition, but it earned Preston a small fortune. After cofounding Ellipsis Ventures, Preston and his partners became somewhat notorious for running their venture firm as he had run BroFest. Their only female employees were young assistants who clicked around the office in stiletto heels and size-zero miniskirts, looking more like runway models than business professionals. Regardless, if Sam was going to oust Rohan, he needed to persuade Preston.

Almost every time Sam had been to Buck's, he'd bumped into an executive or investor he knew, compelling what could, at times, be an awkward conversation. He had suggested more discreet locations for their meeting, but Preston had insisted on Buck's since it was on his bicycle training route, and they were meeting after his morning ride. Inside, Sam looked around for Preston, who had not yet arrived. He observed the various Silicon Valley bric-a-brac that adorned every square inch of the interior—some of it legitimately museum-worthy, such as original silicon fabs from Fairchild Semiconductor, but much of it emblematic of Silicon Valley's more pretentious hobbies, such as an aerodynamic toboggan sponsored by a VC firm that hung from the ceiling. Sam stepped back outside to wait for Preston and filled a thick white mug with black coffee from a communal coffee station outside for waiting customers.

Almost twenty minutes after their appointed time, Sam saw a flock of cyclists, all in matching Lycra jerseys emblazoned with the Ellipsis Ventures logo, descending the hill toward the restaurant, as if it were the final stage of the Tour de France. Sam picked out Preston in full regalia in the middle of the pack. *Jesus Christ, he thinks he's Lance Fucking Armstrong.* Sam stepped into the parking lot toward the group, raising his arm to get Preston's attention, but the riders glided past him as if he were a pothole to be avoided. A few of them effortlessly turned in graceful circles like birds of prey to slow their momentum as others came to rest and squirted water bottles into their mouths, slapping each other on the back. Sam certainly hadn't expected Preston to show up for their one-on-one breakfast with a posse of over a dozen people. He wondered who they all were. It was difficult to recognize anyone through their helmets, wraparound sunglasses, and matching uniforms—probably other partners, or junior associates, or maybe executives in Ellipsis's portfolio companies, members of a club to which Sam didn't belong.

Preston leaned his bike against a tree and reached to his head with his fingerless riding gloves to remove his helmet. It had a long, tapered back, reminiscent of the superlaser operators on the Death Star. Sam hoped it was designed to minimize wind resistance, rather than to serve as a fashion statement. The two made eye contact, though Preston's face remained expressionless as he made his way to Sam. Clicking on the sidewalk in his all-white bike shoes, Preston tiptoed toward him like a giraffe on an ice-skating rink. Sam reached out to shake hands.

"One second," Preston said as he removed his phone from a pouch in the back of his riding jersey and started typing a message. Sam looked on self-consciously, unsure if he should attempt conversation or let Preston finish his oh-so-important text message. He took another prolonged sip of his coffee as he waited, then finally Preston returned the phone to his fanny pouch and acknowledged Sam with a handshake. "Hi, Sam. How are you?"

"I'm good, I'm good. Let's grab a table."

"Sure, but I'm not eating anything. Just a coffee." Preston intended to keep the meeting as short as possible.

"Of course—plus, you don't want to keep your crew waiting. But I'll probably order something, so why don't we sit for a minute," Sam said, indicating to the hostess a table for two.

Preston maneuvered carefully across the hardwood floor and slid his lanky frame into the booth across from Sam. The two sat silently for a moment as Sam perused the enormous laminated menu, settling on a Denver omelet, which he relayed to the waitress. "Just a coffee, please," said Preston. "So, Sam . . . what did you want to meet about?" he asked with the impatient undertone of someone whose time is incredibly valuable—despite mostly spending that time on ski vacations, exotic car collecting, and two-hour bike rides on random Tuesday mornings.

"Oh, I just wanted to catch up," Sam said, pondering how to broach the conversation he intended with Preston. "How was your ride?"

"It was great. Nothing beats a strenuous climb to Skyline at 6:00 a.m. on a beautiful Northern California day."

"No doubt," Sam agreed enthusiastically. "So how long have you been biking?"

"It's *cycling*," Preston responded bluntly.

"I'm sorry?"

"*Biking* is what sixty-year-old guys in black leather on Harleys do," Preston said pedantically. "Cycling is performed with your feet, not with a 1,000-cc engine. I'm a *cyclist*."

"Of course, that's what I meant. How long have you been *cycling*?"

"Competitively, probably ten years now," Preston said. "I just upgraded my road bike."

"Oh—what did you get?" Sam asked, as if he knew anything about high-end bicycles.

"A Pinarello Bolide," Preston replied proudly, as if Sam was supposed to know what that was. This topic was the first glimmer of engagement in the conversation Preston had shown.

"Ooohh, wow!" Sam reacted appropriately, playing along.

"Yeah, I've always wanted one. I got it totally tricked out—with the titanium frame and the disk brakes. It only weighs 2.2 pounds," Preston gestured to the bike, unlocked outside the restaurant. "The thing set me back twenty grand, but on a ride like today, I know it was worth it."

"Wow." *Twenty thousand dollars for a fucking bike?* Sam tried to demonstrate a commensurate level of enthusiasm for Preston's latest material conquest. As nauseating as the expenditure was that exceeded the average annual family income back in Lima, the topic of crazy high-end bicycles had achieved Sam's objective of disarming Preston's defenses. "Sounds like you're really enjoying it. Anyway, Preston, I know you don't have much time, so I'll get to the point," Sam said, taking a thoughtful pause before continuing. "It's about Ainetu. I think Rohan may be improperly accounting for some of the deals to hit the quarterly revenue number. I'm aware of at least three deals, including GGT—the deal that nearly killed me—where I believe two-year contracts were recognized as revenue in a single year in order to inflate the number."

Preston peered suspiciously at Sam, taking a sip of his just-arrived coffee, then asked, "So what are you suggesting I do with that information?"

Sam was taken aback, expecting a bigger reaction to his act of whistleblowing. Tilting his head sideways with a somewhat confused look, he asked, "Well, aren't you *concerned*? As an investor and a board member, I would think you'd want to have confidence in the accuracy of the company's financial statements."

Preston stole a glance around the restaurant. "Is this something you can *prove*, or is it just a *hunch*?"

"Well, I . . . ," Sam stammered, unclear if the question was intended to aid or obstruct further exploration of the topic. "I saw the GGT contract, and it was a two-year deal. Carl, their head of IT, sent it to me by mistake."

"Isn't that company-confidential information?" Preston asked, pursing his lips to the edge of his coffee mug. Sam didn't like the direction the conversation was going.

"Yes, but, as I said, it was sent to me by mistake. He didn't realize I'm no longer at Ainetu. Obviously I don't have access to the company's latest financial statements," Sam lied. "Maybe it's nothing. But I thought it should still be brought to the board's attention."

Preston nodded cryptically, then asked, "Why are you telling me this? What do you hope to gain?"

"I'm not trying to *gain* anything," Sam insisted. "I'm still a shareholder, so I guess I have a financial interest in my stock being worth something someday. And it won't be if the company is based on misleading financials. Look, I'm not saying I know for sure Rohan is doing something wrong. I'm just making you aware of what I suspect so that you can take appropriate action."

"What would that be, in your estimation?"

"I don't know. Maybe bring in an outside accounting firm to do an audit?" Sam suggested. "Couldn't hurt. You're going to need to raise another round of financing soon. Any new investors are going to want audited financials anyway."

Preston took another long pause and gazed intently at Sam, as if trying to gauge the sincerity of his comments. "Honestly, Sam, this seems like sour grapes."

"You think I'm trying to get *revenge* on Rohan? If anything, my motivation to poke into this was simply out of a sense of fiduciary responsibility to the company. I approached you with this because I thought you'd be the most receptive. You've worked with Rohan since the beginning."

Preston leaned forward and said with sudden intensity, "Sam, I've gotta be honest. *I don't care.* A few deals getting exaggerated isn't going to matter for this company. Ainetu's either going to be a home run or a strikeout. If it's a strikeout, it won't matter. Nobody will care. As an investor, it's meaningless for me. Statistically speaking, seven out of ten investments we make are worth nothing at the end of the day. *Zero.* So, when they don't exist anymore, it doesn't matter if they did it ethically or not."

"I guess that makes sense for the companies that fail, but don't you think Ainetu has a shot at being one of the companies that make it?" Sam asked.

"Yes, I do. Which is all the more reason not to fuck it up by worrying about the goddamn GAAP accounting rules for every little deal. Most likely, this is just a simple clerical error. But if it's intentional, as you're suggesting, then I've got to *do* something about it. So I don't want to know. Suppose they are recognizing revenue too aggressively. If that helps them get to the next financing, or to an exit, that's *great.* That's all that matters. Then it becomes somebody else's problem. If they get to a liquidity event, they can always restate their financials and clean it up later."

Sam realized then that Preston knew. But he pressed on. "Who do you think you're going to sell to? At some point, the buck stops. Any serious suitor will immediately discover these discrepancies in the sales figures during due diligence. The deal won't even get out of the gate."

Preston squinted as if he was trying to comprehend Sam's naiveté. "Sam, there's *always* a buyer. As long as the company has perceived momentum, we can exit it. There are the strategics, who just want to do a transaction to bolster their own stock price. They'll overlook minor accounting errors. Then there are the big pension funds and mutual funds.

Those guys are always looking for places to stash capital, even if they find the underlying asset dubious. And if it's major financial transgressions, as you seem to be accusing, then we'll just look to offshore buyers."

"Such as?" Sam asked.

"Such as *anyone*. The Chinese, the Russians, the Saudis—all these guys have sovereign wealth funds with virtually unlimited capital they're eager to stash in Western businesses. The crown prince of Saudi Arabia has so much fucking money, he doesn't know what to do with it. He's looking all over the world for pillowcases to stuff cash into. He doesn't give a shit if the pillowcase is made from the semen of Egyptian silkworms or from polyester recycled from a superfund site. You're just another pillowcase. Someplace he can squirrel away cash and, Allah willing, launder it out the other end. These guys are pretty much running organized crime rings. You think they'll care about a *revenue recognition error*? They're so fucking desperate to get their money into any quasi-legitimate business, they'll invest in *anything*—and Silicon Valley tech companies are at the top of that crap heap. When your alternatives are Russian oil oligarchs, African diamond mines, or Macau casinos, a venture-backed Silicon Valley company that may have overstated some of their financial statements looks like a triple-fucking-A-grade investment."

Holy shit, Sam thought. Preston's perspective was so cynical. His whole investment thesis was essentially indistinguishable from a Ponzi scheme. It wasn't about building great companies. It wasn't even about building respectable companies. It was about building something that some other sucker, further down the line, with more money, less discretion, and untethered morals, would be willing to buy.

"So, if you're smart and you want to make some money, you'll shut up about whatever it is you think you know," Preston continued. "None of these guys will even read the financial statements, but if there's bad press, that's the kiss of death. Bad PR can turn these things into toxic assets overnight. So do the smart thing and keep your little hunch to yourself."

Sam didn't want to commit to anything but nodded in the hope of undoing the conversation. Preston pushed aside his remaining cup of coffee and stood to take his leave. He buckled on his helmet and simply said, "Good luck, Sam. Let me know if there's anything I can do." Then he turned and click-clacked toward the door, his multicolored Lycra clinging to his triangular rib cage.

Sam watched him leaving, feeling like his last chance at redemption was leaving with him. As the waitress placed his Denver omelet in front of him, Sam reached into his pocket and pulled out the USB drive Bill had given him.

He stood to catch up with Preston, thinking of the last thing he had said to Bill—*I promise.*

I promise to keep you out of this.

I promise to protect you.

I promise, you're safe.

He thought about all those things, yet now, here he was, holding up the USB drive in front of Preston's face.

"I have proof."

CHAPTER 17:

BOOST

A COLUMN OF FEDEX TRUCKS merged onto the highway in front of Sam, delivering their cargo of online purchases around the city. He was headed to the BOOST Conference, an annual gathering of tech execs, founders, and investors at the Fairmont Hotel, facing Grace Cathedral atop Nob Hill. Hosted by the eminently well-connected Jason Cauffman, the event was a mash-up of panel discussions, a start-up pavilion, and a demo day in which nascent entrepreneurs gave their pitches to a panel of VCs and angel investors.

Sam was finally ascending the seemingly vertical last block of Taylor Street at the top of Nob Hill and turning alongside the whirring cable car tracks of California Street when his concentration was disrupted by a text message. He pulled his phone from his pocket. It was from an unexpected sender, Ben Bentley, the Ainetu board member from Wellington Ventures: "*Hey, I'm speaking at BOOST today. Any chance you'll be there?*"

Sam pressed and held the button on his phone to dictate a response. "What would you like to reply to Ben Bentley?" the automated assistant asked.

"Yes, I'll be there. I'm pulling up now," Sam said.

"'*Yes, all be scared. I'm pulling a cow,*'" the assistant said. "Would you like to send this message?"

"No," Sam quickly replied. He enunciated his words in a second attempt: "Yes. I'll. Be. There. I'm. Pulling. Up. Now."

"'*Yes, all be there. Am pruning the sow,*'" the assistant replied. "Would you like to send this message?"

"Pruning the sow?" Sam asked out loud. "What is it with the barnyard animals?"

"I'm sorry, I didn't understand that. Please repeat your message."

"Forget it, I'll type it myself," Sam said as he pulled up to the valet.

The BOOST Conference was already packed with eager, young, predominantly male entrepreneurs by the time Sam arrived, nursing their artisan coffees as they mulled about the lobby clad in Patagonia fleece vests, Chrome messenger bags, and Allbirds sneakers. Sam had adroitly navigated hundreds of events like this before, but he suddenly felt like a fish out of water. He was more accustomed to being a speaker or a sponsor, with a PR handler and conference staff catering to his needs. The other attendees would kiss up to him, looking for meetings, jobs, or partnerships. Now he was the one doing the kissing.

With no particular agenda, he drifted somewhat aimlessly into the start-up pavilion, trying to look like he had a purpose in being there. The pavilion was a huge ballroom with row upon row of start-up companies, each paying the conference organizers upward of $5,000 for a single stool and table crammed with a monitor, tchotchkes, and collateral. Sam strolled the length of the room, noting the categories designated by signs hanging from the ceiling: VR/AR, Food/Alcohol Delivery, Dating & Social Apps, Gaming, Fitness Tracking, Cannabis, etc. *Jesus Christ*! Sam thought. *Is this really what the greatest young minds in Silicon Valley have to offer?* "Solutions" to the "problems" of a socially awkward twenty-two-year-old suburban male living in his parents' basement—which many, no doubt, still were.

Much of the crowd seemed to know each other already, products of the same universities or enrollees in the various start-up incubator programs promising to turn their half-baked ideas into full-fledged businesses under their tutelage—and the ability to cherry-pick investments from their graduating classes at pre-negotiated valuations. Young entrepreneurs would wear these private valuations as a badge of pride, bragging to their friends about their equity stake in businesses now valued at millions of dollars, feeling they had it made after a seed-round investment. Most of the companies with a table in the pavilion would be out of business within the year—80 percent of them would never raise a series A. Of those that did, fewer than half would make it to series B. Even for companies that made it through six or seven rounds of financing, 75 percent would still go out of business. The odds of start-up success were infinitesimal, but everyone in that room was convinced theirs was that black swan.

"Want to experience the next generation of multisensory VR?" a young man's voice asked, piercing the din of crowd noise as he intercepted Sam.

"Uh . . . sure," Sam replied cautiously.

"Sweet! Let me just get you wired up," he said, immediately raising a huge set of VR goggles toward Sam's face. He pulled the straps around the back of Sam's head. Suddenly staring at a blank screen inside the goggles, Sam felt the man now applying a pair of noise-canceling headphones over Sam's ears. The man said something inaudible over the white noise.

"*What?*" Sam heard himself ask, aware he was probably shouting the question in his hearing-deprived state.

Lifting one of the earpieces momentarily, the man in his cuffed black polo shirt repeated, "I said, now I'm going to put on the gloves."

"Oh, uh . . . OK. How long is this going to take?" Sam was regretting his reluctant willingness to get "wired up."

"Just a few more pieces of equipment," the man explained. "We need to get all your senses activated."

Sam didn't like the sound of that. With the goggles and headphones back in place, he felt the man take his hand and shove it into what felt like hockey gloves. Surely, he was almost ready, but no—the man was applying some sort of chin strap.

"What's that you're doing?" Sam asked, again trying to avoid shouting.

"It's our patent-pending flavor strip, for olfactory sensations," the man explained.

"Wait, *what*?" Sam asked with alarm, involuntarily jerking his head away from the chin strap. He again lifted one of his earpieces to hear the reply.

"It's just a vapor-emitting strap that releases chemical compounds that let you experience digitized smells," the man reassured, as if it were perfectly routine. "It actually tricks your brain into thinking you can taste things too."

"Can I do it *without* the flavor strip?" Sam asked, realizing the same gear had likely been strapped to the faces of dozens of other people with varying degrees of upper respiratory health.

"Well . . . That's sort of the part of the experience that's ours. The headset, headphones, and even the tactile gloves are all off-the-shelf. At Olfabulous, our mission is to add smell, and eventually taste, to the VR experience."

Sam was starting to feel disoriented and slightly nauseous. *But I don't want smell and taste added to my VR experience. I'm not sure I even want a VR experience,* period. But he felt bad dashing the sincere ambitions of this eager young entrepreneur, so he reluctantly agreed to the flavor strip—convinced he looked like a complete moron, and momentarily wondering if this whole thing wasn't some *Candid Camera* "punk the old guy" prank.

"OK, ahh'mm stahtting thuh sim-yoo-laashun," was all Sam could hear.

The black screen two inches in front of his face flickered to life, and Sam saw what appeared to be an auto mechanic's garage.

"Go ah-head ahnd moove a-rouhn," the man recommended.

Sam staggered forward a step or two in what, in his actual reality, he knew was a three-foot-square patch of carpet and promptly bumped into the demo table.

"Yooo cahn piick up thuh gaas cahn."

"Huh?" Sam asked, bewildered.

"Piick up thuh gaas cahn," the man repeated, guiding Sam's gloved hands toward a can of gasoline on the virtual garage's floor. As he touched the can, Sam felt the gloves provide simulated resistance, as if he were touching a real object. Sam stood with the virtual can and felt himself careening off-balance to his right, crashing into the neighboring demo table and sending marketing literature flying. The man steadied Sam by the shoulders as he apologized to the adjacent demo'er, likely not for the first time that morning. Sam's motion sickness was rapidly escalating from mild nausea to the hairy edge of projectile vomiting.

"Doo yooo smehll thaat?" the man asked with anticipation.

Sam was about to respond that he couldn't smell anything, or maybe he was just so focused on his sudden and profuse perspiration that his olfactory sensation had shut down. Then it hit him, a caustic aroma that felt as if someone had spritzed his nostrils with lighter fluid.

"Jesus *Christ*!" Sam shouted involuntarily, his head whipping back.

"Yooo smehll eht?" the man asked in confirmation.

"Yeah, I fucking smell it!" Sam blurted out. "I don't think I have any nose hairs left." Feeling faint, Sam desperately groped at the goggles on his face, constrained by the wires tethering his still-gloved hands. "This demo is over."

"Awww . . . you're just about to get to the best part," the man said, trying to convince Sam to continue.

"What?" Sam asked, the goggles now ensnared with the headphones on his forehead. "The part where I pass out and you simulate smelling salts to revive me?"

Sam, who could now see again, discovered that what he imagined was a roomful of people gawking at him was only a few amused onlookers.

"You didn't like the demo?"

Sam could see the disappointment in the face of his demo host, but he was too close to the brink of losing consciousness to continue. "Sorry, I just got a little motion sick."

"Can I at least send you our pitch deck?" the man asked, assuming from his age that Sam was a prospective investor.

■ ■ ■

Sam drifted around the pavilion a few more minutes, trying to find a demo of something, *anything*, that he could actually get excited about. An ad-targeting platform for mobile devices? Nope. An online community of philatelists? Don't think so. A gig economy network for hiring mixologists? Useful the one night per decade you host a party that requires a dedicated bartender. These seemed to be the 80 percenters—the companies that would never raise a series A. Sam couldn't bring himself to sit through their demos, let alone consider the prospect of joining any of these organizations. If he wanted to join a nascent start-up with a cockamamie idea, no product, no customers, and no funding, he could just found one himself.

Looking at his watch and eager to get out of the start-up pavilion, Sam realized the demo-day pitches were about to begin. So he followed the buzzing crowd toward the main auditorium and found a seat. Without intending to, Sam sat down in the same row as Ben Bentley, who immediately noticed him and slid down to sit in the next seat.

"Sam! How are you doing?" Ben said.

"I'm great," Sam said with a subdued smile. "Enjoying some more time with the kids and figuring out what's next."

"That's great," Ben said, smiling. "How old are your kids again?"

"Connor is fourteen—going to high school next year. Mason is eleven. And little Riley is just eight."

"That's fantastic," Ben said. "Family is so important. When I met you, they were still just toddlers. I'm not sure Riley was even born yet."

"Yeah, that's probably right," Sam agreed. Then, pivoting the conversation from small talk, he asked, "So what did you want to talk to me about?"

As Sam posed the question, the lights in the auditorium dimmed and Jason Cauffman emerged from behind a curtain, wearing a slimly tailored blue suit with high-hemmed pants that revealed bright striped socks and orange wing tips that matched his orange tie and perfectly arranged orange pocket square. His receding hairline accentuated his disproportionately large forehead, and fastidious rimless glasses perched on his nose gave him an intellectual air.

"Greetings, ladies and gentlemen, and welcome to the BOOST Demo Day!" Jason proclaimed, grandiosely extending his arms toward the ceiling to invite the applause that ensued. "Allow me to introduce you to today's esteemed panel of judges."

As Jason regaled the audience with how long he'd personally been friends with the three investors who would be judging the day's pitches, Ben leaned in toward Sam and proceeded in a hushed voice. "As you recall, I convinced you to join Ainetu in the first place, so the board thought I should be the one to talk to you today."

"About what?"

"We had a board call late last night. And, well . . . we're prepared to ask Rohan to step down. We'd like you to rejoin the company as CEO," Ben said, pausing to let his request sink in.

Sam tried not to let his expression show the surge of mixed emotions he felt, instead simply replying, "*Really?*"

"Yes. We've lost confidence in Rohan and think you would be a great choice to come back to run the company," Ben said.

Sam contemplated how to respond as he watched Jason smugly sit at a sofa onstage and cross his legs, causing his pants to pull up like clam-diggers and reveal even more of his brightly colored socks. "And now . . . without further ado, I present to you the first BOOST Demo Day pitch: Byron Song with BodyFit!" Jason pointed to stage left just as a spotlight illuminated a young Asian man in a tight-fitting gray T-shirt with "BodyFit" across the front in lime-green lettering, flanked by a taller, pug-nosed white guy in the same T-shirt with protruding muscles.

The man started dramatically, "Imagine a product that could revolutionize fitness as we know it. BodyFit is disrupting the thirty-billion-dollar fitness industry with a transformational workout app to get you as ripped as Sebastian here, *guaranteed*!"

"Sounds like a late-night infomercial," Ben remarked sarcastically as videos of tight-bodied women performing some sort of synchronized aerobics appeared on the big screen.

"Is this because I can prove he's committing fraud?" Sam finally asked.

"Well," Ben replied cautiously, looking around to see if anyone consequential was within earshot. "Let's just say we didn't realize the magnitude of what was going on."

"I was telling you guys for months that Rohan had to go, but you didn't do anything. When I confronted Preston, you know what he said?" Sam asked rhetorically. "He said it sounded like sour *fucking* grapes! He wasn't going to do shit till I threatened him with that USB drive. And *you* . . . when Rohan fired me, you were too busy vacationing in Saint Barts to intervene." Sam felt the rage of the humiliating termination surge into him. There was so much more he wanted to say—how this experience had rattled his self-confidence, compromised his family's financial well-being, challenged his marriage—but, instead, he just stared at Ben in a combination of disbelief, anger, and vindication.

"I know," Ben acknowledged. "I'm sorry, Sam. We dropped the ball on this one."

Sam turned his attention back to the presentation, contemplating Ben's comment as the BodyFit team left the stage, high-fiving each other exuberantly. "OK, thanks, Byron and Sebastian. Judges, per our protocol, I will ask you to hold your feedback until we've heard the first three pitches. Next up: Morten Spence with BudBuddy!"

A pale kid with thick black curly hair and a Vans T-shirt emerged onto the stage, rolling what appeared to be a small refrigerator on casters. The Vans dude started in full Santa Cruz–stoner diction. "So . . .

show of hands, how many of you have found yourself late at night, and you've run out of weed, and the dispensary is closed? *Huh?*" he pressed, prompting three or four hands to rise in the audience. "Well, worry no more. That problem is solved, thanks to BudBuddy!" he declared, whipping open the door of the refrigerator to reveal a large marijuana plant inside. A reaction of surprise and laughter rippled through the audience.

"Yeah, that's what we need—because there's just not enough pot in San Francisco," Sam observed to no one in particular. Then he asked Ben, "Have you said anything to Rohan yet?"

"No." Ben shook his head. "We wanted to talk to you first. This needs to be a clean transition. And, frankly, you're our only option. If word got out about what was happening, we'd have a hard time getting anyone to take the role."

Sam turned from the stage and fixed his gaze on Ben. "You completely screwed me, you know? You practically begged me to join Ainetu. Then, after I worked my ass off to make it successful, in spite of the inept founder that you guys refused to replace, you just kicked me to the curb without a second thought. I'm *forty-five*. Do you know how hard it is to get a good job in Silicon Valley at forty-five? I might as well be a card-carrying AARP member!"

Ben smiled and replied facetiously, "You don't look a day over forty."

"Why should I do this?"

"Well, as you've pointed out, you *are* a major shareholder. Don't you want your equity to be worth something?"

"Yeah, but what's the *goal*?" Sam challenged.

A slightly perplexed look flashed across Ben's face, illuminated by the light reflecting off the stage. "Same as it always is. What do you mean?"

"I mean, *what's the goal*?" Sam reiterated. "The company is running out of cash. We can't do another outside financing. The numbers—the *real* numbers—aren't good enough. We can't sell it—that's off the table. This is a complete train wreck. Unless you guys are willing to do an inside round, but I can't imagine you want to pump in more capital.

Seems like you just want someone to clean up the wreckage and sell the spare parts. That's not me."

Ben let Sam's monologue subside, then he leaned in and whispered, "We have a buyer."

CHAPTER 18:

PARENT NIGHT

"HOLD FOR PETER," the executive assistant said from the other end of the video conference. Sam was already late. Parked a good seven blocks from Jefferson Elementary School with no closer spots available, he knew he'd have to run to fulfill his promise to make it on time to the parent open house at Mason and Riley's grade school that evening. But when Peter Green, his former boss at FusionCommerce turned cryptocurrency billionaire, was available, you made yourself available—particularly when Peter was joining the video conference from the Caymans, his assistant explained, and Sam, who had implored her to find time, had a narrow twenty-four-hour window to make a critical career decision.

"Hey, Sam," Peter said, finally joining the conference. His voice preceded his image, which eventually caught up in jerky spurts. "I don't have too much time. We're just about to break for cocktails."

"Thanks for talking with me, Peter," Sam replied. "Break from what? Are you at an event or something in the Caymans?"

"Oh, it's just The Patio," Peter explained. Sam was vaguely aware of the mysterious, invitation-only conference called simply The Patio. The ultra-exclusive event was hosted by an enigmatic group of top-tier VCs who invited about one hundred of the highest echelon of billionaire tech entrepreneurs to a secret destination. One did not turn down an invitation to The Patio, so named for the networking sessions that took place on the patio of whatever luxury resort the organizers took over for the week. The exact venue was announced only twenty-four hours in advance, so as to discourage media coverage and make it even more inaccessible to laypeople who did not have a private jet at their disposal. Sam suspected Peter was violating some sacrosanct rule of The Patio to even acknowledge he was attending or where it was. The first rule of The Patio is there *is no* Patio.

"Nice!" Sam replied, exuding the expected reaction of being impressed while at the same time projecting as if he were a potential invitee himself. "So, it's in the Cayman Islands this year?"

"Yeah, Grand Cayman," Peter said. "They're doing a whole track on cryptocurrency, so they wanted a location with loose banking laws and lax extradition," he added, only half joking. "Anyway, I only have about five minutes before they start pouring drinks. What's up?"

"OK, I'll be quick then," Sam proceeded. "So I took your advice and learned more about why I was fired."

"And?"

"Long story short, Rohan was overstating revenue to get an acquirer interested," Sam explained. "The board was in denial at first, but now they realize the extent of what's going on. So they're ready to fire Rohan and bring me back as CEO."

"Interesting. Have they pulled the trigger with Rohan yet?" Peter asked.

"I don't think so," Sam replied. "Ben Bentley, who led the series B and recruited me there in the first place, just told me today. He said they wanted to talk to me first—to make sure I'd take the reins."

"Yeah, I know Ben. Good guy, but he may just be probing."

"What do you mean?"

"Have you spoken to the other board members yet?" Peter asked.

"No," Sam replied.

"Keep your guard up till you do," Peter said. "Ben may just be using you."

"How so?"

"Well, *he* may want Rohan out, but if the other board members don't agree, it's not happening. He needs a forcing function. The biggest reason boards don't replace CEOs is they're not sure they can get anyone better. If he's going to set in motion a plan to oust Rohan, he needs to make sure you're available as his next card to play."

"Good point," Sam acknowledged.

"Even if they do bring you back, you need to make sure they're unanimously in support of this transition. Otherwise, as soon as you stub your first toe, whoever is against you will be saying, 'I told you so.'"

"Yeah, I met Preston Lawrence for breakfast, and he couldn't have been less interested in all this."

"I don't know Preston, but that doesn't surprise me," Peter said. "How do you think Rohan will handle it?"

"I don't know. Not well," Sam said. "He's so passive-aggressive it's hard to—"

"That's another thing," Peter interrupted. "VCs always balk at firing founders. They think it makes them look bad. So make sure that guy is out of the building."

"Absolutely. I already told Ben that was one of my preconditions."

"OK, so what are they offering you?" Peter asked, abruptly changing subjects.

"Uhh . . . I'm assuming the comp will be similar to Rohan's, but I actually don't have the written offer yet," Sam replied sheepishly.

"Jesus, Sam. Is this your first fucking rodeo? These guys already screwed you over once. It's like you're walking through the door ass-backward with your pants down."

"I know, I . . . ," Sam stammered. "I just wanted to make sure this is what I wanted to do before negotiating the comp and stuff."

"And *stuff*? What else *is* there? You're not volunteering for a non-profit, for Christ's sake. Get the comp package, and get it in writing before you tell them anything. Their backs are against the wall, so don't settle for anything less than $500,000 base salary plus 50 percent bonus and 10 percent equity."

"OK," Sam said.

"You'll also need full stock acceleration in a change of control and 2X severance in case you're terminated. That's all got to be in writing."

"Right, of course," Sam said, scribbling a note to himself.

Peter sighed as he watched Sam over the grainy video connection. "I gotta say, it doesn't seem like you're really up for this."

"No, I am," Sam responded. "I mean, I really believe in the core business. We need to clean some things up on the product side in order to get our revenue growth going again. But I definitely like the people and believe we can—"

"That's exactly what I mean," Peter interrupted. "You sound like a fucking Boy Scout. You're about to go into a goat rodeo, and you're telling me it's 'cause you like the *people*? You need to get your rodeo face on. Only one of you is going to win—you or the bull."

"What do you mean?"

"*What do I mean?*" Peter asked with exasperation, his delayed image grimacing into the camera. "This is going to be a *bitch* is what I mean! For starters, you'll need to fire a bunch of people your first week to get the burn rate down before this whole thing goes off a cliff. But you need to do it quietly, so the press doesn't find out and declare you dead. Then you'll need to get the financials cleaned up *stat*, because any acquirer will look at you like a pregnant prom queen until you do. That needs to be done discreetly too and blamed on some rogue accounting person, so you don't have the taint of fraud on you. Then, if you somehow manage to thread the needle and get a definitive offer, you'll need to twist the tits of your board members to keep them all in line and not fuck up the deal or cut you out of it. You need to be *ruthless*, and you don't sound ready to be ruthless. Companies are *bought*, not *sold*. If you're going to get this done, you need to have *swagger*. At least you have an offer, so there's a chance."

"Wait, you know about the offer?"

"*Of course* I know about the offer. It's the only reason for you even to be considering this," Peter said.

"What do you know? They're being super cagey with me, saying it's confidential until I sign the offer letter."

"All I can tell you is the acquisition interest is real. Ben isn't bullshitting you," Peter said. "Could be worth half a billion."

"Half a *billion*?" Sam blurted. "No way. Who's the buyer?"

"I can't tell you."

"How the hell am I going to sell a company for that much money once they find out there's accounting fraud?"

"That's what being a start-up CEO is all about." Peter laughed. "Keeping the whole steaming heap of lies and promises alive long enough to get liquidity. If I had a dime for every time FusionCommerce nearly went out of business, I'd have a lot of fucking dimes. By the end there, I felt like my sole 24-7 job was getting out the defibrillator to resuscitate that thing. Then, just when I thought it was finally dead for good, we got bought for $4 billion. You can make this thing a success, but you *gotta* be in rodeo mode. You can't fall off. You can't give up. You can't *ever* give up—no matter what."

■ ■ ■

In a full sweat by the time he reached Ms. Ellison's classroom, Sam tried to slip in the door unnoticed. It was Ms. Ellison herself, Mason's fresh-out-of-undergrad teacher, nervously fumbling through her presentation, who blew his cover. "Welcome—please, come in and find a seat," she said to Sam as he entered, prompting Heather to roll her eyes at his tardiness as he found her across the room. When the teacher's speech concluded, Sam made his way through the students and parents to Heather and Mason, who was beginning to proudly share his various school projects. "Hey, buddy!" Sam said. "Sorry I'm late."

"You're supposed to be in Riley's class," Heather admonished him. "Rosa took her to Ms. Jacobson's, room 23."

"I know, but I wanted to see Mason first," Sam said, trying to cover his slipup. "Graduating fifth grade is a big deal!"

Mason showed them both more of his projects before Sam said, "OK, I need to get to your sister's class. Will you show me the rest of this at home?"

Mason nodded and Sam leaned forward in an attempted hug. But Mason turned to thwart the embarrassing gesture, which turned into an awkward shoulder squeeze. Sam exchanged looks with Heather then left to find room 23. As he was staring at the room numbers, trying to determine which way to go, he heard a voice behind him call out, "Hi, Sam!" It was Lisa Atkins and her husband, Brian. Two of their three children were in the same grades as Connor and Mason, so they bumped into each other at these sorts of events with some regularity.

"Hi, guys. How is Camilla?" Sam asked, referring to their younger daughter, also in fifth grade at the elementary school.

"Great! Just great," Lisa effused. "She's actually performing a piano recital at the reception event this evening."

"Oh, that's impressive," Sam said. In addition to being a virtuoso pianist, Camilla was a straight-A student, star of the school's esteemed theater program, and, somewhat randomly, a nationally ranked fencer. "Is she still fencing?" Sam politely inquired.

"We actually just got back from regionals in Sacramento," Brian said. "She took first place in her age group."

"It should really help her chances of getting into an Ivy," Lisa added.

Sam nodded, pondering what else could already be on the college-application checklist of an eleven-year-old. "So, is she going to La Puerta next year?" Sam asked in reference to their outstanding public middle school.

"Oh, no!" Lisa said with a slight laugh, as if Sam might be joking. "She's going to St. Ignatius like her sister." St. Ignatius was a $50,000-per-year private school that resembled a college campus. "Is Mason going to La Puerta?"

"Yes. Well, that's where his older brother went, so . . ."

"I see—well, it's a good school too," Lisa said encouragingly. "If you'd like, we'd be happy to put in a recommendation for you at St. Ignatius."

"Oh, that's very nice of you," Sam said. "But until we have a liquidity event, we're probably stuck with the public schools."

"OK. Well, I'm sure he'll do fine," Lisa said as Bob smiled sympathetically. "So, will you just do tutoring then?" she asked with a combination of sincerity and pity.

"Mason's a great student," Sam replied somewhat defensively.

"I'm sure he is," Lisa said. "But you can't start prepping for the SATs too early. Our oldest, Lindsey, worked with the most wonderful tutor all through junior high and high school, on top of her outstanding curriculum at St. Ignatius. I'm sure you heard, she was thrilled to be selected valedictorian."

Sam, unsure why he would know the valedictorian selection for a school his children didn't even attend, replied, "Congratulations! That's very impressive."

"Oh, she didn't do it to *impress* anyone. She already got accepted early decision at Princeton back in December, so this won't even be on her transcript. She's just doing it to give back and inspire future generations of St. Ignatians."

"I see," Sam said. "Still, she must be very honored. And *Princeton*—wow! That's a hard school to get into. You all must be thrilled."

Brian proudly put his hand on Lisa's shoulder as she explained, "Yes, it was her first choice. We were just glad we saved up enough to send her to the best school she could get into. But she's going to take a gap year before enrolling. She'll be working with orphans in Guatemala."

"Of course she will," Sam said.

A gaggle of parents was just letting out of Ms. Jacobson's presentation when Sam arrived at his daughter's classroom. He saw Riley showing artwork to Rosa, their nanny, across the room, so he slipped through the crowded classroom to reach them.

"Hi, sweetie!" Sam surprised her with a tickle and a hug.

"*Daddy!*" she cheered and proceeded to proudly share her portfolio of drawings, which he enthusiastically observed.

"Her insulin was at ninety-five an hour ago, so she may need this," Rosa said, handing Sam a juice box. Sam thanked her as she gave Riley a kiss on the forehead and left to get home to her own family. Riley pulled out more assignments, but Sam was finding it hard to remain present. Peter's admonition was stuck in his head, primarily because he knew it was true. This wasn't just a job offer, it was an assignment, a *mission*. The board expected an acquisition. They expected an exit—a return on their investment. If he succeeded and shepherded the deal to a positive outcome, he would be a hero and personally make a fortune. But, equally true, if he failed and the deal fell through, he would be the chump—brought back from being fired, only to shit the bed. *What would my reputation be then?* As Peter said, if he was going to do it, he needed to be ruthless. Only one of them could win—him or the bull.

"And this is our ant farm," Riley said, pulling Sam by the hand toward a glass terrarium along the wall. Ants frantically traversed the tunnels inside, crawling over each other with scraps of food as large as their bodies pinched between their mandibles. "See," Riley pointed. "The male ants bring food to the queen and to all her babies. Those are the larvae." Riley's small finger tapped on the glass, but it did nothing to disrupt the ants' frenetic pace. Up and down the tubes they raced, as fast as they could, hurtling past each other in single file, with barely any acknowledgment except for a microsecond-long tap of antennae. The exchange of pheromones enabled the entire colony to work in concert toward one goal. Devoid of individual identities. Prepared to defend against any threat. Anonymous soldiers, desperate to fulfill their one mission, their *sole purpose*—to provide for their queen.

"What's *that*?" a younger boy who had been watching the ants suddenly asked, pointing indelicately at the ivory-colored plastic disk protruding from Riley's arm.

"It's my blood sugar sensor. It tells me my insulin levels," Riley replied with the practiced pride of all the times she had answered that question. Then, repeating the explanation for the device that Sam had given her, she said, "My daddy got it for me, to keep me safe."

CHAPTER 19:

PRISM

SAM PUMPED AT THE PEDALS of his stationary bike as EDM beats blared over the speakers in a cramped, dark room. The spin instructor shouted to the class, "OK, *dig deep*! Here we go!" Approaching a virtual hill at mile ten, Sam stood on the pedals and leaned into the machine, willing it forward. Immediately in front of him, a row of fit soccer moms in sports bras and spandex leggings rose in unison to confront the virtual climb. Barely winded from his own workout, the instructor encouraged them, "Almost there! You're doing *great*!" Drops of sweat rolled off Sam's forehead onto the handlebar. With a frantic last rotation, he reached the summit. "Great job, everyone!" the instructor said into his lavalier as the class sat upright and gulped squirts from their water bottles.

Sam looked around the class of mostly women. No more spin classes in the middle of a Thursday morning for him. He was prepared to accept the offer to go back to Ainetu—this time as CEO. His initial trepidation had transformed into conviction. Ben had agreed to all the provisions Sam asked to have stipulated in his offer letter—the salary, the equity, the acceleration, the termination clause; it was all negotiated swiftly with the unanimous consent of the full board. Ben remained vague about the identity of their prospective acquirer, assuring Sam he would disclose everything once the employment agreement and NDA were signed. So Sam would have to take a leap of faith, but he wasn't overly concerned. Peter's insight that the offer was legitimate provided more credible assurance of its veracity than anything the board could tell him anyway. That knowledge galvanized his determination. He was finally getting his chance to run a company that was on track for a successful exit. This was restitution. A return to his rightful role in the organization.

Of course, he would discuss it with Heather before making a final decision. He hadn't told her anything about the offer yet. The topic of Ainetu had sparked enough arguments between them, so he was waiting for the right moment. Wanting to get out of the house, he bided his time at the gym down the block from Ainetu's office. To compete with the big tech-company campuses that had their own elaborate on-site fitness centers, Ainetu offered employees discounted memberships at this boutique health club. Sam dried his face with a towel and slung it over his shoulder, following the others out of the spin studio.

Turning toward the gym's café to get himself a post-workout smoothie, Sam abruptly halted at the sight of Rohan leaning casually against the wall in street clothes, typing on his phone. *Shit.* Sam instinctively wiped his face again with his towel and considered evasive maneuvers, but it was too late. Rohan looked up and made immediate eye contact. Someone from the board must have told him. Even though Sam intuitively expected this awkward moment to be unavoidable, he suddenly felt unprepared for their conversation. Still panting from his workout, Sam smiled cordially and walked toward Rohan.

"Hey, man! How have you been? So good to see you!" Rohan declared as if they were long-lost friends, finally reunited. In fact, they hadn't spoken a single word to each other since the day of Sam's firing.

Thrown by the clearly disingenuous greeting, Sam shook hands apprehensively. "Good to see you too."

"Sooo psyched to hear that you're coming back to the company!"

As insincere as Rohan's behavior was, this wasn't the conversation Sam had expected when he rehearsed what he would say when they first spoke. Maybe the board really cut him down to size. "Thanks," Sam replied cautiously. "I'm excited to be coming back. So presumably the board told you?"

"Oh, yeah—we've been talking about this for a while," Rohan said. "I'm totally supportive. We needed to shake things up a little bit. Plus, it will be great for the optics of the company if we have someone who doesn't have all that *founder baggage*."

Sam still wasn't sure how to play Rohan's overexuberance. With his guard still up, Sam asked, "So have you given any thought to what you're going to do next?"

"Well, my chairman responsibilities will keep me pretty well occupied."

"Chairman? Chairman of what?"

"Didn't Ben tell you? I'm staying on as chairman of the Ainetu board."

"What are you *talking* about?" Sam asked, steering Rohan to a table in the corner of the café. "The board assured me you weren't going to be involved in any capacity."

"Yeah, that's not how it's going to happen," Rohan said, revealing a snide grin.

Sam paused in disbelief. His head spun at the prospect of Rohan not only remaining at the company but, in effect, again being his boss. "Well, it's not really your decision, is it? You don't control the company anymore. The investors have the voting rights. They own the majority of the shares."

"They don't have a choice," Rohan said. "The Prism deal isn't going to happen without me. I found it, and I can kill it."

So it's Prism. Sam finally had the answer to his question of who the potential acquirer was. Prism Systems was one of the original relational database vendors that exploded with the rise of client-server computing in the nineties. Already a multibillion-dollar company, their shares ballooned through the first dot-com wave, making their bachelor founder, Charles "Chip" Peterson, one of the first tech multibillionaires. Since the mid-2000s, Prism had used its inflated stock price to gobble up both legacy software companies and start-ups with interesting technology, usually garnering enough of a bump in their stock price to cover the cost of the acquisition. Chip once bragged in a media article that it was like they were acquiring companies for free, which, effectively, they were. Prism was such a logical suitor for Ainetu, Sam couldn't believe it hadn't occurred to him already—an acquisition that would, no doubt, be lauded by industry analysts and rewarded by Wall Street.

"So you're saying you'd scuttle this deal if you're no longer at the company?" Sam asked skeptically. "Why would you do that? You still have your founder's shares."

"Because it's *my* company," Rohan said, now brimming with hubris. "This deal won't happen unless *I* say it will."

Sam leaned back in the metal café chair and thought for a moment. *Is Rohan bluffing? Is this a final decision from the board, or can I change their minds? And why didn't Ben give me a heads-up that they were going to let Rohan stay on in such a prominent role?* He needed to talk to Ben—to get the board's side of the story.

"So are you here just to rub this in my face?" Sam finally asked.

"Sam . . . c'mon—do you really think I'm that petty? No, I actually want you to come back. You're good at the day-to-day operational minutiae. I'm more big picture—don't have time to get into the details like you do," Rohan said in a perfectly executed backhanded compliment. "Plus, this is a chance for you to be part of a big exit."

"This deal's never going to close with you still involved with the company," Sam contended, building his gumption. "I know you've been manipulating the revenue figures. I told the board everything. As soon as the Prism team audits the customer contracts during due diligence, either this deal will blow up or you'll be forced out."

"I'm not worried," Rohan said.

"Your revenue figures are bullshit. It's only a matter of time before they figure that out and demand you be removed from the company."

"Didn't you hear?" Rohan asked, again reveling in the information advantage he possessed. "I guess Ben really hasn't told you anything. We cleaned all that up. I've already told Prism that we found some accounting irregularities. We had to restate a couple quarters of revenue, but they're keeping their offer at $500 million. For them, it's more about the strategic fit than the cash flow. They're buying the tech and the team. They don't care about a couple deals that got booked incorrectly by a rogue CFO."

Sam felt his lungs constricting. The winning card he thought he held over Rohan had been neutralized. Now, with no smoking gun to point to with either the board or the acquirers, Sam had no leverage to get Rohan out of the company. He felt sick to his stomach. He stood abruptly, causing his metal chair to reverberate on the concrete floor.

"You'd better not blame Bill for this," Sam said, jabbing his finger toward Rohan.

"Bill? *Please*—he's a pawn. If you're going to play this game, trying to force me out of my own company, you'd better be ready for a fight!"

Sam slammed his chair under the table and turned to leave. The young woman at the front desk continued folding towels, pretending not to notice the escalating confrontation.

Rohan stood and shouted after him, "Don't you forget, Sam, this is *my* company! The only way I'm leaving is in a body bag!"

■ ■ ■

Walking out into the bright sun, Sam pulled out his phone and pinched his forehead with his hand as he scrolled through his contacts. Coming upon Ben's information, he pressed to dial. The phone rang seven times, Sam's indignation growing with each ring. Just as he expected to go to voice mail, Ben picked up.

"Hey, Sam."

"What the *fuck*, Ben?"

"I know, I know," Ben replied apologetically. "I was hoping to be the first one to tell you, but I've been in LP meetings all morning."

"Well, Rohan beat you to the punch. He told me he's staying on as *chairman of the board*?" Sam stated, looking to confirm Rohan's claim.

"It's a compromise," Ben claimed.

"How so? He's chairman of the damn board!"

"Honestly, Sam, we told him yesterday and he freaked. He threatened to blow up the whole deal if we fired him," Ben said.

"But that's what you promised *me* you'd do. Do you really think the Prism guys won't go through on the deal if he's gone?"

"So he told you it was Prism?" Ben asked.

"Yeah, I probably could have guessed it. Anyway, I actually think it's more likely they'd close the deal if he's *gone*," Sam said.

"I don't know," Ben said. "He's the only one on our side who has spoken with their execs. We on the board have only interacted with the bankers. Maybe we can exit him later, but it's just too delicate right now."

"OK, but why do you have to make him chairman? He'll be undermining my every move."

"It was the only way he'd agree to step down as CEO. I think you're actually the only person he'd agree to pass the baton to. Believe it or not, I think he trusts you. Besides, Kamal and Preston wouldn't agree to this CEO transition unless Rohan stayed on the board. Don't worry—the chairman title is really meaningless. He won't have the power to make any decisions on his own. We won't let him pull any of his bullshit."

"Bullshit like manipulating the revenue," Sam said. "How are you guys comfortable with him still involved with the company? He called them '*accounting irregularities*'! It was fraud, plain and simple."

"Yeah, I was deeply disappointed to hear that Bill was incorrectly recognizing revenue," Ben said.

"Wait . . . *what*?" Sam exclaimed. "I was talking about *Rohan*. He specifically instructed Bill to misstate the revenue."

"That's not what Bill said," Ben replied. "Rohan informed the board that Bill had been doctoring the books. He provided several emails as proof. When we confronted Bill, he admitted everything. Obviously, we had to let him go right away. He was dismissed this morning."

"But that's not what happened," Sam said.

"Well, all we can go on is what those guys said," Ben contended. "And they said the same thing—that it was Bill's idea and Rohan had no knowledge of it. Anyway, we sent restated financials to the Prism team, and it didn't scare them away. So we're hoping we can put the whole thing behind us."

In other words, we've already found our scapegoat. Sam struggled to recompose himself as he watched the next spin class checking in at the front desk. "This is all . . . pretty unbelievable, Ben."

"Look, it's all just part of the ride. Don't let it throw you for a loop," Ben said. "You're making the right decision to come back. This deal is going to get done, and, when it does, it will mean life-changing wealth for you. Don't let go now. We need you to get it over the finish line. We're so close."

CHAPTER 20:

THE GOOSE

CRAVING A BREAK from their makeshift kitchen, Sam suggested he and the kids meet Heather after her work at one of their favorite local haunts, the Dutch Goose. Tucked into a residential neighborhood, the watering hole was a bit of an institution in Silicon Valley, with an eclectic mix of Stanford students, families, and VCs from nearby Sand Hill Road. It was a stark contrast from the luxury hotels and restaurants nearby. Dating back to the sixties, "the Goose" had housed one of the first Atari game consoles and still had a cluster of video games in the back, along with a dozen flat-screen TVs showing sports. Pints of beer and peanut shells were scattered across the tables, which were bolted to the ground. The walls of the cramped booths were adorned with carvings, graffiti, and framed memorabilia crudely mounted with wood screws.

"Only two games each, boys!" Heather shouted to Connor and Mason as they jumped from the booth toward the siren call of the video games.

Sam cracked open a peanut and discarded the shell onto a growing pile. A silence ensued as Heather replied to a text message, Riley played with a rainbow unicorn, and Sam looked up at a basketball game on a screen overhead. "So I heard about an interesting job opportunity yesterday," Sam finally said, licking the foam from his lips after a slow sip of his beer.

"Really?" Heather said, glancing up from her screen. "What is it?"

"You're getting a new job, Daddy?" Riley asked as her unicorn leaped over the pile of discarded peanut shells.

"Maybe, sweetie," Sam replied, then turned to Heather. "Ben said the board wants me to come back as CEO at Ainetu."

Heather pursed her lips and set her phone facedown on the table. "Oh? That's . . . great," she replied. "I told you that pulling on the thread a little would help. So what did you say?"

"I told him I wanted to think about it. That I wanted to talk to you first," Sam quickly added.

"I'm not going to tell you what to do. It's your decision. Do you already have the offer letter?"

"Just got it today. They agreed to everything I asked for—twice my previous salary. I told them I'd make a final decision by tomorrow."

"Well, at least we'd have a second income again."

"Yeah," Sam hesitated. "I can't tell if you think this is a good idea or not."

"It's not an *idea*. It's a *job*," she said. "We need the money, but I guess I'm just a little surprised you'd consider going back there. Are you sure this is what you want to do? Haven't you been telling me they're committing fraud?"

"That's all been cleaned up," Sam said, casually waving his hand. "I really think it's going to be different this time. I'll be able to make all the decisions Rohan was unwilling to make—to get the product right and organize the team the way I want."

"So what's happening to Rohan?"

Sam took another sip of his beer before sheepishly replying. "He's staying on as chairman of the board."

"I see. So same people, just different titles—I'm sure that will make all the difference."

"It *will* make all the difference. I'll be CEO. Ben assured me they won't let Rohan interfere."

Heather nodded but regarded him skeptically as she cracked open a peanut. The boys scurried back to the table, still arguing over who won their video game. "Sam—your order is ready," the voice called over the loudspeaker. Heather redirected Connor and Mason back to the counter to pick up their food.

"There's even some interest from a potential acquirer," Sam said after the boys left.

"Sounds like you've already made up your mind," Heather said.

"Not yet, but I'm leaning toward it. It just feels like . . . a chance for redemption, I guess. Meant to be."

"You should do whatever makes you happy."

"I don't know if it will make me *happy* or not, but it gives me a shot at something I've always wanted: successfully exiting a company. It could be life-changing for us," Sam said.

"Yeah, you made it pretty clear at the winery that's all you care about," Heather said. The boys returned to the table with trays of burgers and fries. Sam quietly picked up his basket in the wake of Heather's remark. His phone started vibrating, announcing an incoming call. Sam pulled it from his pocket to check the caller ID. It was Jessie Hernandez, their VP of HR. He squinted curiously at the phone, then realized she must be calling about the logistical details of his offer.

"I better take this," he said. The kids were too focused on inhaling their food to respond, but Heather acknowledged him with a terse nod. Sam held the phone to his ear. "Hi, Jessie."

"*Sam*! Thank God I reached you!" she said in obvious distress. "I have *terrible* news!"

"What is it?" Sam asked. An expression of concern overtook his face.

"Bill Johnson committed suicide tonight!"

Sam felt the air leave his lungs as if he'd just had the wind knocked out of him. His face blanched as Heather mouthed, "What is it?" He looked at her but didn't reply. "Oh *my God*!" he finally said, standing from the table. "Where are you?"

Jessie was sobbing on the other end of the line. "I'm on my way to the hospital," she said, barely able to get the words out. "I'm bringing clothes to his wife and daughter. They went straight to El Camino Hospital with him in the ambulance," she wailed, unable to continue.

"I'll be right there," Sam said and hung up the phone.

CHAPTER 21:

MIDNIGHT GOLF

"HOW DID IT HAPPEN?" Sam asked after finding Jessie in the waiting room of the ER.

"Overdose," she said numbly, giving Sam a hug. "Sandy found him in the bathroom and called 911. The paramedics tried Narcan, but they couldn't revive him. They rushed him to the hospital. He was dead on arrival." Jessie started to cry and dabbed the mascara running from the corners of her reddened eyes.

"Oh my God." Sam grimaced and pinched the bridge of his nose with his forefinger and thumb. "That's just so *awful*. Have you spoken with her?"

Jessie took a deep, cleansing breath and shook her head. "Not yet. I'm dreading it. Apparently she told one of the nurses to call me and bring some clothes over, since we live close. Our daughters are friends. She specifically told the nurse to tell me what happened." Sam just stared at her under the harsh fluorescent light of the waiting room, still processing the situation. "He left a note," she finally said in a foreboding tone.

The statement preempted Sam's uncomfortable next question of whether the overdose could have been accidental, but the existence of a note had its own implications. "What did it say?" he asked.

Jessie simply pulled an envelope from her purse and handed it to Sam as she started to sob again. He opened the envelope and read the note inside.

Dearest Sandy and Danielle,

With my career now over, it's become clear to me that I've reached the end of my useful life. The decisions I made were mine alone. I always strived to provide for the two of you the best I could. In the end, my best wasn't good enough. I couldn't bear to put you through further humiliation.

– Bill

Sam refolded the letter and inserted it back into the envelope.

"I feel so *guilty*," Jessie sobbed. "This is all my fault. We terminated him this morning!"

"It's not your fault," Sam tried to reassure her. "This was the board's decision."

"I can't face Sandy," Jessie said, not hearing Sam's comment. She looked around the lobby as if she was envisioning the confrontation. "She's going to *hate* me! And *poor* Danielle!"

Sam knew Bill was distraught, but it never occurred to him that taking the fall for the company's financial misdeeds would lead to this. He felt a lump swell in his throat at the thought of their last exchange. The trust Bill had placed in him. The subsequent sequence of events that led to this tragedy—the thumb drive, the board drama, the need to find a scapegoat.

"*Jessie*," Sam said sternly, trying to pull her out of her guilt spiral. "Listen to me. This *isn't* your fault. Bill made his own decisions." Sam looked her in the eyes until he knew he had her attention. "Does Rohan know about this yet?"

Calming down, Jessie dabbed at her eyes again and shook her head. "No. You're the only person besides his family who knows."

"OK. Don't tell him yet," Sam said. Jessie nodded slightly. Then Sam asked, "Why did you call me first instead of him?"

"Because . . . well, you're going to be CEO, right? Ben had me prepare all the paperwork."

"Yes, of course," Sam said. "So you know about Rohan too?"

"Well, yeah—Ben had me prepare his severance paperwork too. HR knows everything."

Sam acknowledged her statement with a pensive nod. Just then, the emergency room doors opened, and a distraught couple came running through. The woman frantically asked the nurse at the reception desk, "Where is my *brother*?"

■ ■ ■

A 747 gradually descended from a queue of planes in the sky, its landing lights piercing the fog over the San Francisco Bay. Sam watched it, transfixed momentarily by the pure physics of a 300-ton fuselage of metal creeping through the air at low speed without immediately plummeting to earth. As the plane roared overhead at low altitude, he returned his attention to the golf ball he had just placed on a tee and struck it into the darkness.

Not wanting to return home, he had meandered aimlessly up Highway 101 until he ended up at Mariners Point—a low-budget golf center jutting into the bay on a former landfill under the glide path of SFO airport. As the last person on the illuminated driving range at ten thirty, Sam slipped a $100 bill to the night groundskeeper, who had been trying to shut down the facility for thirty minutes, to turn on the lights over the course for a round. Heather had called him a dozen times in the last few hours, but he let it go to voice mail each time. He knew she wouldn't understand. As he searched for his ball in the darkness, he glanced up at another airplane emerging from the circling queue to begin its descent.

Despite multiple metallic towers crowned with floodlights, Sam could barely make out the green. What he thought initially was the flag of the hole turned out to be a seagull that took flight as he was about to hit. Sam recomposed himself and squinted through the darkness to locate his target. Then, changing his club, he lined up to take his swing.

The ball arced into the gusty black sky, disappearing briefly from sight. Then it emerged from its shroud, landing with a satisfying thud on the green. Sam picked up his golf bag, which still bore a faintly mildewed stench from the box of office supplies that had shared trunk space with it for the last several months, and walked toward the green.

Turning to look over his shoulder at what sounded like another airplane approaching, Sam noticed a golf cart traversing toward him up the fairway. He figured at first it was the groundskeeper, either chastened by his boss for allowing Sam on the course in the first place or emboldened by his corruption to collect another bribe for the back nine. As the cart grew closer, though, he gradually recognized a discernible silhouette. It was Heather.

"*Sam*!" she scolded as she got within shouting distance. "What the *hell* are you doing out here?"

"What does it look like?" Sam asked. "I'm actually having a pretty good round."

The cart skidded to a stop, ripping up patches of grass. Heather jumped from the driver's seat, obviously furious. "It's *midnight*! The kids are home alone! I called you, like, ten times. Why didn't you pick up your phone?"

"It's bad etiquette to take a phone call on the golf course," Sam replied. "Why did you leave the kids at home?"

"Because I was *worried* about you!" Heather said, her voice cracking slightly. She took an anxious step toward him but stopped when Sam calmly pulled a putter from his bag.

"How did you even find me?"

"Are you *kidding* me right now? You get some urgent phone call from Jessie, then rush out the door without telling me where you're going and don't answer my calls? I've been panicked all night wondering what the hell happened, and the first thing you ask is, 'How did you find me?'"

Sam looked up from the putt he was about to take and pointed with his club at the golf cart. "Yeah, I mean—you tracked me down in that thing like a heat-seeking missile. I was just trying to unwind after a hard day with a little golf. I didn't expect to get the third degree."

Heather stared at Sam slack-jawed as another plane roared overhead, its din compelling her to shout her response. "Well, I'm sorry that I gave a shit about where you might be in the middle of the night after whatever devastating news you got. If you must know, after my tenth attempt to call you went straight to voice mail, Mason used that Find My Phone app to locate you. I didn't even know there was a golf course here. I was so worried. I couldn't imagine where you were right on the edge of the bay!" she said, her voice warbling between anger and relief.

"Yeah, it's a pretty crappy course. Smells like swamp gas. And there are the planes," Sam said, pointing up at another approaching aircraft.

"So . . . you just decided to play golf, by yourself—in the middle of the night?"

"I'm on pace to break forty on the front nine."

"Who *cares* what your score is, Sam? Honestly, are you all right? What was Jessie calling you about?"

Sam broke eye contact and lined up his putt, which he dropped into the cup. "I told you I'm having a good round," he said, retrieving his ball.

"*Sam!* What's going on? What did Jessie want?"

"She was at the hospital."

"The *hospital*? *Why?*"

"Bill Johnson took his own life tonight," Sam said, looking down and tapping his shoe with the end of his club.

"*What?* Oh my God! *Why?*"

"I don't know, really. He left a note, but he didn't really say."

"Didn't he have a wife and daughter?" Heather asked, tears welling in her eyes.

"Yeah," Sam nodded. "His sister and her family were arriving at the ER just as I left."

"Did something happen at Ainetu?" Heather asked, wiping tears from her cheeks.

Sam looked down again, pretending to inspect his ball. "He was . . . *involved* in the fraud stuff. They let him go this morning."

"Do you think the fact that you were asking questions about the accounting . . ."

"I had nothing to do with it. Bill was the one who decided to be complicit with all this."

"You were forcing this whole issue with the board. That's probably what got him fired."

Sam shook his head. "No, he made his choice. I actually tried to help him get out of this mess. But he was too close to it. Collateral damage, I guess."

"*Collateral damage?* Bill was one of your closest colleagues at Ainetu. Don't you feel any sympathy or regret or *anything*?"

"Don't act so innocent. This was *your* idea."

"*What?* I just told you tonight at dinner I didn't think you should do this."

"No, no—you were the one encouraging me to pull the thread, to get my job back."

Heather pressed her index finger into his chest. "I was just telling you to stop feeling sorry for yourself and find a new job. I wasn't trying to push you into a personal vendetta that caused Bill to . . ."

"It doesn't matter now. I'll just need to get people refocused and moving forward," Sam said, hoisting his golf bag on his shoulder and proceeding to the next tee.

"You're not still going back to Ainetu, *are you?*" Heather followed him on the path.

"I start Monday."

"Sam, you *can't*."

Sam leaned over and pushed a tee into the soft grass, placing his ball on top. Then he turned back toward Heather as he took a practice swing.

"I'm going to be CEO of a company that's on track for a big exit. I already know the business and the board. We have a $500 million offer on the table. This is my big shot. It's perfect."

"It's not perfect for Bill's family! Why would you do this?"

"I deserve it! *We* deserve it. Look at this," Sam said, gesturing with his golf club around the darkened course. "Is this what you want? Midnight golf under a flight path on a landfill that smells like ass crack? I want private clubs, private schools, private jets. If it's *private*, I want it. This is my chance to set us up for the rest of our lives."

"I don't want any of that stuff."

"Oh, *bullshit*!" Sam said. "Your pussy was dripping wet watching those rich motherfuckers at the auction!"

Heather abruptly slapped Sam's face. "*Fuck you!*" she shouted. She turned and stomped back down the path to the golf cart.

Sam put a hand to his cheek, feeling a warm throb rise to the surface. He followed her partially back down the path as she left him behind in her haste to get back to the cart. Rather than backing up, Heather abruptly drove the cart forward, leaving huge tire imprints across the green. Sam stopped his pursuit and watched as she screeched back onto the path toward the clubhouse. Standing in the center of the green, he looked up as another plane started its descent.

CHAPTER 22:

THE RETURN

SAM WATCHED THE ELEVATOR DOORS EXPECTANTLY. The ding announcing their arrival had kept him in anticipation for what felt like an eternity, waiting for them to open. Finally, they parted, admitting him into the chamber and out of the faint exhaust smell of the garage. Sam hoisted his box and entered, pressing Ainetu's floor as he had done hundreds of times before. He watched the numbers slowly increase as he ascended to the fifteenth floor. Glancing down at the contents of his box, left largely untouched in his trunk since the day of his firing, he noted the framed photograph of his family, warped from water damage.

Monday had finally arrived. Sam's first day back at Ainetu couldn't come soon enough. He had spent the last two nights on the couch, estranged from Heather and the kids. Wandering the house silently, his face buried in his phone, Sam's brain popped with ideas for how to make Ainetu a success. An email had been sent the night before by Rohan to all employees announcing Sam's return as CEO. Despite Rohan's assurances that he would "still be intimately involved in every aspect of the company," everyone appreciated the significance of the transition. Gratifyingly, Sam was inundated with congratulatory messages from employees when he first logged back into their corporate Slack instance. The external press release officially announcing his return as CEO of Ainetu wouldn't be issued until the following day.

Sam put the picture back in the box and confidently emerged from the elevator. A cluster of employees in the reception area spoke in hushed tones. Their receptionist hurried by Sam toward the group with a cup of tea, barely acknowledging him. As Sam passed, a woman he didn't recognize dabbed her eyes with a tissue. Sam knew all too well the corner office he would be occupying, Rohan's former office. He immediately turned and walked toward it across the central office workspace. Several other employees appeared to be consoling each other near the open kitchen. None of them greeted him.

Having traversed the sea of desks, Sam turned and pushed open the glass door of his new office with his shoulder, his hands still occupied with his box, which he set down on the desk. Dozens of notifications on his phone alerted him to Jessie's announcement about Bill moments earlier. The congratulatory messages on Slack from the night before had been subsumed by condolences. A group of employees had already organized a channel for collecting gifts for Bill's family.

Nicole, their executive assistant, suddenly appeared, tailgating Sam into the office. "Great to see you. I'm so glad you're back! I just wish it were under better circumstances," she said, shuffling in to give Sam a hug, which he half-heartedly reciprocated.

"I guess everyone just heard about Bill?" Sam asked, gesturing toward the pods of huddled employees.

"It's *such* a tragedy," she said, her face downcast. "I can't believe it. I just saw him on Friday. Do you know how it happened?"

"I don't," Sam replied. He removed the stapler from his box and placed it deliberately on his desk. "I'm sure today will be busy. Do you have a schedule for me?"

"Yes, of course—sorry. Here you go," she said, handing him a copy of his schedule on color-coded binder paper with the day's date on top. She could be old-school that way. One time, Sam recalled, Nicole made a company org chart using printed names on cards with Velcro backings stuck to felt poster board with yarn to indicate the reporting structure.

Amanda remarked that it looked like the wall of a 1970s detective trying to crack an organized crime ring. "It should be on your iPhone calendar as well, but I wasn't sure if your account was set up yet or not. We have an exec staff meeting at nine and then a company all-hands at ten."

"Thanks." Sam looked at her expectantly for a moment, then added, "That's all for now."

"Of course, I'm sorry—I'll give you some time to get reacclimated," she said, backing out the door. Sam sat at the desk and inspected the new laptop that had been set up with a sticky note on the cover providing his temporary login. He removed a few more items from his box—an Ainetu-branded water bottle, business cards with his previous COO title on them, printed presentations that were fused together from their previous saturation. He tossed the box with its remaining contents, including the framed photos, onto the floor. Pulling open a drawer, Sam discovered the signs of Rohan's hasty departure—crumpled notes, unused ketchup packets, a smattering of random folders. He assembled it all and discarded it in the trash.

As Sam made his way to the main conference room, other employees parted slightly to let him pass. He greeted the members of the executive team, who stood as he circled the table exchanging handshakes—Amanda, of course, as well as Zhang, their CTO; Anton, VP of marketing; Jessie, VP of HR; Craig, VP of business development; and Kim Hahn, a new hire Sam had not met before who joined a month earlier to run customer support. Ajay Khatri, an accounting director, was in attendance as a battlefield promotion for Bill, representing the finance team.

"Thanks, everyone," Sam said, taking his seat at the head of the table. "I appreciate the warm welcome. Let's jump right in, though, because we have a lot to do. I emailed you all an agenda last night. We're already midway through the quarter, so let's start with a pipeline review. Amanda?"

"Did you want to, maybe, say anything about Bill first?" Amanda asked.

"Oh, of course," Sam said, glancing at Jessie. "Obviously, Bill's passing was a horrible tragedy. I remember when Jessie called me, how shocked I was. I just couldn't believe it." Sam looked around the room at the subdued faces, then continued, "That said, we have a business to run. So, Amanda—give us the pipeline update."

As she started talking, Sam reflected on how quickly he already felt comfortable in the new role. Without having to placate Rohan's ego, the interpersonal dynamics of their executive meetings would be so much simpler. Finally, they could just focus on growing the business rather than navigating internal politics. Each of the other executives ran through their updates. There were no sidebars, no diversions, no distractions, no prolonged pauses while someone waited for Rohan to return his attention to the meeting from his phone.

"OK, final topic: cleaning up our financials," Sam said. "Ajay, I saw you sent around updated financial statements that accurately recognize the revenue from our customer contracts. Thanks for that. I assume you or someone on your team has reviewed every contract to make sure everything is clean?"

"Yes, we actually brought in a team of three auditors from our accounting firm, just to double-check that everything matches the contracts," Ajay affirmed, somewhat nervously.

"Great," Sam nodded. "That was the next thing I was going to suggest. So, how many employees knew that our financials were misrepresented?"

Ajay looked around at the other execs, but no one was bailing him out. "I . . . I'm not sure," he said. "I think most of the people on the finance team knew something was off. But not all of them see the contracts."

"Amanda, what about in the sales team?" Sam asked.

"Not sure. Maybe a couple reps noticed their commission checks were bigger than they expected, but they're usually not going to complain about that."

"OK," Sam said. "We're going to come clean on this in the all-company meeting. I think more people might have suspicions. I want to be transparent—explain the problem and what we've done to fix it."

Everyone nodded in agreement as Nicole poked her head into the conference room.

"Everyone's assembling for the all-hands," she said.

As they all stood to leave, Jessie whispered to Sam, "Can I speak to you privately for a minute?" Sam nodded and waited for the other executives to depart as they both sat back down. "Sorry to hit you with this on your first day, but someone has raised a sexual harassment claim," Jessie said. "It's a female employee, obviously. She wishes to remain anonymous."

"Awww, shit—*really*?" Sam said. "Who is it?"

"I can't tell you. That's what *anonymous* means, Sam. I promised her I'd keep her identity secret. But I've documented the incident, just in case."

"What *was* the incident?" Sam asked.

"Lewd comments, inappropriate touching, it . . . ," Jessie trailed off.

"It what?" Sam asked.

"It happened here, in the office," Jessie said.

"OK . . ." Sam paused. "Can you at least tell me who the alleged perpetrator is?" Jessie hesitated. Sam continued, "Well, I'm sure whoever it is, we can just negotiate an exit and put a nondisparagement in place, right?"

"It's not quite that easy," Jesse said. "It's not an employee. It's a board member . . . Preston Lawrence."

■ ■ ■

Sam walked into their kitchen area, which served as their all-company meeting space. His approach garnered several remarks and scattered applause from those assembled. He recognized fewer faces in the crowd than he expected. Most of these people would be gone within a month if the deal with Prism didn't consummate. Ainetu's burn rate was unsustainably high. If the deal didn't happen, they would go bankrupt unless he made drastic head count reductions.

"Thanks," Sam said, smiling at no one in particular. "I'm very excited to be back at Ainetu. As most of you know, I've dedicated several years of my career to this company. It's a huge market, we have a great product, and we have an incredible team. Many of you are probably wondering what's been going on. Especially after hearing the terrible news about Bill Johnson. My condolences go out to his family. The fact is that we were incorrectly recognizing revenue in our customer contracts. I don't want to dwell on why this happened. There is a lot of pressure to hit quarterly targets. We just got a little overzealous. But we have cleared up that accounting irregularity and restated our financials with confirmation from our auditors. So we're good now."

Sam took a moment to survey the somber faces around the room, then continued—laying out their goals for the quarter and recognizing people on the executive team who had stepped up during this transition period, including Ajay filling in for Bill. "Finally, I want to thank Rohan. He may not be here anymore, but he will always be the founder of this company. It's important that we never lose sight of our original mission. Every day, Ainetu is enabling businesses to make better decisions with their data. By bringing together all data about customers into a single view, customer experiences are better, business is better, the *world* is better. Ainetu is making the world a better place—*never* forget that. OK, let's get back to business. Thanks, everyone!"

Nicole intercepted Sam as the crowd of employees dispersed. "Just making sure you know you have a board video conference in ten minutes."

"Yup, got it all here," Sam said, holding up the paper schedule she had given him.

"And then you have an eleven o'clock call with the Prism team," she said.

"*Shhh!*" Sam reprimanded her, looking around to see if anyone heard the reference to their potential acquirer. "Use the code name."

"I'm sorry, *Spectrum* team," Nicole said, winking and twisting an imaginary key to seal her lips.

Sam pressed his fingers against his temple. Then, with Nicole in tow, he redirected to the coffee machine for a refill. He nodded curtly at a twentysomething employee who was deliberately making himself a peanut butter and jelly sandwich on thick slabs of white bread.

"Sam, have you met Marcus yet?" Nicole asked, ushering in the awkward exchange both Sam and Marcus had hoped to avoid.

"What do you do, Marcus?" Sam asked, grasping Marcus's limp hand.

"I'm a JSON developer," Marcus replied. "I pretty much just code."

"Cool," Sam nodded, clearly hoping to curtail the interaction.

"Zhang said Marcus is really talented," Nicole eagerly interjected to prop up the conversation. "We hired him away from Facebook."

"Oh, that's great," Sam said. "How did you like it there?"

"It was OK," Marcus said. He'd finished preparing his sandwich and reached into a communal bag of Doritos, scooping them onto his plate. Sam watched Marcus proceed to touch various items in the kitchen with his fingers now covered in bright-orange artificial spices.

"What made you decide to join Ainetu?" Sam asked. "Are you excited about working on AI analytics?"

"No, not really," Marcus said, taking a bite of his sandwich and cracking open a Mountain Dew. "Ainetu's closer to where I live. So I can eat breakfast and lunch here. Then I usually order dinner from DoorDash, and it's waiting for me by the time I get home. At night I watch Netflix or Hulu or play Xbox. If I want booze, I get it on DoorBuzz. If I want weed, I get it on Eaze. If I want to hook up, I get it on Tinder." Marcus took another bite of his sandwich and shrugged matter-of-factly, as if life was pretty good.

"OK, then . . . ," Sam said with a cursory nod. "Nice meeting you, Marcus."

Nicole followed Sam into his office. As the door closed, he turned to her and said, "I want him gone."

"Who? Marcus?"

"Yes! That was ridiculous," he said, conjuring up their conversation. "He's here because he wants a shorter *commute*? That's bullshit. I only want people who are dedicated to the mission of this company. There are plenty of other companies that will serve him free food."

"But . . . ," Nicole started. A regretful expression took over her face.

"Talk to Jessie and get it done. I have a call."

CHAPTER 23:

INVITATION

SAM LOGGED IN TO THE VIDEO CONFERENCE a few minutes early, ensuring he would be the first on the call before the board members joined. He self-consciously noticed his own face staring back at him in the corner of the screen and adjusted his hair and the angle of his laptop camera to be more flattering. The video conference was ostensibly an update from Rohan on the negotiations with Prism, but Sam planned to use the forum to inform them about Bill. In the intervening days since Bill's suicide, it occurred to Sam that Bill was one of the few people who could attest, potentially in a court of law, to the fraud and cover-up that Rohan had perpetrated. As he waited for the video conference to start, Sam pulled the USB drive Bill had given him from his briefcase and held it in his hand. It felt as heavy as a gun. That tiny device had already taken one life. He wrapped his fingers around it and tapped it gently against the desk as a tone indicated another person joining the conference.

Moments later, Kamal's face appeared on Sam's screen. "Hi, Kamal," Sam greeted him. Kamal said something but his audio didn't seem to be working, so Sam pointed at his ears. "Kamal, sorry, I can't hear you."

As Kamal fussed with his settings, another chime introduced Ben. "Hi, Ben," Sam again greeted. This time the audio worked, and Ben responded. Two more tones indicated Preston joining, along with their legal counsel, Peggy. Preston's audio worked, but Peggy's did not. "Don't worry, Peggy—as long as you can hear, you can take minutes," Sam said.

"Can you hear me now?" Kamal finally audibly asked.

"Yes! Hi, Kamal. I think we're just waiting for Rohan now," Sam said, noting the irony since it was Rohan who organized the call. Ben said something about the weather, but nobody seemed to be in the mood for chitchat. Finally, another chime announced Rohan. "Hey, guys— sorry I'm late," Rohan said as his image flickered onto the screen.

"Before we get the update on Project Spectrum," Sam said, cringing at the code name for the Prism deal that he had just insisted Nicole use, "I'm afraid I have some very sad news to share. Tragically, Bill Johnson took his own life."

Sam paused for a reaction that didn't seem to come. Rohan and Preston said nothing. Ben seemed to say, "Oh my God," but his microphone was muted. Kamal was adjusting his web camera. And Peggy, whose audio now seemed to be working but who apparently didn't fully hear the statement, asked, "*What* happened to Bill? You were breaking up."

"I said, Bill Johnson committed suicide. He was declared dead from an Oxycontin overdose at 8:23 p.m. Friday night," Sam said sternly.

"Are they sure it was a deliberate suicide?" Preston asked. "Or was he just abusing pain meds?"

"It was definitely a suicide," Sam said. "He left a note to his wife and daughter, so it was clearly a deliberate action. Caused, in part, according to the note, by his dismissal from Ainetu."

Sam again paused for reaction, but it was more muted than he expected. "I see," was all Preston said in response. Rohan again said nothing.

Ben unmuted himself and exclaimed, "How awful!"

Kamal looked pensive. "So do you think this will affect the deal?" he finally asked.

"No," Rohan interjected confidently. "Bill never spoke directly with anyone on the Prism team. They only know him as the faceless guy responsible for the accounting anomaly."

"Good," Ben chimed in. "Don't mention anything to them. It's not relevant. He's not at the company anymore, so we have no obligation to disclose this." Preston and Kamal quickly agreed with Ben's advice.

"So what's the latest, Rohan?" Preston asked.

Sam cocked his head. *Are they really moving on so abruptly after I just delivered news of a former C-level employee killing himself?* It was as if he'd just announced the date of the next board meeting. They had each known Bill personally and attended dozens of meetings with him, yet nobody seemed fazed that the man had just taken his life as a direct result of his termination, leaving his wife and child behind.

"I had another good conversation with the banker," Rohan said in a self-satisfied tone. "Obviously, they have a lot of questions about the CEO transition. They want to talk to Sam."

"You haven't spoken with them yet?" Ben asked Sam.

"No, he hasn't," Rohan answered on Sam's behalf.

"Not yet," Sam admitted. "Of course, it's 11:00 a.m. on my first day back. I'm talking to them right after this. I'll know more today."

"Look, Sam," Preston said with a sigh. "I'm sure you know I had some reservations about bringing you back, but we didn't have a choice. Given the accounting issues, we needed to show we were doing our fiduciary responsibility. But you're in the driver's seat now. You need to get this deal done, *fast*."

"I understand the urgency, but Prism's a big company. I need some time to establish a rapport and figure out how real their intentions are," Sam said, trying to calibrate expectations. Sam still suspected the entire deal could be exaggerated, if not entirely fabricated, by Rohan as a ploy to sustain his involvement at Ainetu.

A long pause ensued as each of the board members waited to see who would speak first. Kamal was first to break the silence. "Sam, I'm beginning to question your ability to get this deal done."

Before Sam could reply, Ben came to his defense. "C'mon, Kamal, you know it takes forever to navigate a deal through a company the size of Prism."

"We don't *have* forever," Preston said. "We're running out of cash. We've got to get this *done*!"

"You're absolutely right, Preston," Sam said. "That's why I'm going to tell Prism they have thirty days to submit a definitive agreement. If they're as serious as Rohan claims they are, they should have no problem with that deadline. Otherwise, we'll need to dramatically reduce our burn rate."

Nobody responded for a moment. Then Ben asked, "Do you have an expense-reduction plan already?"

"Yes," Sam replied. "It starts with eliminating 70 percent of our personnel."

"If we cut that many heads, it will be a giant red flag," Preston said. "Nobody will touch us. We'll have no chance of getting acquired."

"Can Prism get this done before your deadline?" Kamal asked.

"I have no idea," Sam said. "I haven't even spoken to them yet. But we don't have any other suitors, so we don't have a choice. We can't delay expense reductions beyond thirty days or we won't make payroll. So unless you guys want to do an inside financing round, that's the deadline—not only for them, but for us too."

Another stretch of silence ensued before Ben finally said, "OK, keep us posted."

Sam glanced at the five faces on his screen, but no one seemed to have anything more to say, so he closed the app and slammed his laptop shut.

■ ■ ■

Sam had previously met Carlson Mayfield, the investment banker at Bronson & Associates who was representing Prism on the deal. So, not wanting an introduction through Rohan, Sam had reached out directly to arrange their call. If the deal was real, he knew a change of CEOs in the middle of the process could scuttle it. So it was critical to talk to them before the public announcement of his return the next day. Sam dialed into the conference bridge and waited for others to join.

"Hi, Sam Hughes here," Sam said as he heard the tone indicating the call had started.

"Hi, Sam," another voice chimed in. "This is David Budelli, SVP of corporate development at Prism. I've also got Carlson Mayfield from Bronson on the line."

"Hi, guys. Thanks for making time," Sam said. "Anyone else joining the call on your end?"

"Nope, just us," David replied. "So let's start with the elephant in the room—we were a little surprised to hear the news that Rohan was stepping down and you were rejoining as CEO."

"Yeah, well, obviously I'm intimately familiar with the business from my previous tour of duty here," Sam said. "I've already done an executive team meeting, company all-hands, and board meeting, and it's not even lunch yet. So we're not going to skip a beat with this transition."

"Good to hear," Carlson said. "Your board member, Ben, gave me a call Friday to give me a heads-up. He was singing your praises. Sounds like they're glad to have you back."

"I'm happy to *be* back," Sam said.

"You were on our list of people to talk to as part of our due diligence, even before we heard you were returning," David said. "We always like talking to former employees. They're usually the most honest with us. So, tell us, why did you leave in the first place?"

Sam realized that in the haste of his reengagement, he and Rohan had never really coordinated their stories on this subject. "That's a reasonable question," Sam started cautiously. "I assume you asked Rohan that already?"

"Yes, of course," David replied. "He said you wanted to 'spend more time with your family.'"

"I see," Sam paused. "Well, that's true—I did want to spend more time with my family."

"We all do," David dismissed. "But that explanation is usually code for 'got fired.' I would normally dismiss it and move on, but now that they're bringing you back, it begs the question—why did you leave?"

"Creative differences, I guess," Sam said, as if they were a rock band that split up. "Look, you guys know how this goes. Rohan was the founder and visionary for this business. My job as the number two was to make sure all our operations ran smoothly. We just reached a point where we weren't on the same page anymore, so we parted ways. But that process of taking a step back was actually good for both of us. It made us realize that maybe we work well with each other after all. So we got the band back together," he said, rolling his eyes at his own analogy.

The explanation seemed to satisfy David. "Well, I guess you just answered my next question then, which was why did you return?"

"That's an easy one," Sam said, feeling his confidence growing. "It's a great product, great people, and a huge market. It's not often you get handed the keys to a Maserati and just get to drive. This is poised to be a huge success, and we have the team to execute."

"That's good to hear," David responded. "So tell us about these accounting irregularities."

"Honestly, that was all uncovered after I left," Sam said. "Apparently, we were misstating the revenue of some of our multiyear customer contracts. But we've completely cleaned it up and sent you audited financials."

"You don't just *misstate* revenue from dozens of customers," David objected.

Carlson intervened as though he and David hadn't discussed the topic previously. "My understanding from Rohan was that your ex-CFO, Bill something, was the one responsible and was fired. He blamed the whole thing on him. Is that right?"

"Correct," Sam said. "Bill is no longer with the company."

"Well, Rohan must have had his fingerprints on it," David continued, pressing his inquiry. "Otherwise, why was he pushed out?"

"He wasn't pushed out," Sam asserted. "He just reached that point that most founders eventually do—where they realize that they've gotten the company off the ground, but they need to pass the baton to someone with new energy and ideas to take it to the next level. Rohan trusted me to grow this company to its full potential."

"It just seems like a strange time for the founder to step down, when we've submitted an LOI to buy the company," David said.

Recalling Peter Green's advice that companies are bought, not sold, Sam seized on the opportunity to turn the tables. "Why do you say that? An acquisition at this early stage in the business isn't what I'd characterize as our full potential. We're just getting started. We have the best product in the market, including, with all due respect, Prism's so-called AI analytics tool. That's not just my opinion—all the industry analysts see us as the undisputed market leader. So now we're ready to capitalize. If we were just looking to sell the business, Rohan would still be here. As I said, I was brought in to take the company to the next level. That's why we're setting a thirty-day deadline to get a definitive agreement from you guys. We can't afford the distraction, and I'm not going to be dragged along. We have too much else we need to focus on."

David and Carlson were both silent. Sam thought for a moment they had lost their connection and that his mic-drop monologue had gone into the vapor. He was about to ask if they were still there when he heard a new voice join the conversation.

"Hi, Sam. This is Chip Peterson. I've been listening in on the call here in David's office."

Holy shit! Sam thought, immediately worried he'd overplayed his hand not knowing the Prism CEO was listening in. Chip was not accustomed to people declining his solicitations. "Hi, Chip—nice to meet you."

"Sounds like you have a clear mandate from your board to grow the company," Chip continued. "While I appreciate that, I see a real synergy here in joining forces that would be a shame to pass up."

Stay on offense, Sam thought. "Well, we have a lot going on with a new software release and the end of the quarter coming up, but I'd be happy to explore this further with you."

"That sounds great," Chip replied. "Do you play golf?"

"Uh . . . not very well," Sam joked. "I'm an eighteen handicap."

"Good enough," Chip laughed. "Tell you what, why don't you join me down at Cypress Heights tomorrow, and we'll talk through this thing."

"OK, sure—sounds great," Sam said. Cypress Heights Golf Club, near Pebble Beach at the tip of the Monterey Peninsula, was one of the most exclusive golf clubs in the world.

"My EA will be in touch with all the details. See you soon," Chip said, with no further word from David or Carlson.

CHAPTER 24:

CARMEL

"WELCOME, MR. HUGHES, we've been expecting you," an attractive young woman greeted Sam as he entered the sliding glass doors of the private air terminal. "Would you like some champagne or a mimosa for your flight?"

"Uh, no thanks," Sam replied. "Maybe just some water, please."

She gracefully handed Sam a chilled bottle of water from underneath her reception counter. "Mr. Peterson, Mr. Budelli, and Mr. Mayfield will be here momentarily. You can wait in the reception area. Please help yourself to the buffet."

Sam strolled into an atrium overlooking the tarmac and selected a pastry from the expansive spread. He had left the house that morning before Heather or the kids were awake to catch their 6:30 a.m. helicopter flight down to Carmel. Taking a seat and crossing his legs, Sam attempted to assume the indifferent nonchalance of someone who started every day with a private helicopter ride. He looked at his phone for the first time since arriving at the terminal and discovered over twenty unread text messages. The press release announcing his return as CEO had hit the wire, and he was receiving well-wishes from colleagues. He quickly read through them, then opened his LinkedIn app and found dozens of additional messages related to the announcement, which had been posted from the Ainetu corporate account. Sam clicked on the post and shared it with his network, adding the caption, "Very excited to be rejoining the world-class team at Ainetu!"

Sam heard the sliding glass doors open and looked up to see Chip Peterson, flanked on either side by David and Carlson, each deferentially a step behind, enter the terminal like he owned the place. It was likely he *did* own the place. The woman at the reception desk jumped from her seat. "Good morning, Mr. Peterson," she greeted him, largely ignoring the other two.

"Good morning, Lexi," he said without breaking stride. "Ready for takeoff?"

"Absolutely," she replied cheerily. "Steve and Jordan are your pilots today. We're loading up your clubs now and can take off as soon as you're ready."

"Perfect," Chip dismissed her, turning his attention to Sam. "You must be Sam Hughes."

After exchanging handshakes, the foursome proceeded out the doors into the crisp Northern California morning. The blades of the helicopter were just beginning their strained arcs of motion, propelled by the squeal of the engine that intensified in pitch with each rotation. Sam had never been in a helicopter and couldn't help but crouch under the whirling canopy with visions of decapitation running through his still-intact head. He noticed none of the other men altered their posture.

"First time?" asked Lexi, who had accompanied them to the aircraft.

"Is it that obvious?" Sam asked in a voice only she could hear over the roar of the engine.

"Don't worry." She smiled. "The blades can't reach you. And Steve and Jordan are two of Mr. Peterson's best pilots. Enjoy the ride!"

When he heard they were taking a helicopter to Carmel, Sam had envisioned one of those little traffic helicopters with headphones you had to shout into to talk to each other. The offer of champagne should have been his first tip that this helicopter would be different—more like the Marine One helicopter the president flies from the south lawn of the White House. Sam climbed aboard into a remarkably quiet cabin, appointed in tan leather and smelling of sandalwood.

Chip took the frontmost seat, which had already been arranged to his liking with a tightly folded copy of the *Wall Street Journal*, an iPad in a leather case, and a perfectly frothed cappuccino in a white enamel cup and saucer. The other men took seats in the next row, leaving the seat adjacent to Chip for Sam. Chip was in an impeccably tailored dark gray suit with no tie, causing Sam to suddenly self-consciously realize he was the only one in golf attire.

"Can I get you anything?" the flight attendant asked Sam.

"A newspaper would be great," he replied, more out of a desire to appear preoccupied.

David and Carlson were both immediately on their laptops. They looked up to put in orders for custom espresso drinks with the attendant, as if they'd taken this flight a hundred times before. No one seemed particularly conversational, so Sam took his seat and glanced again at his phone, pretending this was just another routine day in the world of business.

With drinks delivered, the helicopter engine accelerated, and they effortlessly left the ground. Sam watched from his large side window as they rose above the bumper-to-bumper traffic beneath them on Highway 101. Within minutes, they were whizzing over the lush Santa Cruz mountains. Sam pretended to be as unimpressed with the view as the others, glancing at his phone in between marveling at the beauty of the Pacific coast.

They were soon over the Salinas Valley, a fertile agricultural region south of the Bay Area. Staring at fields of perfectly straight rows of plants, Sam could see white school buses that looked like they were designed for prison inmates, each towing a portable toilet poised precariously on a trailer. Just as he realized that these vehicles were for transporting farm workers to the fields, Sam heard Chip address him for the first time on the flight.

"In about five to ten years, you won't see those anymore," Chip said.

Lost in thought and not expecting the comment, Sam asked, "Sorry, see what anymore?"

"Buses full of farm workers. In a few years, all those jobs will be automated," Chip explained. "There's no reason to pay illegal immigrants to do work that can be so easily automated by robots at a quarter the cost."

Sam's gaze was fixed on the people below, scattered across fields in their ragtag attire of bright mismatched sweats and long-sleeved T-shirts with straw hats or baseball caps. Even from a distance, he could see how quickly they performed their backbreaking work, no doubt paid by the bushel for the strawberries, spinach, or artichokes they were harvesting. "Yeah, it's pretty monotonous work," Sam observed. "Perfect for robots, I guess."

"It's actually quite complex," Chip said. "Determining that a strawberry is ready to be picked requires a surprising amount of sensory perception—its size, color, aroma. If you pick it too soon, you have a useless, green, underripe berry. If you pick it too late, you have a rotten berry that could spread mold to an entire pint. Automating it requires sophisticated sensors and video analytics, as well as self-learning AI to continuously improve the harvest—not to mention a delicate picking mechanism that won't bruise the fruit."

"Wow. I guess I hadn't thought about how complicated it is," Sam conceded, deferring to Chip's superior fruit-picking expertise.

"Yes, but it's now possible at a price point that farmers can afford. No more labor shortages, no more complaints about working conditions, no more illegals. The entire system will pay for itself within the first season."

"You know a lot about automated farming," Sam said.

"I have an investment in an AI farming company," Chip said. "It's part of our portfolio in my billion-dollar investment fund, GeniusAI. Our entire investment thesis is to focus on businesses that will leverage AI to fully automate labor-intensive services industries."

"Interesting," Sam said.

"Yes, it's been fascinating, actually," Chip continued with budding enthusiasm. "We did an analysis of the largest services occupations in the country and identified those most likely to be automated. Of the ten largest occupations, we've made investments in companies that automate nine of them."

"Impressive."

"Indeed. That's almost twenty million jobs in the US alone that can be completely automated by AI. But you know which job is the hardest one to crack?" Chip asked rhetorically. "Registered nurses—there are almost three million of them scattered across the country, and they earn decent wages since there's a shortage. Most of what they actually *do* can be automated—taking vitals, administering medicine, moving patients around—that stuff is all easy. It's the human interaction, though, that's hard to replicate with a robot."

Sam looked back out the window at the field workers and their white school buses, unaware that a man whose entire investment strategy was to obviate their jobs was literally hovering over them. "Fascinating," he said. "I hadn't really thought about that part of a nurse's job. I can see why that's hard to replicate—the human touch, the emotion."

Chip, leaning back in his leather seat with his legs crossed, took another sip of his cappuccino. "We'll get there eventually. There's a groundbreaking study that was published by two psychology professors at MIT that showed the majority of people actually prefer simulated human interactions over real ones. The researchers hypothesized that the simulated human support was actually more gratifying to the recipients because it was more obsequious. The AI bot never tired of being affirmational and subservient. It learned what the recipient wanted to hear and repeated it indefinitely. It never needed reciprocal emotional support of its own. It's a fascinating next frontier, challenging whether even the deepest human emotions—compassion, companionship, even *love*—can be replicated by AI. We're getting close."

Not catching the abrupt change of subjects, Sam asked, "Do you have an investment in emotional AI as well?"

"No. We're getting close to Cypress Heights," Chip said, pointing out the window as they started their descent toward the spectacular coastline of the Monterey Peninsula. "Anyway, that's why I see Ainetu as so synergistic with our strategy. All these jobs we're talking about can be done more efficiently. There is an optimal way to clean a warehouse, or serve meals in a dining room, or drive on the highway. AI and human-autonomous deep-learning algorithms are *the* enabling technologies to automate all these jobs. Or instruct the few remaining employees what to do. With Ainetu's technology and our infrastructure of salespeople, distributors, and customers, we'll dominate the market. I'm talking 90 percent market share. No one else will be close."

Chip's words hung in the air as they all looked out their windows at the picturesque landing pad along the shore. A black Cadillac Escalade was awaiting their arrival. The helicopter touched down smoothly, and the whir of the engines started to slow as they gathered their belongings and exited the aircraft.

Cypress Heights was the private club for those who found Pebble Beach's $500 greens fee and public accessibility too pedestrian. As the third-ranked golf course in the country, the club's exclusive three-hundred-person membership included celebrities, heads of state, and, most of all, technology tycoons. At the clubhouse, Sam glanced at pictures of famous members and their equally famous guests adorning the walls, while the other men changed into their golf attire. Finally, they made their way down to the first tee. Chip strode confidently to the tee box, placed his ball, and blasted a beautiful drive straight onto the fairway. "That'll play. Sam, let's see what you've got."

Sam stepped up and placed his ball on the tee. Standing over it with his driver, he coached himself, *OK . . . nice steady swing; no need to crush it.* He then promptly disregarded his own advice and swung with a viciousness typically reserved for chopping wood or butchering a side of beef. Met with such blunt-force trauma, his ball whistled up on a disconcerting trajectory before spinning into a glorious slice into the Pacific Ocean.

"You can drop up there," Chip remarked, perhaps regretting the decision to suggest golf as their activity. David and Carlson both hit respectable drives, and the foursome embarked on their round.

"Good timing for you to come back to Ainetu," Chip said as the two of them pulled off in their cart.

"Possibly," Sam conceded. "Depends on where things go from here. A nonbinding LOI is a long way from a signed definitive agreement." Sam had been through the acquisition dance enough times to be cynical about the acquiring party's intentions. The tactics were almost as predictable as the plot twists in a romantic comedy—lob in a generous but nonbinding offer, to get the target company on the hook; insist on an exclusivity period during which the acquiree is prohibited from shopping the deal; perform extensive due diligence with an army of investment bankers and analysts; promptly share the confidential information turned over in diligence with their own internal teams so they can replicate the target company's product and business model; entangle the target company so long that they have no choice but to accept a lowball offer; or simply use the knowledge gained through the process to put the target company out of business. It is a brutal, lopsided fight, and it risks preoccupying the target company so completely that they never recover if a deal fails to consummate. "It's already been three weeks since the LOI, and it doesn't seem like we're making much progress."

"David tells me the delays have been on your side, what with the CEO transition," Chip said.

"Fair enough," Sam said, dropping a ball approximately where his went soaring out to its life at sea and hitting a more respectable shot, though still well short of the green.

"I'll be honest with you," Chip said as he pulled up to his ball. "I've been skeptical this deal is going to happen."

"Why is that?" Sam asked.

"Because there's obviously something wrong if you have an accounting snafu, fire your CFO, and replace your founder in the middle of an acquisition process," Chip said, glowering at Sam intensely, then turning to hit his second shot perfectly onto the green. "So, tell me . . . what the fuck is going on?"

Sam gathered himself as he adjusted his golf glove. "OK, I'll be honest with you. Our CFO, Bill Johnson, had been doctoring the books. It wasn't a huge amount—just enough to make sure we made our number each quarter. But after Rohan fired him, he took his own life."

"*Jesus* . . ." Chip sighed. "I'm sorry to hear that." He glanced over at Carlson, who was preparing to take a shot, then turned back to Sam. "Still, Rohan must have known about it if the board replaced him too."

"Not exactly," Sam said as the cart pulled toward the green.

"I feel like you're fucking with me, *Sam*," Chip said impatiently as they screeched to a halt. "I'll kill this deal right now, and you can walk home to Palo Alto."

"I'm not fucking with you," Sam said calmly as he pulled a club from his bag. "Isn't it obvious? The board knew they couldn't keep Rohan as CEO because if the deal happened and you all suspected Rohan knew about the bad financials, you'd sue us. But they couldn't fire him either because he was the point person on the deal and you all might pull out. So, they cut the baby in half and made him chairman."

"That doesn't make sense. If they thought he was complicit in the fraud, they should have fired him. Period. I don't give a shit about him."

"That's not what he told us. According to Rohan, you guys begged him to acquire the company and have him lead your AI business unit. Without him, the whole deal falls through."

"Ha!" Chip scoffed. "Rohan reached out to one of our VPs. I don't know him very well—Sanjay or something. Anyway, he connected Rohan with David, and we decided to take a closer look. The LOI was a good-faith gesture to show we're serious. But the tech is all we're interested in, not Rohan. Frankly, I never trusted the guy. He seemed passive-aggressive. Like he was going to fuck me over, the way he fucked you over."

"Obviously, you've done your diligence," Sam said, tacitly acknowledging the circumstances around his departure.

"I don't drop half a billion dollars without doing some homework." Chip said, lining up his putt and dropping it into the cup for a birdie. He pointed his putter at David, who was walking up to his shot. "I told David to figure out what was going on, and he called an HBS classmate of his who is a partner with your board member, Kamal, at OakGrove Capital."

"He told me Rohan fired you because of something you said at a conference," David said as he lined up his own putt.

"That was the reason given to the employees," Sam said. "But the real reason is I caught on to the accounting issues. When I confronted Rohan about it, he fired me."

David and Carlson exchanged glances, but Chip squinted at Sam skeptically. "Why didn't you raise it with the board?" he asked.

"I did. That's why they eventually brought me back—to clean it up."

"I don't like it," Chip said, addressing his remark to David and Carlson as if Sam were suddenly no longer there. "Sketchy financials, founder drama, a board asleep at the switch—it's more trouble than it's worth." He waved his hand as if swatting away a gnat.

"You won't need to worry about any of that. The financials are cleaned up, and I'll personally see to it that Rohan is gone once and for all, so there will be no founder drama."

"Give me one reason I shouldn't kill this deal right now," Chip demanded.

"You said it yourself on the flight down here. We'll dominate the market. This is a no-brainer. You can't lose. A $500 million deal is chump change for you guys, especially since this is an all-stock transaction. Prism's market cap will jump by way more than that when this deal is announced. A 1 percent increase in your stock price is worth, what, $2 billion? Ainetu's a hot company. This deal could give you a stock pop of 5 percent or more. No other acquisition you're considering has that potential. Plus, you have a 10b5-1 scheduled stock sale coming up in a month, Chip, so we better get this announced before then."

Chip stared intently at Sam for a moment. The other two men held their putters in silence, awaiting a cue from their boss. Then, with a slight chuckle at Sam's moxie, he asked, "Speaking of equity, what did they put yours at?"

"About 8 percent," Sam replied.

"Not bad. You should be at ten, but eight's not bad. And what are preferences?" he asked, referring to the guaranteed return venture investors received from their preferred shares.

"Just over one hundred," Sam answered.

"Great, so you'll make a huge return for your investors and pocket $40 million yourself, before tax," Chip said. "You'll be set for life."

"That's the plan," Sam said, allowing himself a slight smile as the foursome returned to their carts.

"You know, I think you could have real potential within Prism," Chip said, steering the cart through a winding path. "We've done over twenty diligence calls on you, and the feedback has been very positive. I could see you running our analytics division. Do you know what that role pays?" Chip asked. Sam shook his head. "One million in annual base salary, plus a 100 percent bonus and a stock options package that could earn you millions more."

"That sounds like an incredible opportunity," Sam said. "But a deal needs to happen first before my potential with Prism can be realized."

"Don't worry. We'll get it done. So, how do you like the course?" Chip asked as they pulled up to the next tee.

"It's incredible," Sam replied, juxtaposing the breathtaking coastline with his recent round on the landfill at Mariners Point. "A once-in-a-lifetime experience."

"It doesn't have to be once in a lifetime," Chip said. "If this deal closes, I'll recommend you to the membership committee."

CHAPTER 25:

COPIER ROOM

THE BAY WAS ALWAYS SO MESMERIZING in the early morning. As the fog fought to hold on to its overnight reign, the rising sun burned away the remaining wisps to reveal a bright blue sky above the morning bustle. From Sam's vantage point in his office, he could see a wide expanse of the city's panorama, from Alcatraz and Coit Tower to the Ferry Building and Bay Bridge. A flock of seagulls frolicked among the vintage trams traversing the Embarcadero. A Princess cruise ship the size of a ten-story hotel disgorged its passengers onto Fisherman's Wharf. A pontoon ferry transported commuters from Marin who impatiently stood on the deck with their bicycles. A tugboat escorted a gigantic freighter stacked impossibly high with shipping containers in from the Pacific Ocean. A tower crane lifted building supplies to a construction crew high in the steel skeleton of a new building. An endless stream of cars on the Bay Bridge flowed like corpuscles into the arteries of the city. These and hundreds of other diversions momentarily distracted Sam from the more urgent issues preoccupying his mind.

Since his golf outing with the Prism team, their due diligence had picked up pace. Sam had misgivings about providing so much confidential information to a company that was, in effect, one of their top competitors. Yet failing to do so would ensure the deal would die. No acquirer would spend $500 million without such a degree of visibility into what they were buying. Each shared file, however, made him wince. Maybe Prism was just playing a game, entangling Ainetu in a courtship they never intended to consummate. If a deal was going to happen, it needed to happen quickly. Prism had agreed to Sam's thirty-day deadline, but it came with a price—they insisted on an exclusivity period during which Ainetu could not shop the deal to other potential acquirers. Already, they were halfway through the thirty days.

Turning from the panorama in his window, Sam saw Jessie through his glass office wall. She had just arrived and looked exhausted, but she indicated she needed to talk with him. Sam waved for her to come in.

"What's up?" he asked as she opened his office door.

"I have an update on the sexual harassment claim I told you about," she said. "I sent some emails to a few other HR leaders I trust. About a half dozen replied and said they'd had complaints about Preston as well."

"*Really?*" Sam said.

"Yes, really," she said. "And that was just from reaching out to HR people I know. I haven't even gone to other Ellipsis portfolio companies or start-ups who pitched them. I'll bet there are dozens of women who would make claims against him."

"Have any of them gone public?" Sam asked.

"Not as far as I know," Jessie said. "But everyone I spoke to had documented the accusations with their HR teams, since the incidents took place either with employees or at company events. There were two from BroFest—shocker, I know. Another was a former admin at Ellipsis who quit when he wouldn't stop groping her. A female founder who was pitching Ellipsis said Preston pinned her to a wall at a company holiday party. And so on."

"Wow," Sam said, shaking his head.

"Yeah," Jessie replied. "He's basically a predator."

Sam nodded, then asked, "Who here even interacts with him, though? Nicole talks to him from time to time about board logistics, but he mostly ignores her. I've never seen him show an interest in Kelly at the front desk. Other than that, it's just the exec team. But that's almost always in a group setting. The only time I can think of where we got into a smaller group was around the sales numbers with . . ." Sam froze his train of thought, knowing he'd arrived on the victim. "*Amanda*." Jessie looked down at the table, her silence providing all the confirmation Sam needed. "OK. I need to talk to her."

"She wanted to remain anonymous. I promised her," Jessie said.

"I understand. I'll make it clear you didn't tell me," Sam said.

"What are you going to say?" Jessie asked.

"I just want to hear directly from her what happened," Sam said.

Jessie regarded Sam intently as she considered her next words. "I don't suppose I can change your mind," she finally said.

"Look," said Sam. "I've worked with Amanda a long time. She's the first person I hired. I'll handle this discreetly."

Jessie let out a restrained sigh. "Then I guess you might as well have this," she said, pulling a CD from the file folder on her lap.

"What's that?" Sam asked as she slid it across his desk.

"It's a video," Jessie said. "The whole incident was captured on one of the security cameras."

"*Jesus Christ*. So is she going to press charges?" Sam asked.

"I don't think so. Like I said, she wants to be anonymous," Jessie said, shrugging her shoulders. "She never even would have reported it to HR if it weren't for the video."

Sam gave her an inquisitive look. "So how did *you* get the video?"

"It just showed up in the mail," she said, standing from her chair. "Bill must have sent it. He managed the facilities team, so he probably had access to the security footage. There was a sticky note on it in his handwriting that just said, 'This is the only copy.' So keep that in a safe place."

As Jessie left his office, Sam held up the CD, tilting it in the sunlight, reflecting a spectrum of colors against the wall. Then he spun his chair around to face the tapestry of the city outside his window. His gaze stopped on a small sailboat bobbing among the chop of the bay. Despite its fully deployed mainsail, the boat made only painstakingly gradual progress in the unusually calm morning breeze. Larger ships navigating the bay at faster speeds seemed barely to avoid capsizing the vessel. Ferries, freighters, and tugboats all generated conflicting wakes that crashed against the sailboat's hull. It wasn't entirely clear which direction it was trying to head, with its mast at an odd angle as it tacked across the bay. Gradually, he lost sight of it behind a skyscraper.

■ ■ ■

Sam entered the conference room where the executive team was assembled. Their chatter subsided as he took a seat at the head of the table. Sam let the ensuing silence hang expectantly for a few moments, making sure he had their full attention. "As you all know, we have some difficult decisions in front of us," Sam began. "Rohan and Bill really painted us into a corner. I'm exploring some strategic options."

"You mean selling the company," said Anton, their head of marketing, looking to clarify. "James thinks we're getting acquired," he added, referring to his husband.

"Possibly," Sam said. "But I don't want us all to get distracted by something that most likely isn't going to happen. And with the recent financial irregularities, it will be difficult to raise money from a new investor. So we need to assume that the cash we have is all the cash we're going to get."

"What does that mean?" Amanda asked.

"It means we need to prepare for the scenario where we are self-sufficient—cash-flow breakeven," Sam said. "And that will require a head count reduction of about 70 percent of our employees. So I want each of you to send me your cut list by the end of the day. Assume we're letting go of seven out of ten people in your organization. Some teams will be more, some will be less, so send me your list in order of priority—from the most essential employees to the least."

"*Jesus*, Sam," Amanda said. "If I cut that many sales reps, our revenue will go off a cliff. I can't just expect the remaining reps to pick up all that quota."

"The cuts won't be as deep on the sales team, but we can't let revenue decline," Sam replied curtly. "If we do, then we'll just need to cut head count further. We are counting on the sales reps who remain to hit the revenue number."

Amanda looked down at the pen she clenched between her fingers. "I can't hit our revenue target with half the sales team, Sam."

"Yes, you can. We have to," he replied. "Each of the reps will pick up new leads from the folks who aren't here anymore. Plus, they'll get paid full commission on those deals. So this is a chance for the reps who are still here to make a lot of money."

Amanda tapped her pen against the tabletop and squinted quizzically at Sam, clearly questioning the viability of his proposal but not wanting to challenge it further in front of the group.

"All this because of Bill?" Zhang, their CTO, asked.

"Yes," Sam replied. "And Rohan. We just don't have many options. Let's all keep our fingers crossed that an acquisition comes through, but we need to prepare for the worst."

Ajay, their acting head of finance, had remained silent. "Are you tracking this, Ajay?" Sam asked him. "I know you and Bill worked closely together and it's a lot to take in. But I need you to create a new budget that consolidates the cost reductions and gets us into the black."

"It's not that," Ajay said quietly without altering his detached expression. "He sent me an email."

"Who did?"

"Bill, on the day he died," Ajay said, transfixed by his own thoughts. "He sent it to my personal email. All it said was 'Double-check the accounts payable' in the subject line."

"Accounts *payable*?" Sam asked. "It was our *receivables* where we had the fraudulent accounting. Why would the invoices we pay other vendors matter?"

"I think I know," Ajay said. "Give me some time this morning to research it."

"OK, let me know what you find out. In the meantime, we need to find a path to profitability ASAP, so send me your cost-reduction plans by the end of the day," Sam said. He looked around the conference table, but nobody had anything more to say. "OK, you know what you need to do, folks. This is why they pay us the big bucks."

As the executive team began to disperse, Sam caught Amanda's attention. "Can you hold up for a minute?" he asked. Amanda nodded and sat back down in her chair. Once the conference room was empty, he turned to her and said, "So Jessie informed me there's been a sexual harassment complaint filed against one of our board members." Amanda stiffened in her seat but didn't say anything. "She said the alleged incident took place right here in the copier room, so there's surveillance-camera footage of the whole thing."

"Why are you telling me this?"

"Well . . . besides Jessie and Nicole, the only other female employee who has regular interactions with our board members is *you*."

"*Goddamn it!*" she burst out, her face flushed. "I *knew* I shouldn't have told Jessie! I told her to destroy that video. I don't want anybody to know about this."

"I totally respect that," Sam replied. "And, if that's what you want, I will keep it *100 percent* confidential. But don't get mad at Jessie. She had to report it to me. And I just guessed it was you."

Amanda was fuming. She was normally so calm and collected. Sam had never seen her like this and couldn't tell if the expression on her face was anger, embarrassment, frustration, or all of the above—and more. "You don't need to worry about it," she finally said, her nostrils flaring.

"I *am* worried about it," Sam replied. "I'm worried about *you*. I want to make sure you're all right. You know I always have your back."

"I don't need you to defend me," she said. "Not everything is a problem for you to fix, Sam. I can defend myself. This has happened to me before. That's why I formally lodged the complaint. So if it happens again, I have this incident on the record."

"Wait, you've been harassed before? *Here? At this company?*" Sam asked.

"No, I mean it's happened before in my *career*. It happens to a lot of women in tech."

"OK. Are you planning to expose him?"

"And ruin my career, like he threatened to do? Why would I do that? Do you have any idea how much bullshit I've had to endure to become a head of sales in the Valley? It comes with the territory. I'm not going to throw that all away just 'cause a board member grabbed my crotch."

"OK, I get it," Sam said. "Honestly, that's also the best thing for the company. It wouldn't exactly be great publicity as we're trying to close this deal."

A scornful look flickered across Amanda's face before she said, "I agree. Like I told you, I'm fine. Get this fucking company sold."

■ ■ ■

The camera was hardly hidden. Easily discovered with a cursory inspection of the copier room ceiling, it was one of only two security cameras on their floor, the other in the lobby. It had been placed there for what purpose Sam could only imagine. *Were we worried about employees stealing toner cartridges?* He recalled his last time in this room, the hushed conversation with Amanda moments after he was fired. Protecting office supplies was perhaps not the motivation for the camera at all—more so the secret meetings that tended to happen in this room, one of the only private places in the entire office. The thought caused Sam to realize his fire alarm pull was potentially caught on the other camera, sitting in some video archive on a server waiting to be discovered.

"I figured out what Bill was referring to!" Ajay said, bursting into the copier room holding his laptop in one hand and pointing at the screen with the other.

Sam startled, less from the abrupt entrance than the fact that he had been caught pondering the scene of the crime. "*Dammit*, don't sneak up on me like that."

"Sorry," Ajay said, catching his breath as if his act of spreadsheet sleuthing had required physical exertion. His demeanor, simultaneously agitated and eager, had completely changed since the exec meeting minutes earlier. "Here, look at this." Ajay set his laptop on the counter and again pointed to the screen. "After we found those deals where we were misrecognizing revenue, it got me wondering about recurring revenue from older customers. I was curious what the durations of some of those earlier deals were, so I looked at the contracts and I noticed something interesting. A bunch of them are actually *holding* companies based in the Cayman Islands. I always wondered about these customers. They renewed their subscriptions every year, they always paid on time, they never called customer support, but I noticed that I also couldn't find any users from those companies actually *logging in* to our software."

"That's odd," Sam said.

"Yeah, curious, right? But that's not even the interesting part," Ajay replied. "I also checked our accounts payable, as Bill's email suggested. I remembered Rohan had me paying a bunch of random marketing consultants, so I checked those first. I was never sure what these firms were actually doing, but he told me just to pay them. And *guess what*? When I added it all up, the amount we billed these offshore companies was the exact same amount we paid these marketing consultants—$3,975,000," he said, pointing to the figure highlighted in yellow on his spreadsheet.

"Holy *shit*," Sam moaned. He glanced out the copier room entrance to make sure no employees were nearby, then continued in a whisper. "Are you telling me that we laundered almost four million dollars through our company and recognized it as revenue?"

"I'm afraid so. And that was just in the last year. This has grown each year over the last four years—the cumulative now is over ten million."

"*Unbelievable*," Sam said, shaking his head. "How is it that *nobody* on the finance team discovered this?"

"I know," Ajay said. "I just . . . I always had questions about these customers and the expenses. Whenever I mentioned it to Bill, he told me not to worry about it. I guess I just never put two and two together until now. I never imagined he was hiding something like this."

"*Shit, shit, shit!*" Sam said, his hand pressed to his forehead as he stared at Ajay's spreadsheet. He was fucked. He had unwittingly taken the helm of a company built on a giant fraud. If Prism found out, the deal would surely be dead. If he hid this information, he would be complicit in committing a crime. The walls of the copier room felt like they were closing in on him.

"There's something else," Ajay added cautiously.

"Oh, wait . . . there's *more?*" Sam said sarcastically.

"All these customers who have been paying us and all these agencies who have been invoicing us are owned by the same parent company."

"Paragon Enterprises, Incorporated," they said in unison. Of course; it was Preston's dad's media conglomerate.

"Jesus Christ," Sam sighed. "Shouldn't the auditors have caught this?"

"They probably *should* have," Ajay said. "Then again, the auditors were recommended to us by Preston. We've never worked with them prior to this audit."

"OK . . . ," Sam said. How was it possible he'd been at the company most of that time without realizing something was off? This couldn't be blamed on a bookkeeping error. This was obvious, outright fraud, hiding in plain sight. And their previous scapegoat was already dead. Rohan, Preston, Ben, Kamal—they had all fucked him. Had they brought him back simply to be the patsy?

"What do you think we should do?" Ajay finally asked.

"I don't know yet," Sam said, looking up at Ajay. "Just keep it to yourself for now, until I figure out what to do."

CHAPTER 26:

TREADING WATER

BEAMS OF SUNLIGHT PIERCED the family room window, illuminating a constellation of dust particles that encircled Sam. He sat on the couch staring vacantly at his laptop, lost in the thoughts that had awakened him hours earlier. Heather was still asleep. Not that it mattered. They had eased back into a tentative détente since Sam's midnight golf outburst—exchanging only desultory remarks, each avoiding the lightning rod subject of Sam's decision to return. Listening to his latest problems at Ainetu was the last thing she would want to hear, and he was equally uninterested in the "I told you so" he was apt to hear in return. As the birds outside began greeting the sunrise, Sam returned his attention to the open spreadsheet and the grim reality he was facing at the company.

They were running out of cash. That was the bottom line of the analysis Ajay had prepared. They couldn't wait any longer to reduce their expenses, and there wasn't enough time to raise another round of financing—even if they could do so under reasonable terms. The lunch with the Prism team, which had finally been scheduled for that day, was make-or-break. They would either have a definitive acquisition agreement ready for signature by Thursday, or Sam would need to lay off the majority of the company.

As unlikely as the acquisition already seemed, it felt preposterous given the additional revelations Ajay and Jessie had uncovered. Not wanting the incriminating files residing on Ainetu's corporate network or even his company-issued laptop, Sam had taken to stashing the evidence on the USB drive—like a digital Rosetta stone of the company's misdeeds. In addition to the documents Bill had meticulously organized that decoded the accounting scheme, Sam had uploaded a list of the fake customer accounts, incorporation documents linking those shell companies to the media empire of Cameron Lawrence, and invoices for promotional services that were never rendered. He even created a folder that contained the HR complaint Jessie had compiled detailing Amanda's sexual assault, along with the grainy black-and-white video of the incident itself caught on the office security camera—the original CD promptly put through the shredder. It was all there on the USB drive, waiting for Sam to decide what to do with it.

So far, in the ensuing week, Sam had decided not to do *anything* with the new information, beyond sequestering it on the drive. He just couldn't be sure who on the board besides Preston was in on the fake accounts, and there was no point in disclosing the fraud to Prism when he wasn't even sure if they were going to submit a definitive acquisition offer at all. Best for now, he thought, to hold on to that information until they showed their cards.

Eager to meet, Sam was the first to arrive at Boulevard for lunch. The restaurant, with stunning views of the waterfront and Bay Bridge, was a favorite of San Francisco's old guard. Waiting for the others to arrive, Sam took a seat at the mahogany bar near a multitiered tower of seafood. The once-threatening claws of lobsters and crabs now dangled inanimately. Sam had also invited Ben Bentley to the lunch to represent the board. Shortly after Ben arrived, David from Prism and Carlson, the investment banker from Bronson & Associates, strode through the revolving door and they all were seated at a prime table facing the bay.

After some small talk and placing their orders, Sam zeroed in on the purpose of the meeting. "So, I'm eager to hear where we stand, given Thursday is the end of our thirty-day exclusivity period," Sam said.

"Yes, understandably so," Carlson said. "First, thanks for being so forthright through this process. Your team has been expeditious in providing the documentation we need for our diligence."

"Of course," Sam said, bracing himself for the "but" that seemed likely to follow. "It's all part of the process. If we expect you to move fast, we have to move fast ourselves."

"As you know, the price we proposed in our LOI was . . . very generous," Carlson continued. "It was predicated on a projected growth rate, and, even then, it was a very high multiple of revenue."

Sam shot a glance at Ben but remained silent. He could see where this was headed but wanted them to at least provide a rationale.

"What Carlson is diplomatically saying is there's no way we can keep our offer price at $500 million," David interjected. "We just can't justify a 10X multiple to the Street at your current growth rate."

Sam took a moment to process David's comments. They seemed to be taking Ainetu's revenue numbers as reported, at face value. The justification for a lower offer didn't seem to be based on any new information, so Sam decided to push back. "But you've had the restated financials for over a month now and didn't amend the offer price in your LOI. What changed?"

David and Carlson looked at each other before Carlson picked up the "good cop" side of the conversation. "Nothing really *changed*, per se. We just hadn't yet had the opportunity to put the deal through our model." As the banker, Carlson was trying to walk a fine line. While Prism was indisputably his client, he only got paid his commission if a deal was consummated. So his incentive was to play the role of intermediary and bring the two sides together.

David was more impatient. "Look, you guys also don't exactly have a strong balance sheet. With less than a quarter of operating cash, you don't have a lot of options."

"We don't need a lot of options. As I mentioned before, I was brought back to *run* the company, not *sell* it," Sam said. "We're entirely prepared to walk away from this deal."

"When you say 'we,' I'm not sure exactly whom you mean, but I can assure you that not all your board members share that view," David said in a mildly threatening tone.

"Well, that will depend on the offer price, won't it?" Ben said, having been silent to that point. "I'm here on behalf of our board today."

"So . . . where do we stand?" Sam asked, pressing the issue as he turned back to David and Carlson. "Are you prepared to submit a definitive offer, or have we reached the end of the line?"

"Yes," Carlson intervened, again trying to temper the conversation from becoming adversarial. "We're still prepared to submit a definitive offer, but we want to set expectations that the price will be lower. And there will also be some . . . *conditions* in the agreement. To protect us from various downside scenarios. I'm sure you understand."

"Obviously, we can't assure you that whatever you're offering will get approved, but Ben and I will at least present it to our full board. So let's start with the important part: *What's the number?*"

"Right," Carlson proceeded cautiously. "This is still a very generous offer. It has the potential to be a $200 million deal."

"What do you mean *potential*?" Sam asked skeptically, already choking on a number that was a fraction of their original offer.

"We're proposing we structure the deal in stages, with an earnout based on the company's future performance," Carlson said.

"So the *max* would be $200 million?" Ben asked.

"That's correct," Carlson nodded.

"And what would be the *minimum*?" Sam asked. "What are we guaranteed?"

"That would be the *initial* offer amount, which would be $100 million," Carlson explained.

Sam bristled at the figure. Leaning forward, he asked incredulously, "You're telling me that after entangling us in an exclusivity period for the last month, you're coming back with an offer that is *20 percent* of your original offer?"

"I wouldn't characterize it that way," Carlson said, as David allowed himself a subtle but self-satisfied smirk. "You have the opportunity to earn twice that in the final consideration. Achieving the milestones for the additional earnout should be a no-brainer."

"What did you have in mind for the performance milestones?" Sam asked.

"Well, you're forecasting revenue next year of about $50 million, right?" Carlson started. "We think the business can do better than that, so we have next year's revenue target at $75 million. Then with Prism's sales machine, we think we can be on a 2X ramp the next two years."

"So, like, $150 million in year two and $300 million in year three?" Sam calculated.

"Precisely," Carlson said, as if the expectation were exceedingly reasonable.

"So you expect us to close over half a billion in revenue in three years, in order to earn another $100 million in potential deal value?" Sam asked.

"Yes, but powered by the synergies of Prism's global distribution infrastructure," David said.

"No offense, but your '*global distribution infrastructure*' can't sell this product for shit," Sam said. "Your sales reps only get business apps. They don't understand AI—that's why you're struggling so much with your current analytics product. It's a different skill set, different call point, different competitors. You can't just hand your reps a data sheet and expect them to grow this business tenfold in three years! That's a ridiculous assumption. We'll never see that earnout. This is a *nonstarter*, guys!"

Sam stared expectantly at both men. He had known all along that a $500 million deal was improbable. Why would Prism pay such a steep premium when Ainetu had no other suitors and so little remaining cash? He also recognized his soapbox tirade was completely undermined by what he now knew about the fraudulent accounts. At that moment, though, he didn't care. Here these guys were, throwing their weight around to screw him over—just as he had expected them to do. Was their bait-and-switch tactic any less ethical?

"I've sold a lot of companies in my career," Ben interjected. "But I've never seen an acquirer cut their offer by 80 percent days before closing. I'd hate for word to get around to other start-ups that Prism operates in bad faith."

Carlson looked to David for a cue on how to proceed. "OK," David conceded, for the first time taking a slightly less contentious stance. "Maybe we can go back and sharpen our pencils with the earnout milestones. But that basic structure of an up-front payment and milestones over the next three years is the only way we're going to get our number and your number to meet."

Their entrées arrived and an uncomfortable pause in the conversation ensued as the waiter described their dishes. Closing this deal seemed like an increasingly lost cause. If Prism had stuck to their original price, then Sam could have disclosed the fake customer accounts—clearing his conscience but, hopefully, still salvaging a deal, albeit likely at a lower price. Now there was no room to maneuver. The likelihood that Prism would just walk away at the news of a second financial transgression seemed almost certain. His only course, it seemed, was to secure their reduced offer in writing and then decide how to proceed. At least then he would have a bird in the hand.

Sam broke the silence. "OK. As I said, I think it's unlikely we will accept that offer, but it will be up to our board," he said, gesturing toward Ben with his fork. "Send us the details that you're proposing, and we'll review it. Can you get that to me by Monday?"

Carlson picked his phone up from the table and typed a quick message. "I'm having the definitive agreement sent to you now," he said. The fact that the documents were already drawn up was further proof of how confident they were that Ainetu would have no choice but to accept their lower offer.

Sam felt his face flush with anger. He was going to fail. Every doubt that Rohan and Peter and the board had expressed would come true.

He didn't have what it took to get the deal done. Already, he'd lost $400 million in deal value, but even at the reduced price he saw no possibility of closing it. Between the revenue irregularities and the fake accounts and the sexual assault, Prism would certainly leave him at the altar. He would immediately have to cut head count in a desperate attempt to stay in business, if he didn't get fired again first. He'd be finished—his reputation in the Valley destroyed. Even if the deal somehow did close, he wouldn't even make any money since his stock would be worthless at that price. But at that moment he was motivated more by the fear of failure than the fruits of success. *Stay on the horse. Don't fall off. Don't give up. Don't ever give up—no matter what,* Sam told himself as he quietly finished his meal.

■　■　■

"Well, that sucked," Sam said the moment he and Ben exited the restaurant.

"Why do you say that?" Ben asked calmly.

Sam stopped walking and turned to look at Ben. "The whole reason I came back was to do this deal. They just totally screwed us. They know we don't have any other options, so they're just going to lowball us. If we agree to one hundred, who's to say they won't cut it again to fifty, or twenty?"

"That's not going to happen," Ben reassured. "This is a negotiation, Sam. We'll get more than $100 million as a starting offer. This Carlson guy at Bronson is a nobody. I know Blake Bronson from Stanford GSB. I was on the deal that put his shitty little investment bank on the map. I've been waiting to play that card. But with a written offer on the table, it's time for me to call Blake and tell him what it will take to get this deal done."

"That's great for you, but unless it's over $120 million, it won't matter—we'll be below the liquidation preferences. So all the proceeds would go to the preferred shareholders—you and the other VCs. The *common* shareholders, including me, will make nothing."

"Yeah, that price isn't great for the common shareholders," Ben acknowledged. "But it could work out fine for you." He looked pensively up and down the Embarcadero, then asked, "You want a coffee? Let's go to the Ferry Building."

"How do you figure?" Sam asked as he pressed the button at the crosswalk.

"Well, you're right that your stock will be worthless, but we'll set up an executive carve-out for you and any other execs you select," Ben explained. The ping of alternating sound waves invited them to cross the busy intersection. "It would be a fixed percentage—usually around 10 percent of the final sale price."

Sam, who hadn't been fishing for such an offer, briefly contemplated its implications. Although he would personally pocket millions, it was, in effect, a bribe to go along with a deal that was very unfavorable to every other employee.

"OK . . . but there's another problem. We found more fraud. Nearly a dozen accounts that don't really exist. They're shell companies. Part of Preston's dad's media empire. They pay us for imaginary contracts, and we pay them for imaginary advertising buys."

Ben contemplated the bay as they walked along the Embarcadero, weaving through joggers, dog walkers, and rickshaws filled with tourists. "There's nothing wrong with buying services from a customer who also buys services from you," he responded. "It happens all the time."

"*Bullshit!* They haven't even logged in to our software. And the sum of their expenditures on Ainetu precisely equals the amount of supposed services we've purchased from them. This is washing each other's laundry, to the tune of almost $4 million in revenue last year alone. We're just swapping imaginary business to fluff up each other's top line."

Ben was momentarily silent again as they entered the Ferry Building. "How did you discover this?"

"Ajay in our accounting department found it," Sam replied in a hushed voice to avoid being overheard. "But it wasn't hard, frankly. All you needed to know was which accounts to look at and then be capable of second-grade math. How are we going to close this deal knowing there's significant additional fraud on our books? They will find this. We have to divulge it or clear it up somehow before the deal closes."

"Uh-huh," Ben said as they stood in line to order coffee, then found a quiet corner to wait for their drinks. "Look, Sam, this wouldn't be the first time Prism has been sold a bill of goods. Shit, they bought Blue Onyx, and those guys didn't even have a functioning product. Chip knows the biggest win is the stock pop they get from buying a hot new tech company. We have a great product, great customers, great employees. It's a great acquisition for them. At the end of the day, it's not going to matter if there's a little hair on the deal."

"This is more than just 'hair on the deal.' This is outright fraud. There's no way to sugarcoat it. We would be personally liable."

"Nobody's going to get sued, Sam. Not after the deal closes. You think they would let this information get out to their shareholders? You've got to put this in perspective. We're talking about *Prism* here. They're one of the largest companies in the world. Chip is a billionaire a gazillion times over. Who *cares* if they pay a little extra for this deal? They have the money."

Sam contemplated Ben's comment for a moment. There was undeniably a bit of "steal from the rich" Robin Hood appeal to how Ben characterized the situation. *Who am I protecting, after all?* The Prism team had just jumped at the chance to screw him over. Why was he looking out for *them*? Wasn't there a certain justice to screwing them right back? Sam retrieved their coffees, and they exited toward the docks as a ferry to Sausalito began boarding.

"You seem pretty confident," Sam said, blowing on the rim of his cup.

"I wouldn't call it confidence. I'm just saying we're not fucked—not yet, at least," Ben said. "I think we can get to a definitive offer. That's not the problem. The problem is Rohan. We need him out."

"Seriously?" Sam said, turning to scowl at Ben. "I've been trying to get him out of the company since I started, but you guys won't do it."

"No, that's not what I mean. We don't just need him out of the company. We need to get back his founder's shares. Otherwise, we won't be able to fund the carve-out."

They sat on a bench facing the bay. Ben took a slow sip of his coffee as seagulls gathered around them, hoping for crumbs.

"So, how do we get him out?" Sam asked.

"Well, you tried to do it before, but you didn't understand the board dynamics," Ben said. "We saw the mismanagement, but each of us had our reasons for keeping him around. For me, I didn't want to jeopardize the Prism deal. But that's not a concern anymore. For Preston, he and Rohan go way back, but that's not his reason. His real concern is the false accounts—he has to trust that you won't let that get out."

"And go to jail over it?" Sam asked.

"I'm just telling you how to navigate this," Ben said. "Kamal is the trickiest. He doesn't know about the false-account stuff, but he's extremely loyal. Rohan is his cousin."

"What? I never knew that."

"Yeah, but he's a high-integrity guy. If he finds out there was wrongdoing, maybe he would flip—even though Rohan is family."

Sam tapped the side of his paper cup and watched the ferry ignite its engine in a plume of smoke before it set off into the bay. "So all I have to do is secure a definitive agreement for more money, enlist our board members to oust our founder, then close the deal without anyone discovering the steaming pile of fraud underneath, and maybe, just *maybe*, I'll get some ambiguously promised carve-out? Is that the plan?"

"Yeah, pretty much," Ben agreed, smiling at Sam's sarcasm. "You're just forgetting one thing."

"What's that?" Sam asked, shooing a pigeon away with his foot.

"Who else knows what's on that USB drive?"

CHAPTER 27:

VENTUREMASH

SAM LOOKED DOWN AT the sidewalk, onto which were projected the words *Welcome to the Battery* in crisp white light. Passing a homeless man slumped against a potted plant, Sam entered the impossibly hip, invitation-only private club at the corner of Battery Street and Pacific. Inside, a hostess led him through the dimly lit retrofitted loft space of exposed brick to the glass elevators leading to the roof deck. The Battery hosted exclusive events for its members, from luxury tequila tastings to burlesque shows, spinning classes to charity benefits—and, occasionally, it hosted parties.

VentureMash was one such party. Held each year in an ever-more dazzling location, the event was the blowout annual soirée for Bernstein & Levin, one of the premier venture law firms in the Bay Area. Gathering upward of five hundred attendees, most of the top VCs and start-up CEOs were there. Sam had attended for years and could always count on the event for bumping into folks he knew. With the Prism deal dangling by a thread, Sam felt like he was on an impossible mission. He needed a drink.

Weaving his way through the crowd toward the bar, Sam encountered Joseph Levin, the founding partner and host. "Sam Hughes! Great to see you," Joseph said as they shook hands. Joseph was a wine aficionado and prodigious collector, so he always stocked the event with cases of premium wines from his personal cellar. His capacity to remember the names of rare vintages was exceeded only by his photographic memory of the names of everyone on the invite list.

"Great to see you too, Joe. What are you pouring tonight?" Sam asked with a nod toward the bar.

"There's an unbelievable Sangiovese from Umbria," Joseph said, leaning in conspiratorially. "It's under the bar, but tell them I sent you and they'll pour you a glass. It'll blow your mind."

After procuring a glass of the secret wine, which was spectacular, Sam made his way to the hand-carved charcuterie station for some impossibly paper-thin slices of prosciutto, which were clipped to a canopy of wires by clothespins. As he dangled a slice into his mouth, Sam noticed Quinn Randall from *TechWrap* approaching quickly.

"Sam Hughes, fancy seeing you here," Quinn said with atypical enthusiasm. "I have to say, I'm impressed."

Sam tilted his head sideways in a curious expression. "Why's that?"

"You did it," he declared. "You turned it around. I thought Ainetu was veering toward the dead pool, but I heard today you're about to get acquired. Congratulations!"

How the hell does he know this? As Sam stammered for a reply, he realized Quinn could just be fishing based on a rumor. Literally, all *TechWrap* cared about was scoops, so he couldn't do anything that would reveal what was really happening.

"What gives you that impression?" Sam finally asked deadpan.

"Oh, just a little birdie whispering in my ear. But I don't know yet who the buyer is. Say nothing if it's Salesforce."

"It's not Salesforce," Sam replied, immediately regretting taking the bait.

"So you *are* getting acquired then," Quinn said with satisfaction at the trap he'd laid.

"Quinn, you know I can't tell you anything, sorry," Sam said.

"*C'mon!* I'm ready to publish this story, but you've got to at least confirm a deal is in the works, and, preferably, who the buyer is."

"Not a chance, Quinn."

"Not a chance of *what*?" Quinn would not relent. "That you'll tell me who the *buyer* is? Because . . . if you weren't getting acquired, you'd tell me 'we're not getting acquired,' and you're not saying that."

"You're overthinking it, Quinn," Sam replied. "I'm just telling you I don't have anything to tell you right now."

"But if there *wasn't* anything to tell me, you'd tell me that, and you're *not* telling me that," Quinn persisted.

"Jesus, Quinn—you're like a dog with a bone," Sam said. "Look, I don't know what you've heard, but as soon as there's something to announce, you'll be the first to know."

"You *promise*?" Quinn asked.

"Yes, Quinn, I pinkie *fucking* promise," Sam said, extending his pinkie finger. "Now, stop harassing me. I'm going to have to get a restraining order, for Christ's sake!"

"OK, I'll let you off the hook for now," Quinn relented. "But I get this scoop, right?"

"Yes, I promise. Now, let me do some networking," Sam said, placing his hand on Quinn's shoulder and pushing past him into the crowd.

Who leaked that to him? Sam pondered as he walked away. Possibly someone on the Prism side, but if that were the case, Quinn would have known who the potential acquirer was. That suggested the leak was on their side. Probably Rohan, trying to create momentum behind the deal—maybe get another bidder interested. Quinn could post something to *TechWrap* at any time. If any article did appear and mentioned Prism, it could kill the deal. They were disciplined about avoiding bidding wars for companies and would not look kindly on a tactic meant to provoke just such a scenario.

Sam was scanning the room for his next conversation, but it found him first. Closing in was Cory Campbell, the founder of Marvel.io and sparring partner on the SaaStr stage. "Hey, Sam. I didn't know you guys were raising money again already."

"Hi, Cory," said Sam. "What gives you that idea?"

"Why else would you be at VentureMash if you weren't kissing up to the VCs?"

"Oh, I just come here for the charcuterie. How are you doing?"

"We're *crushing* it!" Cory interjected before the question was fully out of Sam's mouth. "We've just totally hit that inflection point of exponential growth, you know? The VCs are practically throwing money at us. Our last round was oversubscribed 5X. What about Ainetu? I heard after your onstage meltdown they actually brought you back as CEO."

"Yup, I just rejoined a couple weeks ago," Sam replied, trying hard not to get annoyed.

"That's fitting—brought back to be the captain of a sinking ship," Cory said, reaching past Sam to snare an appetizer from a passing tray.

Sam took a moment with a "go fuck yourself" grin on his face as he watched Cory pop the morsel into his mouth. "Funny you say that, because I was just fending off Quinn Randall—you know, from *TechWrap*—who was pestering me with rumors about Ainetu getting acquired. I couldn't tell him anything, of course."

Cory perceptibly winced and the two looked past each other to scan the room for a few seconds. "Anyway, I've got to meet up with some private equity guys who've been bugging me to invest, so I'll catch you later," Cory said.

"Good luck with that," Sam said. "Not that you need it, *right?*" Cory started to take his leave without saying anything more. Then Sam added under his breath, "Sit down, you punk-ass bitch." Cory abruptly looked back at Sam as if he might have heard the remark. "Hey, I just say what other people are thinking," Sam said before Cory again turned and walked away.

The altercation made Sam surly. *Do I really have to spar with douchebags like that, or can I enjoy my fucking Sangiovese in peace?* Sam thought as he tilted back another glass of wine. He surveyed the room, but all he saw were douchebags. Everyone had an agenda. The overzealous founders trying to hide their desperation as they gave breathless elevator pitches. The VCs bragging about their latest hot investments nobody had ever heard of. The big company execs pretending they didn't need to be there but knowing their companies were endangered species. The lawyers and accountants and IT contractors and PR people who fed off the whole ecosystem like birds on the backs of animals in the Serengeti. A bunch of posers all slinging their bullshit. *Fuck it.* If he was going to get drunk, this was a good place to do it—downing $100 bottles of someone else's wine.

After procuring his fourth glass, this time a rare Napa cabernet, Sam made his way over to another food station—a caviar bar arranged on a chest-high block of solid ice. The selection of roe in different sizes and colors was presented in recessed bowls carved directly into the ice slab's surface. Collectively, the stash was easily worth $10,000. Guests used mother-of-pearl spoons to scoop the caviar onto freshly made blinis cooked at a nearby station.

As he piled his blini high with caviar, Sam heard a cheer and turned to discover two young women in tight skirts pouring custom-made creams through a liquid-nitrogen funnel to produce ice cream shots. The crowd around the apparatus applauded every time the girls ceremoniously poured a creamy concoction into the funnel. Sam watched as a paunchy middle-aged man pumped his fists in celebration as one of the girls fed him his custom ice cream with a flirtatious shrug, licking the spoon suggestively in his face.

We're all going to hell, thought Sam as he regarded the long waiting line.

"That shit is amazing," came a voice from behind him. Sam turned to see Preston, exactly the guy he was hoping to find, staring past him at the girls. "The ice cream tastes like sawdust, but having that chick pour it into your mouth is like eating wet pussy."

"So do you have a frequent-buyer card?" Sam asked.

"Hell yeah—I've been through the line three times already," Preston said, then focused his attention on Sam. "So Ben tells me your little helper at Ainetu found some more accounting issues."

"I guess you could call it that," Sam said, finishing off his caviar. "Either that or fraud."

Preston nodded ambiguously, stealing a fleeting glance at the ice cream girls as they poured another shot. "Look, it was a long time ago. We needed more revenue, or we were never going to close our series A. It was one of those 'you scratch my back, I'll scratch yours' kinda deals. I'm not saying it was right, but we never would have made it to where Ainetu is today if we didn't have that revenue."

"The end justifies the means," Sam said.

"*Exactly*," Preston agreed. "And that 'end' could be a nice exit for all of us, if we just keep all this under the rug."

"That's not all we need to keep under the rug," Sam said, sipping his wine.

"What do you mean?"

"I think you know. Amanda shared the details of an . . . *incident* involving you with our head of HR."

Preston looked at Sam gravely without saying anything for a second. "Whose side are you on, Sam?" Preston finally asked. "Are you going to man up and get this fucking deal done, or are you going to spend your time investigating unsubstantiated HR violations?"

"Oh, I plan to get this deal done," Sam said with a terse smile. "That's what you brought me back to do, right? This is just another wrinkle we need to navigate." A waitress appeared with a tray full of cocktails, and both men grabbed a glass as she took their empties.

"What do you want, Sam?"

"I want Rohan *out*. Fully out—not on the board, not an observer, not an advisor, not even a shareholder." Preston considered the request as he carefully lifted his cocktail to his lips, trying to prevent it from spilling out of the overflowing martini glass. "And I want a 10 percent executive carve-out in writing, to be paid when this deal is closed. You guys can fund it from Rohan's portion and still be ahead."

"Do you think the Prism deal still has a shot?" Preston asked.

"It's not exactly a layup," Sam said. "More like a half-courter at the buzzer. But, yes, I do. I'm not giving up. They pulled a bait and switch on the bid price, but we're still negotiating it. At least we have a formal offer in writing now. The big question is the deal swaps. Most likely they will discover them in their final diligence. Even if they don't, we may want to disclose it, so it doesn't bite us in the ass on the other side. Either way, I'll do my best to make sure it doesn't get back to you or Paragon."

Preston looked around the room, showing little interest in Sam's disclosure. "The problem is we don't have any leverage," Preston said. "We need another buyer. Right now, they can fuck with us all they want. They know we don't have any other options."

"Agreed, but easier said than done," Sam said. "We don't have time to pitch this to other buyers. Besides, we agreed to exclusivity, so we couldn't shop it anyway."

"The no-shop is for acquirers," Preston said, intercepting another server to procure a fresh drink. "It doesn't prevent us from talking to *investors*."

"What investors?" Sam asked. "We don't have time to raise another round either. We won't make payroll in a month. If we don't sign a definitive acquisition agreement with Prism by Thursday, I need to cut 70 percent of the team."

"We won't need to do that," Preston replied. "I'm already talking to a new suitor, and they're interested. It will technically be a private equity buyout. They will own 90 percent of the company."

"*They* who?" Sam asked.

"One of the Saudi crown princes is good friends with my father. His sovereign wealth fund is trying to compete with Softbank and is itching to get into US tech deals. They'd come in at a billion-dollar valuation, minimum."

"Holy shit," Sam said. "That would be . . . helpful."

"You *think*? If I get them to the table, though, none of this shit can get out. Do you understand?"

"Yes, of course," Sam said. "Rohan out, 10 percent."

Preston returned his attention fully to the tall blond ice cream girl extending her nubile body to pour her concoction into the liquid-nitrogen funnel. She was distractingly gorgeous. Sam tried not to stare at her as he waited for Preston's acknowledgement of their agreement.

"Listen, you should come with me to Cabo," Preston finally replied.

"Oh . . . ," Sam said, unsure what exactly Preston was proposing. "Yeah, we should totally do that some time."

"No, I mean *tonight*. My jet is fueled up and ready to go. We'll be wheels up by midnight and have our toes in the sand tomorrow morning," Preston said, peering at Sam expectantly over the rim of his cocktail.

"Ummm . . . ," Sam stammered. "I'd love to, but . . ."

"But *what?*" Preston said, then nodded toward the ice cream girls. "They're both coming. The blond one even asked about you."

"Sounds awesome," Sam said. "I just . . . I don't know."

"Are you kidding me, *Sam*? Don't be such a limp dick. Look at them. It's too much pussy for me to fuck in one night. I need a wingman. Meet us at the private jet terminal at SFO by midnight. Give them this card, and tell them you're my guest."

Preston handed Sam a card without breaking his gaze, then took another sip of his drink. Sam looked at the card that read "VIP Access" as he pondered his decision.

"OK . . . I'm in."

CHAPTER 28:

BOARD MEETING

THE STACK OF PAPERS SAT in the passenger seat, heavy enough to occasionally trigger the fasten-seat-belt notification. Sam stole sideways glances at the cargo each time the traffic came to a standstill. Defying his expectations, the final acquisition documents from Prism had arrived by courier earlier that morning. True to his word, Ben had pulled some strings with Blake Bronson. The eponymous head of the investment bank had convinced Prism to boost their offer to $180 million guaranteed up front with another $50 million in earnouts. Though it was still below preferences and well short of the $500 million they had initially dangled, it was still almost a 4X multiple on Ainetu's forecasted revenue. Plus, now they had a definitive agreement ready to be signed—a bird in the hand.

The birds in the bush remained elusive. Preston had come forth with no further information about the purported Saudi investment fund and their generous offer. After scant details during their thirty-six-hour Cabo boondoggle, Sam was starting to suspect the deal was as fictional as the customer accounts owned by Paragon Enterprises—concocted by Preston to obfuscate the allegations against him of fraud and sexual misconduct. At least he had Preston's trust and support, though Sam was now also compromised. He knew incriminating pictures on Preston's phone could be sent to Heather by text message at any moment, for any reason.

Pulling into his parking space in the garage, Sam drummed his fingers on the steering wheel, delaying his exit from the car as if it could delay the events of the day. He couldn't get his hopes up about some illusory Saudi investor. Until he had something definitive, it was all party small talk. Despite his misgivings, selling to Prism was the obvious path. Even at the reduced offer, the deal would mean life-changing money and prestige for him personally. That said, the Prism deal had nothing but hair on it. Sam knew they couldn't simply sign the documents that sat in his passenger seat. They would need to disclose the discovery of the fake accounts and consequent fake revenue. Failure to do so was just too risky. Prism was a US-based public company, so the FTC and SEC would be involved. *I'm not going to fucking jail over this.* There could also be shareholder lawsuits, which would expose Sam and the board to civil liability. Sam could truthfully assert he didn't perpetrate the fraud, but his plausible deniability was gone. His conversations with Ajay, his possession of the USB drive, his disclosure to Ben, these would all become evidence that Sam knew exactly what had happened and failed to disclose it.

Even if the deal did, somehow, consummate, it would be a shit sandwich for Ainetu's employees. Sam's personal windfall, assuming it happened as promised, would be thanks to the 10 percent executive carve-out Ben had secured—hush money to go along with a deal that was only favorable to the preferred shareholders. As Sam and the VCs made off with the proceeds, the employees would quickly realize they were holding on to worthless stock. Those who were lucky enough not to lose their jobs in the transition would find themselves embedded in the bowels of a huge company—anonymous drones in a sea of cubicles.

Pushing ahead with the deal under these circumstances was unethical at best, illegal at worst. Sam knew there was no gray area, yet he had managed to rationalize one for several weeks now. Of course, he told himself, he would eventually divulge all this information to Prism, when the time was right. But that time never seemed to come. With Ainetu already teetering on the brink, it seemed any negative news would sink them. *And for what?* Every employee would be fired, investors would lose all their money, and Sam's reputation would be destroyed. All that would be left is a giant crater. *Who would that help?* The thought bolstered his resolve to somehow successfully get this deal done.

Stepping off the elevator onto Ainetu's floor, Sam tersely greeted Nicole. His executive assistant was the only other person in the office. She had arranged the conference room for their board meeting that morning with a breakfast buffet as well as printouts of the board packet and Ainetu-branded notepads and pens on the table. Sam closed his office door and quickly scanned his inbox for anything that might alter his circumstances. Finding nothing, he looked up to notice Jessie, their head of HR, enter the office. He had given her a heads-up that he wanted her at the board meeting to capture whatever HR issues might ensue after he confronted Rohan. The trap was set—it was time to get him out.

The other board members started arriving, so Sam joined them in the conference room, exchanging handshakes. Peggy Croft, their legal counsel, suddenly appeared in the conference room—possibly returning from the restroom, since Sam hadn't seen her come in. Finally, the elevator doors opened, and Rohan emerged, typing something on his phone as he strolled toward the conference room. Jessie, having noted Rohan's arrival, slipped into the back of the conference room herself to be present for what would follow. Sam called the meeting to order as Rohan entered.

"OK . . . thanks, everyone, for the early start today," Sam said. "Obviously, we have a lot to cover. I've asked Jessie Hernandez, who runs human resources here, to join us today, as she will be critical to our transition planning. Ajay Khatri on our finance team is also on standby if we need to review any financial terms with him. And, of course, Peggy from our law firm will be keeping minutes, as usual."

Peggy interjected, "You all should have received the final definitive agreement paperwork by courier early this morning." The board members nodded that they'd received the documents, while Rohan continued typing on his phone.

"Great," Sam said. "Of course, the main order of business today will be consideration of this definitive agreement to be acquired, in full, by Prism Systems. I want to leave plenty of time for any last questions or discussion before we vote on that deal. But before we do—"

"Do we *really* need to discuss this?" Rohan interrupted. "I mean, guys . . . I brought us an offer of five hundred million, which Sam managed to negotiate down to one eighty, but it's still a good deal for us. What else do we have to discuss? I move to approve."

Sam glanced around the room, then said, "I'm afraid it's not that simple, Rohan." He plugged his laptop into the projector and brought up a spreadsheet that itemized both the false customer accounts and the correlating false services invoices. "Unfortunately, we've discovered more irregularities in our financial statements. This spreadsheet shows eleven customer accounts, totaling almost $4 million in revenue last year, that don't appear to exist."

"What do you mean, they don't *exist*?" Kamal asked, the only person besides Peggy for whom this disclosure was a revelation.

"I mean they're fake accounts," Sam said. "They're shell companies, without any employees or actual users of our software. And if you look at our expenses, you'll see invoices from these advertising agencies for services we never received. Notice that the amount of revenue we've booked from these companies in column D precisely equals the amount of invoices we've paid to these other companies in column G. In other words, both the customer accounts and service providers are fake— fabricated to prop up our revenue."

Sam let the accusation sink in as everyone else sat in varying degrees of stunned silence. Peggy's hands hovered over her keyboard, unsure if she should be capturing minutes that confessed to a potential crime.

"This is *bullshit*!" Rohan was the first to speak. "You don't know what you're talking about."

"Actually, I *do* know what I'm talking about," Sam said. "Don't you find it rather unusual that no user from any of these accounts has ever logged in to our product, and, yet, they gladly, without negotiation, renew their contracts each year? Several even increased their spend with us, in exact lockstep with the increased invoices from the agencies. They never talk to a sales rep, they never call customer support, they always pay their invoices promptly. It's almost like they're too good to be true, which is *exactly what they are.*"

Judging from his reaction, Kamal seemed completely unaware of the issue. "How is this *possible*?" he asked with considerable alarm. "Shouldn't the auditors have caught this?"

"You would think," Sam replied. "Of course, Rohan hired the auditors and likely paid them off to keep this quiet. This was a scam, Rohan—plain and simple."

"I don't know anything about this," Rohan said, attempting to assume a casual demeanor as he spun a pen between his thumb and forefinger.

"Oh, you most certainly *do* know about it," Sam said. "In fact, you explicitly directed it and extorted Bill Johnson to perpetrate it. Before his suicide, Bill shared over forty emails from you, as well as the voice mail in which you threatened to fire him if he didn't cooperate with your scheme."

Rohan pulled out his phone and glared anxiously at the screen, as if he were expecting an urgent message rather than just using it as a prop to avoid eye contact. He put the phone down on the table, then picked it up again and flipped it over several times in the palm of his hand as everyone stared at him, waiting for a response. The muscles in his jaw twitched. "I didn't want to do this," he finally said. "It wasn't my idea."

"*You* were CEO of the company," Kamal immediately said. "Whatever happened here happened under *your* watch. We need to know if these accusations are true." Rohan dropped his phone onto the table but said nothing, an admission in his silence. "*Rohan Vishwanath Sharma!* Your mother would be *ashamed*!" Kamal suddenly scolded him like a recalcitrant child. The admonishment drew puzzled looks from around the room. Peggy, who hadn't typed another word, looked like she would give anything simply to leave.

"You know Rohan's mom?" Preston finally asked.

"I should think so," Kamal replied emphatically. "She's my Aunt Lenore."

"Wait . . . ," Preston said, struggling to put it together. "So you guys are *cousins?*"

"You should be grateful," Kamal said to Preston. "We never would have led the series C if it weren't for the family connection." He then turned to Rohan and said, "Rohan, I have defended you on this board many times before, but I can't defend this behavior. It's too much. I can't put family ahead of my integrity. An accounting error is one thing, but I won't be a party to blatant fraud."

"*Kamal,*" Rohan implored, but Kamal continued unmoved.

"I hereby move that you be put on an immediate leave of absence from the board until we can conduct a complete internal investigation. You'll need to recuse yourself from the remainder of today's board meeting. As chair of the compensation committee, I will inform you of any disciplinary action, including your likely termination from the company, once we've had a chance to review the evidence presented today. Peggy, please have the minutes reflect that Rohan, at this point, has left the board meeting," Kamal concluded, staring at Rohan.

Peggy, who had been completely dumbstruck since Sam had first projected the list of fake accounts, hastily returned her suspended hands to her laptop keyboard, presumably capturing Kamal's directive. She then looked expectantly at Rohan, waiting for him to fulfill what she had just transcribed as having happened.

Rohan suddenly stood, propelling his chair backward, and leaned over the conference table, propping himself up by his fingers. "If I'm gone, this deal with Prism is gone too. Sam will never get this deal done. Ben—you know that."

"Why would the deal not get done if you're no longer here?" Ben asked.

"I'll call Chip. I'll tell them we reject their offer," Rohan replied, picking up his phone as if to underscore the threat.

"I already told Chip you've been terminated," Sam said. "He couldn't care less."

"*Preston*," Rohan said, shifting his attention. "You can't let this happen. We had a deal!"

Preston looked down at his hands but said nothing. With everyone watching him, Rohan regarded the stack of Ainetu notebooks on the table and picked one up along with the pen he had been mindlessly spinning. "You're not going to ruin me. I need to document my side of the story," he said enigmatically, as if some scribbles in a notebook would exonerate him. "I don't know what you *think* you know, Sam, but you're *wrong*! And I can *prove* it. I fired you before, and I'll do it again."

"Good luck with that," Sam replied calmly.

Rohan grabbed his chair and slammed it against the wall. "I swear to God, Hughes—if you fuck this deal up, I will *melt your fucking face off*!" he shouted, pointing at Sam with veins bulging from his temples.

"By the way, once these allegations of fraud are substantiated, which Bill has, in fact, already done, by the terms of your employment agreement we will be reclaiming your founder's shares," Sam said. "You'll have nothing."

A look of helpless bewilderment overtook Rohan's angry expression. One by one, he checked the faces of each of the board members, but all were resolute. He then emphatically turned and stormed toward the door of the conference room. Shoving it open, he paused at the threshold, turned, and, pointing to the screen, said, "You left out one fact, Sam. These businesses are all owned by Paragon Enterprises. Maybe Preston can explain that one to you." They all watched through the glass wall as he swept a random computer monitor off its desk, sending it crashing to the floor. Then he kicked open the emergency exit to the stairway with one foot and disappeared down the fire escape.

Peggy nervously typed something on her keyboard as the board members exchanged glances. Sam looked around the room, then stood and said, "Well, that was fun. I need a muffin." He strode to the buffet to grab a pastry and coffee.

"Is that true?" Kamal asked, directing his question at Preston. "Are these businesses all owned by your father's company?"

Preston leaned forward in his chair and pointed to the screen dismissively. "My dad's organization owns lots of companies. I'm sure Ainetu does business with many of them. There's nothing unusual about that."

"Sure. And I suppose it's just coincidental that it happens to equal the exact amount of revenue from these customer accounts," Kamal said.

"Look," Sam said, trying to regain control of the situation. "At this point, it doesn't really matter. We will need to disclose this to Prism and restate our financials, *again*. It's just too risky to sell ourselves to a public company knowing we have falsified financials."

"Unless there's another offer on the table," Preston interjected.

Sam held up his hand to pause the conversation as he returned to his seat. "Thanks for sitting in, Jessie. You can leave now." Jessie gathered her items and pointed to her notebook, indicating to Sam she had captured the incident with Rohan.

Ben, who had been largely silent, was now sitting upright in his chair. "What other offer?" he asked, after Jessie left the room. "Is this a hypothetical?"

"Preston has suggested another acquirer may come forward, but we don't have anything definitive yet, and if it's going to happen, it needs to happen today," Sam said.

"It doesn't matter," Kamal said. "We can't proceed with a sale to *any* acquirer under these circumstances. We are sitting on millions of dollars of fraudulent revenue. Even if you had ten suitors, this will all be discovered during diligence. Besides, I'm less concerned with how we spin this to outside buyers than I am in getting our house in order. Preston, you appear to have colluded with Rohan to fabricate revenue. That's unacceptable. I'm not comfortable with that."

"Maybe you'll grow more comfortable when you hear the terms of the new offer," Preston said, glancing briefly at Sam. "One-point-two billion. In cash."

Kamal's head flinched back on his shoulders. "One point two *billion*?" he asked, as if he had heard the number wrong. "That doesn't make any sense. Who would offer that? That's over 6X the offer we have on the table, and almost 25X our forward revenue. It's irrational."

"You would stand to make twelve times your investment in less than two years, almost $250 million," Preston said to Kamal. "You'll return your entire fund in this one deal. Your IRR will be off the charts. You'll be on the Midas list. You'll be able to do whatever you want—raise another fund, start your own venture firm, retire. *Anything.*"

Kamal listened thoughtfully, rotating his cup of tea, which sat on the table in front of him.

"So I think we can all agree that we don't need to worry about what did or didn't happen with these deals," Preston said, walking to the buffet to refill his coffee.

"You still haven't told us who the offer is from," Ben said.

"Ufuq Jadid," Preston said, casually stirring artificial sweetener into his coffee.

"What's that?" Ben asked.

"Aren't they part of the Saudi sovereign wealth fund?" Kamal asked.

"To be precise, it's a new $500 billion private equity fund, run by the family office of the Saudi royal family, specifically focused on technology investments," Preston said.

Sam remained circumspect. Ufuq Jadid wasn't exactly a household name in Silicon Valley tech circles, so he didn't know much about them—besides the fact that they had limitlessly deep pockets and were eager to do a big deal to put themselves on the map. But the number was preposterous—*$1.2 billion, all cash*? It sounded made up. Further, it came through Preston as the sole intermediary. Sam had not even met with or heard from anyone at the firm yet. For all he knew, Preston had fabricated the entire thing.

Still, it was a tantalizing prospect. The offer, if it was real, meant spectacular wealth for everyone. Sam would likely clear $100 million, or more. Most of the executive team would make over $10 million apiece. Every employee would make money they'd never dreamed of. Even Kelly, their front desk receptionist, would be a millionaire. Beyond the eye-popping price, a Saudi sovereign wealth fund would exhibit much less financial scrutiny than a publicly traded company subject to SEC jurisdiction. As a private offshore business, Ufuq Jadid was out of the reach of US regulators. It seemed unlikely they would ever discover the financial transgressions, and, if they did, it seemed equally unlikely they would care. There would be no investigations or lawsuits, just bags of cash to drag to the bank.

"When will we have this in writing?" Ben asked.

"I expect the definitive agreement from their bankers tonight—first thing in the morning their time," Preston replied.

Kamal and Ben smiled at each other. Then Peggy meekly interjected, "So are we going to vote on the Prism offer? They are expecting an answer back today. What should I tell them?"

"Tell them to go fuck themselves," Preston said. "We got a better offer."

CHAPTER 29:

DRIVE

BACK IN HIS OFFICE, Sam sat in his chair and focused his attention momentarily on the ever-changing canvas of civic activity outside his window. All these other commercial industries—transportation, tourism, real estate, construction, financial services, retail—they were all, in fact, extensions of one industry: *technology*. None of these other sectors in San Francisco would have any vibrancy without the core, unstoppable, *insatiable* economic engine of technology and the vast wealth it created. Tech wasn't simply the strongest sector of the economy. It *was* the economy. Without tech, everything else was flatlining.

As he watched the bustle below him, Sam contemplated his next move. Now, against all odds, there might be a plan B. But as enticing as the prospect of a Saudi oil sheikh backing up a dump truck of money was, Sam had to assume it was still a long shot. Plus, with the entire deal brokered through Preston, it could be complete fiction—there was nothing Sam could do but wait to see if a definitive agreement materialized. In the meantime, plan A remained getting the deal done with Prism—decidedly *not* telling them to "go fuck themselves," as Sam had quickly clarified with Peggy. But that path made him sick to his stomach. The only thought that gave Sam hope was Ben's insistence that Prism wouldn't be fazed by the discovery of new irregularities. *Every start-up has funky financials. The only one who thinks this is a big deal is you,* Ben had argued. It was possible he was right. Maybe this was just about the jump in stock price for Prism. They didn't exactly have a track record of successfully integrating the technology or customers of the companies they acquired. They often seemed more motivated by the stock rally, thanks to the short attention span of Wall Street, and the elimination of a potential competitor.

Since Prism adjusted their offer back up to $180 million, the deal had been brokered by Ben. Sam had not had any interaction with anyone on their side. The final paperwork arrived with a cover note from Carlson Mayfield, the investment banker at Bronson & Associates, that effectively said, "Take it or leave it." But Sam also knew Carlson had a strong incentive to get the deal to fruition and earn his commission. Carlson would know Prism's motivations for doing the deal and whether they would consider the latest transgression a showstopper or not.

Jessie tapped the glass door to his office, looking to debrief after the board meeting. "Well, that went about as I expected," she said after coming in and closing the door behind her.

Sam nodded. "Rohan's the least of my worries. I need to figure out how to navigate this issue with Prism."

"So you haven't told them about any of this yet?"

"They know about the overrecognition of revenue, but not about the fake customer accounts," Sam said.

"Or the sexual assault by one of our board members," Jessie added.

"Right, that too," Sam said. "I'm going over to Bronson right now. Their office is only a couple blocks away. I need to talk to Carlson face-to-face."

"Carlson? Isn't he just the investment banker? Why not call the guys at Prism directly?" she asked.

"Because I need his help to smooth this over," Sam said. "Ben doesn't think it will be a big deal. So my plan is to feel out Carlson. He'll know his client. If he agrees it's not a problem, we can proceed in good faith. Or, if he thinks it will raise concerns, he can help us position it with Prism."

"What was Preston referring to in the board meeting? Is there another offer?" Jessie asked.

"Not until we get something in writing," Sam said, pulling on his jacket. "Maybe Preston will pull a rabbit out of his hat, but we can't count on that. Right now, it's just Preston's word."

"That and three dollars will get you a cup of coffee," Jessie said, delivering her joke more like a threat. "That guy has no credibility in my book. He conspires with Rohan around all these fake accounts—Rohan gets fired for it, but nothing happens to Preston? He sexually assaults one of our executives, but nothing happens to Preston? Where does it end? What's the line for holding him accountable?"

"Yeah, well—that's what happens when you dangle a billion-dollar deal in front of a boardroom." Sam shrugged as he pulled open his office door to leave.

"Well, he's not going to get away with it much longer," Jessie said. "Amanda changed her mind about remaining anonymous. When I told her about the other victims, she decided she couldn't stay quiet. She's ready to press charges against Preston."

Sam froze, then stepped back into his office. "That would be a problem," he said. Sam knew if the Ufuq Jadid deal did happen, the biggest landmine was not the accounting issues, it was the assault. The investment firm's founding partner, Hamza Ali Ahmad, had been accused of sexual improprieties by a secretary in their London office. She sold her story to the tabloids. Although the charges were dismissed by a British court, the Saudi kingdom, eager to burnish their reputation in the West around the treatment of women, had allegedly warned Ahmad that another transgression would not be tolerated. It was hard for Sam to imagine UJ (as they'd already taken to abbreviating the firm's name) would continue with a billion-dollar-plus acquisition if an accusation of sexual assault arose against one of Ainetu's board members.

"I think she has a very strong case," Jessie said. "Given Preston's history and the other accusers who are likely to come out against him. Plus, the security-camera footage I gave you makes it pretty definitive. Have you watched it?"

"No, I haven't. I trust Amanda."

"It's disturbing." Jessie's expression crumpled in disgust with the recollection. "When she initially wanted to remain anonymous, she asked me to delete the video. I'm glad I didn't. You still have it, right?"

"Right here," Sam said, presenting the USB drive before nestling it into his pocket.

■ ■ ■

Sam pulled up the collar of his jacket and leaned into the stiff breeze channeling between the buildings along Montgomery Street. The bright glow of a huge electronic stock ticker welcomed him to the Financial District, its symbols and numbers racing across the screen with green or red arrows to indicate the day's winners and losers. Looking up, he saw the letters *PSI* fly by, the symbol for Prism Systems, Inc.—a green arrow pointed up 2.3 percent, an increase of almost $5 billion in one day. Walking past marble columns and through an Art Deco revolving door, Sam entered the lobby of Bronson & Associates.

"Do you have an appointment?" the security guard at the front desk asked.

"No," Sam said. "But I'm working on a big acquisition with Carlson Mayfield that's supposed to close today. So I need to meet with him immediately."

"Well, you're not on the schedule," the guard said, shaking his head.

"Yes, I *know* I'm not on the schedule. I just told you I don't have an appointment. Can you just call up to his assistant, please?"

The guard reluctantly picked up the phone, pinched the headset under his ear, and slowly dialed the extension, as if each button required exertion. "*Name?*" he asked, without looking up.

"Sam Hughes."

"*Company?*"

"Ainetu."

"Hey," the guard said into the phone. "I've got a guy named Sam Hughes with A-notu . . ."

"*Eye*-netu," Sam corrected him.

"A-net-you," the guard said, annunciating his mangled pronunciation. "Said he wants to see Carlson Mayfield. Yeah . . . OK. OK." The guard hung up but said nothing. Finally, he handed Sam a temporary badge on a plastic clip. "Seventeenth floor. Put your keys, phone, and wallet in here," the guard said, handing him a small plastic bowl. Sam stepped through the metal detector.

Carlson's assistant met Sam as the elevator doors opened. "Mr. Hughes, we weren't expecting you."

"Well, a $180 million acquisition may just be another day around here, but it's kind of a big deal for me."

"Of course. Carlson will be here in just a minute," he said, depositing him in a conference room.

"Sam Hughes, what a surprise," Carlson said as he entered moments later. "How did the board meeting go today?"

"It went . . . pretty well," Sam replied in a measured tone as they shook hands.

"Uh-oh," Carlson said. "What happened?"

"Well, we don't have approval on the deal yet," Sam said. "There's a delicate little wrinkle we discovered as part of our own process that I wanted to run by you."

"OK, shoot."

"So you remember Bill Johnson, our former CFO who, tragically, took his own life?"

"Of course, so awful," Carlson said.

"It really was. Anyway, we found some additional anomalies in the financials, beyond the revenue-recognition issue we disclosed earlier." Carlson was silent, so Sam continued. "In fact, we found several customer accounts that are . . . *unusual*."

"What do you mean?" Carlson asked.

"We had some customer accounts that were paying us money, but we were buying the same amount of services from affiliated companies," Sam explained, trying to put the best spin on it. "So . . . we really shouldn't have recognized that as revenue—more of an in-kind contribution to each other."

"I see," Carlson replied. "How much revenue are we talking about?"

"A few million dollars over the last couple years," Sam said, cringing as the words came out of his mouth.

"Kind of a 'you scratch my back, I'll scratch yours' sort of arrangement," Carlson said.

"Yes, *exactly*," Sam replied, seizing on the positive spin Carlson seemed to be putting on it. "That's what one of our board members said—that this sort of thing is fairly common when companies are just getting started. Anyway, even though it's not a large percentage of our total revenue, we wanted to be fully transparent with you guys."

"OK," Carlson said before a prolonged pause. "So I assume you're going to amend your financial statements again?"

"Yes, I'll have our finance director, Ajay, upload new financials to the online deal room," Sam said cautiously. "So . . . can we go ahead and approve the definitive agreement as it stands?"

"Look, Sam." Carlson sighed. "I don't want to speak for the Prism guys, but this is over. I've been the one keeping this thing on the rails. Then Ben got Blake to twist Chip's arm and up the offer to one eighty. That really pissed him off. Now you're coming back and telling us you have fake customer accounts? This isn't just an accounting error, this is fraud. You know it, I know it, and Chip knows it. There's no way this deal is happening."

Sam was silent. He started to reply but all that came out was a prolonged sigh.

"Sorry, Sam. You seem like a nice guy. I know you didn't do this. You're just the messenger," Carlson said with a softened tone. "I'll run it by Chip and David, but you should expect the answer to be no."

"OK, that's fine," Sam said. "That makes this an easy decision."

"Decision about what?" Carlson asked.

"Truth is, we have another offer," Sam said. "It's actually a substantially *higher* offer. I thought the strategic fit was better with Prism, but *fuck it*—we'll take the money. So I guess you can tell Chip to go fuck himself after all."

"Sam, I don't know what else to tell you . . . ," Carlson started, but Sam was already out of the conference room and headed back toward the elevators.

He impatiently jabbed at the down button. Seeing the elevator was on another floor, he turned and slammed his way through the door to the men's room. Grasping a sink with both hands as if he were going to rip it off the wall, Sam looked up at his reflection in the mirror. Then he kicked open the door to one of the stalls. Pulling the USB drive from his pocket, he turned it over once in his hand, then tossed it into the toilet and flushed it.

CHAPTER 30:

LIFELINE

"WHERE'S AJAY?" SAM ASKED NICOLE as soon as he walked into Ainetu's lobby.

"Would you like me to find him?" she asked.

"Yes," Sam said, pushing the door open to his office. He typed a text to Amanda, then sat down and drummed his fingers on his desktop impatiently.

Ajay appeared a minute later, carrying his laptop as he always did. He gave Sam a nervous look as he entered. "You wanted to see me?"

"Yes, sit down, please," Sam said, indicating the chair facing his. "Ajay, I appreciate your contributions to this company, particularly after Bill's passing. But I'm afraid we're going to have to let you go." Ajay looked down at his computer, cradled between his legs. "I realize these financial irregularities were not your doing, but you should have discovered them earlier. For us to have such lax financial oversight is unacceptable—a real breakdown in your organization. There needs to be accountability. And, unfortunately, with Bill gone, the buck now stops with you."

With his shoulders hunched inward, Ajay began rocking slightly in his chair. Tears began welling in his downcast eyes. He swallowed then said, "Yes, of course. I understand. I'm sorry."

"I'll need your laptop and badge," Sam said, extending his hands toward the computer.

"Of course," Ajay said. His hands made an adhesive sound as they released the machine, as if they were fused to its plastic case. Without the prop of his ubiquitous laptop, his hands were unmoored, making him appear even more emotionally fragile. He briefly clenched them timidly between his legs before giving them a new assignment. Reaching to his belt, he unclipped his employee badge from its extensible cord and handed it to Sam as well.

"Jessie can go over all the details with you," Sam said, pointing to Jessie, who was now waiting outside his office holding a manila folder.

Ajay slowly stood, his narrow frame still arched as if sheltering himself from a rainstorm. He extended his hand toward Sam. "Thank you for the opportunity."

Still seated, Sam tentatively shook Ajay's hand. "Good luck to you, Ajay."

■ ■ ■

"Hey. Now work for you?" Amanda asked, peering through the door of Sam's office in response to his text for a quick "walk and talk."

"Yeah, let's go," Sam said. Not wanting to be inadvertently overheard by any employees, they waited to start their conversation until they had descended the elevators and emerged onto the street.

"*So . . .* ," Amanda started expectantly. "How did it go with the board this morning? What's the latest?"

"Do you want the short version or the long version?" Sam asked.

"I want *any* version!" she insisted. "Last I heard, Prism was at five hundred. Do we have it in writing now? Did the board approve the deal?"

"It's a little more complicated than that," Sam said hesitantly. "As you know, we had to disclose the deals that were incorrectly accounted for, and that freaked them out a little bit."

"I can imagine," she said. "So did they cut their offer price?"

"Yes, and structured the deal to have an up-front payment followed by earnouts if the business hits certain revenue milestones," Sam explained as he watched her facial expression shift from optimistic to concerned.

"That doesn't sound good," she said. "So what's their new price?"

"Well, it *was* $100 million," Sam started.

"A hundred million?" she blurted out. "That's only 2X forward revenue! We're worth *way* more than that!"

"I know, I know," Sam reassured her. "They've since increased it to $180 million. Plus, with the earnouts, we could get another $50 million over the next two years."

"We'll never see those earnouts," she said cynically as they strolled by an artisan coffee roaster with a line of tattooed hipsters waiting for drinks, thumbs dancing over their phones. "But one eighty is a little more reasonable. I'd clear almost three million from that," she estimated.

"Unfortunately, that's not the case," Sam said. "We need to clear the investor preferences."

"Right, but that's just the $60 million that's been invested, right?" she asked.

"Not quite. It's a 3X participating preference, so all the proceeds would go to the investors. Your stock will be worthless."

"*What?*" she asked. "How did I not know about that?"

"Because Rohan never told you. He never told me," Sam explained. "I just found this out when I came back as CEO."

"So why didn't you tell me then?" she asked.

"I didn't think it would matter," Sam said. "I figured we would clear preferences and all would be good. Now we'll be lucky if the Prism deal happens at all."

Amanda suddenly stopped walking and was nearly sideswiped by a guy on an electric scooter doing twenty-five miles per hour on the sidewalk. She didn't even notice. "This is *bullshit*, Sam. I'm not letting Preston and the other investors make off with all the money after what he did to me. Fuck it—I'll go public. I already told Jessie I want to press charges against Preston."

"You could do that, but I think you need to be prepared for him to really come after you. He's going to be ruthless—calling you a liar, questioning your character, saying you're just doing it to extort money. Plus, it will be your word against his. You'd probably never work in the Valley again," Sam said.

"I don't care. If I'm going to get screwed on this deal, then why should I hold back? Besides, it won't be my word against his—there's the security-camera video."

"Look, there may be another option, but you have to trust me. You have to promise me none of this stuff comes out." They both paused and regarded a homeless woman slumped like a rag doll with her legs splayed out and her back propped up against a trash can. Her tattered brown sweatshirt bore the stains of life on the street, incongruously accentuated by a pink tutu. She was either strung out or deranged, mumbling loudly but incoherently as she combed her hair with a plastic fork. A young man walking toward them wearing AirPods and a tech company–embroidered hoodie stepped over the woman's outcast leg without looking up from his phone.

"What do you mean 'another option'?" Amanda asked as they navigated their way around the woman's sprawling legs.

Sam looked back at the homeless woman. Even though she was in her own world, he wanted to wait to answer until they were out of earshot. "We may have another buyer. I don't have it in writing yet, but, if it goes through, you'd be set for life."

"How much?"

"One point two billion," Sam said.

"Holy *shit*! Who's the buyer?"

"A Saudi private equity fund," Sam said. "They are what we'd call *price insensitive*."

"What about Preston? How much does he make on all this?" she asked as they walked past a cannabis dispensary adjacent to a gelato stand.

"Well, Ellipsis was in early, so he'll do quite well. As a firm they'll probably make over $400 million."

Sam could see Amanda was roiling, going through in minutes the same emotional roller coaster of greed, envy, and spite he'd endured the last several weeks. They were now crossing Mission Street, close to the Millennium Tower, an ultra-luxury high-rise of condominiums that was gradually sinking into the unstable San Francisco soil. Amanda nodded her head toward the Salesforce Tower on the next block. "That thing looks like a giant fucking dildo," she observed. "The perfect monument for the tech industry: a bunch of billionaires waiting for the perfect moment to fuck you with their thousand-foot dick."

"That's a vivid metaphor," Sam said. "Look, I know it sucks, but the managing director of this fund, Ufuq Jadid, had an . . . *incident* himself. So, if this came out, it would scuttle the deal."

Amanda shook her head. "It's just . . . not fair."

"No, it's not," Sam agreed. "But it is what it is."

Amanda didn't reply. She just stood staring up at the tower, sparkling in the afternoon sunlight, as the stream of busy pedestrians eddied around them. Sam studied her face, trying to read her emotions. As the traffic light at their intersection turned red, a column of traffic came to a halt before them. They were joined by a man wobbling on a single fat-wheel mono board, two Teslas, a tinted-glass Google bus bound for Mountain View, a pair of tourists packed into a tiny yellow convertible go-kart, and a giant mobile billboard advertising some new brand of ultra-premium tequila. A homeless man with a cardboard sign staggered through the stopped traffic in search of donations.

"You said you had my back," Amanda practically hissed.

"What are you talking about? I *do* have your back. You'll make a shitload of money off this deal—probably twenty million before tax."

"I don't care about the fucking money, *Sam*! I care about Preston walking off with $400 million and no consequences. *That's* what I care about!"

"Look, I get that it's not fair—especially after what he did to you."

"Guys like that always get away with this shit. Nobody ever stands up to them."

"Amanda, I don't have a choice," Sam insisted. "The Prism deal is most likely going to fall through. If it does, we'll need to lay off most of the company before we run out of cash. This Ufuq Jadid deal could be our lifeline. You make money, I make money, the investors make money, all the employees make money."

"And Preston makes the most money," she added.

"Yes, you're right—Preston will make the most money, but he also was the original investor and found the acquirer, so it's not entirely unfair."

"I can't believe this," Amanda said.

"Can't believe what?"

"That I *trusted* you. I thought you were on my side. But you're just like every other guy."

"What do you want me to do?" Sam asked. "Blow it all up? Tell them about the fraud and the sexual assault and just completely shit the bed? You'll be set for life after this. We can't fuck this up."

"No, *you* can't fuck this up, Sam," Amanda shouted, pushing her finger into Sam's chest. "I'm out!"

Sam watched Amanda turn and walk away, floundering for the words that would change her mind. *She's right.* That thought wrapped itself around his throat, momentarily choking off his rebuttal. But were they really going to lose the deal over this? "Amanda, *wait.*"

Swirling around to face Sam, she regarded him intensely and demanded, "Look me in the eye and tell me you think you're doing the right thing."

"It doesn't matter if it's the *right* thing. The reality is it's the *only* thing," Sam said. "We're out of options."

Amanda glared at him. "You're so full of shit! What about 'building a great company'? What about being 'transparent' and 'doing the right thing'? What about 'making the world a better place'? Do you remember saying *any* of that? Or don't you believe your own *bullshit?*"

"I need to hear you say you won't go public with this," Sam said.

"*Jesus*, Sam! What happened to you? I followed you to this damn company. I *believed* in you!"

"*Exactly*—and I believed in you too. I took a chance on you. You were just a regional manager when I hired you. Nobody else would have given you this opportunity. And now, thanks to me, you're going to make millions of dollars. You *owe* me."

Amanda's shoulders sagged, her spirit demoralized. She looked up again at the tower, then finally nodded and said, "Fine . . . I won't go public."

"Thank you," Sam said. "I'll make sure you're taken care of. I'll send you an e-signature for an additional share allocation, along with a non-disclosure agreement, of course."

Amanda reacted with a melancholy nod. "Goodbye, Sam," she said, then turned again and walked westward toward the setting sun along Mission Street. Her long shadow cast backward, lingering next to Sam on the sidewalk a moment more.

As Sam watched her walk away, he pulled out his phone and tapped open the text message that had arrived minutes earlier. It was a group text from Preston to Sam and the full board. "*We have the docs from UJ.*"

Sam clenched the phone in his hand and pumped a fist up at the sky. He reread the message with his thumbs poised over the screen, then typed, "*Awesome! We're good to go.*"

CHAPTER 31:

LAST CELEBRATION

IT WAS THE MOST EXPENSIVE BOTTLE of champagne for sale at their neighborhood liquor store. Nuzzled in the top shelf of the refrigerated case, the ninety-dollar bottle of Dom Pérignon was a bit bougie but sufficiently special for the occasion Sam wanted to celebrate. Heather wasn't home from work yet, and the kids were sequestered in their rooms doing homework. Sam rifled through the cabinets, looking for their champagne glasses. Before he could find them, the front door creaked open, and Heather entered, tossing her car keys onto the sideboard in their cramped entryway.

"Have you seen our champagne flutes?" Sam asked as Heather placed her coat on a chair.

"The ones from our wedding?"

"Yeah, do you know where they are?"

"I think they're still in one of the boxes near the pantry." Heather plopped onto their living room sofa, exhausted from her day at work, and slowly extracted her feet from her heels. "Why? Are we celebrating something?"

Sam emerged from the kitchen with the bottle of champagne and the now-procured flutes. "As a matter of fact, *yes!*" Sam grinned as he placed the glasses on the coffee table in front of her. He ceremoniously presented the bottle of Dom Pérignon with a towel over his forearm like a sommelier, then commenced fiddling with the foil top and wire enclosure.

"Do tell. You're keeping me in suspense," she said.

271

"We're signing the deal to sell Ainetu tonight," Sam said as he wrestled the cork free with a satisfying pop.

"You *are?*" Heather asked. "With Prism or the other one?"

"The other one, Ufuq Jadid," Sam said as he poured them each a glass.

"*Right* . . . I'd never heard of them before you mentioned the name. So they just came in at the last second with an offer out of the blue?"

"One point two *billion* dollars! I just got the unanimous approval back from our board, so it's ready for their countersignature first thing tomorrow in Riyadh, which is in about three hours."

"*Really?*" Heather asked with a look of incredulity, taking the glass from Sam.

"You sound like you don't believe me."

"No . . . I'm just surprised. That's a *huge* number, and it happened so quickly. You were working on Prism for weeks. It didn't sound like you even thought Ufuq Jadid would put in an offer."

"Gotta strike while the iron's hot," Sam said, raising his glass to toast against hers. "Preston told them the Prism deal was ready to sign, so they moved fast. He managed to get them to submit a definitive agreement before they'd even done diligence."

"Oh . . . ," Heather said, tilting her head contemplatively as they clinked rims. "Do you think that's a good idea? Won't they discover the accounting issues?"

"I doubt it. Preston said the managing director there, Hamza, doesn't really dig into the details. All he cares about is the PR splash of putting their firm on the map."

"Didn't that guy sexually assault his secretary?"

Sam looked inquisitively at Heather for a moment as he took a sip of his champagne. "As a matter of fact, yes. Well, technically, he was *accused* of it and ultimately acquitted. But how did you know about that?"

"Well . . . like I said, I'd never heard of them, so I did some research. It's the first thing that comes up when you google Ufuq Jadid. It got a ton of press."

"Yes, it did." Sam shrugged his eyebrows.

"I'm amazed they'd do this deal, given the situation with Preston. You know—and Amanda."

"Well . . . ," Sam sighed.

"Or did you not disclose that either?"

"We *couldn't*," Sam insisted. "It would have killed the deal."

"I'm sure it would have. You're lying about everything else. So why not lie about that too?"

"We're not *lying*. We're just being selective about which information we divulge. If they don't bother with due diligence, why would we volunteer negative information?"

"You're fucking *unbelievable*!"

"You're not supposed to say the f-word," said Riley, who had silently crept into a corner of the living room without Sam or Heather noticing.

"You're right, sweetie," Heather said. "You should never say that word. That's an adult word. Did you have a good day?" Riley nodded as she cautiously approached the couch to give her mom a hug. "I missed you today. But Mommy and Daddy are having a conversation right now, so can you brush your teeth and read a book? I'll be back in a few minutes to tuck you in."

Riley nodded again without speaking. Sam and Heather looked at each other as she walked back to her bedroom. "I didn't have a choice," Sam finally said when she was out of earshot. "I couldn't risk it. We needed to get this deal done. It's OK—I talked to Amanda about it. She understands. She agreed it was the right thing to do."

"Of course she agreed not to say anything—if that's what you told her. She'd do anything for you, Sam. You know that."

"That's ridiculous. She's perfectly capable of standing up for herself."

"Yes, she is. But she viewed you as a mentor. I can't believe you'd take advantage of the trust she put in you. That you'd sell her out like that."

"*Sell her out?* How am I selling her out? She's going to make a ton of money from this deal. I'd hardly call that selling her out."

"Is that how *she* saw it? When you asked her not to say anything?"

Sam looked away, crossed his arms, and leaned back on the sofa.

"What are you guys arguing about?" Mason asked as he entered the living room.

"Nothing, honey," Heather said, standing to give him a hug. "How did your biology test go today?"

"Fine," Mason replied. "It sounded like you guys were in a fight."

"No, we weren't fighting. We're celebrating, actually," Sam said, pointing to his glass of champagne.

"What are you celebrating?"

"Dad had a good day at work, that's all," Heather said.

"We sold our company today. We're going to be able to afford a much bigger house now," Sam said.

"Wait . . . we're *moving*?" Mason asked with sudden urgency.

"There's *no way* I'm moving!" Connor, their older son, said emphatically as he entered the living room as well. "I'm not leaving my friends!"

"No, we're not moving. We're not going anywhere," Heather reassured them.

"Why is Dad talking about getting a bigger house then?" Mason asked.

"He's just speaking hypothetically. There's nothing to worry about," she said, shooting a micro-expression at Sam that revealed her irritation in the unspoken language of a long-married couple. "Boys, can you go back to your rooms, so your father and I can finish our conversation?"

Mason picked up a football and tossed it up in the air to himself.

"Mom! I'm done brushing my teeth!" Riley shouted from the back bathroom.

"OK, I'll be back in just a minute," Heather replied.

"*Here*," Connor said, his hands up, beckoning for the football from his brother. The ensuing pass bounced off a table, knocking a stack of mail to the floor and nearly toppling a lamp, which cast undulating beams of light across the room from its wobbling shade.

"*Boys!* How many times do I need to tell you? No balls in the house!"

Heather glared at them as Connor hurriedly gathered the scattered envelopes. "Get back to your rooms."

As the boys shuffled down the hall giggling with each other, Sam turned to Heather. "See, we need a bigger house. The boys need more space."

"We *just* remodeled this one! We're not even done yet." Heather said, waving her hand toward their still-unfinished kitchen. "Besides, it doesn't matter how big our house is; I don't want them turning it into a football field."

"We could install an indoor football field for what we'll be worth."

Heather gave him a dubious expression, as if she didn't need to dignify such an outrageous statement with a response. Then, the words came to her. "Why would we spend money on something as frivolous as that? If we really had so much money, I'd like to think we'd find more worthy things to spend it on than a personal sports field. You went on and on at Isabella's birthday party about how stupid it was of the Costas to spend obscene amounts of money on a soccer field."

"That was different. That was just an ostentatious display of wealth."

"Oh, so an indoor football field wouldn't be ostentatious?"

"I was *joking*! I wouldn't really do that. I was just making a point."

"Making what point? That you'll be so rich you can buy *anything?*"

"Yeah, I guess," Sam conceded. "I thought you'd be excited. This is what we always wanted."

"This is what *you* always wanted! I just wanted a normal marriage, a normal family. Crazy money was never my dream—especially not this way."

"What do you mean 'this way'? It's not like I broke the law or something."

"*Sam* . . ." Heather paused, her mouth agape as if her forthcoming sentiment was so self-evident it barely needed stating. "You're covering up misstated revenue, fake customer accounts, and a sexual assault by one of your board members. I'm not a corporate attorney, but that seems pretty much like breaking the law. You can't lie to get the company sold. That's not you."

"Or maybe this is just what it takes to make it," Sam said. "Maybe I've just been the nice guy too long—grinding away, working my *ass* off my whole career, trying to do things the 'right way,' whatever the hell that means, and not even realizing it's the guys who lie and cheat and manipulate who make it. I'm *forty-five*! I don't have that many more shots on goal. I've *got* to get this win."

"*Why?* Like you said, you're only forty-five. You have half your career in front of you."

"No, I *don't*." Sam shook his head and wiped the condensation from the side of his glass. "Not in tech. Maybe I could have a second act as a VC or an angel investor or a board member. But none of those things happen if I don't have a big exit. That's what opens the doors. Besides, we'll make more money than we'll know what to do with."

"How many times do I have to tell you, I don't *want* that. I don't *care* about the money! That's not why I married you. I married you because you're smart and nice and honest. Who cares if you never make a ton of money? You're a great husband and father. Why isn't that enough for you?"

"Because it's *not*!" Sam shouted. "I came here to do something special—to be a *success*. I didn't just abandon the family business to jerk off into a cup and call it a day. I came here to conquer and earn the fame, fortune, and respect that comes with it. To prove I can make it. To make my dad proud!"

"Your dad wouldn't be proud of this."

"Awww, *bullshit*! My dad would shit his pants if he knew how much money I'm about to make. It's enough to buy a thousand Hughes Rentals. He couldn't imagine success like this in his wildest dreams."

"*Jesus*, Sam, you're starting to sound like Preston."

"What's wrong with Preston?" Sam asked. "He takes what he wants. He gets shit done. When we needed a lifeline, he got us this deal with Ufuq Jadid. He saved our asses."

"He also groped Amanda's crotch! That doesn't bother you?"

"Of course it bothers me, but what am I supposed to do? Hamza would have killed the deal if he'd found out about it. He can't be associated with another incident."

"So you're not only protecting one sexual predator, you're protecting *two*."

"Something like that," Sam said, looking down at a text message on his phone. It was from Peter Green and simply said, "*Congratulations!*"

"Sam, she got sexually assaulted! You've worked with her for over five years. She's your friend. You're the only person who can support her side of the story."

"I already told you, she's not going to go public with the accusation."

"*Accusation?* I'd call it more than an accusation. You have proof, from the security-camera footage."

"There's no proof. There's no footage."

Heather slammed her glass down on the table and glared at Sam. "What do you mean there's no proof? You have the entire incident on video. Jessie gave it to you."

"Nope." Sam shook his head.

"*Nope?* That's all you have to say? Sam, you had firsthand video evidence of Preston sexually assaulting Amanda. Do you know how hard it is to prove a sexual assault case? It's always 'he said, she said' and the guy gets off. That video was the only way she could prove what happened was true."

"Not anymore. I flushed it."

"You *flushed* it? You mean, like, flushed it down the toilet?"

"Yes, literally—I flushed it down the toilet," Sam said, flushing an imaginary handle with his fingers.

"You've got to be *fucking* kidding me!"

"No. No, I'm not fucking kidding you. There's no way I was going to risk blowing up a $1.2 billion deal over this. Besides, why are you so bothered? I thought you hate Amanda."

"*Hate* her? Why would I hate her?"

"I don't know. I guess I just thought you were a little jealous."

"Yes, you're right—I am a little jealous. She's beautiful and successful and intelligent. She's also been a victim of sexual assault multiple times in her career."

"How do you know that?"

"We're in the same support group together."

"Support group? I thought it was a book club."

"Yeah, a book club where every book we read happens to be about a woman who survived sexual assault."

Sam paused as the significance of Heather's comment sank in. "So you were sexually assaulted? I mean . . . *when*? Who did it? Why didn't you ever tell me?"

"Not everything is about you, Sam. This happened a long time ago, when we first started dating. I didn't tell you for the same reasons a lot of women don't tell anyone. I was embarrassed. I felt like it was my fault. I thought nobody would believe me. I didn't want you to think differently about me. Etcetera and so forth."

"What happened?"

Heather set her glass down and inhaled deeply, mustering the mental energy to lay out the story. "It was at a trade show in Vegas. I was working the booth all day, and a bunch of us went out for drinks afterward. I probably had too many and ended up at an after-party in the hotel room of one of our regional VPs. He'd been flirting with me the whole day, but he seemed harmless and there were five or six of us in the room. Anyway, a couple of us were dancing when someone pushed me onto one of the beds from behind. I didn't know who did it, but I heard one of the other girls scream. He was pressing me down between the shoulders and took his penis out with his other hand. I was able to crawl across the bed as he started grinding on me. Then I fell to the floor on the other side. He stood and started coming around the bed with his pants around his ankles and a possessed look in his eye. If I had been alone, I have no doubt he would have raped me. Thank God there were still other employees in the room. A couple of them grabbed him, which gave me just enough time to get up off the floor. He was yelling incoherently at that point, pushing everyone away. The only other guy in the room was a sales rep who worked for him. He started trying to reason with his boss—telling him to chill out and put his pants back on. The rest of us got the hell out of there as fast as we could." Tears were streaming down Heather's cheeks, but her words were steady and organized, as if she had told the story several times before.

"Holy shit," Sam said. "What happened to the guy?"

"Nothing." Heather quickly wiped a tear off her cheek, her voice catching in her throat for the first time. "The sales rep didn't want to lose his job, so he told HR it was all just a joke—a misunderstanding. The company pretended to investigate it, but everyone was drunk, and their stories were inconsistent. Plus, the guy was running the top-performing sales region, so the head of sales wanted to believe his side of the story. By that point, I just didn't know how far I wanted to take the whole thing. I didn't have proof, and the guy was calling me a liar, and none of the people who witnessed it were really credible. I didn't know what to do. So when the CEO and the head of HR met with me and told me how inconvenient a sexual assault case would be for the company, I let it go."

"Jesus, Heather—I had no idea." Sam reached for her hand, but she immediately withdrew it.

"So, to answer your question, *that's* why it bothers me. Amanda trusted you. She looked up to you. She did what she thought you wanted her to do. And you had the power, the *proof*, right there to do the right thing. But, instead, you destroyed the evidence."

"Honey, you've got to believe me. I didn't have any other choice," Sam protested. "Amanda's not the only person at the company. I have over a hundred other employees I need to worry about."

Heather set her glass on the table and looked at him earnestly for a moment. "You know, you don't need to go through with this."

"*Yes, I do*," Sam said. "If we don't do this deal, I'll need to lay off most of those employees. I'd be fired too. They'd just kick me out of the company and sell it anyway. Then we'd get *nothing* for all the blood, sweat, and tears I've put into this thing."

"No, I mean you could walk away from this whole thing," Heather said sincerely. "Just quit. We'll sell this damn house and move back to Ohio."

"You're not even from Ohio, *remember*?" Sam said.

"Who cares? Like you said, we could afford a huge house out there for the price we'd get for this money pit. You could take over your dad's company and make all those improvements you were talking about—turn it into a profitable business."

"Yeah, and you could run my uncle's chicken farm. It's perfect," Sam said.

"Don't be such an asshole," she said, dismissing his sarcasm. "I'm just trying to point out that you have alternatives."

"What alternatives? I don't know how to do anything else. My entire career has been in tech. All my experience and contacts are in tech. It's like my entire *identity* is built on the scaffolding of tech. I've invested over twenty years of my life trying to be successful here. I'd be throwing that all away. And to do *what*? I don't even know. It would be one thing if I shitcanned my whole career because I always wanted to be a bronze sculptor, or play saxophone in a jazz band, or raise sustainable salmon, or—"

"Become a chicken farmer," Heather interjected.

"*Exactly!* Become a chicken farmer. But I don't want any of those things. I've been striving my entire professional career to achieve this elusive dream of making it big in Silicon Valley, and here I am at the doorstep. I can't fall off the horse. This is my last chance."

"Last chance for *what*? To make a bunch of rich VCs *richer*? Why are you defining yourself by the esteem of others? Why are you measuring your self-worth by the size of this acquisition? Why are you succumbing to this one narrative of success?"

"I'm doing this for *us*!"

"No, you're *not*. Not really."

"How can you say that? This money will set us up for life. We won't have to struggle like my parents did. The house remodel, the medical bills, the college tuition—we won't have to worry about any of it."

"Give me a break, Sam. You're not doing this for your family. All I see motivating you is your own greed and pride. Ever since you lost your job, you've been trying to repair your bruised male ego at all costs. You're fixated on this exit, like it's going to prove something. You've compromised your morals. You've sold out your friends. You're jeopardizing our family. And for what? Greed and pride and ego. I don't even know who you are anymore."

"Maybe you'll remember when our bank account has nine digits in it."

CHAPTER 32:

THE FLOCK

THE MORNING SUN CAST LONG SILHOUETTES of the giant redwood trees along Skyline Boulevard. The fog had just lifted along the winding rural road that straddled the ridge of mountains separating the Peninsula from the Pacific Ocean, revealing a dazzling blue sky. Sam squinted through the trees toward the coast and watched the bright sun pursue the last remaining clouds into retreat. He took a sip of coffee from a paper cup as he loitered outside Alice's Restaurant with the usual weekend-morning crowd—Harley-Davidson enthusiasts, a Lamborghini club, and dozens of cyclists.

By noon, the expansive deck and picnic tables outside Alice's would be overtaken by families, gobbling down paper-lined baskets of burgers and hot dogs to sustain their weekend outings—hikes through the hills, horseback riding, drives along the scenic coast. The spot was one of the Hughes family's favorites, anytime they made their way up to Skyline. Sam recalled selecting pumpkins for Halloween, driving to the beach to go surfing, and cutting down their Christmas tree. Maybe Heather would be here later today with the kids, he thought.

The kids . . . Heather . . . His dislocated family. The sudden flood of memories tore through him like a knife to his gut, triggering an expulsion of breath that threatened to escalate into a sob. All the normative details of his prior life, from the mundane to the joyous, piled up in his memory. *Why hadn't it been enough?* The school drop-offs, the date nights, the parent events, everything he'd taken for granted, replaced by attorneys, settlements, and visitation rights. Looking into the sun with a vacant stare, Sam again conjured his first glimpse of Silicon Valley, descending from the Altamont Pass. All his hopes and aspirations encapsulated in that sunset. The promised land of everything he dreamed of achieving, right there on the road ahead. *What was I trying to prove? To whom?* Only with the benefit of hindsight, having finally captured wealth beyond his wildest ambitions, did he appreciate the immeasurable price. The limitless spoils of his professional success, but no one to share them with. The achievement of what he came here to do, but the failure to heed his own advice.

Sam slowly exhaled and wiped the corner of his eye. Then, tilting his head back, he finished his coffee, crumpled the cup, and tossed it into a nearby garbage can. It wasn't time to get nostalgic. He would need to stay focused for the remaining ride. Sam pulled his Lycra shirt, still damp with the sweat of his climb, away from the freshly shaved skin on his chest. Releasing the fabric, the Ellipsis Ventures logo on its front snapped back into place. Sam adjusted his helmet as Preston walked down the stairs from the restaurant.

"Ready?" Preston rhetorically asked the group of a dozen similarly clad cyclists. Sam swung his leg over his bike and pulled a pair of fingerless gloves over his hands. "We've got another thirty miles," Preston said as he coasted his bike out onto the road. Sam looked back at the restaurant one more time, then clicked his shoes into his pedals and continued to ride.

ACKNOWLEDGMENTS

Publishing a first novel is not an individual effort—particularly when the novelist in question had no idea what he was doing at the outset. One might assume from the characters in this novel that I have worked with terrible people over my career. The reality is quite the opposite. I am so thankful for all the amazing, diverse, and intelligent people I have had the privilege of working with at so many wonderful companies. Thanks in particular to all the friends and colleagues who endured early drafts and provided invaluable feedback, including Alex, Bob, Conrad, David, Deborah, Erin, Keith, Jon, Laila, Liam, Linda, Mark, Marysue, Mike, Rudi, Tom, Wendy, and many others. Your encouragement inspired me to write this novel.

Turning a rough draft into a real book required more than inspiration; it required expertise. I can't offer enough gratitude to my developmental editor, Joshua Mohr, who helped transform a mediocre manuscript into something I'm truly proud of; my copyeditor, Ryan Quinn, who brought an incredible attention to detail; and David Provolo, who designed the perfect cover and interior to encapsulate this story.

For getting this project over the finish line, I'm incredibly grateful to Brooke Warner, Shannon Green, and the rest of the editorial team at SparkPress for steering me through the publishing process, and Crystal Patriarche and BookSparks for driving market awareness with their publicity acumen. Without your expertise, this book would have been dead on the vine.

Finally, thanks most of all to my family, who supported me in this endeavor—my sons, Cole and Chase, who cheered me on, and especially my amazing wife, Leslie, who provided everything from editorial feedback to moral support, affording me the chance to pursue my lifelong dream of writing a novel.

ABOUT THE AUTHOR

Mike Trigg was born in Kentucky and raised in Wisconsin. He earned a BA from Northwestern University and an MBA from University of California, Berkeley. Over his twenty-five-year career in Silicon Valley, he has been a founder, executive, and investor in dozens of venture-funded technology start-ups, as well as a contributor to *TechCrunch, Entrepreneur,* and *Fast Company*. He lives in Menlo Park, California, with his wife and two sons. *Bit Flip* is his first novel.

SELECTED TITLES FROM SPARKPRESS

SparkPress is an independent boutique publisher delivering high-quality, entertaining, and engaging content that enhances readers' lives, with a special focus on female-driven work. www.gosparkpress.com

Riding High in April: A Novel, Jackie Townsend, $16.95, 978-1-68463-095-0. *Riding High in April* takes us across the world as one man risks it all for a final chance to make it big in the tech world. At stake are his reputation, his dwindling bank account, and his fifteen-year relationship with a woman grappling with who she is and what really matters to her.

Indelible: A Sean McPherson Novel, Book 1, Laurie Buchanan, $16.95, 978-168463-071-4. Murder at a writing retreat in the Pacific Northwest, but this one isn't imaginary. Authors only kill with words. Or do they?

Firewall: A Novel, Eugenia Lovett West. $16.95, 978-1-68463-010-3. When Emma Streat's rich, socialite godmother is threatened with blackmail, Emma becomes immersed in the dark world of cybercrime—and mounting dangers take her to exclusive places in Europe and contacts with the elite in financial and art collecting circles. Through passion and heartbreak, Emma must fight to save herself and bring a vicious criminal to justice.

The Sea of Japan: A Novel, Keita Nagano. $16.95, 978-1-684630-12-7. When thirty-year-old Lindsey, an English teacher from Boston who's been assigned to a tiny Japanese fishing town, is saved from drowning by a local young fisherman, she's drawn into a battle with a neighboring town that has high stakes for everyone—especially her.

The Cast: A Novel, Amy Blumenfeld. $16.95, 978-1-943006-72-4. Twenty-five years after a group of ninth graders produces a *Saturday Night Live*-style videotape to cheer up their cancer-stricken friend, they reunite to celebrate her good health—but the happy holiday-card facades quickly crumble and give way to an unforgettable three days filled with moral dilemmas and life-altering choices.

Hostile Takeover: A Love Story, Phyllis J. Piano. $16.95, 978-1-940716-82-4. Corporate attorney Molly's all-consuming job is to take over other companies, but when her first love, a man who she feels betrayed her, appears out of nowhere to try to acquire her business, long-hidden passions and secrets are exposed.